Magnolia
PARK

Magnolia
PARK

KATE McCABE

POOLBEG

Published 2013
by Poolbeg Press Ltd
123 Grange Hill, Baldoyle
Dublin 13, Ireland
E-mail: poolbeg@poolbeg.com
www.poolbeg.com

1

A catalogue record for this book is available from the British Library.

ISBN 978-1-84223-546-1

Typeset by Patricia Hope
Printed by CPI, Cox and Wyman

www.poolbeg.com

About the author

Kate McCabe is married with two children and lives in Howth in County Dublin. She is a former journalist and recently began writing fiction full time. Her first novel *Hotel Las Flores* was published by Poolbeg Press in 2005 and became an Irish bestseller, as did her following novels *The Beach Bar, The Book Club, Forever Friends* and *Casa Clara*. Kate's hobbies include reading, music, travelling and walking along the beach in Howth while she thinks up plots for her stories.

Acknowledgements

I would like to thank the usual suspects.

My family for their continuing encouragement and support.

All the professionals at Poolbeg Press.

The booksellers who helped me get this book into the hands of the public.

Marc Patton who has always been available to iron out computer problems.

And most of all, you, dear reader. I hope your good taste and loyalty are amply rewarded.

Enjoy!

This book is for my newest fan,
Alex Patton (aged one)

Chapter 1

Amy Crawford lay back on the recliner and faced the sun. Close by, the sound of water tinkling from a fountain gently lulled her senses. She could hear the birds chattering in the branches of the jacaranda trees and the drowsy humming of the bees around the flower-bed.

This was exactly what she needed. She had been looking forward to the holiday for months. Just thinking about it had carried her through the long, dark winter with its cold frosty mornings and the damp and rain. Whenever she felt low, she would imagine Spain and Magnolia Park and immediately she would feel her spirits lift and a smile return to her face. And now that the holiday had finally arrived, Amy was determined to extract every ounce of enjoyment from it.

Beside her, her boyfriend Sam Benson was beginning to doze off. She fixed her sunglasses firmly on her face and closed her eyes. A gentle breeze caressed her cheeks and carried with it the sweet perfume from the rose bed. She settled down to work on her tan. But as she allowed her thoughts to drift away, she could never have imagined what lay ahead and how the next two weeks would prove to be a turning point in her life.

Amy had been up since four o'clock that morning, making sure that everything was in order. She always fussed over journeys and especially holidays. She remembered with horror the occasion when her friend Debbie Fox had arrived at the airport all gung-ho for her holiday only to discover that her passport was still sitting where she had left it on her dressing-table back in her apartment in Rathmines. Debbie missed her flight and had to buy another ticket and the airline hadn't even shown the least smidgen of pity or sympathy at her plight.

So Amy had been up before dawn, ticking off the items she had made on her must-do list till she was certain that everything was in place. She had double-checked the luggage, her credit cards, the changes of clothes, the book she was bringing and the all-important boarding passes which she had printed off her computer the night before.

Only when she was satisfied did she allow herself a cup of strong, sweet coffee while she studied the directions she had been given to Magnolia Park. The internet advert had described it as a quiet gated development of eighty apartments and townhouses modelled in the Moorish style and situated right in the centre of Fuengirola on the Spanish Costa del Sol.

The advert went on to say that Magnolia Park was only a short walk from the beach and the port and had a wide selection of restaurants, shops and supermarkets nearby. But it was the description of the gardens that had really sold it to her. The advert talked about the beautiful flowers that bloomed all year round, the swimming pool, the cool fountains and the shady courtyards. And to prove it, there right before her eyes was a photograph of a terrace ablaze with flowering geraniums, their scarlet faces open to the sun. Amy was hooked. She went ahead at once and booked a ground-floor apartment for two weeks for herself and Sam.

So far, everything had gone exactly to plan. The flight from Dublin had arrived at Malaga airport just before noon. From there, it was a twenty-minute taxi ride to their destination and Magnolia Park had turned out to be everything she had been promised.

The apartment was in a three-storey block and had direct access to the garden at the end of which the pale blue water of the swimming pool sparkled enticingly. The pool was surrounded by two more blocks of three-storey apartments. All were painted white. In another part of the complex near the gates and the road was a square of townhouses, at the centre of which was a quaint little courtyard with a bar.

Their apartment had been cleaned just that morning and sparkled like a new pin, the floors swept and the bed linen placed in a neat pile on top of the mattress. They quickly showered and changed. Then it was a dash to the supermarket to stock up on basic provisions and lunch at a little *tapas* bar near the train station.

Now it was three o'clock and Amy just wanted to relax, chill out and soak up the sun. She had a paperback novel and some magazines to read. She had a glass of wine on the little table beside her. The cool blue water of the swimming pool was only yards away if she should get too hot. She stretched her legs and uttered a sigh. She had two weeks of uninterrupted peace stretching ahead: no ringing phones, no distractions and no boring job to go to. This was the holiday she had dreamt about for months. Not even an earthquake was going to be allowed to spoil it.

The holiday had actually been Sam's idea. He had come up with it one damp evening in November while they were sitting in the kitchen of their apartment in Dublin, staring gloomily at the rain running in streams down the window pane.

"I'm sick to death of this bloody weather," he grumbled, pushing away the remains of the pizza which Amy had picked up on her way home from work. He was out of sorts and Amy knew why. Tonight was one of his football nights and she knew how much his football game meant to him.

It had begun as a simple opportunity to get some exercise but it had grown to be much more. Now it was a weekly ritual where he would meet his friends, burn off some calories and exchange news and gossip afterwards in the changing room. But the foul weather made it almost certain that the game would be cancelled.

As if reading her thoughts, he lifted his eyes and shrugged. "I'll bet they'll call it off. There's no way we can play in this rain."

She felt sorry for him. She loved Sam. She went to him, kissed his cheek and stroked his handsome brow.

"The forecast said it would clear away tomorrow."

"Tomorrow's no use," Sam said dismally. "I've got a meeting with a client tomorrow."

"Maybe you could go for a jog afterwards."

"It's not the same, is it? There's no competition. That's what makes the football game so enjoyable."

He got up and walked to the window where he stared out into the dark, inhospitable night. Just at that moment, his phone started to ring. He quickly opened it and clamped it to his ear.

Amy watched his face as he absorbed the bad news.

At last she heard him say: "Oh well, can't be helped, I suppose. See you next week."

He put the phone away and turned back to her with an air of defeat.

"Just as I predicted, the game's been cancelled. This bloody rain is beginning to get me down."

She put her arms around him.

"I'm sorry," she said.

"It's not your fault," he replied. "You don't control the weather."

"I know. But I want you to be happy. Why don't I drive to the video store and pick up a DVD? You can take a shower and get changed. We'll open a bottle of wine and spend a cosy evening in front of the fire."

At this suggestion, his face brightened.

"You know something, Amy? That sounds like a very good idea."

And then, suddenly, he clapped a hand to his head. "I've just had an inspiration," he said. "There's one way we can be certain of good weather."

"What?"

"We could book a holiday in Spain."

Amy and Sam had been living together for almost a year. This had been his idea too. He said it would save money and besides they were mad about each other, so what was the point of living apart?

He was right. They *were* mad about each other. Amy was

4

twenty-eight and had been in and out of relationships since she was seventeen but nothing had ever lasted till she met Sam. They had been seeing each other for nine months which was the longest relationship she'd ever had with any man. So when he suggested that she move into his smart, two-bed apartment overlooking the sea at Sutton, it immediately got her full attention.

"Are you serious?"

"Totally. And it isn't just a spur-of-the-moment decision either. I've been thinking about it for weeks. I love you, Amy. I want to share my life with you."

She felt her heart melt at these words. What a lovely thing to say! She could think of nothing better than to share her life with this wonderful man. But some instinct warned her to be cautious. This was a big step to take and she didn't want to give Sam the impression that she was gagging to move in with him.

"Let me think about it."

"Okay but don't take too long – I might change my mind," he laughed, gathering her into his arms and smothering her with hot kisses.

At the time, she was sharing a flat in Clontarf with three friends from work and she was quite cosy there. They got on extremely well. They socialised together, swapped clothes, shared sympathy, advice and gossip. She had been contented with her life until Sam showed up out of the blue one evening in the Zhivago Bar in Dawson Street and swept her off her feet.

The Zhivago was their favourite watering hole with its shiny zinc bar counter and its bright lights and comfortable seats for lounging in. It was close to work and it was a place to meet interesting people of their age which was mid-twenties to early thirties. And it always had an exciting buzz. You never knew when some celebrity actor, fashion designer or visiting rock star might drop by.

She had spotted Sam earlier standing at the counter with a group of his friends. He was hard to miss. He was maybe thirty-five years old, at least six feet tall, with dark, flashing eyes, broad shoulders and a mane of thick black hair. He was wearing a light cashmere jacket, white shirt and blue tie. When he sat down beside her uninvited and asked what she was drinking, she could see the faces of her companions drawn like magnets to this handsome, dark-eyed devil.

She held his gaze for a moment before replying.

"My mother warned me never to accept drinks from strange men."

"I'll bet she did. She sounds like a wise woman, your mum."

"You got that much right."

"Well, I'm Sam Benson."

He held out his hand and she found her own hand enclosed in a warm, firm grip.

"What's your name?"

"Amy Crawford," she replied.

"So now that we've been introduced, what would you like to drink?"

Amy asked for a gin and tonic and Sam caught the attention of a passing waiter.

"Now, tell me why a ravishing creature like you is out on her own without a minder?" he asked.

She found herself warming to him at once. He was brimming with confidence and certainly knew how to flatter a girl. But he also had this direct, no-nonsense approach that she found appealing.

"Why would I need a minder? I'm perfectly capable of looking after myself."

"There are certain advantages, you know," Sam said.

"Like what?"

"Do you really need me to explain?"

Before long, they were deep in conversation. He told her that he was a creative executive with a big advertising agency located in nearby Baggot Street. She hadn't a clue what it meant but when he talked about his job he made it sound very glamorous. It seemed to be a constant round of parties and product launches and meetings with exciting people. He dropped the names of showbiz personalities and actors and models as if they were his very best friends.

Amy was swept away. This was a life she'd only read about in the glossy magazines. She thought of her own job as a tele-sales rep with a busy insurance company. She never got invited to swish parties. She never met exciting people. The highlight of her working life was the annual Christmas party when her boss took the staff to a nearby restaurant for a meal. It occurred to her that Sam could be right. Maybe there were advantages to having a minder, as he so quaintly put it.

Two hours later, when everyone was preparing to leave, they were still wrapped up in conversation. He offered to share a taxi with her but she declined, saying she had to go home with her friends. He looked disappointed and asked if he could keep in touch so she gave him her phone number.

She wasn't sure if she would ever hear from him again but the following morning, as she was going through the post, her phone rang and it was Sam. He asked if she was free to go for dinner with him to a new restaurant in Howth. As it happened, Amy was planning an early night with a good novel and a mug of hot chocolate. The idea of a nice meal in Sam's witty company was very appealing, so she agreed. He turned up right on time driving a blue 2011 Porsche and dressed immaculately in a dark suit and tie.

The meal was a great success. The restaurant was at the edge of the pier and outside the window they could hear the sea growling while they sat inside, warm and cosy. The food was superb, the atmosphere romantic. The candles on the table cast shadows across Sam's handsome face.

When he dropped her home, he kissed her gently on the lips and stared longingly into her eyes. She could feel her heart flutter. He asked if he could see her again and she said yes. Before long, they were seeing each other almost every day. That was how their relationship began.

Back in those days, Sam never grumbled or complained about the weather or wanted to play football with his pals. He was content to spend all his free time with her. In the beginning, everything was smooth as silk. He was constantly in good spirits, witty and charming. His manners were impeccable. He was everything a woman could wish for in a man: generous, humorous, even-tempered and handsome to a fault. Sam was a dream partner.

Amy quickly discovered that the stories he had told her about the hectic social life of an advertising executive were true. Before long, she was immersed in a giddy round of parties and receptions and opening theatre nights and was learning how to deal with the envious glances from Sam's many female admirers. It was like living in a movie that would never come to an end.

Amy was an attractive young woman and very sure of herself. She was five feet seven inches tall, had a firm bust, a slim waist, brown hair, blue eyes and a pale complexion. When her hair was cut and washed and hung down over her shoulders and her blue eyes sparkled, she could turn men's heads.

Everyone who knew her agreed that she had a warm personality. She was intelligent and sympathetic and fiercely loyal to her friends. She was considerate and dependable. She wasn't jealous or scheming. She didn't say things behind people's backs or smile into their faces while secretly plotting to cut their throats like some she could mention. But she could also be tough and independent if necessary and she didn't appreciate being lied to or taken for granted, as many men had found to their cost.

People said they were a perfect couple. Amy was beautiful and Sam, well, Sam was something else. He was drop-dead gorgeous. He was charming. He lived a glamorous lifestyle. He had a well-paid job. All her friends thought he was the dishiest man they knew. No wonder people said it was a match made in Heaven.

Chapter 2

When Amy told her friends over coffee the next morning that Sam wanted her to move in with him, they were unanimous in their approval.

"Some people have all the luck," Tara Brady babbled, barely able to contain her envy. "What a hunk! You agreed, of course?"

"I told him I needed time to think about it."

Tara almost spilt her coffee, she was so surprised. "Are you crazy? What is there to think about? If he asked me, I'd be in there like a shot. And I'll tell you something else. He'd never get me out again."

"Us too," the others nodded in agreement.

"Move in tonight," Tara insisted. "This is a no-brainer. There's no time to waste."

This response was music to Amy's ears. She loved it when they heaped praise on Sam and told her how fortunate she was. Their words of encouragement served to reinforce the views that were rapidly crystallising in her mind.

Already she was beginning to dream about what life would be like when she was living with Sam. She would cook nice meals for him. She would organise his apartment, buy some new furniture and drapes. Like most men she knew, Sam had no taste when it came to decor. They would share all their free time. She would wake up every morning with her head on the pillow next to his. Life would be wonderful. She couldn't think of a more exciting existence.

"It's nice of you all to be so positive," she said. "But I don't want to rush into anything."

"Why not?" Tara replied as if she was talking to an idiot. "Rush away! Rushing is good. In fact, if you want my opinion, rushing is absolutely essential in a situation like this."

But not everyone was so encouraging. She knew her parents would have reservations, particularly her mother who had strong views about this sort of thing. Mrs Crawford believed that people should wait till they were married before sharing a roof together. Amy rang her mother that evening when she knew her parents would have finished dinner. At once, she heard the disapproval in Mrs Crawford's voice.

"Nobody did this in my day," she said.

"Times change, Mum."

"It's hardly respectable. Your father won't like it."

"It's not unusual. Lots of people do it."

"That doesn't make it right. You were always an independent woman, Amy. You didn't use to follow the herd."

"I'm not following the herd, Mum. This is my own decision. This is something *I* want to do."

"And when is this going to happen?"

"I'm not sure. I have to talk some more to Sam."

"Well, before you do, there's something you should consider. What will happen if he gets tired of you and throws you out? You'll look like a reject."

Her mother's words stung.

"I might leave *him*," Amy said, defiantly. "Have you thought of that?"

"That's not the way it usually happens," her mother said.

Amy had been expecting some opposition from her mother but the reaction of her friend, Debbie Fox, took her completely by surprise.

"Are you sure you know what you're doing?" Debbie asked the following evening after Amy had broken the news over a quiet drink. "You'd be a fool to throw all your cards away."

Amy looked at her in amazement. "How do you mean?"

"If you move in with him, he'll get everything he wants. What will you get?"

"The same as he does."

She went over the advantages. They would save money. They would be together. She realised that she sounded just like Sam as she listed all the positives of living together.

Debbie slowly nodded. "So, if he's so keen on you, why doesn't he ask you to marry him?"

Amy was stunned. "Who said anything about marriage?" she replied. "We just want to get to know each other better."

"You can do that without living together. Marriage means a commitment. Has it never occurred to you to wonder why he's not prepared to give it?"

"You sound very old-fashioned," Amy snapped.

"I'm just being practical," her friend replied. "I don't want to see you getting hurt. I've seen it happen before."

"Well, you don't have to worry on that score," Amy said. "It's not going to happen to me."

"I hope you're right, Amy. But please be careful."

Debbie Fox's comments had hurt Amy. She had been expecting her friend to react like all the others, with gushing approval. Instead she had been given a lecture and she didn't like it. It was none of Debbie's damned business what she did. But later, when she was alone, she found herself wondering if perhaps Debbie might be right.

What if she moved in with Sam and ended up being an unpaid maid, cook and bed companion? Perhaps she should hold off till she was more certain of his intentions. Sam had told her that he loved her. But he had never once mentioned marriage. And Amy was reminded of the old adage: *Actions speak louder than words.*

But over the following days, she cast her doubts aside. By now she was being carried away with the thought of them living together. It seemed so exciting. She told herself it would bring them closer together. It was a statement to the world of their faith in each other. She would view it as an experiment, a test drive to see if they were really compatible and could form a steady long-term relationship that would endure. What was there to lose? If her mother and Debbie Fox were correct and things did not work out, she could simply move out again.

She made up her mind to move in with Sam no matter what others might think. It was her life and the more people raised objections, the more determined she became. She thought of all Sam's strong points: his thoughtfulness, his charm, his good manners, not to mention his stunning good looks. Tara Brady had been right. She would be stark raving mad not to jump at his offer.

But there was one final thing she must do.

The next occasion when they were alone together she asked him bluntly: "How do I know you won't get tired of me and throw me out?"

A look of shock came over his face. "Why on earth would I do that?"

"You might. It's happened to girls before."

"It won't happen to us. I'm not so stupid. Throw out a gorgeous creature like you? I'd need to have my head examined."

He drew her closer and kissed her warm lips.

"Once I get you into my apartment, I'm going to bar the doors and windows to make sure you don't escape," he said. "I might even chain you to the radiator, if necessary. I'm not going to mess up the opportunity of a lifetime."

This was all the assurance that Amy required. She went back to the flat she shared with her friends and began to pack her belongings in large cardboard boxes: her books and CDs and her laptop computer. She carefully packed her clothes and shoes. By the time she had finished, there were six boxes, two big suitcases and several bags stacked in the hall waiting for Sam to come and pick them up in the van he had rented for the purpose.

On the final night, the four flatmates went out for a farewell drink to a nearby pub. Everyone was sad, especially Amy. She had been very happy in the flat with her friends. They had shared good times together and she had many happy memories.

But she was comforted with the thought of having Sam Benson all to herself and the wonderful life they would have together. It wasn't as if she was saying goodbye to her friends forever. She would see them every day at work. She would have plenty to tell them. And no doubt they would be green with envy when they heard how well the adventure was working out.

Nevertheless, she left the pub at closing time with an ache in her heart and fell asleep with tears welling in her eyes. But her sad feelings were banished the following morning when she heard Sam's van pulling up outside the front door. She drew back the curtains and saw him step out of the driver's seat dressed in a casual shirt and Levis. He kissed her before carrying her belongings outside and stacking them carefully away in the back of the van.

Amy said goodbye to her friends and promised to give a dinner party in their honour once she had settled into Sam's flat. Five minutes later they were driving along the Clontarf Road and Howth Head was gleaming green and brown in the bright morning light.

The first things to greet her when he opened the front door were a huge bouquet of flowers and a streamer stretched across the hall saying WELCOME TO YOUR NEW HOME. Sam unloaded Amy's boxes and carried them carefully into his flat. Then he marched into the kitchen and opened a bottle of champagne and poured two glasses. He proposed a toast.

"To us," he said. "Health, joy and happiness!"

Amy sipped her champagne. It tasted crisp and refreshing and the bubbles tickled her throat. It suddenly dawned on her that this was a very significant occasion in her life. They should have got someone to take a photograph. Sam produced a set of keys and pressed them into her hand.

"Those are for you – and, Amy, the banner means what it says. This is your new home and I want you to be happy here."

She felt giddy with pleasure but Sam quickly brought her smack down to earth. He led her to the dining table, pulled out two chairs and sat down beside her.

"Now before we begin, I thought it would be a good idea if we drew up some guidelines," he said, turning businesslike. "Just so we both know where we stand. It's important that we have our own space so we don't end up getting in each other's hair. Don't you agree?"

"Y-yes," Amy replied wondering where this conversation was leading.

"So I suggest you should have the second bedroom. You can put your clothes in there and we'll get a desk for your computer and some shelves for your books. Then when you want to be alone, you can just go in there and close the door."

"Okay," Amy replied.

"We should also draw up a roster for cleaning and shopping and things like that. That will save arguments later on."

Amy had never had an argument with Sam and didn't anticipate any but she nodded her agreement.

Sam smiled. "I also think it's important that we are allowed to lead our own lives."

Suddenly, Amy began to hear alarm bells ringing in her head. "How do you mean?"

"If I'm working late, I don't want you getting concerned and wondering why I'm not home. The same thing applies to me of course. What I'm trying to say is that we have to learn to trust each other. Lack of trust has killed more relationships than any other single thing."

"Are you planning to work late very often?"

"Oh no," he said, quickly waving her worries aside. "That's not what I meant. But I don't want you ringing me in the middle of some important business meeting and demanding that I drop everything and come rushing home."

"I've never interfered in your business," Amy said.

"No, of course you haven't. But the situation has changed. Now we're living together so it's important that we set down guidelines."

"Is there anything else?" she asked, feeling slightly uneasy.

He suddenly laughed and ruffled her hair. "No. And don't be worrying. Everything is going to work out just fine. I'm delighted that you have agreed to move in here and share my life. This is an auspicious day for both of us."

He finished his champagne and stood up.

"Now I have some stuff to take care of. Why don't you start unpacking and later we'll go out to some nice restaurant and celebrate."

Amy sat nursing her champagne which was slowly turning warm in the glass. She stared out of the big wide windows at the sea and the Dublin Mountains. The uneasy feeling persisted. Why hadn't Sam mentioned these rules before she moved in? Why had he waited till it was a done deal? Had he been afraid that she wouldn't have come?

But she quickly brushed these concerns aside. She was worrying over nothing. Today she had reached a defining moment in her life. It would be foolish to dwell on petty misgivings. She should be happy. She was sharing a roof and a bed with the most desirable man in Dublin. She should look to the future with confidence.

Chapter 3

Amy soon settled into her new life in the apartment. It was a stunning ground-floor home with two large bedrooms, two bathrooms, a modern kitchen and an enormous lounge and dining room with views across Dublin Bay. As they ate dinner in the evenings, they could watch the yachts sailing almost up to the window.

Once she had turned the second bedroom into an efficient study with a comfortable couch, desk, office chair, CD player and bookshelves, with Sam's approval she began the task of giving the apartment a feminine touch. Even though Sam had spared little expense on furniture and fabrics, it still retained the look of a bachelor pad. So she got on the internet and read every home-decor article she could find and consulted with some people Sam knew in the interior-design business.

When she had decided what she wanted to do, she got in the decorators and gave them instructions to repaint the lounge and master bedroom in soft pastel shades. Next, she purchased new furnishings and fabrics and bought curtains and some nice modern paintings for the walls. Finally, she went off to a garden centre and installed some trailing house plants. When she was finished, she had put her stamp on the place and Sam had the good grace to concede that the apartment looked much brighter and smarter.

But she still wasn't finished. She made herself mistress of the kitchen and took great pleasure in creating wonderful meals which they enjoyed together over a bottle of wine when Sam returned from work. She organised the dinner party she had promised for her former flatmates, cooking roast lamb with broccoli, carrots and potatoes and finishing off with a delicious strawberry flan she had bought in a delicatessen at Sutton Cross.

They drank lots of wine, giggled quite a bit, kept repeating how wonderful the apartment looked and confessed that they envied the hell out of her, the jammy bitch with her hunky boyfriend and this beautiful pad. She had to send them home in a taxi.

For the first few months, Amy was deliriously happy. Each night, they made passionate love and she fell asleep in Sam's arms and woke with his strong body pressing against her. She left for work with her heart bursting with joy. They partied and went out to fancy restaurants and celebrity events or ate alone at home with the sound of the sea whispering in their ears. Everything she had been promised had come to pass.

It took a while before small cracks began to appear in this perfect situation. Despite Sam drawing up a roster for sharing the chores, Amy soon found the burden of the work falling on her shoulders. At first she made excuses for him. He was very busy. He was working hard at the advertising office. But she was working hard too and she often felt irritated when she returned in the evening to find a stack of unwashed dishes piled up in the sink waiting for her to wash. And it wasn't just dishes. She quickly discovered that Sam was very untidy. He never cleaned the shower after he had used it. He left socks and underwear lying around in the bedroom for her to pick up and put in the laundry basket. He often didn't bother to put the milk back in the fridge after he had used so that it went stale and had to be poured away. There were so many small things that got on her nerves.

And he had no sense of timekeeping. He left everything to the last minute. She began to lose count of the number of occasions when she had to hurry him out the door in the morning with his shirt collar unbuttoned and his tie undone lest he be late for an important appointment. Or the times she had spent preparing a nice dinner for some special occasion and Sam would turn up late and the meal would be ruined. And this wasn't all. He was spending more and more of his time in the pub after work, drinking with his buddies. Then he would arrive home tired and collapse into bed and fall fast asleep. Those cosy nights they had spent together were becoming fewer and fewer. Amy couldn't escape the feeling that Sam was taking her for granted.

She decided the time had arrived for a heart-to-heart talk. She waited till the weekend when they had more time together and broached the subject on Saturday morning after breakfast.

"Remember that roster we drew up?" she began in a deliberately pleasant voice because she didn't want this discussion to turn into an argument.

Sam put down the golf magazine he was reading. "Of course, it was my idea in the first place."

"So why don't you stick to it?"

He immediately went on the defensive. "I do stick to it."

"No, you don't. You leave the dishes piling up. You leave dirty clothes lying around for me to pick up."

"That's only when I'm in a hurry. I always look after them later when I have time."

"You don't, Sam. I'm the one who looks after them. Don't you see the message you're sending out?"

His face went blank. "You've lost me," he said.

"What you're saying is that your time is more valuable than mine."

He began to defend himself. "You're taking this up wrong, Amy. That's not what I mean at all."

"But it's what it boils down to. You're too busy to do these chores but little old me, my time doesn't count."

He sighed and put up his hands. "I'm sorry," he said. "You're right."

"That's not all. How many occasions have I cooked dinner for you and you didn't bother to turn up on time?"

"There's always been a good reason for that," he protested.

18

"Such as?"

"I could be in the pub and I get caught up in a round of drinks."

"That's another thing. You're spending more and more time in the pub. And meanwhile, I'm sitting at home and the dinner is getting cold. It shows disrespect for me, Sam. It sends a message that I'm not important."

"Of course you're important. You're the most important person in my life. I don't know what I'd do without you."

He stood up, took her in his arms and held her tight.

"I'm sorry," he said. "I'll pay attention to what you've said. Now let's not argue. I can't stand it when we have disagreements."

After this intervention, Amy noticed a definite improvement. Sam appeared to be taking her concerns to heart. He shouldered his share of the household jobs. He made an effort to be more tidy. He tried to be punctual. She began to believe that he had changed. But her hopes were short-lived. Slowly, he began to slip back into his bad old ways.

She was at a loss what to do next. She had tried confrontation and it had only worked for a while. Meanwhile, the cosy life she had dreamed of was turning into a mirage. Sam's behaviour was making her depressed. For the first time, she began to doubt whether she was still in love with him. Then one day at work she read a magazine article which said that handsome men were more likely to be selfish than plain men. The article said this was because people were always admiring them and the constant attention gave them an exaggerated sense of their own importance. A lot of the time, they weren't even aware of their selfishness. They just accepted it as their entitlement.

She put down the article and stared off into space. It could have been written about Sam. It described him to a tee. He was extremely handsome and was used to women fawning all over him and falling in with his every wish. It was this constant attention that had made him the way he was. It made her wonder if his selfishness was so deep-rooted that he might never change.

Why had she not spotted it before? Either she was too starry-eyed to notice or Sam had been very good at hiding it. Another thought struck her and sent shivers down her spine. Was it possible that his selfishness might lead him to cheat on her? She shook the thought away. No, Sam would never do a thing like that. But now that the idea had entered her head, it was difficult to dislodge it. With selfish people, anything was possible.

Something would have to be done and quickly. Sam would have to be forced to confront his selfishness. If it wasn't checked, it would get worse and put their relationship under serious strain. She knew one thing for certain: she couldn't live for the rest of her life with a selfish man. It would be unbearable.

She made up her mind to have another showdown, a serious one this time. She would give him an ultimatum to change his ways or else. But each time she tried to broach the subject, Sam found some excuse for avoiding it. Gradually time slipped away and before she knew, it was April and the holiday in Spain was fast approaching. In a few weeks' time they would be off to spend two weeks in Fuengirola. She had been looking forward to this holiday for months. If she had a big bust-up with him now it could spoil everything.

No, she decided. The best thing was to wait till they got back to Dublin and then she would have it out with him. And if he didn't change she would be gone. It would be embarrassing. Her mother and Debbie Fox would have been proved right. But she would just have to live with that.

So she put her misgivings aside and tried to concentrate on the holiday. She devoured the holiday guides and the tourist brochures. She made a list of things they must do and see. Her mind filled with thoughts of the sun and the scent of orange blossom floating on the breeze.

She dreamt of pleasant meals at little open-air cafés, the sound of guitar music wafting on the sultry night air, the heavens lit by stars. Fuengirola was to be the Promised Land, the reward for enduring the long, dull Irish winter.

And now it was May and the time had arrived. Everything had gone to plan. Amy had looked forward to this for so long. She was determined to enjoy this holiday come hell or high water.

Chapter 4

Betty Parsons glanced over the balcony of her top-floor apartment and saw the two young people sunning themselves on the lawn beside the fountain. They hadn't been there when she'd popped out earlier to check her mail-box so she assumed they had just arrived. She decided they must be staying in the ground-floor apartment which the Pilkingtons rented out in the summer because they couldn't stand the heat.

Betty had always thought that rather strange. Why go to all the trouble of purchasing an apartment on the Costa del Sol if you didn't like the heat? It just didn't make sense. The heat and the sun were what most people came for. She had asked June Pilkington about it one time and she mentioned something about wanting to spend the summer with their grandchildren in Cornwall. Cornwall was very nice. Betty had been there. But the weather was unpredictable. Not like here in Fuengirola where the sun shone all day long and you could go for weeks on end without seeing a cloud or a drop of rain.

Of course, it was none of her business what people did with their lives. Betty's philosophy was 'live and let live'. As long as people didn't bother her, she didn't bother them. So she decided to say nothing about the young couple on the lawn, although, strictly speaking, sunbathing was confined to the pool area. It was in the regulations somewhere and she knew some of the residents objected. But Betty didn't mind. They seemed a nice young couple and they weren't making noise or dropping litter, unlike some of the guests who had rented the Pilkingtons' apartment in the past.

She remembered, with a shudder of distaste, the stag party which had arrived a few years ago and caused mayhem running around the complex at all hours, drinking cans of lager and jumping into the swimming pool in the middle of the night, and causing so much trouble that the *policía* had to be called. Thank God, they had only stayed for a weekend.

Then there was the family who had stayed for a whole month last summer. They had three teenage boys who made an awful racket playing football and broke the plants. Not to mention turning up the volume on the television late at night when Betty was trying to get to sleep. And she needed her sleep. She had cut an article out of a magazine one time that said a minimum of seven hours' sleep was required for a healthy mind and body. If she didn't get a good night's sleep she felt washed out the next day and hadn't an ounce of energy.

That was the problem with letting your apartment. You never knew who you would get. It was all done on the internet and people could tell you anything. How were you supposed to check? They could say they were Buddhist monks and turn out to be devil worshippers performing Satanic rituals on the lawn in the light of the full moon. Not that anything like that had ever occurred at Magnolia Park, of course. But it *could* happen. That was her point.

Betty was a small, bird-like woman of sixty, slim and blonde, and she lived alone. She had come to Fuengirola for a holiday twenty-five years ago with her husband, Alf, and had fallen head over heels in love with the place. At the time, Alf was very busy with work. He owned an electrical store in London, selling everything from televisions to washing machines, and was planning on opening more.

Magnolia Park was just being built and Betty was so captivated with Fuengirola that she took one look at the developer's plans and persuaded her husband to put down a deposit on an apartment. She thought they would be able to use it as a holiday base and come out several times a year for breaks so that Alf could relax and get away from all the pressure of business for a while.

Back then, sterling was very strong and the cost of living in Spain was cheap. You could buy a slap-up meal in a very good restaurant for about a fiver. And that included wine. But it wasn't just the cost of living. There were all the other things that attracted her. There was the lovely weather and the flowers that bloomed all year round. There was the sea and the mountains. There was the relaxed Spanish lifestyle and the ferias and fiestas that brought music and excitement and spectacle to the streets.

But things hadn't worked out exactly as she planned. Any time she asked Alf to come away to Magnolia Park, he said he would love to but he just couldn't find the time. So she started coming out during the school holidays with their son Josh. Then Josh grew up and Betty was left to come alone.

It was a bit odd at first. She had planned the apartment for family holidays and now neither her husband nor son would come. The first few times she came on her own, she felt lonely. But gradually she started to get to know people. She joined the Amigos, a society which organised trips and lunches to raise funds for the local amateur English drama group who owned their own theatre, an old converted cinema. And she helped out occasionally at the second-hand shop run by a cancer charity.

Betty was an outgoing woman and before long she had made loads of new friends, many of them widows or single ladies. They took it in turns to hold little dinner parties in their homes. But Betty didn't particularly enjoy these occasions. Instead of opportunities to relax and have a chat, they became competitions, with each hostess trying to outdo the one before. Betty's friends found it odd that she had a husband who didn't spend time with her but they were too polite to say anything. She had a suspicion that behind her back they felt sorry for her.

Gradually, her periods in Spain grew longer till she was living the whole year round in Magnolia Park and only went back to London once or twice a year. The situation had been completely reversed. Then one day, she made a startling discovery. She realised that she didn't really miss Alf all that much. She could get along perfectly well without him.

This revelation came as a shock to her. They had been married for almost forty years and until she started coming regularly to Spain, she had never envisaged a day without her husband. Alf was her first and only lover. Theirs was an old-fashioned marriage. Alf was the provider and head of the household. She looked up to him and left him to make all the major decisions. And she never had a moment's regret.

He was a good husband. He worked hard at his business. He was successful. He wasn't mean or penny-pinching. Once the business took off, they moved to a nice house in Wandsworth and Alf provided the money to fill it with the very best furniture and accessories. He wasn't domineering or abusive and he was utterly faithful. Betty trusted him implicitly. Yet here she was at sixty and she suddenly realised that if Alf was run over by a bus tomorrow, her life would just go on exactly as normal.

This discovery made her feel guilty. It didn't seem right. Alf was her husband after all. He was the father of their son. He had worked every day of his life to provide a good living for them and here she was thinking of him as if he meant no more to her than some character in a television soap opera. Surely after all these years she should have stronger feelings for him?

She decided to ask some of her friends. There was one woman in particular she was close to, Gladys Taylor. She knew she could confide in her. Gladys had been married three times, divorced twice and widowed once when her husband, George, had been carried off by a massive heart-attack while pressing weights at the local gym. But Gladys hadn't allowed these tragedies to get her down. She didn't go around with a long face. She dressed well and had her hair nicely styled. She was always laughing and full of fun. And she had plenty of admirers. She often turned up at the theatre functions with a man on her arm and Betty couldn't help noticing that many of these men were much younger than she was.

One afternoon when the Amigos were having their regular

lunch, Betty made it her business to get seated beside Gladys. She waited till the meal was over and they had served the brandy before raising the topic that was on her mind. She had planned in advance how she would handle it. She began by asking Gladys if she ever missed any of her husbands.

Gladys let out a loud belly laugh that had heads turning in their direction.

"Well, not the first two, darling. They were proper bad 'uns, they were. Tell you the truth, I don't know why I ever got involved with them in the first place. Brought me nothing but grief, they did."

"Really?" Betty said, opening her eyes wide in encouragement.

"Oh yes. The first man I married, Freddie Bates, he was a gambler. Mind you, I was only seventeen when I met him. He was twenty-seven. Real lady-killer he was – dark eyes, wavy hair, nice snappy dresser. I thought I was in love, you see. Well, I was only a kid, what did I know?"

"Of course," Betty said. "You were inexperienced."

"Freddie Bates promised me the moon and the stars, settled us in a couple of rented rooms in Streatham and promised me that within a year we'd have the money to buy our own house. And I believed him. Six months later we had to skip in the middle of the night because he had pawned every stick of furniture in the place and owed the landlord three months' rent.

"Well, I should have learned from that but, of course, I didn't. He told me it was only a temporary cash-flow problem. He claimed to be in the antique business, said there was good money to be made and in no time we'd be rolling in lolly. Well, *I* never saw any of it, that's for sure.

"Then I discovered he was gambling, betting on anything that moved: horses, dogs, poker, slot machines, two flies walking up a wall. In the next three years we moved digs fifteen times because people were coming after him for the money he owed. We never had a red cent. In the end, I couldn't take it any more. I just packed up one day and went back to my mum."

"That must have been dreadful," Betty said. "I don't know how you stuck it so long."

"Love," Gladys said, taking a swig of brandy. "I was a sucker for love. That was how I met my next husband, Joe Thompson. If you think Freddie Bates was bad, Joe Thompson was a total one-hundred-per-cent gold-carat bastard and no mistake."

Betty shrunk back a little at the bad language. "What did *he* do?"

Gladys put down her glass and rolled up her sleeve to show an ugly scar on her arm.

"He attacked me with a carving knife."

Betty gasped and raised her napkin to her mouth in shock. "You mean he did that to you?"

"He sure did and might have done more only I managed to get away. He was one of them psychopaths."

"My God," Betty said. "That's terrible."

"Damn right it is. Of course, it didn't start right away. In the beginning, he was nice as ninepence, used to buy me flowers, boxes of chocolates, jewellery. You'd think I might have learned from my first experience but not me. He bowled me over, he did. We were married within six months.

"But within a year, Joe Thompson was coming home at three and four in the morning, pissed as a newt. And the smell of cheap perfume, it would knock you down, it would. If I opened my mouth to complain, out came the fist. He was one brutal bastard, thought nothing of knocking me around.

"Well, I stuck that for another eighteen months till he went at me with the knife one night and I decided I'd had enough. I wasn't going to hang around till he murdered me, was I?"

"I should think not," Betty said, cringing at the thought.

"Straight round to the police station and lodged a complaint. Coppers nicked him before he knew what was happening. He was charged with grievous bodily harm and got two years in the slammer. When he got out, I was gone."

By now, Betty was completely captivated by Gladys's story. She could have sat all afternoon listening to her talk.

"So where did you meet your third husband?" she asked.

"Battersea public library."

"Really?"

Gladys laughed and took another swig of brandy. "Odd place to find a man, isn't it? But love can lurk in the strangest places. I was browsing the shelves one evening looking for a good romance and I noticed this well-dressed bloke standing beside me. So we just fell to talking. It turned out he was taking part in a general knowledge quiz and was looking for books on opera. That was to be his special subject. So I helped him find a couple of books and then he invited me to come along to the quiz night and I thought, why not, what have I got to lose? And that was how it started." She smiled.

"Strange, isn't it?"

Betty laughed. "It's certainly unusual."

"George Taylor was a lovely man," Gladys went on. "He was a perfect gentleman. He was a scrap-metal dealer. Knew how to treat a lady and was very skilled in the romantic department, if you catch my meaning. Pity I didn't meet him sooner but it was not to be. And then he was snatched away so cruelly just when I had finally found the love I'd been searching for all my life. Massive coronary, he went out like a candle, dead before he hit the ground." She sighed and drained her glass. "That's life, I suppose. At least he didn't suffer."

"That's a fascinating story," Betty said. "You've had a very interesting life, Gladys. Have you ever thought of writing your autobiography?"

"Get away. Who would want to read it?"

"I would for one and I'm sure there'd be plenty of others. Do you ever miss George?"

"Well, I do think of him now and then. But what's the use of grieving? It's not going to bring him back, is it? In my opinion, life is for living. Better to press on and make the most of what you've got. And you know something? There are lots of people worse off than me. Sure here I am sitting in the Spanish sun enjoying myself without a care in the world."

After she got home, Betty poured a glass of wine and sat on her terrace, looking out at the flowering bougainvillea climbing the wall of the apartment next door. Her little talk with Gladys Taylor had been very instructive. It was the first time she had heard another woman talk so frankly about her married life.

She thought of the terrible times Gladys must have had with her first two husbands. Alf had never been like them. He had never beaten her or run up debts and pawned the furniture or got drunk and chased other women. He had been a model husband in those respects.

But, on the other hand, he hadn't been particularly skilled in the romantic department, as Gladys had so delicately put it. Alf had always been working too hard to have much interest in sex. After siring Josh, he had lost interest. And, eventually, he had moved bedrooms with the excuse that Betty's snoring kept him awake at night. Not that it bothered her. She had always suspected that the first flush of passion wouldn't last forever.

All in all, she thought she hadn't done too badly with Alf. He had bought her this lovely apartment and paid her a monthly allowance that made sure she had no financial worries. He came out a couple of times a year and spent a few days beating a golf ball about and watching Sky Sports on television. If he didn't want to spend more time here, that was his loss. Why should she feel guilty?

No, Betty decided. She should take Gladys's advice and make the most of her situation. *Life is for Living* would make a nice motto to stick on the kitchen fridge. And there was a little shop in the old town that made lovely wooden ones. She would call in the next time she went past and ask if they would make one for her.

Now, she gazed down at the young couple sunning themselves on the lawn. They weren't much older than Alf and she had been when they got married. They have all their life ahead of them, she thought. I wonder what it will bring.

And then an idea came floating into her head. I'll just nip down and introduce myself, she thought. Have a little chat. Welcome them to Magnolia Park.

Chapter 5

Sam came awake when he heard footsteps approach along the path that bordered the lawn where he and Amy and were sunbathing. He had dozed off but before that he had been thinking about where they would go for dinner that night. Eating out was one of the pleasures he enjoyed most about a holiday. Sam liked to think of himself as a gourmet diner, willing to try new food, and travel had given him plenty of opportunities.

He had many happy memories of wonderful meals he had eaten abroad, including a magnificent repast he had enjoyed one time in Florence at a little place called Ciro's. It wasn't a famous restaurant – in fact he could easily have passed it by without noticing. But the hotel clerk had recommended it and Sam had sought it out. He had found it in a little back street behind the cathedral and never again had he eaten lamb that tasted so good. And it was at this restaurant that he had first been introduced to the marvellous Italian liqueur called Strega.

Before coming away, he had a quick look on the internet to check out the cuisine of this part of southern Spain. Every article he read had stressed the wonderful range of seafood dishes that were available, from prawns and squid right through to wild sea bass. This was perfect. He could get meat and chicken anywhere but good fish wasn't so easy to find.

The internet articles had mentioned a number of restaurants and Sam had written them down. Two of them were here in Fuengirola port which was only fifteen minutes away. They would go there tonight. He had visions of a nice steamed lobster or a grilled sole with a crunchy salad and chilled white wine. He would enjoy that. He would mention it to Amy later. She wasn't a fussy eater and normally fell in with his plans.

He adjusted his Ray-Bans and stretched his face to the sun. Sam had a naturally dark complexion so he wasn't hung up about getting a tan. He was just here to unwind and recover his breath after the last frantic month spent in the offices of Burrows Advertising Executives in Baggot Street, working on one of the most testing projects of his entire career.

He still had nightmares when he thought about it. He had been put in charge of an advertising campaign for a designer clothes company called Slimline Fashions, which claimed to give a slender, youthful look to the gullible women who could afford to pay their outrageous prices. It was a big account and stood to earn the company a hefty commission.

The project itself wasn't particularly difficult. In normal circumstances it would have been a piece of cake. The problem lay with the owner of Slimline Fashions, an utterly impossible individual called Herbie Morrison.

Never in his years in advertising had Sam come across a client who had been so fussy and contrary and difficult to please. He thought of the constant arguments, the rewrites, the doubts, the last-minute changes of mind. He shuddered when he remembered the irate phone calls and the relentless hassle.

It was like working in a lunatic asylum. Several times he had been on the verge of telling Herbie Morrison where to stick the campaign but Sam's boss, Ron Burrows, had insisted that he must give the client what he wanted. There was a lot of money riding on this contract but it was easily the worst job he had ever worked on. He had heaved a massive sigh of relief when he finally got the project finished just in time to pack his bags for Magnolia Park.

He opened his eyes when he heard a voice close by. He took off his sunglasses and found a small, thin, middle-aged lady peering down at him. He sat up with a start and blinked at her.

"I hope I didn't startle you," the woman said. "My name is Betty

Parsons. I'm your neighbour. I live in the top-floor apartment in your block."

She pointed up to her apartment. Sam could see the top of a yellow umbrella poking above the terrace railing.

He stood up and grasped her outstretched hand. "Pleased to meet you," he said.

By now Amy was also getting to her feet. Sam made the introductions.

"I'm Sam Benson and this is my partner, Amy Crawford."

"Hi," Amy smiled.

"I spotted you a few minutes ago and I thought I'd nip down and say hello," Betty continued. "Have you just arrived?"

"We got here a few hours ago," Sam explained. "But first we had to get in some provisions and grab a bite of lunch."

"I hope you like your apartment. Is everything to your satisfaction?"

"Oh yes," Amy replied. "The apartment's beautiful."

"Well, that's good. June will be pleased. That's June Pilkington. She's the owner. She always goes to Cornwall for the summer." Betty lowered her voice and whispered, "She doesn't like the heat." She chuckled. "I've never understood it. That's what most people come here for. How long are you staying?"

"Two weeks."

"Well, you couldn't have chosen a nicer place than Magnolia Park. Have you been to Fuengirola before?"

"No," they both said.

"You're going to love it. Everything you could want is here. And the weather is going to remain nice and sunny. I check the forecast every morning, you see."

Amy brightened up at this prospect. "That's good news," she said. "It was overcast when we left home."

"And where is home, dear?"

"Dublin."

"Well, isn't that a coincidence?" Betty exclaimed. "My husband has a shop in Dublin. He's in the electrical trade."

"What's the shop called?" Sam asked.

"Parsons Electrical, The Friendly Store. It's in Dundrum shopping centre. I don't suppose you know it?"

"Afraid not, we live on the other side of town."

"Well, he loves going to Dublin. He says the Irish are great people for a party. He says they really know how to let their hair down."

"They're not partying very much since the recession began," Sam said glumly.

"Do you live here all the time?" Amy asked.

"More or less," Betty said. "But I do go back to the UK occasionally. My husband and son are in London. They're both involved in the family business."

"I envy you," Amy said. "It must be wonderful to wake up every morning to that beautiful sun and the sound of water splashing from the fountain."

"And the birds chirping – the dawn chorus. There's nothing to beat breakfast on the terrace with the sound of the birds and the sun shining and all the flowers in bloom. Makes you glad to be alive."

"I'll bet it does," Amy said, making a mental note to have breakfast on the terrace the following day.

"Well, I hope I haven't disturbed you," Betty said. "If you need anything or want any directions just knock on my door. I'll be delighted to help you. Goodbye."

"Goodbye, Mrs Parsons," Amy said.

"Oh, no, you mustn't be so formal. You must call me Betty."

She began to turn away and then suddenly stopped.

"I've just thought of something. Have you got anything planned for tomorrow afternoon?"

Sam and Amy shook their heads.

"Good," Betty said. "Why don't you call up and see me about four o'clock? We'll have a nice glass of wine and I'll tell you everything you need to know about Magnolia Park."

She smiled and waved goodbye.

"Toodleoo!" she said and Sam and Amy watched her disappear down the garden.

Partner, Betty thought as she skirted the rose bed and made her way past the swimming pool. That's the term they use now. In my young days it was girlfriend or, if you were really polite, you might say 'my young lady'. Fiancée, of course, was only used if you were formally engaged. Using 'partner' had something to do with what Josh called the equality agenda and women's rights. She must get into the habit of using it. Move with the times. But the trouble was, the times were moving very fast now and it was difficult to keep up.

On the way back to her apartment, she ran into Antonio the gardener and stopped to have a chat. Antonio's little boy had come down with an ear infection and wasn't able to attend school. So Betty spent some time assuring him that these minor ailments were all part of growing up and everything would turn out alright in the end.

Then she left to call on old Mrs Gilbert who lived further along the block. She was a widow and lived alone. Betty was planning a trip to the supermarket tomorrow and usually picked up some items for the old lady. When she finally got back to her apartment, she made a pot of tea and sat on the terrace to drink it.

She was glad now that she had taken the trouble to go down and introduce herself to the young couple. They seemed to be nice people, not at all the type to be having mad parties or playing loud music late at night. They were Irish and, of course, Alf was mad about Irish people. She suspected they took him out carousing all over Dublin any time he went over to visit the store. That was why he was always so keen to go back.

She was just pouring her second cup of tea when her phone rang. When she answered, she heard her son's voice.

"Hi, Mum," he began.

"Josh! What a lovely surprise. How are you, dear?"

"I'm a bit tired to be honest. I'm on my way back from China."

"You certainly must be exhausted!"

"It's been a tough four weeks and now I need a rest. I thought I'd come down and join you for a few days."

Betty felt her heart leap at this news. "Oh Josh, that would be lovely. When are you coming?"

"Tomorrow morning. I'm in Madrid right now. I'm catching an

early flight. I should be with you around nine o'clock. What's the weather like?"

"It's beautiful and there's a nice cool breeze. You'll enjoy it."

"Okay, I'll see you tomorrow. And Mum, don't do anything special."

"I have to prepare your room, dear."

"Yes, but nothing else. I don't want you fussing over me. You know I don't like that."

"Of course not, Josh."

She heard him laughing.

"*Adiós,*" he said.

She put down the phone and smiled to herself. What a nice surprise! It would be wonderful to see her son again. And then she remembered that she had invited the young Irish people for drinks tomorrow at four o'clock. She wondered if she should cancel. No, she decided. It would look rude. She would introduce them to Josh and have a jolly little party.

Sam took a sip from his wineglass and carefully touched his mouth with his starched white napkin. He had just eaten a wonderful meal of grilled sole, potatoes fried in garlic and a mixed salad and now a sense of contentment was settling over him. He looked across at Amy. They were seated at a pavement table outside *La Rueda*, one of the restaurants down at the port which had been recommended on the internet. The sun was hanging over the ocean like a ball of fire and, just a few feet away, the yachts and cruisers creaked in the gentle swell of the sea.

He gave a loud sigh. "This is the life," he said. "What a wonderful setting! Where would you get it?" He reached out and took Amy's hand. "Are you enjoying the holiday?"

"Of course, this is what I've been dreaming about all winter. And so far it has come well up to my expectations."

Sam smiled. He loved moments like this, just him and Amy alone, no jangling phones or unhappy clients to distract them. He could feel the peace settling around him like a comfort blanket.

"Fancy some dessert?" he asked.

"I'm not sure I have any appetite left!"

"Maybe we could share one?" he urged. "Why don't we have some tiramisu?"

"Okay," Amy agreed.

"And a small brandy?"

"I don't think so," she replied. "The last time I drank brandy, it gave me a headache."

Sam called the waiter and asked for a portion of tiramisu.

"I was thinking of that woman, Mrs Parsons," he continued.

"What a nice lady," Amy said. "It was kind of her to drop down and welcome us today. And it's always good to have someone to go to if we need anything."

"But we don't want to get too friendly, do we?" Sam said. "We're here to relax, to get away from people and be on our own. We don't want to get involved with a whole new set of people we don't even know. To be honest, I'm beginning to regret this invitation tomorrow afternoon."

Amy gave him a look of surprise. "Why? What harm can it do? Besides, we've already accepted. We can't back out now."

"Of course, but we shouldn't get too close, if you know what I mean. I don't think we should get tied down."

"I don't think that's likely to happen," Amy said. "It's just a glass of wine. And we might pick up some useful tips."

"It's a bit odd her living here and her husband living in London."

"She seems happy enough," Amy replied.

"Well, I don't think it would suit me. What about you?"

"Hmmm," she said. She looked around at the water lapping at the wall of the harbour and the sun sinking into the sea in a blaze of orange light. "I do believe I could get used to it."

He leaned across and kissed her.

"You wouldn't last a wet week without me," he laughed. "So don't pretend otherwise."

"Don't bet on it," she said.

He gave her a quizzical look. Amy was becoming increasingly enigmatic. Sometimes he found it hard to know when she was serious.

Chapter 6

Josh Parsons put down the phone after speaking to his mother and a slight smile played around the corners of his mouth. It was good to hear her voice. He was looking forward to his visit to Magnolia Park. He knew he would be able to unwind there and perhaps talk to his mother about the problem that was bothering him. It would do him good to unburden himself and Betty was a good listener. She might even be able to give him some advice.

Josh was thirty-two years of age but already he had led a very chequered life. It had begun smoothly enough. As an only child with a wealthy father, he had been cosseted and fawned upon. At primary school he was the boy with the best designer runners, the largest collection of comic annuals, the most pocket-money and the shiniest bicycle. He didn't even have to walk to school like most of the other pupils. Each morning he was dropped at the gates in his father's silver BMW car. At three o'clock he was taken home again by one of the company's van drivers.

Of course, there were some begrudgers among his schoolmates who objected to his conspicuous wealth and expensive clothes. They tried to bring him down a peg by calling him a snobby creep and other abusive names. But they were in the minority and easily dismissed. Most of Josh's school friends were happy to suck up to him in return for invitations to watch TV at his house or accompany him on trips to the cinema at weekends. From a young age, Josh had been led to expect that people would pamper him and do his bidding.

But this sort of upbringing was not good for him. He became a self-centred little boy who was used to getting his own way. He had only one real friend and that was his mother. His father, who might have set an example for the growing boy, was too busy building up his business to spend much time with young Josh. While other boys of his age were being taken to football matches or swimming lessons by their dads, Josh was left in the gentle care of his mum.

His mother loved him, of that there was no doubt. But she loved him too much and that was the problem. Betty was loath to correct him or teach him that there were limits to his behaviour beyond which it became unacceptable. Josh quickly became a master of the strategic sulk and the extended silence. He never had to resort to foot-stamping or tantrums. It was enough to let his mother know that she had offended him for Betty to cave in and give him whatever he wanted.

There were those who witnessed Josh's antics and said he was a spoiled little brat and what he needed was a good thump. Some even said that Betty Parsons was building up problems for that boy when he finally went out into the big wide world. But Betty would no more have thought of chastising Josh than she would have considered cutting off her big toe with a meat cleaver.

However, at age thirteen, two things happened to shatter this sheltered lifestyle. The first was that his mother started disappearing to Spain for extended periods. The second was he was sent to boarding school. Both events were traumatic. Alf Parsons had already decided that his son was going to follow him into the business. Josh was never consulted. It was simply assumed that he would be delighted to inherit a chain of electrical stores.

Alf was a self-made man who had little education and had prospered by sheer hard work and good business sense. But like many men in this position, he had a secret admiration for those who had been to public schools and could talk knowledgably about affairs of state. So he began to make discreet enquiries.

He soon discovered that getting his son into a good public school wasn't as easy as he had assumed. Some of them insisted that a brother or an uncle or parent should have been a past pupil. Others had waiting lists a mile long. For some of the very top schools, parents were known to have put the child's name down at birth.

Alf quickly realised what he was up against. It was the old-boy network. Alf had plenty of money but that wasn't what counted. What counted was class and breeding and unfortunately for Josh, his father had neither. But Alf persevered, slowly working his way down the ladder till at last he hit upon Willowfield Academy for Boys. This was a very minor public school which was strapped for cash and happy to take Alf Parsons' money.

The fees cost £10,000 a year but Alf considered it money well spent. Josh would get an education that would hopefully see him into university where he could study Business Management and be in a position to take over the reins of Parsons Electrical whenever Alf retired or, more likely, dropped dead from overwork.

And there was another advantage. Alf believed that Josh would rub shoulders with the type of boys who would go on to become captains of industry and masters of the financial universe. These contacts would stand Josh in good stead when eventually he had to make his own way in the world.

Willowfield Academy was housed in a crumbling old house in rural Kent. Josh hated it from the minute he set foot on its gravelled driveway. Here, Parsons Electrical meant nothing. In fact, it was a positive drawback and Josh became a subject of scorn and ridicule. The majority of the boys had fathers who held down middle-ranking jobs in the civil service or the professions. Class snobbery was ingrained in them. To them, Josh was a little twerp whose old man was a money-grubbing shopkeeper.

He was bullied unmercifully and quickly became the butt of cruel jokes. They sneered at his accent, his manners and his physical appearance. They soon coined a nickname for him – Parsnips – which followed him all over the school. And there was another problem. By the time he arrived at Willowfield, the pupils were already organised into little clubs and cliques and Josh was systematically excluded from each one and socially ostracised.

To make matters worse, the masters were distant and unsympathetic, the food was awful and the bunk bed he was allocated in a dormitory shared by twenty-nine other boys, was hard and uncomfortable. For the first month, he cried himself to sleep every night with the blankets pulled over his head so that no one would hear.

Josh couldn't understand how his fortunes had changed so dramatically. From being the centre of attention where his every whim was catered for, he had become a social outcast without a single friend. His existence was pitiful. He saw himself as Oliver Twist in the Dickens' story he had read. His first reaction was to demand that his parents take him out of the school immediately. But his father was not the pushover that his mother had been. He had gone to considerable trouble to find this place for his son and he wasn't going to throw it away lightly.

Yet Willowfield Academy was to be the making of Josh, although not in the way that his father had foreseen. Despite his sheltered upbringing, Josh was a bright, intelligent boy. After the initial shock had subsided, he soon came to the realisation that he was stuck with Willowfield school. And something told him that snivelling and complaining would do him no good at all. It would probably invite even more abuse. If he was to survive in this hell-hole, he had to become good at something. The obvious thing was sport.

Recreational facilities were not high on the list of priorities at Willowfield Academy. But in the true tradition of British public schools, Willowfield did manage to have a rugby fifteen which trained once a week on a field borrowed from a neighbouring farmer. Although they rarely won any games, members of the rugger team were regarded as the élite of the school. These were the heroes and all the pupils looked up to them. Josh set himself the goal of joining them.

However, he suffered from another major handicap. He had never been keen on sport and knew absolutely nothing about rugby. But, he was determined and after careful consideration, he drew up a plan of action. The first thing was to watch the team at close quarters so as to learn the basic rules of the game. The second was to get his father to buy him books about the sport so that he could study it in detail. The final step was to get fit enough to play.

There was one thing that stood in Josh's favour. He was developing into an athletic young man despite the best efforts of the catering staff to stunt his growth with the awful diet he was fed. He was taller than most boys of his age. And he had a solid frame which was suited to a tough physical contact sport like rugby. But he still had a mountain to climb.

The rugby coach was a former player called Mr Cartwright. He looked Josh up and down, ran a tape measure over him, weighed him and reluctantly agreed that he could join the training sessions but not actually play. His first outing was a nightmare. He had to endure a barrage of catcalls and derision as he made a stumbling attempt at the press-ups and stretching exercises which formed the basis of the fitness programme. But he persisted until he had mastered the techniques and gradually the abuse began to subside.

However, Josh wasn't content to rely on the weekly training sessions. Each day, after class was over, he spent an hour jogging around the sports field to improve his fitness. He also persuaded his father to purchase a membership for him at a gym in the nearby town of Kirkwood. At weekends and half-days, he inveigled permission to visit the gym where he trained with weights to build up his strength and endurance. Within four months, through sheer persistence and dogged determination, Josh had made himself fit enough to take the place of a player who had been injured.

There was stunned incredulity throughout the school that Parsnips, of all people, had been selected to play for the rugger team. He was a wet and a wimp whose father turned up at the annual parents' day meeting wearing a leather jacket instead of a pin-striped suit like the other fathers.

However, there was also a code of honour at Willowfield Academy. Every boy at the school was duty bound to support the rugby team. There was absolutely no question of anyone jeering at a boy who ran onto the pitch wearing the Willowfield rugby jersey. He was representing the school and the prevailing ethos demanded that he must be supported.

But Josh knew he had to do more. This was his big opportunity and he might not get another. If he fluffed it, he would never be allowed to forget it and his life would become totally unbearable. The night before the game, he took half a sleeping tablet he had cajoled from his mother and enjoyed eight hours of the deepest sleep he could ever remember.

He woke fit and refreshed. He forced himself to eat a large breakfast of porridge and eggs to stoke up his energy. On the way to the game, he sat silent on the team coach and focussed all his mental concentration on the task that lay ahead. The team they were due to play were the reigning league champions and everyone expected Willowfield to lose. The only question was by how much. But Josh didn't even allow this consideration to enter his head. Even the best team could be beaten. They were fifteen boys just like themselves. They were human and therefore fallible.

Because of his size, Josh was selected to play on the back row. The game started badly for the school and by half-time they were trailing their opponents by five points and already showing signs of tiredness and defeat. Josh consoled himself that so far he had managed to hold his own and hadn't disgraced himself. However, much more was required. If Willowfield went on to lose he knew who would be blamed.

In the second half, the margin widened when their opponents scored several more points. It looked like the game might descend into a rout. Then suddenly, out of the blue, Josh found himself in possession of the ball. This was his moment. He put his head down and charged down the field like a bull.

It was an amazing spectacle. Opponents hurled themselves at him to no avail. He ducked and weaved and brushed them aside like minor irritants till somehow he managed to struggle across the line with two opponents still clinging on to him. He had scored a try. There was uproar from the Willowfield supporters. The try was converted and the gap was narrowed. Suddenly, it appeared that the school might be back in the game.

Josh's try seemed to have the effect of galvanising the rest of the team. They played with fresh confidence and now it was their opponents who were under pressure. Then, fifteen minutes from the end, Josh got possession of the ball for a second time. He looked around and saw a gap in the opponents' defence. Off he went once more on a solo charge.

No one had seen anything like it. He was a boy on a mission. Opponents were tossed aside as he ploughed down the pitch to plant the ball firmly across the line and score a second try. The spectators went wild. This try too was converted and now Willowfield were ahead by three points. Somehow, they managed to hold this slender lead till the final whistle blew and victory was theirs.

The scenes after the game had never been witnessed before. Josh was a hero. The wimp who had been scorned and ridiculed had been transformed into a champion who had scored two tries and inspired Willowfield Academy to go on and win their first game in six months. He was carried shoulder-high from the field and warmly congratulated on all sides.

The fact that he accepted this praise with due humility and no hint of triumph only served to strengthen his popularity. Now his erstwhile tormentors were forced to review their opinion of him and decide that old Parsnips wasn't such a bad chap after all even if his father sold electric toasters for a living.

The game was a turning point in Josh's life. From that moment on, he became a regular feature of the team and in due course became captain and led Willowfield to its first ever success in winning the Schools Cup. Overnight, he had become accepted. Boys who had shunned him now wanted to become his friend. Social circles that had been closed to him suddenly opened up. By the end of his stay at Willowfield, Josh had become the most popular boy in the school. The younger pupils looked up to him and tried to gain his approval. In his last year, he was elected Head Prefect by popular acclaim.

But the experience had taught him several important lessons that he would never have learned if he had remained under the shelter of his mother's wing. The first was that determination and application could overcome apparently insurmountable odds. The second was never to make snap judgments about people based on class or position. And the third was the crippling and demoralising effects of bullying. Josh made himself a promise never to subject another human being to the withering sarcasm he had endured in his early months at Willowfield Academy.

In due course, he successfully completed his exams and moved on to university. His time there was largely happy. He enjoyed his studies. He continued to play rugby. He made lots of new friends and for the first time in his life, he began to meet young women. But this experience was mixed. He had been educated in an all-male environment and had no sisters, so his initial contacts with girls were awkward.

Josh had grown into a tall, handsome young man with a shock of blond hair. Women found him attractive but he felt uneasy in their company. He missed the back-slapping camaraderie of the rugby club and envied those fellow students who socialised easily with girls.

At the end of four years, he left university with a first-class Honours degree in Business Management. By now, he had accepted the inevitability of his father's plans for him to take over the family firm. He began his career working as a sales assistant in the store in Hackney and gradually got to know the business from top to bottom. Parsons Electrical had grown to a total of forty-five stores and had a turnover of millions of pounds a year. But other people had got the same idea of selling electrical goods at discount prices and the competition was fierce.

Josh persuaded his father to hire a couple of bright young marketing graduates to raise the company's profile and appointed a Head of Sales to oversee distribution. He drew up plans to diversify into other product ranges, particularly computers and electronics, when the day finally arrived when he would assume the reins of the company.

But at age sixty-five, Alf was showing no signs of handing over. He was still working twelve-hour days, which was only a slight improvement on the fifteen and sixteen hours he had put in when he was starting out. It wasn't that Alf didn't trust his son to run the business. It was simply that he didn't know what else to do with his time. Alf Parsons' whole life had been spent in the electrical business. Letting go would be like turning off a life-support machine.

Several times, Josh talked to his father about retiring and taking a well-earned rest. He was now a very wealthy man. And despite the punishing regime he had subjected himself to, he still enjoyed good health. Apart from the large family home in Wandsworth, he owned a comfortable apartment on the Costa del Sol where Betty spent most of her time and he had the funds to purchase an even grander one if he so desired. He could retire out there and take life easy. He could play golf and let Josh worry about the business.

But Alf wasn't interested. He kept saying he would think about it in a few years' time. Josh was beginning to believe his father would never retire. It looked as if Alf Parsons would be found dead some morning at his desk clutching an invoice for 5000 electric kettles.

Josh had no intention of following his father's example and submerging his life in the family business. He wanted a social life. He had enjoyed the company of many attractive women, though it wasn't till he met a young actress called Nina Black that he fell in love. But sadly, this relationship had come to a shuddering end.

Chapter 7

Sam had gone to bed with Amy's remark still ringing in his ears. Had she been serious when she said that she could quite easily live down here without him? He tried to remember how many glasses of wine she had drunk with the meal. At least half a bottle. That was it, he decided. She must have been tipsy.

Of course, it had to be a joke. Amy idolised him. He had plucked her from the Zhivago Bar and swept her off her feet. He had provided her with a beautiful apartment and given her carte blanche to redecorate it. He took her to fancy restaurants and glitzy social events where she would never have been invited without him. Sam knew that all her friends envied the hell out of her. Why on earth would she even think of giving it up?

And yet, he had noticed an independent streak creep into her manner in the past six months. There was that lecture she had given him about being selfish and not doing his share of the household chores. It had taken him aback. Sam had never regarded himself as selfish. But he did hold down a responsible job as a creative executive in a major advertising company which meant he was always busy. He didn't have time to wash dishes and do laundry so he tended to leave that sort of stuff for Amy. But since that little heart-to-heart talk he had tried to do his best to please her.

This business of visiting Mrs Parsons tomorrow was a very good example. He didn't really want to go and listen to her rattling on about her husband's electrical stores and how Mrs Pilkington didn't like the heat. But Amy had insisted and he had given in and agreed to go for the sake of quiet life. That was a good example of how co-operative he could be.

Sam had long ago come to the conclusion that women were strange creatures. It was difficult to know what went on in their heads. It was best to humour them. With thoughts of the lovely grilled sole he had eaten for dinner still fresh in his mind, he rolled over, pulled the bed-sheet around him and soon was fast asleep.

The following morning, Amy was up early, determined to start the day on a high note. She had slept well and felt refreshed. She had been very impressed with Betty Parsons' description of breakfast on the terrace and was eager to sample the experience. But first she had to get some fresh bread.

Their apartment consisted of a large bedroom with an en-suite bathroom, a lounge, another bathroom, and a small kitchen. The size of the kitchen didn't really matter since they wouldn't be doing much cooking anyway. They had already decided to have their main meals out. Yesterday they had bought basic provisions on their shopping trip – things like milk, butter, ham, cheese, coffee and fruit. But bread had to be bought fresh each morning. There was a bakery at the gates of the complex. She checked her watch. It was a quarter to nine. It should be open now.

Careful not to wake the still-sleeping Sam, she got dressed in the bathroom, quietly closed the front door and set off. Already, the sun was bright and it promised to be another beautiful day. Her route took her through the gardens. They were magnificent in the bright morning light, the roses and geraniums in bloom, the clematis and bougainvillea in vivid colour and the air filled with the chirping of birdsong.

Amy was in wonderful form. She could feel herself settling into a relaxed holiday mood. As she passed through the gardens, she couldn't help thinking once more how wonderful it would be to have this magnificent spectacle to look forward to each morning.

She envied people like Betty Parsons who lived here all the year round. What a marvellous life it must be!

On her way, she passed the square of townhouses set around the quaint little courtyard and, as she approached the gates, her eyes were drawn to another striking sight. Both sides of the path were lined with magnificent magnolia trees, their bright white and pink flowers opening to the sun and filling the morning air with their sweet lemony perfume. It was from these wonderful trees that the development got its name.

She opened her bag and began to rummage for her keys. But at that moment, she noticed a tall blond man approach from the street outside. He was dressed in a light linen suit with open-necked shirt and was carrying a travelling bag. He quickly unlocked the gate and politely held it open for her.

"*Muchas gracias*," she said and hurried through. As she passed, she couldn't help noticing his eyes. They were a most appealing colour of cornflower blue.

"My pleasure," the man replied and gave her a warm smile before closing the gate and walking quickly away.

What a polite man, Amy thought, and handsome too. From his accent he obviously wasn't Spanish. She walked the short distance to the bakery and was met with the wonderful aroma of freshly baked bread. The young assistant smiled in welcome

"*Sí, señorita?*"

"*Dos baguettes, por favor*," Amy said, remembering the little bit of Spanish she had picked up from her phrasebook. A few minutes later with the bread tucked under her arm, she was making her way back through the gardens to their apartment.

When she arrived, she found Sam was already up and showered. And he had laid out knives and forks on the table on the terrace and set the kettle to boil. She was pleasantly surprised. He kissed her warmly on the cheek.

"*Buenos días*," he said and grinned.

Amy quickly put out some ham and tomatoes and honey and made a pot of coffee.

"Another hellish day in Paradise," Sam quipped as he sat down and applied butter and ham to a chunk of warm bread. Apart from the splashing water of the fountain, the complex was so still you might have heard a pin drop.

"You know, Mrs Parsons was right," he continued, as he took a mouthful of strong hot coffee. "This is the way to begin the morning. You've no idea what it feels like to get away from that madhouse where I work."

"I think I do," Amy smiled. "I have the very same feeling. This is sheer pleasure."

"So what have you planned for today?"

"Nothing. I think I'll just laze in the garden and maybe have a swim."

"Sounds good to me," Sam replied and poured another cup of coffee.

After they had cleared the breakfast things away and washed up, Amy changed into her swimsuit and Sam carried the sun-beds out to the garden. The sun was now quite strong and Amy positioned herself close to the shade of the trees so that she wouldn't get burnt. She spent the morning reading and whenever she got too hot, she took a dip in the cool water of the swimming pool. Beside her, Sam soaked up the sunshine and listened to his pocket radio.

She thought again how pleasant it must be to enjoy this lifestyle all the time. Her mind returned to Dublin and its weary hustle and bustle and the unpredictability of the weather. How she envied people like Betty Parsons. Her thoughts were interrupted by Sam's loud snoring. He had fallen asleep again. She looked at his handsome face and felt her heart go out to him. He had been working very hard on that Slimline contract, too hard indeed, and now he must be exhausted. But it was good to see him relaxing at last and getting some benefit from the holiday.

At one thirty Sam stirred again, strode to the pool and dived in. He swam for fifteen minutes then came and stood beside her while he towelled himself dry.

"Got to think of some lunch," he said.

"What do you have in mind?"

"We could return to that little *tapas* bar we visited yesterday."

"Good idea. Give me a few minutes to change clothes."

Sam pulled on some light trousers and a sports shirt while Amy changed into shorts, tee-shirt and sandals and they set off to walk the short distance to the bar. It was down beside the train station. It was cool inside and they decided to take a break from the intense heat so they sat down at the counter and surveyed the range of food on offer.

Amy chose a dish of meatballs in tomato sauce and a slice of tortilla. It came with a little basket of fresh crunchy bread. To accompany her meal, she had a glass of white wine.

Sam was more adventurous and opted for a dish of grilled octopus and another of sardines in vinegar. He drank a glass of beer and heaved a loud sigh.

"This is the life," he said.

"My sentiments entirely," Amy replied. "I was just thinking this morning how wonderful it must be to live here all the time."

Sam laughed. "It's a pipe-dream, Amy. You'd still have to work. You don't find the Spaniards lying around sunbathing all day long."

"Some of them do."

"Just the ones who are on holiday like us."

"I might win the lottery," she laughed.

Sam grinned. "Yes, you might. And pigs might fly. Believe me, if you lived here permanently, you would soon get bored."

But a wistful look had crept across Amy's face.

"I'm not so sure you're right about that," she said.

Sam was enjoying his lunch so much that he ordered another dish of octopus and more beer and they sat chatting peacefully in the gloomy little bar till Amy suddenly glanced at her watch and gave a loud exclamation.

"My God, is it that time already?"

"What time?" Sam said, startled.

"Three thirty. And we have to visit Mrs Parsons at four. C'mon, Sam, drink up. We've got to go."

He gave a loud groan. "Damn," he said. "I don't suppose we could skip it and stay on here?"

"We can't, Sam. It would be very bad manners."

"Why did she have to invite us in the first place? Why couldn't she just leave us alone?" he complained. "We don't even know her."

"She did it because she's a nice, friendly person and she's trying to be helpful."

"She's probably just a busybody who can't wait to poke her nose into our affairs."

"I'm sure that's the last thing on her mind," Amy replied. "I think she might be lonely with her husband stuck in London most of the time. She probably enjoys a bit of company. What's the harm in a couple of drinks?"

"A couple?" Sam said, aghast. "I thought she said a glass of wine?"

"She said she would tell us all about Magnolia Park," Amy coaxed him. "We might learn something to our advantage."

At last, they paid their bill and walked back to the apartment.

Amy went straight into the shower. As she got dried, she examined herself in the mirror and was delighted to see a healthy glow on her cheeks and arms and shoulders.

"What do you think?" she asked Sam who was fastening the belt of his trousers.

"You look ravishing, as always. A few more days of this sunshine and you'll be as brown as a Spaniard. No one will recognise you when you get home."

This cheered her up and she started to get dressed.

Just then, Sam's phone gave a loud ring. He opened it and clapped it to his ear.

"Ron!" he bellowed. "What's going down, man?"

Amy glanced up quickly at the mention of the name. The only Ron she knew was Ron Burrows, who was Sam's boss at the advertising agency back in Dublin. She hoped this wasn't bad news.

"Problem?" she heard Sam say. "What kind of problem?"

Amy shot him a nervous glance. He looked at her, covered the mouthpiece with his hand and vigorously shook his head. For good measure, he walked out onto the terrace and slid the glass door behind him so that she couldn't hear him talk.

Amy concentrated on getting dressed. She took out a white linen dress and held it up to the light. It would go well with a pair of jewelled sandals she had picked up in the New Year sales. And it had the added virtue of being comfortable.

She glanced at the clock on the wall beside the kitchen and saw the hand edge up to three fifty-five. Outside on the terrace, Sam was deep in conversation and he was still only half-dressed. She watched as he began to prowl the terrace with a frown of concentration darkening his brow. At last, she saw him snap the phone shut and slide the door open.

"That was Ron Burrows," he said.

"I know. Why does he want to bother you when you're on holiday?"

"They're having a spot of bother back home."

"Well, that's their hard luck," Amy said, thrusting a shirt into his hands. "If you don't get a move on, we're going to be late."

It took Sam some time to finish dressing, brush his hair and run the electric razor across his face. As a result, it was quarter past four when they finally climbed the stairs to Betty Parsons' apartment. Amy clasped the bottle of Rioja they were bringing as a present and pressed her thumb to the doorbell.

It was opened almost immediately.

She blinked and stepped back as a small gasp of surprise escaped her lips. The man holding the door open was the very same man who had opened the gate for her that morning on her way to the bakery. She would have remembered those cornflower-blue eyes anywhere.

Chapter 8

By the time Josh Parsons had completed his business trip to China, he was so exhausted he felt like he just wanted to sleep for a week. China was a major source of the electrical goods that the company sold in high streets up and down the UK. It was a trip that his father had been making every year for the past fifteen years but Josh convinced him that if he was going to take over the company eventually, it might be a good idea if he got to know the suppliers.

His father reluctantly agreed, so the meetings with the Chinese were arranged, the visas were obtained and the accommodation and flights booked. Josh set off with a feeling of anticipation. He had never visited China before and he was looking forward to the experience.

The first week consisted of a whirlwind succession of factory visits, discussions with manufacturers and hard negotiations over prices followed by lavish banquets at which Josh was placed at the top of the table and treated as the guest of honour. He found the whole thing enormously enjoyable and managed to conclude several lucrative deals with the assistance of an interpreter who his father had engaged.

But it was very tiring. Josh wasn't used to the lengthy schedules the Chinese businessmen set for themselves. His typical day began at 6am with a wake-up call at his hotel then a shower and breakfast and a car journey to whichever factory he happened to be visiting. Often, he didn't get back to his hotel room till one or two in the morning after he had sat through a three-hour banquet and numerous toasts to his good health. He was looking forward to the weekend when he hoped to get a break and perhaps take in a little sight-seeing.

But when Friday came around, he discovered to his dismay that he was expected to do the same thing all over again on Saturday. When it was suggested that he also visit a washing-machine factory on Sunday, he politely put his foot down. Sunday was his day of rest, he informed his hosts. It was against his religion to work on this holy day. As it transpired, he spent the entire day lying on his hotel bed watching English-language movies on a pay-to-view channel and trying to recover his strength for the rigours of the week to come.

Because of the expense involved in this trip, his father was determined that Josh should visit as many places as possible and conclude as many business deals as he could. The trip was scheduled to take in Beijing, Shanghai and Hong Kong and several smaller centres in between. By the end of the third week, Josh could feel his energy draining away.

Besides testing products, visiting factories and conducting negotiations through the interpreter, he also had to arrange for transportation of the goods back to the UK and pay the various handling charges in advance. This all added to his workload. By the time the four weeks finally came to an end, Josh felt that all he wanted to do was crawl into bed and never get out again.

It was the most exhausting business trip he had undertaken since joining the company. However, there had been many benefits. As well as the orders he had placed, he had established good relations with the Chinese suppliers which would stand him in good stead in the years to come.

But now he needed to get completely away from work and recharge his batteries. His mind turned automatically to his mother and the apartment in Magnolia Park. It would be ideal to slip off and spend a few days with her just soaking up the sun, playing a bit of golf and unwinding. When he returned to London, he would be a new man.

But he had barely arrived at Magnolia Park and unpacked his bags when Betty announced that she had organised a little drinks party for that afternoon. Josh felt his heart sink. This was exactly what he didn't want her to do. He had met so many people on his visit to China that he no longer welcomed the prospect of making small talk with strangers. However, he was anxious not to upset her.

"I thought I said I didn't want you to fuss?" he scolded.

"It's not actually a party," Betty quickly explained. "It's really just a young Irish couple who are staying downstairs in the Pilkingtons' apartment. I met them yesterday and invited them up for a drink. I had already done it before you called to say you were coming. And I might invite Mrs Gilbert. She enjoys a bit of company, poor old dear."

"Oh well," Josh said, "if it's already arranged I suppose we'll just have to go ahead with it."

"That's exactly what I thought, too."

"When are they coming?"

"Four o'clock."

"So, it should be over by six. Why don't we go out for dinner afterwards? I'll fill you in on everything that's been going on back home."

"What a lovely way to round off the day!" Betty agreed, thinking of all the news she would pick up from Josh. "What are you planning to do now, dear?"

"Play a round of golf."

He stuck his golf cap firmly on his head and took out the spare set of clubs he kept in a cupboard in the utility room.

"I'll only be gone for a few hours," he said. "I'll be back in plenty of time for your party."

He gave her a peck on the cheek and was gone out the door, leaving his mother in a tizzy of excitement.

The drive to La Ronda golf club took fifteen minutes on the motorway. It was a beautiful course, one of the best on the Costa del Sol. It was an oasis of calm, set amongst stunning scenery between the mountains and the sea. When Josh got there, he found only a handful of players out on the fairways. He dispensed with the offer of a buggy and set off with his golf bag slung across his broad shoulders. The exercise would do him good.

There was a time when Josh had been an excellent golfer but his busy life in the family business had left no time for practice and now he was a little rusty. Indeed, his recent work load had allowed little time for relaxation of any kind. It had completely disrupted his social life and, he thought ruefully, it had also played a part in the break-up of his relationship with Nina Black.

He felt his pulse quicken as he thought of her and memories of their time together came rushing into his mind.

He had met Nina through a dating agency. Normally he would have run a mile from the very idea but he was working so hard for his father that he didn't have time for the more conventional methods of meeting members of the opposite sex. In the end, he convinced himself that a dating agency was the quickest and most efficient way to find a partner.

There were dozens of internet sites he could have used but he was wary of these. Who knew what sort of weird people were lurking in cyberspace? So, after making some discreet inquiries, he chose an agency called Executive Introductions. It was an upmarket outfit and boasted a success rate of 90 per cent. The brochure they sent him showed pictures of happy smiling couples with the slogan *We Met through Executive Introductions*. The fee cost him a cool £1000. He had to attend an interview at an office in Mayfair where he was asked to fill out a questionnaire about himself and the type of person he hoped to meet.

A week later, an envelope arrived in the post with the names and telephone numbers of three women who had been chosen for him by computer because they matched the profile he had submitted. He was invited to make contact with them.

The first introduction was a disaster. After speaking by phone to a lady called Elaine, Josh arranged to meet her at a restaurant in Soho. He arrived early and found her already waiting. He had specified women aged between twenty and thirty-five but the woman who met him in the restaurant lobby was closer to fifty. She was plump, wore a lot of fake jewellery and her dark hair was obviously the result of a session with a very bad hairdresser.

They made small talk as they sat through an awkward meal. Elaine told him she was a widow with two teenage children and worked as a secretary for a travel company. She was a pleasant woman with a bubbly personality but she was not what Josh was looking for. Apart from the fact that she was too old for him, it soon became clear that they had very little in common. At last the evening came crawling to an end. He paid the restaurant bill and saw her into a taxi feeling like a cad and with a heavy heart returned home to his penthouse apartment in the Docklands.

As a result of this experience, he made up his mind to have nothing more to do with dating agencies. His very first date had been an embarrassing fiasco and he had a sneaking suspicion that he had been conned by Executive Introductions. But his resolution didn't hold. A few weeks later, he was tempted back again. There was a possibility that he had just been unlucky. And besides, he had already paid £1000 and still had two names to try.

Nina Black was actually the third person on the list but for some reason the name appealed to him. The voice that answered the phone sounded dark and sultry. Josh explained who he was and how he had got hold of her name. They chatted for a while and arranged to meet in a bar in Notting Hill. When he put down the phone, he had a strange feeling that he might be about to meet the woman he was seeking.

On the appointed day, he set off nervously for his destination, dressed in his best casual clothes – an open-necked shirt under a blue woollen jacket and dark trousers. This time, he was the first to arrive. It was a warm evening and the sounds from the street came drifting into the quiet little bar. He ordered a beer and sat at a corner table where he could keep an eye on the door.

She was ten minutes late. But when she came bustling in, Josh knew at once that his instinct was correct. He reckoned Nina was aged about twenty-seven. She was tall and slim and had a mane of dark hair that hung down to her shoulders. He had always favoured brunettes. She was dressed in a dark-red skirt, black jacket, white blouse and high-heeled shoes. He couldn't take his eyes off her.

She accepted a glass of wine and they began to talk. He quickly discovered that she was an actress and lived in Fulham. She was originally from Bath where her parents still lived. Her father was a retired university professor and her mother was a writer. She had come up to London aged eighteen to attend drama school and had stayed. She told him she had secured several small parts in theatre productions but her goal was to break into films.

When he came to explain his own background, Josh felt uneasy. A career in the electrical retail business sounded flat and uninteresting compared to Nina's exciting background. But she didn't seem to think so. She was genuinely impressed when he explained how his father had built up the business single-handedly. She listened with interest to his stories about his experiences at Willowfield Academy. All the time she kept up a stream of bright, intelligent conversation. At the end of the evening, Josh took her home and they made a date to meet again in a few days' time.

On this occasion, they went to the theatre to see a play that one of her colleagues had a part in. Afterwards, they went backstage to meet the cast and she introduced him to her friends. They ended up having supper in a West End restaurant. When at last he dropped her back to her apartment in Fulham, they kissed in the taxi.

He woke the following morning with a wonderful feeling of lightness and joy. It was something he had never experienced before. Suddenly the world seemed a bright, exciting place filled with golden opportunity. He set off for work with pep in his step. He had met the most wonderful woman. She was witty and beautiful and intelligent. He knew she was the one he had been looking for. And she appeared to like him too. He couldn't wait for their next date.

This time it was a Saturday afternoon. He took her to lunch at a little pub beside the river at Hammersmith and afterwards they went for a walk along the embankment and watched the swans gliding gracefully across the water. Later, he drove her back to

Fulham and she invited him in for coffee. The door was barely closed when he took her in his arms and their mouths were locked in a passionate embrace. Frantically, they tore off each other's clothes as a wild desire swept over them.

The bells of a nearby church roused him the following morning. He was in Nina's bed and she was lying naked beside him. She woke and pulled his head down and kissed him hard on the mouth. Josh's heart swelled with desire. He had met the woman of his dreams.

When he had finished his round of golf, Josh called into the clubhouse and had a quick lunch of hamburger and salad washed down with a beer. He had enjoyed the few hours of peace and quiet on the silent golf course. Already, he could feel himself beginning to relax. After a few more days of this regime, he would be back in trim again.

It was twenty minutes to four when he parked the car at Magnolia Park and went bounding up the steps to his mother's apartment. He found he was now looking forward to the little party she had arranged. It would be pleasant to have a few drinks and some light conversation with the people she had invited. And he had a nice dinner to look forward to in the evening. He would ring immediately and book a table at Campesina restaurant. It had a beautiful little cobbled courtyard with bougainvillea. He had taken Betty there before and she had loved it.

When he came into the apartment, he found old Mrs Gilbert already sitting by the open door to the terrace with a glass of sherry in her hand. He bent to give her a kiss and congratulated her on how well she was looking. The old lady giggled like a shy teenager.

"You always tell me that. You're a flatterer, that's what you are!"

"It's true," Josh said, playfully. "You look younger every time I see you."

"I'll be eighty-one my next birthday," Mrs Gilbert said. "They're getting me ready for the knacker's yard."

"Not a bit of it," Josh replied. "I'll bet you could find some handsome admirer if you set your mind to it, a good-looking woman like you."

"A handsome admirer? I wouldn't take the gift of one," the old lady cackled and almost spilled her drink. "I had one husband and that was enough. What would I do with another one?"

"Oh now, I'd say you could find some use for him," Josh joked.

"Get away with you!" Mrs Gilbert replied but Josh could see that she was delighted at his compliments.

He turned to his mother. "I'll just have a quick shower and get changed. Won't be long."

"Take your time!" Betty called after him. "There are fresh towels in the drawer."

He was whistling as he stepped into the hot shower and began soaping himself. Afterwards, he got dried and put on a pair of tan slacks, loafers and a sports shirt. He brushed his hair, sat down on the bed, got out the address book and found the number of the Campesina restaurant.

"Can I have a table in the courtyard?" Josh asked.

"For how many people?"

"Two."

"That's fine, sir. We will reserve a table for you. What is your name?"

"Parsons," Josh replied.

"What time would you like?"

"Eight o'clock."

"Good, Mr Parsons. Your table will be waiting."

As he stepped back into the lounge, he heard the doorbell ring. Betty was getting up to answer it.

"Relax," Josh said. "I'll get it."

He opened the door and found a young couple standing on the threshold. The woman blinked at him and seemed to give a start.

"Have I frightened you?" Josh laughed.

A deep blush crept over her face.

"Oh, no," she said. "It's just, I met you this morning. You held the gate open for me."

Josh peered closer to examine her. "So I did. Well, I'm Josh Parsons, Betty's son. Come in and make yourselves comfortable."

Chapter 9

Sam had been down in the dumps as he climbed the stairs to Betty Parsons' apartment. Chatting with strangers was the very last thing he wanted to be doing right now. He had been reluctant to come here from the start and now he was even more reluctant after that phone call from his boss Ron Burrows.

The news had not been good. The Slimline campaign, which he had been slaving over day and night for the past month, had been scrapped because the clients had changed their minds again. Now Ron was asking what could be done to salvage the situation. Sam knew that sooner or later his boss was going to ask him to come back to Dublin and work on a new campaign. And Amy was not going to like it.

He should never have brought his phone. That was a big mistake. If he had left the damned thing at home he would now be incommunicado and no one would be able to contact him. He would have been able to enjoy his holiday in peace.

So he'd been in a foul mood by the time they arrived at the Parsons' apartment. He glanced at his watch. It was quarter past four. He would stay till exactly five o'clock just to be polite and then he was off. There was a lively social scene here in Fuengirola and he was anxious to sample some of it. Life was too short to waste time sipping wine with geriatrics like Mrs Parsons while she regaled them with her boring stories about her husband's electrical shop.

The door was opened by a tall, blond man in his early thirties. Sam saw Amy's expression change and next moment they were chatting like long-lost friends.

Inside, he gave the room a quick look-over. It was a big apartment and very cosily furnished. The door out to the terrace was open and a cool breeze ruffled the curtains. Outside, Sam could see a garden table and chairs and pots of flaming geraniums.

Beside the open door, he spotted Mrs Parsons chatting with an old lady with rinsed hair who looked as if she might be her mother. I knew it, he thought. It's a meeting of the local pensioners' club.

Mrs Parsons was already getting up. Sam forced a rigid smile onto his face and shook hands while she guided him to the seat beside the old lady, who on closer inspection looked to be a hundred.

"This is our neighbour, Mrs Gilbert. Why don't you sit here and keep her company. But be warned. She has an eye for good-looking young men."

"What a terrible fibber you are, Betty," the old lady giggled.

"Now what would you like to drink?" Betty asked Sam.

"A beer would be nice," he replied.

She trotted off to the kitchen and returned with a can of Budweiser. Meanwhile, out of the corner of his eye he could see Josh pouring a glass of wine for Amy and sitting down beside her on the settee.

His attention was distracted by the old lady talking in his ear.

"Where did you say you are from?"

"I'm from Dublin," Sam announced.

"I went to Dublin years ago," she said. "I was only a teenager back then. I kissed the Blarney Stone."

"That's in Cork," Sam said.

"Is it? I could have sworn it was Dublin."

"They must have moved it. It was in Cork the last time I checked," Sam said curtly.

"Well, the people were very nice. We had a lovely time. We stayed in the Ritz Hotel."

"That's in Paris."

"Are you sure?"

"Well, I know it's not in Dublin."

"Maybe it was Paris. I remember the people didn't speak English." She paused and took a good look at him. "What did you say your name was?"

"Sam Benson."

"Do you come down here often?"

"This is my first time."

"Do you like it?"

I might if I wasn't dragged off to stupid drinks parties, Sam thought. Not to mention getting ominous phone calls from my boss. He glanced in Amy's direction once more. She was now deep in conversation with Josh. He could have sworn she was gazing intently into his eyes.

Betty was back with a bottle in her hand.

"More sherry, Mrs Gilbert?"

"You're trying to get me tiddly," the old lady said and gave a loud cackle.

"Oh come now, Mrs G. It won't do you the least bit of harm."

"You'll have to carry me home."

"I'm sure Mr Benson would enjoy that, wouldn't you?" Betty replied and nudged Sam gently.

"I was just telling him I was in Dublin once," Mrs Gilbert piped up. "I kissed the Blarney Stone."

"That's why you are such an interesting conversationalist," Betty replied. "They say it gives you the gift of the gab."

"Does it?" Mrs Gilbert replied. "I can't remember." She stared across the room to where Amy was sitting on the settee. "Who is that woman over there talking to Josh? Is that his girlfriend?"

Betty couldn't suppress a laugh. "No, that's Amy. She's Mr Benson's girlfriend. They're staying downstairs in the Pilkingtons' apartment."

"And where are the Pilkingtons?"

"I told you before," Betty replied. "They've gone to Cornwall."

"Cornwall? What are they doing there?"

"They are visiting their grandchildren. They do it every year."

Mrs Gilbert gave a sigh and took a sip of her sherry. "I find it all very confusing." She looked across the room again. "If that woman is Mr Benson's girlfriend why is she sitting with Josh?"

Why indeed, Sam thought. He could feel his frustration mounting by the minute. He was trapped here listening to this inane gobbledegook and could see no way of escape. He checked his watch. It was half past four. He had to endure another half hour of this torture but he wasn't sure if he could make it.

Meanwhile, Josh was telling Amy about his recent visit to China.

"Were you able to eat the food?" she asked. "You weren't presented with anything . . . strange?"

Josh shook his head. "No! The food was delicious. The only problem was the quantity." He patted his stomach and gave a smile. "I think I might have put on some weight."

"You don't seem overweight to me," Amy said quickly.

"Well, the scales in my mother's bathroom tell a different tale."

"How long were you there?"

"Four weeks. It was pretty exhausting. The Chinese worked me very hard. But I managed to conclude some good deals for the company. We source a lot of our products in China."

"Was it all work? Didn't you get any time to yourself? Did you manage to see any of the sights?"

"Not really. It was mostly business."

"What a pity. China must be fascinating. And there you were cooped up in stuffy meetings the whole time."

"I did get to see a lot of factories," he laughed. "My hosts were very big on factory visits."

"You must have found the whole thing very tedious."

"It wasn't so bad. You make it sound like four weeks in a Siberian salt mine."

"Well, there are only so many factories you can visit. But now that you're here, how long are you planning to stay?"

Josh shrugged. "I'm not sure. That depends on whether my father needs me back in London."

"I think Magnolia Park is beautiful. Your mother is a very lucky woman being able to live here all year round."

"I agree," Josh said. "And Fuengirola is the best spot on the Costa. Some people prefer Marbella but I find it far too pretentious. And it's more expensive. Fuengirola is a proper Spanish town and it's got everything you could wish for: good beaches, plenty of bars and restaurants and lots of shops. Plus it's only twenty minutes from the airport." He paused to take a sip of wine. "How long are *you* here for?"

"Two weeks."

"You should hire a car, get around and see a few places. Seville is only a few hours away and so is Granada. The Alhambra Palace is well worth a visit. And Malaga is right on our doorstep. It's a beautiful city."

"Do you come out often?" Amy asked.

"Not as often as Mum would like."

"If I owned a beautiful apartment like this, I'd use it every spare moment I could."

"If you're really interested, there's nothing to stop you buying one. They come on the market from time to time. Mum could let you know. She usually hears all the gossip around the community."

"How much would I be expected to pay?"

Josh shrugged. "Depends what you want."

"I think a one-bed would suit me fine," Amy said.

"A one-bed beside the swimming pool went a few months ago for €120,000."

Amy closed her eyes briefly. Perhaps Sam was right. It was all a silly dream. Where was she supposed to get €120,000 to buy an apartment in Spain?

"I think I should talk to my bank manager first," she said and Josh laughed.

At that moment, Amy became aware of a sudden movement across the room. Sam had put down his glass and was standing up. From the look on his face, Amy could tell that something was bothering him.

"It's time to go," he announced.

Amy glanced at her watch. It was a quarter to five. They had barely arrived. She shot him a beseeching look.

"So soon?" Betty asked. "I was just about to fill up the glasses again. Are you sure you won't stay a little while longer?"

"I'm positive," Sam replied. "Amy and I have to get ready for dinner."

He looked at her and her face turned pale. She was shocked at Sam's bad manners.

"But that's all right," Josh intervened. "Mum and I are going to dinner at Campesina restaurant later. Why don't you join us? We'd love to have you."

"Yes, why don't you?" Betty urged.

Out of the corner of his eye, Sam could see Amy looking at him in appeal.

"That's not possible," he said through gritted teeth. "We've arranged to meet some friends."

Amy looked aghast. Sam was behaving like a barbarian. What had got into him? In all the time she had known him she had never seen him like this.

"What a pity," Josh went on. "Maybe we could have dinner some other time? I'm going to be around for several more days."

"Yes," his mother added. "Why don't we do that? We know lots of lovely restaurants."

"Perhaps," Sam replied. He reached for Amy's arm and drew her up from her seat.

"Thank you very much for your hospitality, Mrs Parsons. And you too, Mrs Gilbert."

He held on to Amy's arm and marched her to the door.

"Have a nice dinner," Josh called after him. He smiled at Amy and added, "I enjoyed talking to you."

Sam started down the stairs. Amy followed behind him, silent with anger. Already he was beginning to regret his rash behaviour. He knew as soon as they got inside their own apartment, they were going to have the mother-and-father of a row. Well, maybe it was time for a few home truths.

Chapter 10

Josh closed the front door and returned to his mother and Mrs Gilbert. That was all rather abrupt, he thought. He had noticed the tension between Amy and Sam and realised that all was not well. She had seemed happy to stay longer and to take up his invitation to have dinner together. But Sam was determined to get away as quickly as possible. Josh hoped it was not something he had done which had caused the strain between them.

"That young man didn't have much to say for himself, did he?" Mrs Gilbert said. "One of those strong, silent types, I suppose. Some women like that."

"I think it was our fault," Betty confessed. "I feel a bit guilty."

"Why do you say that?" Josh asked.

"Well, you were talking to his girlfriend the whole time and he was left with Mrs Gilbert and me. I think he felt excluded."

"I don't think he wanted to be here," Josh went on. "I could tell the minute I opened the front door that he was uneasy."

"Maybe he was jealous of you," Mrs Gilbert said. "Some men can be very possessive. I remember a boyfriend I had one time. He wouldn't let me out of his sight. I had to give him up in the end."

Josh smiled.

"Would you like to come to dinner with us?" Betty asked the old woman.

"Oh no, I can't eat anything after five o'clock. I wouldn't be able to sleep."

She got unsteadily to her feet. "In fact, it's time I went home. My soaps will be starting soon. Thank you very much. I really did enjoy myself."

"I'll go with you," Josh volunteered. "And make sure you don't come to harm."

The old lady put on her cardigan and Josh helped her down the stairs. But his mind was elsewhere. He kept thinking of Amy. It was a pity the way things had turned out. She was a very interesting young woman and quite attractive. He would have enjoyed talking with her some more.

As he passed the door of the Pilkingtons' apartment, he thought he could hear the sound of raised voices. But he didn't comment. He guided Mrs Gilbert out through the main door to the garden and safely back to her own place. On the way back, the clash of angry voices could still be heard coming from the downstairs apartment. Oh dear, he thought. It sounds as if they are having a row. Why is it that people seemed to argue more on holidays than any other time of the year?

"Did you have to behave like that?" Amy exclaimed. "Did you have to treat me with such contempt?"

They had barely got the door closed when the argument had begun.

"Contempt?" Sam spluttered, hardly able to contain himself. "I was the one treated with contempt. I was left with two geriatrics for company while you made googly-eyes at that blond guy."

Amy caught her breath. "I beg your pardon?"

"You heard what I said."

"You didn't want to go in the first place. You made that plain enough. And then you proceeded to sulk like a little boy."

"That is simply not true," Sam thundered.

"You dragged me out of there. You embarrassed me in front of those people. You treated me as if I was a child with no will of my own."

"I didn't drag you anywhere. You could have stayed if you wanted. You can go back right now, if you like."

"Don't be ridiculous!"

"Let's be honest here, shall we?" Sam said. "You weren't really interested in Mrs Parsons. This is all to do with that blond Lothario, isn't it? He fastened on to you like a limpet the minute we walked into the apartment. You think I'm blind? You think I didn't notice? And you were lapping it up, weren't you? You were purring like a kitten."

"You're talking nonsense. I didn't even know he was going to be there. And Josh was simply being polite. He has good manners. It's a pity I can't say the same thing about you."

"Thank you for the compliment," Sam replied, sarcastically. "But it seemed to me there was a bit more involved than good manners. He was doing his best to impress you and you were doing nothing to discourage him."

"What was I supposed to do? Ignore him?"

"Did you pause to consider my feelings? He's chatting up my girlfriend and I'm forced to listen to a batty old lady who insists that the Blarney Stone is in Dublin."

"You're crazy. He wasn't chatting me up. He was simply being a good host."

"And that nonsense about buying an apartment, where did that bright idea come from? I don't remember you ever discussing it with me."

"If I want to buy an apartment somewhere, that's entirely *my* business."

"Oh? And where would you get €120,000, might I ask?"

"I could take out a mortgage. I've got savings of my own. You seem to forget that I'm an independent woman. I don't need to consult you whenever I want to do something."

"So you don't mind living with me rent-free while you save up to buy a love-nest in Spain?"

Amy's face went bright scarlet.

"Excuse me," she declared. "Who is talking about a love-nest? And while we're on the subject, I pay my share of the household expenses and I clean up after you and do most of the cooking. And in case you have forgotten, it was *your* idea for me to move in with you in the first place."

"No-one is keeping you prisoner," Sam snapped back. "Feel free to move out any time you like."

"You want to know something? I might just do that."

"Go ahead. I won't stop you."

By now, Amy was exhausted. "You know what your problem is, Sam? You're a selfish brat. Everything has to be about you. You have no consideration for other people, least of all me."

He gave a hollow laugh. "That's rich coming from you. Have you ever stopped to consider your own behaviour? Have you ever thought how you demand your own way in everything? Well, if you must know, I'm sick of it."

"I hate you," she said and, burying her head in a cushion, began to sob bitterly.

"That's right," Sam said. "Turn on the waterworks. When you can't win an argument, start to cry."

He went into the bedroom, found his jacket and put it on. He checked that he had his wallet.

"I'm going out to get some fresh air," he said.

Amy didn't reply. As he closed the door, she still had her head buried in the cushion and was weeping uncontrollably. This was their first big fight and it had left her shattered.

Sam was boiling with rage as he made his way down to the seafront. To add to his irritation, the sun continued to pour down and in the confusion of the argument he had forgotten to bring his sunglasses. By now the perspiration was streaming down his forehead. He took off his jacket and wiped his face with a handkerchief but it made little difference. It wasn't till he had reached the seafront that a breeze began to blow to cool him a little.

He was mad as hell with Amy. If he hadn't got out of that apartment, God knows what might have happened. He needed a drink to calm himself down. He came to a little bar, went in and ordered a large brandy then sat in a cool corner and considered his next move.

Sam was in righteous mood and he took comfort in the fact that it was Amy who had provoked the fight. Besides, it had been building for some time. He was glad he had got some things off his chest. She needed to be told the truth. Her behaviour in the Parsons' apartment had been outrageous. She had been practically flirting with that Josh guy right before his eyes. How was he supposed to react? And what would she have thought of him, if he had just sat there and taken it on the chin?

He swallowed a mouthful of brandy and continued to wallow in a warm sea of self-justification. He thought of everything he had done for her – the presents he had bought her, the dinners, the parties, not to mention inviting her to live under his roof rent-free for the past year. And this was how she repaid him – by making a fool of him in front of a bunch of strangers.

He had been right about that drinks party. They should never have gone. They should have ignored Mrs Parsons and stayed at the *tapas* bar. If they had done that, none of this would have happened and he wouldn't be sitting here staring at the ruins of his holiday. For that was what it had come to. He knew Amy too well. She didn't like the truth and he had said some things that she didn't want to hear. She would go into a mope until he apologised. Well, he had no intention of apologising. She had said some cruel things herself. She had even accused him of selfishness. His lips parted in a cynical smile. That was rich coming from her. It was a classic example of projecting your own faults onto someone else. He was the least selfish person he knew. He was forever thinking about her, complimenting her, buying her flowers, going out of his way to please her. And this was the thanks he got.

He finished the brandy and ordered another. By now he had begun to calm down a little and gradually he began to see the situation in a slightly different light. Perhaps he had said some things which would have been better left unsaid. He had told her she could move out of his apartment. It was just the sort of stupid thing she might do. He wondered if he should apologise after all. He would give her a little time to settle down and then he would ring her. He felt in his pocket for his phone and was relieved to find it there.

He scavenged for something positive to retrieve from the incident. He told himself that every couple had arguments. In fact some couples he knew seemed to spend their whole time fighting with each other. It was a wonder that Amy and he hadn't had one before. Wasn't it a measure of how well-suited they were that it had taken so long before they had their first major row?

He told himself that the showdown had been necessary. It had cleared the air and now they had a better idea of where they both stood. But it was a pity that it had been accompanied by some harsh words. Another thought came into his mind. This talk about buying an apartment out here – where had that come from? She had never mentioned it to him before. Was she serious? Was it some secret fantasy she had been harbouring or just something she had come out with on the spur of the moment to impress that Josh guy?

By now, his mood was beginning to soften and with it came the realisation that he had better call Amy. He checked his watch and saw that it was six fifteen. He had been gone for an hour, enough time for Amy to have got over the row. Besides, he was beginning to get hungry again. They would have to make arrangements for dinner. He took out his phone and dialled her number while he mentally prepared what he would say.

The phone rang for a few seconds and then stopped. He stared at it. Had she switched the bloody thing off? He thought about having another drink but decided it wasn't a good idea, not on an empty stomach. He left the bar and wandered down to the port. It was sparkling in the evening sun, the light glancing off the yachts and cruisers berthed along the piers. There were people drinking and chatting at the tables spread out on the pavement. He sat down, ordered a coffee and rang Amy once more.

Again, he heard the phone ring and then stop abruptly. Damn, he thought, she was giving him the silent treatment as a way of punishing him. This thought caused his anger to flare again. So, she was playing hardball, was she? Well, two could play that game. Instead of calling her, he would let *her* ring *him*. When the waiter arrived with his coffee, Sam ordered another brandy, leaned back in his seat and stretched his face to the sun.

An hour later, he was still sitting at the pavement table and his phone had not rung. He picked it up once more and made another attempt to call Amy but again he got no reply. By now, he was ravenous. La Rueda restaurant, where they had eaten the night before, had opened for business and the smell of grilling fish drifted past his nose. He made one final attempt to call her. He heard the phone ring and then the line went dead.

That's it, he decided. This matter has gone beyond a joke. He briefly considered going back to Magnolia Park but the thought of what might be waiting made him hesitate. If she was still angry, the whole thing could blow up again and he was just not in the mood for another row. He made up his mind. He drained his glass and walked the short distance to the restaurant.

It was ten o'clock when he left. He had enjoyed a delicious meal of grilled turbot, fried potatoes and salad and had consumed a fine bottle of wine. To round off, he had treated himself to another glass of brandy and a cigar. Now he felt a little tipsy as he strolled out into the warm summer air and saw the moon reflected in the still waters of the port.

He walked a little unsteadily to the row of taxis waiting outside the Palmeras Hotel. Ten minutes later, he was alighting at the gates of Magnolia Park. He found his keys, let himself in and made his way through the gardens towards their apartment. There was a heavy scent of flowers on the night air and the sound of insects chirping in the dusk.

When he arrived at the apartment, it was in darkness. He let himself into the warm interior. He took off his jacket and draped it over a chair. The bedroom door was closed. When he tried it, he found it locked. He pressed his ear to the keyhole but heard only silence. He tapped lightly on the door but there was no response. He tried pushing it but met stiff resistance.

She's locked me out of the bloody bedroom, he thought. What a bitch! Where am I supposed to sleep? He opened a cupboard and found some sheets. He got undressed and stretched out on the settee and pulled a sheet around him. The troubles of the day began to drift away. Two minutes later, he was fast asleep.

Chapter 11

Sam was wakened by a loud noise ringing in his head. He sat up with a start. He was in the lounge and his shirt and trousers were tossed carelessly on a chair. He was stretched out on the settee. His neck felt stiff, he had a raging thirst and there was a throbbing ache at the back of his skull which he recognised as the beginnings of a hangover. Suddenly, the events of the previous day came rushing back. He'd had a row with Amy and she had locked him out of the bedroom. He felt a black cloud smother him in its gloomy embrace.

The ringing noise was growing more persistent. He grabbed his jacket from the chair and dug into a pocket till he found his phone. He clasped it to his ear.

"Hi," a voice announced. "It's Ron here. I hope I didn't disturb you."

Sam looked at his watch. It was a quarter past nine which meant eight fifteen back in Dublin.

"Hello, Ron," he managed to say.

"Are you awake?"

"Of course."

"Good, good. I wasn't sure if you'd be sleeping."

"No, I'm wide awake. What can I do for you?"

Sam glanced around the room. The sun was filtering in from the terrace, seeping under the gaps in the drapes. The bedroom door remained firmly closed.

"It's about that problem I mentioned yesterday, the Slimline Fashions campaign. The clients have been on to us again. I'm afraid they're getting quite nasty."

Sam felt his heart sink. It was turning out exactly as he had feared and much faster than he thought.

"How do you mean nasty?"

"They're threatening to take the contract elsewhere."

"They can't do that."

"Oh yes, they can, Sam."

"But we delivered on our side."

"Not to their satisfaction."

"God," Sam groaned, "I spent a month of my life on that campaign. I did everything they asked. I turned cartwheels. I stood on my head. When I left, they told me they were happy."

"They've changed their minds."

"You know what, Ron? Why don't you just tell them to go and screw themselves?"

There was a shocked silence.

"I take it that was meant to be a joke?"

"No, no joke. I've had it up to my back teeth with the Slimline campaign. The very thought of it sends shivers down my spine. I'm not a performing seal. I'm a creative artist and I've had enough."

"And what do you propose we should do if they take the contract somewhere else?"

"Sue them."

He heard Ron give a brittle laugh.

"Now I know you're joking. Can you imagine the adverse publicity if we went to court? Our competitors would be rubbing their hands with glee."

Sam uttered a loud sigh. The ache in his head had now grown into a grinding pain, as if someone was boring into his skull with an electric drill. Any moment soon, he was going to scream.

"We can't let a major contract like this one slip through our hands," Ron said. "We'd never get work from them again."

"Excellent," Sam said. "That would make me very happy."

"I'll ignore that remark," Ron Burrows said.

"So what's the alternative?"

"We just have to give them what they want."

"But they don't know what they want. That's the bloody problem!" Sam shouted.

"We have to help them, Sam."

"What exactly does that mean?"

"You'll have to come back."

Sam felt the pain in his head reach crisis point. He gritted his teeth and tried to keep his voice steady.

"I'm on holidays, Ron. Do you expect me to drop everything I'm doing?"

"I'm afraid so. I don't think we have any other choice."

Sam gave a loud groan.

"When?" he managed to ask.

"I need you here by tomorrow."

Sam let out a cry like a wounded pig. "*Aaaaagh!*" he yelled.

Five minutes later, when he switched off his phone, Ron had given him an ultimatum. Get back to Dublin on the next available flight or start looking for another job. He sank his head in his hands. He had never felt so helpless, so deflated, so utterly defeated. All the fight had gone out of him. When he looked up again, Amy was standing before him in her dressing gown. She was looking at him like he had just crawled out from under a stone.

He managed to stand up and walk unsteadily into the kitchen. She followed him and stood silently with her arms folded while he made coffee and drank it in greedy gulps.

"Well?" she asked. "Aren't you going to say something?"

"I have to go home," he said. "They want more work done on the Slimline account."

He sat down wearily at the kitchen table and took a deep breath.

"When?" Amy asked.

"Today. As soon as possible. The Slimline clients aren't happy with the campaign and Ron wants me to do it over again."

He turned his bleary eyes to her.

"Look, I'm sorry about yesterday," he said. "I apologise for the things I said. I was angry. I wasn't thinking straight."

"You said some very hurtful things."

"Well, I regret it. I wish it hadn't happened."

"Do you really mean that?"

"Yes."

"Okay, I accept your apology. And I forgive you. We need to have a serious talk, Sam, but this isn't the time. Have a shower and tidy yourself up. I'll start trying to book a flight for you."

"You're an angel," he said and rushed at once into the vacant bathroom.

Five minutes later, he had showered. When he emerged from the bathroom, he found Amy coming off the phone.

"I've managed to find you a flight. I've paid by credit card. It's leaving at midday so you'll have to hurry. Get dressed and start packing your bag. I'll ring for a cab to take you to the airport."

He did as she said. Fifteen minute later, he was ready. As he came out of the bedroom, Amy was switching off her phone.

"That was the cabbie. He's at the front gate. Do you want me to help with your bags?"

"No," he said. "You've done enough. Thanks again, Amy. You're a star. You really are. I'll let you know when I arrive in Dublin."

He opened the front door and bright sunlight flooded into the room. He gave her a quick peck on the cheek and next minute she heard the door close and his footsteps echo along the path.

Amy uttered a deep sigh. Despite what he had said and done, she couldn't help feeling sorry for Sam and the predicament he now found himself in. To be dragged back from his holiday was just too much. Now she wished the argument had never occurred and the harsh words had not been spoken. But they had and they couldn't be taken back. He had said he was sorry and she had accepted his apology and forgiven him. The thing to do now was to put it behind her. When they were back again in Dublin they would sit down and have a frank face-to-face discussion about the difficulties in their relationship.

Coming to this decision made her feel better. She showered and put on her dressing gown then went into the kitchen and made tea and toast. She took it out to the terrace and sat down at the little wrought-iron table. The sun had already crept halfway across the lawn and a family of sparrows was bathing in the fountain.

She stared at the garden and the roses in bloom.

From previous experience, she knew that Sam could be tied up on the Slimline campaign for a long time. He might not return for the remainder of the holiday. She wondered if she should go back and join him. But what would be the point? He'd be working fourteen-hour days and practically living in his office. She would scarcely see him.

Besides, her holiday had just begun and she had been looking forward to it for a very long time. She would just have to stay and make the most of things. But it wouldn't be easy. She was on her own. She would probably get lonely. And Betty Parsons was sure to ask awkward questions. But it was better than going home to the cold and the rain.

She would start right now. She stood up and carried the breakfast things into the kitchen and rinsed them in the sink. She put on her bikini and gathered her radio and book, her sunglasses and bottle of water. She would spend the morning in the garden listening to the birds and the sound of the fountain. And then around one o'clock, she would go off and find somewhere to eat.

Chapter 12

Sam arrived back in Dublin to be greeted by grey skies, a chill wind and a steady drizzle of rain. He was tired, irritable and hungry. Since leaving Fuengirola that morning he had been in a constant state of panic as he rushed from taxi to airport to terminal to plane. It wasn't till he was fastened into his seat on the flight to Dublin and the engine was revving up that he began to calm down.

But, almost immediately, his anger and frustration came boiling to the surface again. He had a lot to be annoyed about. He had been looking forward to his holiday in the sun since last November but no sooner had he got his backside onto a recliner than everything had started to go pear-shaped.

He felt his anger surge at the indignity he had been subjected to. *To be ordered back to the office.* It was the worst insult he had suffered in fifteen years working in the advertising industry. Never in all that time had he been offered such an embarrassing affront. It was an attack on his professional integrity. It was a slur on his creative independence. He was an artist, for God's sake, not a junior secretary! He blamed his craven boss, Ron Burrows. But ultimately, he blamed the Slimline clients.

He had known from the very beginning that they were going to be trouble. He bitterly remembered the day they had come into the office five weeks ago, waving their cheque book and promising to spend shed-loads of money on a big advertising campaign. But it soon became obvious that they hadn't a clue what they were looking for. He had seen their type before. They had no imagination, no originality. They were the sort of people who didn't know what they wanted till they saw it on somebody else's billboard.

At that first meeting, Sam had talked to them for almost two hours, throwing out suggestions, tossing around ideas, envisaging concepts. But every suggestion he made was met with a blank stare. The boss of Slimline Fashions was a thin, nervous little man called Herbie Morrison who looked back at Sam as if he was speaking in Urdu. Sam decided to dispense with the advertising jargon and talk to them in plain English which he hoped they would understand.

The line they were trying to sell aimed to make women look thinner. The trouble was that dozens of rival clothes designers were trying to do exactly the same thing. Sam tried to explain that they needed something creative, something original that would jump out and grab people's attention. In the end, it was agreed that he should go away and come up with some catchy slogans. And that was when the trouble began.

They didn't like any of his ideas. He went off and tried again but they still weren't satisfied. Meanwhile, Ron Burrows had his sights fixed on the juicy cheque that was riding on this campaign and was urging Sam to come up with anything that would keep the clients happy. Finally, Sam went back to his desk and devised a brilliant campaign that featured the one-line slogan: *Slimline: Release the Inner You.*

He thought it was one of the best slogans he had ever created. It had the perfection of a Beethoven concerto. He sat down again with clients and explained the beauty of the concept. It was direct, it was short, it was eye-catching and it was memorable. Above all, it was simple.

He went on to propose a series of billboards and short television adverts to promote the idea, get people talking and more to the point, have them snapping up the Slimline products by the cartload. To his immense relief, the clients bought the idea. Ron Burrows was beside himself with joy.

Sam immediately set to work designing the adverts. He already had a model in mind, a waif-like figure who looked about fifteen but was actually twenty-six. Her name was Topaz Maguire. All she had to do was wear some of the clothes and smile. She didn't need to speak. She didn't even need to appear slim. She already looked like she had been on a starvation diet for the past three months. She would be perfect.

He busied himself hiring Topaz Maguire and arranging the photo shoots. He had already told Ron about the holiday and the fact that he would be spending two weeks on the Costa del Sol in May. Ron agreed that was not a problem so long as he got the campaign finished on time.

Sam set to work like a slave. He put in fourteen and fifteen-hour days. He worked through weekends. He got the campaign finished with only a day to spare. Everything was in order. The ads were designed, the television slots agreed and the billboard locations booked. He set off with Amy for Fuengirola with the joy and expectation of someone who has just been released from prison.

Then everything started to go wrong and Ron Burrows had left him in no doubt that unless he came up with a whole new campaign his career was on the line. He had exactly one week to retrieve the situation. He stepped off the plane at Dublin airport with all the confidence of a man who was facing a firing squad at dawn.

By now, the hangover that had greeted him earlier had evaporated and he thought of a drink to steady his resolve for the ordeal that lay ahead. But he decided against it. He had to be stone-cold sober when he confronted Ron Burrows at the office in an hour's time. He was also starving. He'd had nothing to eat apart from a rubbery cheese sandwich on the flight from Malaga. He disembarked from the plane at Dublin in a foul temper.

He went straight into a restaurant in the arrivals lounge and ordered a large coffee and a hamburger. At least it would put some ballast in his stomach. As he ate it, Amy came into his mind. She'd always had a stubborn streak. He remembered the resistance she had put up when he first suggested that she move in with him. It had taken her two weeks to make up her mind when any other woman would have jumped at the chance of his offer. And she had a sharp tongue. He was still smarting at some of the things she had said to him. However, he didn't want to lose her so he had to get back in her good books again. She had relented a little this morning and forgiven him after he apologised to her. And she had organised his flight for him and paid for it with her own credit card which was very decent of her. But to fully win her over he would have to be on his best behaviour. He would phone her later and have a little chat. In the meantime, he decided to send her a text to tell her he had arrived safely.

He finished his hamburger and went off to the Gents. In his haste this morning, he hadn't had an opportunity to shave. Rather than go to the trouble of unpacking his toiletries, he purchased a razor from a dispensing machine and quickly removed the stubble from his cheeks and chin. He washed his face with cold water and brushed his hair. He straightened his tie and pulled down the lapels of his jacket. Despite his recent ordeal, he looked quite presentable. At a newsagent's shop, he purchased a packet of mints and popped a couple in his mouth to sweeten his breath. Then he marched out of the terminal and joined the queue at the taxi rank.

The taxi dropped him off at the offices of Burrows Advertising Executives in Baggot Street. He had already phoned Ron from the cab to tell him he had landed and was now on his way in. He paid the fare and carried his bag up the stairs to his boss's office. Around the walls were framed certificates and posters of award-winning advertising campaigns of the past. A glass display cabinet held plaques and medals and the trophies of success. He found his boss sitting behind his desk with a sheet of drawings in his hand. He looked up as Sam came through the door.

Sam was in a belligerent mood. He had decided in the cab that his best tactic was to go on the offensive. He dropped the bag on the floor and launched into a tirade.

"I hope you realise you have ruined my holiday," he began. "A holiday which I have worked hard for and which I was looking forward to for a considerable time. I hope you appreciate that."

"Sit down," his boss said.

Sam remained standing. He wanted Ron to know how angry he felt at being dragged back from Fuengirola.

"I am also dismayed that you should side with a bunch of idiots who haven't a clue about advertising against your senior creative artist. That's hardly what I would call a vote of confidence."

"Sit down," Ron said again with more force.

Sam pulled out a chair and sank into it.

There was a loud cough and he turned to see Herbie Morrison sitting in a corner behind the door. His face showed that he hadn't appreciated Sam's description of him as an idiot.

"What is this?" Sam protested. "An ambush?"

"It's just a business meeting," Ron replied and turned his attention to Herbie Morrison. "Tell him what you don't like about the campaign."

"It's all wrong," Herbie began.

"In what way wrong?" Sam countered. "What do you mean?"

"Take that model for a start. She looks like a drug addict."

Sam's face went red. "A drug addict?"

"Yes. She looks like she's got anorexia or something. How is that supposed to appeal to our customers? That's entirely the wrong image."

"But you insisted on a slim look, didn't you?"

"I didn't want someone who looks like she's on famine relief. We know our market. They are middle-aged ladies who want to recapture some of their youthful figures. They just want to look smarter and a little bit thinner. They don't want to look like freaks."

Sam was flabbergasted. "Do you know who she is? That's Topaz Maguire. She's one of the top models in the business."

"I don't care if she's Naomi Campbell. She's not appearing in our advertising campaign. I'm paying for it and I don't want her."

By now, Sam could feel the energy draining out of him. He was tired, he was harassed and he was on the wrong side of a battle he couldn't win.

"Have you any better ideas?" he asked.

"Yes," Herbie replied. "Unless you get rid of that woman, I cancel the contract here and now and we take our business elsewhere."

"If we drop her, she'll still want to be paid."

"That's your problem."

Sam uttered a low moan.

"All right, everybody, let's all calm down." Ron butted in. He turned again to Herbie. "Sam's just got off a plane from Spain. He's probably jet-lagged. And he's an artist. He's highly strung. Now here's what I propose. We're agreed that the main thrust behind the campaign is fine, isn't that so?"

Herbie reluctantly nodded.

"And you're happy with the slogan *Slimline: Release the Inner You*."

"I suppose so."

"Okay, now Sam, I want you to sit down with Herbie, show him a portfolio of models that are available, pick one that you both like and go out and hire her." He turned to Herbie. "I want you to have a hand in this every step of the way."

Herbie brightened up.

"So Sam, pass everything over to Herbie for his approval. I want you both singing off the same hymn sheet. We don't proceed with anything till Herbie has agreed. Is that clear?"

Sam felt any remaining resistance seep out of him. He was totally defeated. He thought of the work involved in cancelling the television slots and the billboard locations that had already been booked and all the trouble he was going to have getting Topaz Maguire and her agent off his back. Not to mention the humiliation of having Herbie Morrison interfering at every hand's turn. But if this was the price of holding on to his job, what choice did he have?

He nodded meekly. "Yes."

"Herbie, are you happy?"

Herbie looked like he had won the lottery. "Sure," he said.

Ron clapped his hands. "Good, that's what I like to hear. Teamwork, that's the key to success."

Chapter 13

Betty Parsons saw Amy sitting on the lawn as she passed through the gardens on her way to have lunch with the Amigos. She briefly considered stopping to say hello and have a quick chat. But Amy's eyes were closed as if she was dozing and, besides, Betty was running late so she continued on to the front gate where she intended to pick up a cab to take her to the restaurant.

So far, the morning had been quite hectic. Josh had left at eight to play golf, telling her he would grab something to eat at the clubhouse. He wasn't expected back till the afternoon. At nine o'clock, Betty had an appointment at the hairdresser's and no sooner had she returned than Mrs Gilbert rang to ask if she would pick up some medication for her at the *farmacia*. Betty had just returned from carrying out this task when the phone rang again and this time it was Gladys Taylor wanting to confirm that she was coming to the lunch.

"Oh certainly," Betty replied.

"You know where it is?"

"El Toro, on Avenida Los Boliches."

"That's correct. Do you know how to get there?"

"I'll be coming by cab but I think I know where it is."

"Good," Gladys remarked. "See you at one o'clock. We'll have a bit of fun. I'm looking forward to seeing you again, Betty."

"Me too."

Betty put down the phone with a mild suspicion buzzing around in her head. Why was Gladys so anxious to ensure that she got to this lunch? Gladys was a bit of a livewire. What was she up to? But Betty had no time to give the matter any more thought. She had barely got dressed and fixed her make-up when the clock on the mantelpiece showed it was half past twelve. She locked up the apartment and set off into the hot midday sun.

Luckily, there was a cab waiting at the rank. She gave her destination to the driver and settled back on the cool upholstered seats with a small sigh of relief. Unless there was a traffic hold-up, which was unlikely, she should get to the restaurant on time. Gladys Taylor's phone call came into her mind once more. She had sounded conspiratorial. What was going on? Betty was still mulling this over when the cab eventually deposited her at the door of El Toro restaurant.

She recognised it at once. Josh had brought her here one time for dinner. El Toro was an imposing building with solid mahogany furniture and walls lined with bottles of wine and pictures of famous bullfighters. The interior was dark and cool but there was also a garden at the rear. Hopefully, the lunch was being held out in the garden. It would be so much brighter.

There was another thing she remembered. El Toro specialised in meat – gigantic steaks and chops, spare ribs, loops of red and black sausages. Betty hoped there was something else to eat on the lunch menu. Many of the guests had dainty appetites and some of them had heart problems. It wouldn't do if the Amigos starting killing off some of its members.

As she got out of the taxi, her eye was drawn to a shiny black Mercedes parked beside the pavement. Who did that belong to, she wondered. She didn't remember anyone arriving in a Mercedes before. She paid the fare, stepped inside the restaurant's dark interior and immediately heard a loud voice call her name. She blinked and saw Gladys Taylor sitting at the bar in the company of a tall, silver-haired man.

"So there you are," Gladys announced in a cheery voice. "You made it all right?"

"Oh yes," Betty replied.

"Well, it's good to see you, ducks."

She wrapped her arms around Betty and planted a wet kiss on her cheek, smudging her make-up in the process.

"There's someone I want you to meet. This is Nigel Smyth. Nigel, this is the lady I told you about. Meet my pal, Betty Parsons."

The tall man leaned forward and took Betty's hand in a firm grip. He was a good-looking man, perhaps in his late fifties, with broad shoulders, a bronzed face, blue eyes and a full head of wavy greying hair. He was smartly dressed in slacks, open-necked golf shirt and blazer.

"Pleased to meet you," Nigel said. "Can I get you a drink? I was just about to order."

"A glass of white wine would be nice," Betty replied and gave Gladys a puzzled look but Gladys simply smiled enigmatically.

Nigel turned to the barman and gave the order.

"Are there many people expected?" Betty inquired.

"About twenty-five. It'll be nice and cosy, ducks. We're having lunch in the garden."

"I hope the menu isn't all meat?"

"Not at all," Gladys replied with a chuckle. "They've already thought of that. There's fish and chicken and plenty of salads. I've had a gander."

"Well, thank God for that," Betty said.

Nigel handed her the glass of wine, put a gin and tonic in front of Gladys and kept a glass of beer for himself.

"Cheers," he said and took a long swallow of his beer.

"Nigel used to be in the motor trade," Gladys said.

"Oh," said Betty. "Was that in the UK or here?"

"The UK," Nigel replied.

"When Gladys says you used to be in the motor trade, does that mean you've retired?"

"Sort of. My daughter is running the business but she comes to me for advice."

What a clever arrangement. Betty thought of Alf. Why didn't he do that?

"So are you living down here now?"

"Well, that's the plan," Nigel said.

"Nigel's got a magnificent villa in Marbella," Gladys cut in. "You should see it sometime. It's like a mansion."

Nigel gave a modest smile. "You're exaggerating again, Gladys."

"No, I'm not. It has these fantastic views of the sea. On a clear day, you can see Morocco. How many rooms has it got, Nige?"

"Ten," he said.

"That does sound big," Betty went on. "Your wife will have her hands full with a house like that."

Gladys gave her a warning look.

"My wife is living in Brighton," Nigel said. "We're getting divorced."

"Oh," Betty apologised. "I'm terribly sorry. I didn't mean to pry into your personal affairs."

Nigel gave a hearty laugh. "Don't worry, it's all very amicable. We just came to the conclusion that we didn't want to live with each other any more. She's got a partner. Nice bloke. He's a banker."

"So now Nigel is free as a bird," Gladys chuckled. She gave Betty a meaningful look. "Some lucky woman is going to land herself a very handsome catch."

At that moment, a gong sounded to announce that lunch was about to be served. Betty picked up her wineglass and they all proceeded out to the garden where a large table had been set beneath an awning to shade them from the sun. Gladys suddenly darted away to greet someone and Betty was left alone with Nigel.

"What's the drill?" he enquired. "Do we wait to be seated?"

"Oh, no, it's all very informal," she explained. "You just sit wherever you like."

Around them, people were beginning to take their seats. She sat down and Nigel sat beside her. She lifted the menu card and immediately spotted several things she could eat. She'd had a light breakfast and now she was feeling quite peckish.

"I think I'll have the bacon and cheese salad to begin," she said. "And then the sole. What about you?"

"That sounds fine," Nigel said. "Have you been here before?"

"I came with my son one time. It's very good for meat. He had a gigantic T-bone steak. I don't know how he managed to finish it but he did."

"Gladys told me you lived alone?"

"Did she indeed?"

She looked across the table at Gladys who waved back in encouragement.

"I do live alone," Betty continued. "But my son comes out to visit from time to time. He's here right now, as a matter of fact."

"Where is it you live?"

"Magnolia Park. Do you know it?"

"Afraid not. I've only been down here for a few months. I'm still finding my feet."

The waiter approached and took their order. Nigel asked if she would like another glass of wine and Betty accepted.

"So this place you're living, is it nice?"

"Well, I like it," Betty said. "I've been living there for a long time and I've never felt the urge to move."

"It must be nice then."

"It is. It's right in the centre of town but we might as well be living out in the country it's so quiet and peaceful."

She proceeded to tell him all about Magnolia Park: the gardens and the pool and the fountain and the lovely neighbours who lived there.

He pointed to her wedding ring.

"Are you married, Betty?"

"Yes, but my husband runs the family business in London. He comes out to Spain whenever he can."

"What sort of business?"

"Electrical goods."

"There's good money in that."

"He built it up from scratch. Now he's got forty-five outlets all over the UK and Ireland."

Nigel looked impressed. "He sounds like a good sharp operator."

"What about your villa?" Betty asked.

"It's a bit big for one person," Nigel said.

"It does sound rather large. Why did you buy it?"

"I didn't. A business contact owed me some money and couldn't pay so he offered me his villa instead."

"That means it was Fate," Betty said. "You were meant to live there."

Nigel chuckled. "You think so? I think it has more to do with my friend's business going bust."

The meal proceeded very well. The food was excellent and the waiters kept ferrying out the courses with scarcely any delay. Betty had several more glasses of wine and began to feel quite relaxed. She was enjoying herself. Beside her, Nigel kept up a stream of interesting conversation. From across the table she could see Gladys Taylor smiling at her from time to time and giving the thumbs-up sign.

After dessert was served they listened to a jolly speech from the chairman who thanked everyone for their continuing support and announced that the next lunch would be held in the Gondola restaurant in Mijas.

When it came time to pay, Nigel took out his wallet and insisted on picking up Betty's bill as well as his own.

"How are you getting home?" he asked.

"I'll get a cab."

"Not at all, I'll drive you."

"Are you quite sure? I don't want to take you out of your way."

He smiled and shook his head. "It's no trouble," he said.

On the way out of the restaurant, he took out his mobile phone. "Would you mind giving me your telephone number, Betty?"

"What for?"

"I might want to keep in touch."

Betty thought it would be rude to refuse so she gave it to him and he entered it on his phone. When they got outside, he led her to the shiny Mercedes she had seen earlier. Fifteen minutes later, he was dropping her off at the gates of Magnolia Park. He said he'd had a lovely lunch and had thoroughly enjoyed her company. Then he sounded the horn and waved as he drove away. Betty walked home through the gardens in the afternoon light. What an interesting man, she thought. I don't know what to make of him at all.

As soon as she was back inside her apartment, she took out her phone and rang Gladys Taylor.

"Hello," Gladys said. "You certainly enjoyed yourself."

"You set that up," Betty said. "Don't pretend you didn't."

"Of course I did. I was doing you both a favour. Old Nige is lonely."

"He's not so old," Betty interjected.

"No, you're right. What age do you think he is?"

"He's sixty. The same age as me."

"How do you know?"

"I asked him," Betty said.

She heard Gladys's throaty laugh. "You don't hang about, do you, girl? I hope he took good care of you?"

"Oh yes, he did," Betty said. "He was very charming. He was a perfect gentleman. He even insisted on paying my bill."

"There you are, then. You should hold on to him. Nigel is loaded."

"But aren't you forgetting something?" Betty said. "I'm a married woman."

"In name only," Gladys said.

Chapter 14

Amy had spent the morning in the garden, reading her novel, listening to the radio and soaking up the sun. To avoid being disturbed, she switched off her phone. After the turbulence of the past twenty-four hours, she just wanted some peace and quiet. She found the experience very soothing.

Eventually, she packed up and returned to the apartment. She changed into a light skirt, tank-top and sandals, put on a golf cap and sunglasses and set off to find somewhere to have lunch. She had been in such confusion that morning that she had only picked at her toast and now she was feeling hungry. Her journey took her into the heart of the old town.

Here, the streets were lined with tiny whitewashed houses and quaint little shops. The shops were beginning to close for the siesta but the *tapas* bars and restaurants were still conducting a busy lunchtime trade. She found a little bar that appealed to her, sat down at a pavement table and ordered a ham omelette with salad and a bottle of sparkling water.

The day was sultry but she was close to the Paseo Maritimo here and a cooling breeze wafted up from the sea. While she waited for her meal, she took out her phone and checked her text messages. There were half a dozen from various friends and work colleagues. But, tucked among them, she found one from Sam.

She stared at it. **Have arrived safely. Will ring you later. PS: It's raining.**

She replied to the texts from her friends and then she read Sam's message again. It was written in a light style, as if the events of the previous day had never happened. She quickly tapped out a short response. **Glad to hear it. Hope everything goes well.**

It was good to hear from Sam. She was glad that he had got back to Dublin safely. She looked forward to hearing his voice again when he called her in the morning.

When she looked up, the dark-haired waitress was setting down her meal.

"Enjoy," she said.

"I think I will," Amy replied as she lifted her knife and fork and prepared to eat.

After speaking to Gladys Taylor, Betty went into the kitchen and made a pot of tea then took it out to the terrace. She looked down from the balcony rail and saw that the garden was empty. Amy and her sun-bed were gone.

She's a wise young woman, Betty thought as she poured out a cup of rich brown tea and added a spot of milk. Too much sun was not good. She had reason to know. Just a few years ago, one of her dear friends, Sally Bannister, had contracted skin cancer and came close to death. She had been lucky to survive but it had given Betty a scare.

She loved the Spanish sun and the brightness it cast over everything. It was a vast improvement on the dull skies she remembered from London. But it had to be treated with respect. Of course, what people did was their own business. But it did give her the shudders to see the way some of them thought nothing of lying in the sun all day long. Young women were the worst. She had seen them at the pool stretched out on their recliners like sausages on a barbecue grill. She was glad that Josh had put on his cap this morning before he left for the golf course.

She sipped her tea. This was one British tradition Betty clung to resolutely. It was much more refreshing than the coffee which the

Spanish drank endlessly. She made a trip once a month to the Iceland store to stock up on it. As she sat in the quiet of the afternoon, her thoughts went back to Josh. She was worried about him. He put on a brave face but Betty could see behind the mask. She knew he was unhappy.

Josh was thirty-two and so far he had shown no inclination to get married and settle down. The truth was he didn't seem to have much luck with women. The few relationships he had struck up hadn't lasted more than a couple of months. And then Nina Black had come along and Betty had immediately noticed the change that came over him. She was certain this was it – Josh was in love. Nina was the girl he was going to marry.

She remembered the joy that shone from his eyes and the lightness in his step. He had brought Nina out here to visit and she had never seen him so happy. Betty could tell when a man was in love and Josh showed all the signs. She used to hear him whistling in the shower in the morning and all day long he seemed to float on air. Then something happened to destroy it all. She didn't know what it was and she had never asked. But the light suddenly went out of Josh's eyes. It was sad because Betty liked Nina. She was a sensible young woman and a talented actress. She was just the type of partner that Josh needed to make him happy. And she was beautiful with her long black hair and those dark flashing eyes that reminded Betty of the gypsy girls she saw at fiesta time with their flamenco dresses and the combs in their hair and their clicking castanets.

Now the sparkle had gone out of Josh's life. He kept up the pretence of being happy but it was just for show. Betty could tell. Of course, there was nothing she could do. She knew better than to interfere or give advice. Josh would have to find his own way out. She just hoped he wasn't going to turn out like his father, married to the business and drowning himself in work to the detriment of the other aspects of his life.

This brought her back to the earlier conversation with Gladys Taylor. She thought Gladys had been rather rude with her remark about Betty being a married woman in name only. But she had forgiven her because it was Gladys's nature to be outspoken and, besides, what she had said was the truth. Betty *was* married in name only. She had known that for a long time.

She only saw her husband for about six weeks in the entire year. The rest of the time Alf was too busy with Parsons Electrical. And when he did come out to visit, he spent most of his time playing golf. Of course, they also spoke several times a week by phone but it wasn't the same. And Alf had long ago deserted the marital bed. Betty couldn't remember the last time she had felt a man's warm body curled next to her. Gladys was right. She might as well be a widow or a divorcee.

These thoughts brought her to Nigel Smyth. What was she to make of him? He was certainly a fine figure of a man, tall and broad-shouldered with nice blue eyes and that beautiful wavy hair. And he was only sixty which Betty considered young since it was her own age. Nigel must have been a dashing man when he was younger. Indeed, he was still fetching. And he seemed very interested in her. He had insisted on getting her phone number before he left.

She felt a little tingle of pleasure as she remembered the attention Nigel had paid her and the charming way he had behaved. She had certainly enjoyed it. He had made her feel like she was a young woman again being courted. It gave her a sense of self-worth and importance that she hadn't experienced for a very long time.

Of course, she mustn't write herself off just yet. Gladys was sixty-five if she was a day and she was still being pursued by admirers. But it was so many years since Betty had viewed herself in this light. From the day she had married Alf, she had always been faithful and had barely looked at another man, certainly not in a romantic way. And suddenly, here was Nigel and she just *knew* he was keen on her.

She wondered what it would be like to have a man in her life again. He would want to take her out to dinner, go to parties and functions and he would want to buy her nice presents. Before long, word would get around. She knew how gossipy her friends could be and Gladys certainly wouldn't be able to keep her mouth shut. She would want to claim credit for her role in the affair.

Betty felt a delicious thrill run through her as she thought of the envious glances she would attract from the other ladies, especially when they learned that Nigel was loaded, as Gladys had so neatly put it. She closed her eyes and let her imagination soar. What would be the harm? It wasn't as if she was stealing someone else's husband. Nigel was separated from his wife and in the process of getting divorced. He was lonely down here and in need of some feminine companionship. Plenty of women had platonic relationships with men. Would it be so awful?

But some sneaking thought told her that Nigel would want more than company. He was a strong, healthy man and she had seen that look in his eye. He would want *sex*. It was natural. How was she going to handle that? Well, this was where she would have to draw the line. It would mean a rejection of her marriage vows and a terrible betrayal of Alf. And Betty knew she wouldn't be able to live with herself if she did that. While she might be prepared to indulge herself with a little male society, there was no way she was going to allow Nigel into her bed.

She gave a gentle sigh. Perhaps it might be best to nip this thing in the bud before it got out of hand. Otherwise she could be accused of encouraging Nigel and leading him on, although that was certainly not the case. She had been careful to let him know that she was married and had a husband back in London.

She took another sip of tea. She could see that she would shortly be confronted with a dilemma. But it was a pleasant dilemma and one she never thought she would have to face.

But the fact remained. What *was* she going to do when that inevitable phone call came and Nigel invited her out to dinner?

Chapter 15

While Betty was thinking about Nigel Smyth, Josh was tucking into a healthy salad and drinking a beer at La Ronda golf club while he considered what he should do that evening. He had been toying with the idea of visiting the English theatre with his mother and afterwards having supper in some restaurant in town. He wondered if they would need to book tickets.

He was glad he had come down to Fuengirola. He could feel the visit was doing him good. But he still hadn't managed to escape from memories of Nina. There had never been a single day since their break-up that he hadn't thought of her. Even in China, in the midst of his hectic schedule of factory visits and negotiations, Nina hadn't been far from his mind. Often he would wake in some strange foreign hotel and Nina would be the first person he would think about. And she would be the last person he thought of before he fell asleep at night. He was still obsessed with her.

He kept wondering where she was and what she was doing and if she ever thought of him. Sometimes he felt an intense hatred for the man who had taken her away from him. In his rational moments, he knew this was unhealthy. The relationship was over. He should move on. But Josh was finding it incredibly difficult. He was sure that they were meant for each other. He was certain that he could never be happy without her. And he was convinced that some day she would realise this too and come back to him.

Their relationship had begun on a high note. Nina was exactly the sort of woman that Josh had been looking for. She was attractive, intelligent, independent and vivacious. He was drawn to her from the start and she appeared to feel the same way about him. He loved being in her company. He loved hearing her voice. When he was waiting for her in the corner of some crowded pub, she would light up the room the moment she appeared. The omens were very good.

For the first few weeks they saw each other almost every day. Sometimes it was just a snatched hour for a quick drink or a hurried snack. On other occasions, they spent the whole day together, going to see avant-garde movies in some little film theatre or visiting museums and art galleries. The highlight was when they could spend the whole night together making love and then waking up wrapped in each other's arms.

But there was a restless itch in Nina that wouldn't allow her to keep still. She was driven by ambition. She was totally determined to make a career in the film business. And Josh supported her in this goal. He had seen her perform on stage and knew she wasn't just a star-struck amateur in love with the limelight. She was a talented actress. She had the determination and the potential.

But he had also seen how the acting profession worked. It wasn't enough just to be talented. There were dozens of actresses more successful than Nina who hadn't half as much talent as she had. What she needed was that lucky break – a part in a successful production that would give her the opportunity to show off her skills and draw attention. A good agent was essential. So were the services of a producer or director who would take her under his wing and promote her career.

He kept encouraging her. At times when she was depressed he urged her on, assuring her that her chance would come. In moments of doubt, he kept her spirits up by reminding her how good she was. She had to stick with it. She had to have faith in herself. She had to think positively and one day that elusive chance would come and her career would blossom into greatness.

He had known from the beginning that this would not be a

normal relationship. Nina's job involved a lot of disruption. There were lengthy periods of rehearsing, travelling, working long hours and sudden alterations of plan. Matters came to a head one Saturday afternoon as they lay in bed in her flat in Fulham. At six o'clock, she was due to leave for a performance of a play she was appearing in at a little theatre in Hampstead.

"Are you really sure you want to get involved with me?" she asked.

Josh kissed her. "What a silly question."

"You see the kind of life I lead. There's no certainty, no permanence. Next month, I could be working in Manchester or Glasgow."

"I'm prepared for that," he said. "My own career is hardly nine-to-five."

"But it's more than that. It's so disruptive. If we ever decided to get married, how could we plan a family?"

He stroked her long black hair, which fell in strands across her full ripe breasts.

"Aren't you getting a little ahead of yourself? Who knows what the future will bring?"

"Most men I've been involved with found it difficult. That's why the relationships broke down. Some of them even wanted me to give up my career."

"I would never ask you to do that," Josh said.

She looked at him with her beautiful sloe-dark eyes. "Are you sure?"

"I'm certain."

"Because I'm growing very fond of you and I'm beginning to get afraid. I don't want either of us to get hurt."

Josh drew her close. "You know how I feel about you?"

"Yes."

"Then why are you afraid? I love you, Nina. I think I've loved you from the day we first met. And I'm not the type of man who gives up easily."

She melted into his arms, their mouths met and he thought: I don't believe I will ever be happier than this.

Over the next few months, the affair went from strength to

strength. But he soon began to understand what Nina had been hinting at. Josh quickly lost count of the number of cancelled dinner appointments, the last-minute phone calls to say that something had come up and she wouldn't be able to keep their date. It was frustrating but he told himself that he had entered this relationship with his eyes wide open. It wasn't as if he hadn't been warned.

Besides, it wasn't all one-way. On several occasions it was Josh who had to cancel an appointment because his father suddenly wanted him to travel to some town to sort out a problem that had arisen in the local Parsons Electrical store. But instead of discouraging him, these forced separations only stoked his passion for her and the next time they met they would fall into bed like drunken sailors who had been away too long from land.

There was an episode a few months later when they were at a party together. It was a theatrical party at the apartment of one of Nina's friends. Josh felt slightly out of place. The room was filled with shrill people, air-kissing and hugging each other like long-lost friends.

As the evening progressed, he noticed that she had become locked in discussion with a tall, older man with thinning hair and a little goatee beard. Their heads were bent together in intense discussion. Josh suddenly felt a surge of jealousy towards this man who seemed to have commandeered his girlfriend's attention.

Eventually, they moved across the room and Nina introduced them.

"This is Harry Pender," she said. "He's one of the biggest agents in London. And guess what, Josh? He has agreed to take me on."

Harry Pender tried to look suitably modest. He held out his hand.

"She's exaggerating as usual," he said. "I'm pleased to meet you."

"It's mutual," Josh replied. "We'd both be delighted if you can assist Nina's career in any way."

"Nina is an exceptionally talented actress."

"I agree."

"I think I can predict a glittering future for her. All she needs is to get the opportunity to display that talent for everyone to see."

"Those are my sentiments exactly," Josh said.

At that moment, a waiter went by with a tray of champagne. Harry stopped him and lifted three glasses. He gave one to each of them and raised his own glass in a toast.

"To Nina's career!" he said.

"I'll drink to that," Josh replied.

From then on, Harry Pender assumed an increasing role in Nina's life. She seemed to have fallen completely under his spell. She pinned all her faith on him. Harry was the person she had been looking for to give her career the push it needed.

She was constantly on the phone to him. Even during intimate moments when she was alone with Josh, the phone would ring and she would break off whatever she was doing to engage in conversation with the agent. Josh realised that Harry was important to her. He was a man who knew the industry inside out and had the right contacts.

But it didn't prevent him from resenting the elderly, balding agent.

There were occasions when he even suspected that their relationship might be more than purely professional but he knew this was ridiculous. Nina was young and vivacious but she was also principled. She would never condescend to have an affair with a man like Harry Pender no matter how many advantages it might bring. Nevertheless, he had to grudgingly accept that there were now three people in their relationship where once there had only been Nina and him.

One evening about three months later, Nina turned up with an excitement in her eyes that he hadn't seen before. They were sitting down to dinner in a little Italian restaurant in Islington that one of her friends had recommended. They had barely given their order when she drew him close and whispered across the table.

"I just got some great news today."

"Well, don't keep it to yourself," Josh said. "Spit it out."

"I got a call this afternoon from Harry."

"And?"

"He thinks there's a pretty good chance that he might be able to get me a film deal."

Her face broke into a rapturous smile. "Isn't that fantastic?"

Her pleasure was so obvious that Josh immediately put aside his dislike of the agent, drew her to him and kissed her.

"It most certainly is. In fact, I think it calls for champagne."

But she quickly laid a restraining hand on his arm.

"No," she said. "It's bad luck to be presumptuous. There's nothing definite yet. Let's wait till we know for sure."

"Okay, if that's what you want. How confident is Harry?"

"He says it's ninety per cent certain."

"And when will he know for sure?"

"He says another week. I don't know how I'm going to stay calm."

"Just try not to think about it. What sort of part is it?"

"It's not the lead but it's still a pretty substantial role. This story is about a love triangle: a wife, her husband and this girl he meets and falls for."

"Which part will you play?"

"The other woman. But look, Josh, I don't really want to get too far ahead of myself. I haven't definitely got the role. No contract has been signed. In fact, I haven't even seen the script. I'm only going on what Harry has told me."

He reached out and caressed her hand. "You'll get it."

"Don't say that. I told you it's bad luck."

"So Harry has come up with the goods?"

"It looks like it. Isn't he an angel?"

Josh knew about the vagaries of the film industry and the multiple hurdles that had to be crossed before a movie finally got made. He knew that nothing was certain in the business. He had heard stories about contracts being signed and finance secured and, at the last moment, the whole project falling apart. But he had a good feeling that this venture would go ahead and Nina would get her break at last.

It was a while before they heard any more news. Then one afternoon Nina rang him at work. She was bursting with excitement.

"Guess what?" she said. "Harry's got a deal!"

He felt a surge of joy. "Oh, Nina, I'm really delighted for you."

"I'm so happy, Josh. You've no idea what this means to me."

"Oh yes, I do. Why don't we go out this evening and celebrate?"

"I'd love to but I can't," she said, quickly. "I've got to see Harry. In fact, I'm going to be terribly busy for the next couple of weeks. I've got to meet the scriptwriter and the director. There are so many things I've got to do. I'm going to be running around like a scalded cat."

"Okay," Josh said. "Call me whenever you're free."

It was several more weeks before word came through that the contract had at last been prepared. When it finally arrived for her signature and she showed it to Josh, he was surprised at the small fee she was being offered. It wasn't much more than she was already earning in the theatre. But Nina brushed his objections aside. She said the fee was not important. The big thing was that she had got the part. Now she could put it on her CV. It meant she was on her way. The big money would come later.

Next she had to negotiate her release from the production she was currently playing in but luckily they had a good understudy available to take over her role. Then there were further discussions with the film company but she left Harry to do that. That was his job. It was the reason she was paying him 20 per cent of her earnings.

All along, Josh had assumed that filming would be carried out in London and that he would continue to see her between breaks in her frantic schedule. But it wasn't till the script arrived that he realised this would not be the case. The story centred on a remote Irish village. She was to play the part of a young teacher who is recruited to the local school and gets involved with the village doctor. After glancing at it, he put it down as the doubts began to surface.

"Where is this film going to be made?" he asked.

"A place called Clifden. It's in County Galway, in the Irish Republic."

"At least it's not LA. So I'll still be able to see you?"

He saw a cloud come over her face as she shook her head.

"It's not possible," she said. "The director is very strict about this. We'll be living on the set till the movie is completed. We won't be able to leave. And we can't receive visitors either. He insists we must give this project our complete concentration."

"He sounds more like a dictator than a director," Josh said, feeling disappointed. "What's his name?"

"Lorenzo Morelli. He's young. He's Italian. He's very intense, very passionate. I think you'd like him, Josh."

"And how long will you be filming?"

"Eight weeks if everything goes smoothly."

"And if it doesn't?"

She shrugged. "Who knows? Could be three months."

Once Harry Pender had negotiated her release from the play she was appearing in, the theatre insisted that she leave immediately so that the understudy could take over. It opened up a gap of several weeks before Nina had to leave for Clifden to begin filming. For the first time since they had met, she was free of work commitments.

Josh had a brainwave.

"We're not going to be seeing each other for a while," he said. "Why don't we make the most of the intervening time?"

"What have you got in mind?"

"My mum has an apartment on the Costa del Sol, a town called Fuengirola. She'd be delighted to have us stay with her for a while."

"That sounds like a brilliant idea," Nina replied. "Just what I need – the calm before the storm, you might say."

Josh had read his mother's mood perfectly. When he rang Betty to tell her, she was overjoyed at the prospect of a visit from her son and his girlfriend.

"How long will you be staying?"

"A week, ten days, it depends on the weather."

"The weather is perfect. It's not too hot. You'll enjoy it. You need a break, Josh. Your father is working you far too hard. He's trying to teach you all his own bad habits."

Betty immediately set about preparing the apartment. It was already spotlessly clean but Josh was bringing a young lady and she wanted make sure that everything would be perfect for her visitors.

Then, in the middle of the preparations, she had a moment of doubt about the sleeping arrangements. She had a spare bedroom which Alf and Josh used for visits but Josh had never brought a woman before. Did they expect to sleep together? In her dilemma, she consulted Gladys Taylor who laughed so loudly that Betty had to hold the phone away from her ear.

"Which century are you living in, Betty?" she said. "Of course they'll want to sleep together. This is 2011. It's not the Middle Ages."

"Are you sure? I don't want to cause any embarrassment."

"You'll cause embarrassment if you *don't* let them share a bed."

"You think so?"

"Betty, I'm telling you. Give them a room together. If they don't like it, one of them can sleep on the floor. But I wouldn't bet on that happening."

"Okay," Betty said. "If you're sure it's alright."

"I'm certain – and light some scented candles. Some couples like that. It gets them in the mood."

Betty was actually relieved at Gladys's suggestion because she had nowhere else to put them unless she gave up her own bedroom and slept on the settee and that didn't appeal to her.

"Thank you for your advice. You're always so knowledgeable."

"It's a pleasure. I'm thinking of offering my services to the local paper as an agony aunt. Do you think I'd be any good?"

"You'd be wonderful," Betty said.

Betty immediately prepared the spare bedroom, put fresh sheets on the bed and new towels in the bathroom. She wanted her guests to be comfortable but she also wanted to create a good impression with Josh's new girlfriend. He had told her she was an actress and Betty was anxious to meet her.

It was April and one of the best times of the year. The flowers and trees were in full bloom and the garden looked magnificent. And, as Betty had reassured Josh, the weather was warm but the temperature hadn't yet climbed to the heights of high summer when it could become humid and uncomfortable.

Nina and Betty hit it off at once. Betty was pleased that Josh had met such an attractive, intelligent young woman. She wanted him to be happy and Nina seemed the person who could achieve this.

Josh hired a car and each day they set off to explore the area. For the first couple of trips, Betty was happy to accept Josh's invitation to join them. Then she found an excuse to withdraw and leave them alone together. In the evening, they all had dinner at some nice restaurant and afterwards sat on the terrace in the moonlight chatting till the early hours.

Josh and Nina stayed for ten days but the time passed too quickly. In the flash of an eye, the little holiday was over and they had to go back to London. Harry Pender had called to say that everything was now ready and filming was due to commence in Clifden in eight days' time. Nina had lots of things to prepare.

Before she left, Betty took her in her arms and kissed her.

"I've enjoyed having you. You really brightened things up."

"I've loved being here. Thank you for having me and making me feel at home."

"It was a pleasure. You're welcome any time you want a break. You don't even have to give me any notice."

"I might take you up on that," Nina replied.

Josh stowed their luggage in the hired car, sounded the horn and they set off for Malaga airport.

The next week was an absolute whirlwind of preparation, packing, confirming travel arrangements and signing last-minute documents. An advance party had been sent ahead to Clifden to prepare the ground and the film crew were already in residence. Accommodation and catering facilities had been secured for the actors and the small army of electricians, lighting men, make-up artists and sundry other individuals whose presence was required to shoot a movie.

Josh had consulted a map of the area and discovered that Clifden was a small town set among beautiful scenery on the edge of the Atlantic Ocean. It was about an hour's drive from Galway on minor country roads that led through the mountains. He could see at once that the place was quite isolated and would not be easy to get to even if visitors were allowed.

The time came for Nina's departure. She was scheduled to fly from London to Galway where transport would be waiting to convey her onwards to her destination. They spent the last night together in her bed at the Fulham flat.

"How do you feel?" he asked, as he cradled her in his arms.

"I'm excited but I'm also sad to be leaving you behind. This is the first occasion we will be parted for such a long time."

Josh felt exactly the same way but he disguised his feelings. He wanted her to leave in good spirits and not with regrets.

"Even if I can't visit you, we can still talk. You're not going to the Amazon jungle, you know. They have telephones."

"I'm going to miss you terribly."

"I will miss you too but it's not forever. You'll be so busy that you won't notice the time flying by."

"I'll think of you every day."

"You might be better concentrating on your lines. This is the big chance you've always wanted."

"I'm also apprehensive," she confessed. "What will happen if I make a mess of it?"

"You mustn't think like that because it's not going to happen. If this Lorenzo guy has even half a brain he couldn't fail to be overwhelmed by your talent."

She curled closer. "You're so good for my confidence," she said. "How do you feel?"

He turned her face towards him so that he could look directly into her eyes.

"Bereft," he said.

The following morning he drove her to the airport and waited while she passed through the security checks and out of sight. Once she had said farewell and kissed him goodbye she never turned to look back. She had already told him that she couldn't trust herself not to weep. Josh felt the same.

He drove back into town feeling gloomy and depressed. It wasn't till she had finally left that the reality struck home that the woman he loved was gone and now he was alone. He was worried about what Nina had said about filming possibly taking up to three months. There were always delays and hold-ups. Sometimes scenes had to be shot as many as twenty times before the director was satisfied. But he consoled himself with the thought that over-runs cost money and Lorenzo Morelli would be under strict instructions to complete the film on schedule. Nevertheless, he knew it could be a long time before he saw Nina again.

They had agreed to keep in regular contact by text. Phoning was going to be more difficult because Nina could never be sure when she might be on set and the director discouraged phone calls while the cast was working. As chance would have it, his father asked Josh to make an overnight visit to Manchester to shake up the local manager who he suspected was not pulling his weight. Josh was happy to take on the task. It gave him something to do and helped keep his mind off Nina.

That evening as he was eating dinner in the dining room of his hotel, he found a short text from Nina saying she had arrived on the set and was ensconced in a cramped mobile home which she was sharing with the actress who was playing the married woman in the love-triangle. Her name was Maggie Bolton. The journey had been tiring and everything was chaotic but the local scenery was absolutely stunning. She ended by saying that she felt lonely and was missing him terribly.

He immediately replied saying he was eating alone in a grim dining room on the outskirts of Manchester and knew exactly how she felt. He said he was missing her too. He asked her to ring him when she got a chance so that they could talk directly. He had a drink in the bar with a travelling salesman from Birmingham and retired to bed for an early night.

The following day, he called on the local manager, gave him a pep talk and started back for London. The visit had been purely psychological in its aim: to keep the manager on his toes and let him know that they hadn't forgotten about him just because he was far away.

He returned to work and, for the next few days, Nina and he swapped text messages. She didn't seem very happy. She complained about the quality of the food, the endless hanging around with nothing to do, the boredom and the lack of privacy in the caravan she was sharing with Maggie Bolton. He tried to encourage her. He told her that once filming began her mood would change. The following morning he was at work in his office when the phone rang and he heard her speaking.

"Thank God I've managed to talk to you at last. You've no idea what it's like here. There is absolutely nothing to do and the boredom is driving me crazy."

He was thrilled to hear her voice again.

"It sounds awful," he said.

"It is. It's like being in prison."

"When is filming due to start?"

"Tomorrow morning at seven. That's why I'm calling. The cameramen want to catch the early light."

"Well, that's progress, I suppose."

"I'm sorry if I sound like a moan. I have to say it is absolutely beautiful here. But I'm lonely as hell."

They talked for a few more minutes and then she said she had to go.

"I love you," he said, reluctant to let her go.

"Me too."

There was a click and the line went dead.

He was right. Once filming began, he noticed a big change in Nina's attitude. Getting an opportunity to speak to her in private was still difficult but, whenever he did, she sounded upbeat and excited. Gone was all the dark broody pessimism. She told him that working with Lorenzo Morelli was a fantastic experience. He was a creative genius who already had several successful movies to his credit and had won a prize at the Cannes film festival. She found him inspiring. Under his direction, she was learning an awful lot about the movie business.

Slowly the film began to take shape. The weather was ideal and Nina was working twelve and fourteen-hour days. The phone calls and texts became less frequent. Josh mightn't hear from her for days and then she would call him, bubbling with excitement. Lorenzo liked her work. He was very encouraging. He said she was a natural film actress. The camera liked her.

Meanwhile, Josh was also busy. A Swedish company had developed a new dishwasher and Alf was keen to secure the UK distribution contract. He asked Josh to go to Stockholm to take a look at it. The trip was organised, the hotel was booked, the flights arranged and a visit to the factory was scheduled. The Swedish manufacturers were looking forward to meeting him and demonstrating their new product.

One morning in the middle of these preparations, he received a call from Nina. He thought he could detect a note of concern in her voice. She asked if he could come and visit her.

"But I thought visits weren't allowed?"

"They're not but I might be able to sneak off to Galway on some pretext, tell them I've got to see a doctor or something. We could meet there."

"Won't they need you for filming?"

"Filming has been suspended. The weather has turned bad. I need to talk to you, Josh. I need your advice about something."

"Tell me now."

"I can't. I need to talk face to face in privacy."

"Has it to do with your career?"

"I can't say."

"You make it sound very mysterious."

"Please, Josh, you need to come. We have to talk."

"This is a very bad time, Nina. I'm leaving for Stockholm tomorrow morning on company business."

"Can't you postpone it for a few days? Can you reschedule the flights?"

He could hear the disappointment in her voice.

"It's not possible, Nina. All the arrangements have been made. What exactly do you want to ask me about?"

"I can't say on the phone. I'm in the mobile home. There's no privacy. Someone might overhear."

"Can you email me?" he asked. "And as soon as I get back from Sweden, I'll come over there and we can meet."

"I'll try."

"How long do you expect filming to be suspended?"

"It's difficult to say. Till the weather improves."

"In any case, when I'm finished in Stockholm, I'll fly directly to Galway."

"Well, when we recommence filming it will be difficult to get away to see you. But I do need to see you so much."

"Alright," he said. "We'll work something out. Try to keep in touch. I think about you every day. I love you."

He heard what he thought was a sob.

"Oh Josh, don't say that. You'll make me cry."

As it turned out, the trip to Sweden took longer than planned. Once the Swedish manufacturers had got him to Stockholm, they wanted to show him other products. Parsons Electrical was a major customer and the Swedes were anxious to do business. By the time Josh returned to London and reported back to his father, the weather in Clifden had changed and filming had commenced again. Nina said it would be extremely difficult to get away to see him as they were working flat out, with hardly time to eat or sleep.

He waited anxiously for her promised email but it never arrived. And the text messages and phone calls became fewer. When he did finally manage to contact her, she sounded harassed and their conversation was brief and hurried. He sensed that some of the passion had gone out of her voice. He began to have a nagging worry that her feelings towards him might be changing.

He put it down to the separation and the long hours she was forced to work. Once she was back in London again and free from the isolation of Clifden, they would be able to pick up where they had left off. But now he began to see the film in a different light. Before, he had regarded it as a marvellous opportunity, now he saw it as a stumbling block to their relationship.

Nina had set her heart on a career in films. This movie was to be her breakthrough and he had no doubt that other projects would follow and other lengthy separations while she flew off to strange locations to work. How were they going to handle that? He began to realise what she had been hinting at that day when they lay together in her bed in Fulham and she had asked him if he was sure he wanted to get involved with her.

But he set these doubts aside as he counted the days till the film was completed and she would be home again.

Eventually, he got the phone call he had been waiting for. Nina rang one morning to say that it was finished. Lorenzo had viewed all the scenes they had shot and was satisfied. Her work was done. Now the film would be cut and edited, the music would be added and it would be prepared for release.

He met her off the plane at Heathrow airport. He swept her into his arms and kissed her so passionately that passers-by stopped to stare.

"You don't know how much I've waited for this moment," he said. "How was the flight?"

"It was fine. Everything went very smoothly."

"Let me take your luggage."

He eased the two heavy bags from her grip and they walked out to his car and started on the journey into London.

"You must be delighted to be home. That experience sounded like boot camp."

She shrugged. "The work wasn't so bad. It was all the waiting around. It was getting all psyched up and then being told that filming was cancelled because the light wasn't right or the weather had turned. And then the constant retake of scenes. That could be quite an ordeal. But on the whole, the experience was very rewarding. I've absolutely no regrets about doing it."

By now they were approaching central London. Nina suggested they go somewhere quiet for a drink. There was a pub in Chelsea which they liked and they went there. Josh found a parking space and they went into the pub and ordered their drinks. He couldn't wait to get her back to the Fulham flat and under the clean sheets.

They sat at a corner table and sipped their glasses of wine. For a while they indulged in small talk. Josh got the impression that Nina had something on her mind. He noticed the way she avoided his eyes and stared at her glass.

At last, she said: "There's something I've got to tell you."

He felt his heart miss a beat. "What is it, Nina?"

"I won't be staying in London."

"Why?"

"I'm moving to Rome."

He stared at her with an open mouth.

"Rome?" he repeated.

"Yes. Lorenzo has asked me to join him."

It took a few seconds for him to grasp the full implication of what she was saying.

"You're leaving me?"

"Yes."

She reached out and stroked his cheek. "Don't take it badly, Josh."

He tried to laugh. "How do you expect me to take it? I love you, Nina, and now you're telling me you're leaving."

"This isn't easy for me," she said. "I've thought about it long and hard. It's for the best, for both of us."

"But –"

"No, listen to me. My life isn't going to change. You've seen how difficult it was because of this film. But that was nothing. Lorenzo is convinced I have a big future in movies. He was really impressed with my work. It's going to mean lots of travelling, lots of disruption. It's going to put an enormous strain on our relationship."

"I told you I was prepared for that," Josh said.

"You don't know what it means. This is what I wanted to talk about when I asked you to come to Clifden that time. Don't you see, Josh? This film has provided the breakthrough. Lorenzo can promote my career. He's got all the contacts. He knows all the important players. He can mentor me. He'll be able to open doors."

"What does Harry Pender have to say?"

"Harry agrees. He says I'd be mad to turn it down. He says I might never get another chance like this."

"Lorenzo wants to get you into bed," Josh said bitterly. "It's the oldest trick in the book."

"No," she protested. "It's not like that, at all. He is genuinely interested in my career."

He looked at her. "I thought we had something Nina, something good. I thought we could build a future together, you and I. Now it looks like I was wrong."

She bit her lip. "I'm sorry you see it like that."

He stood up. "Do you want me to take you home?"

When she looked up, there were tears in her eyes. She shook her head. "I'll get a cab."

He went outside and brought her bags in from the car. He left a ten-pound note on the table to pay for the drinks.

"Goodbye, Nina," he said. "If you ever change your mind, you know where to find me."

Chapter 16

After her lunch in the old town, Amy returned to Magnolia Park via the seafront. She found the beach packed with sunbathers and groups of youths noisily playing volleyball on the sand. On the horizon she could see the cruise ships ploughing along the coast towards Malaga. Eventually, she came to the Palmeras Hotel and started back for Magnolia Park.

When she arrived, she found the complex dozing in the sun. She decided to take a chair and umbrella and sit in the garden beside the fountain with a book. Later, when the light began to fade, she would think about venturing out again.

She opened the apartment door and entered the cool interior, then went into the bedroom and changed into shorts and a tee-shirt. She picked up the paperback she had been reading and took it out to the garden.

She felt her sense of serenity return. It was quiet and peaceful here, the only sound the gentle buzzing of the bees around the rose bushes. Amy settled herself comfortably, opened her book and began to read. She was settling well into the plot when she became aware of someone standing close by.

She sat up, removed her sunglasses and saw Josh Parsons gazing down at her, a golf-bag over his shoulder.

"That must be a very interesting book you're reading," he said.

She looked up at him and smiled.

"I hope I'm not disturbing you," he went on.

"Not at all, I was just catching up on my reading."

"Why are you on you own? Where is Sam?"

Immediately, she felt flustered. A blush crept into her cheeks.

"He . . . er . . . had to go back to Dublin this morning."

"Not trouble, I hope?"

"Oh no, just something that has cropped up at work. His boss needs some alterations to a project Sam was working on. The clients want it finished in a hurry."

"Poor sod! Maybe he'll get back again. You're here for two weeks, aren't you?"

"That's right."

"Well, I'm sure he'll be back before too long. So how are you surviving without him? Finding plenty to do?"

"That's just the point," Amy replied. "I don't want to do anything. I came here to relax and soak up the sun."

Josh made a tutting sound. "Don't let my mother hear you say that," he warned. "She has a thing about the sun. One of her friends got skin cancer and almost died."

"But I take care. I don't stay out too long and I use a good sun cream."

"Well, so long as you know what you're doing. See you later."

"See you."

He was turning to leave when he halted and turned back to her.

"What are you doing about dinner tonight?" he asked.

"I haven't decided yet."

"Well, we can't have you eating on your own. I was thinking of taking my mother to the theatre this evening – to see the English amateur drama group – and afterwards for a bite of supper. You're very welcome to join us."

She sat up straight. "Won't that be rather late?"

"Not really, unless you're absolutely starving. The play should be over around ten. We'll find lots of restaurants open. The Spanish are late eaters."

"Are you sure it will be convenient?"

"Absolutely certain, my mother will be delighted and so will I. It won't be anything grand. You don't have to dress up."

"In that case, I'd be happy to accept."

He nodded. "Well then, it's settled. I'll ring the theatre now and see if we can book seats. If not, we'll go out to dinner anyway. Would you mind giving me your number?"

He entered it into his mobile phone.

"So, we'll pick you up about seven o'clock."

He hefted his golf-bag higher on his shoulder, waved goodbye and was gone.

Amy watched him go. What a pleasant surprise, she thought. An evening with the Parsons would be something to look forward to.

When Josh returned to the apartment, he found Betty waiting for him. She was sitting on the terrace with the tea things on a little table beside her.

"Have you made any plans for this evening?" he asked.

"No. Why do you ask?"

"I was thinking of going to the theatre. And I've invited Amy along. It's not too late to book tickets, I suppose?"

"I don't think so," his mother assured him.

"And afterwards I thought we could go somewhere and have some supper. What do you think?"

"I think it's a wonderful idea. I'll ring the theatre right away."

Josh went into the bathroom and had a shower. He came out dressed in his bathrobe and poured himself a gin and tonic. He took it onto the terrace.

"That's all organised," Betty said. "They had some spare seats. I paid by credit card."

"Excellent."

"Where's Amy's young man?" she asked. "Didn't you invite him too?"

"He's gone back to Dublin. Some business he had to finish."

"Oh dear," Betty said. "What a pity. He had barely arrived."

"That's the reason I invited her. She's on her own."

"That was very thoughtful, dear. How are you enjoying your little break?"

"So far, so good."

"You're not missing work, are you?"

"After four weeks in China? Are you kidding?"

"I wish your father shared your attitude. Sometimes, I think he's going to kill himself with work."

Josh smiled. "I think we both know Dad well enough by now. He'll have to be removed from his office with cutting equipment."

"I suppose you're right," Betty sighed. But she felt a sudden surge of contentment come over her. Josh was in good form and that made her happy. He seemed to be looking forward to this evening. Perhaps the cloud she had noticed hanging over him was finally beginning to lift.

Amy stayed in the garden till six o'clock when the sun began to lose its heat. When it came time to leave, she put her book and glasses away in her bag and carried the chair and umbrella the short distance to her apartment. Then she began to get ready.

She had a shower and washed her hair. Then she spent fifteen minutes deciding what to wear. Among the clothes she had brought were a couple of smart little dresses. She tried them on and examined herself in the wardrobe mirror. In the end she opted for a slim, white dress which not only displayed her figure to good effect but also complemented the healthy suntan she was beginning to acquire.

She put on a simple gold chain and then sat down at the dressing table in her bedroom and brushed out her shoulder-length brown hair. Finally, she applied some make-up. When she was finished, she studied the effect and was pleased with the result. She was trying on a black shawl when there was a knock on her door and when she opened it, she found Josh and Betty waiting outside.

"Ready to go?" Josh asked. He was dressed in a white linen suit, brown shoes and an open-necked shirt.

Amy thought he looked very cool and sophisticated. Betty put her arms around her and gave her a hug and they all set off.

"Josh told me about Sam having to go back to Dublin in a hurry. That's terrible news. I hope it hasn't spoiled your holiday, dear?"

Amy gave a nonchalant shrug. "I'm used to it by now. It happens all the time with his job."

"Well, I hope you're not feeling lonely. We can't leave you all on your own. It's not very neighbourly. You must come up and have afternoon tea tomorrow."

"Yes," Josh agreed. "We'll take you under our wing till he comes back."

They strolled towards the theatre at a leisurely pace. Now that the sun was setting, the air was much cooler and lots of people were out walking.

"What's the production?" Amy asked.

"*Evita.*"

She grasped Betty's arm. "You don't mean the musical, do you?"

"That's right," Betty said. "Have you seen it before?"

"Several times. And I love it. I've got the soundtrack on CD at home."

"Then we're going to have a ball. It's a marvellous show. It's been drawing good crowds and getting excellent reviews. They're all amateurs, you know."

"Really?"

"Well, maybe not entirely amateur. Many of them have worked in the theatre before. But I think you'll be surprised at how good they are."

"Well then, I think I'm in for an enjoyable evening."

Amy sneaked a sidelong glance at Josh. He was smiling as if he was looking forward to a pleasant evening too.

Betty was right. It *was* a marvellous show. The singing, the acting, the sets and the dancing were all so accomplished that it was difficult to believe this was not a professional performance. The cast received a standing ovation and five curtain calls before the audience began to drift out into the cool night air.

By now, Amy was feeling very hungry. They found the streets packed with people strolling and chatting and drinking at pavement cafés. Josh led them to a restaurant in a square where the balconies were hung with baskets of flowers and a man with a guitar was playing flamenco music.

She looked up and saw the sky was lit with stars. Across the table, Josh was smiling at her. She closed her eyes and breathed in the heady scent of the flowers, heavy on the night air.

"Are you playing golf again tomorrow?" she heard Betty ask her son.

"No, I was thinking of taking the car for a spin along the coast to Marbella. I haven't been down there for a while. Do you feel like joining me?"

"Oh no," Betty replied quickly. "I've seen Marbella often enough. Why don't you invite Amy? She might like to go."

He looked across the table at Amy.

"What do you say? Would you like to come? It'll give you an opportunity to see some more of the Costa."

Amy caught her breath. This was totally unexpected.

"I er . . ."

"I'll show you around the place and we can have lunch." He paused and his eyes were smiling at her. "Unless you have made other plans?"

"No," Amy replied. "I'm free."

"So what's stopping you? Shall we say ten o'clock?"

"Yes," Amy said. "Ten o'clock will be fine."

At that moment, their attention was distracted by the arrival of the head waiter with the menus.

Afterwards, as she lay in bed, Amy kept thinking of the wonderful evening she had just spent with the Parsons – the music, the stars, the scent of the flowers. And Josh had been an excellent host. He had displayed perfect good manners and charm and had kept smiling at her throughout the meal to make her feel at ease. It reminded her of something and then, with a start, she realised what it was. It was uncannily like the early days of her romance with Sam Benson when he had swept her entirely off her feet.

She wondered if she was doing the right thing accepting this trip to Marbella. But it was too late now. She could hardly back out without looking foolish. Besides, what was there to worry about? It was just his way of being neighbourly. She was alone and so was he. He was probably happy to have her company. Satisfied that she had settled her doubts, she prepared to sleep.

It was only as she was drifting off that the thought occurred to her that Sam hadn't called as he had promised he would.

Chapter 17

When Amy woke the following morning, thoughts of Sam were still on her mind. Why hadn't he kept his promise to call her? She knew he would be busy – but too busy to pick up the phone? She felt herself beginning to get angry then stopped and took a deep breath. Josh was taking her on a trip to Marbella today. She wasn't going to spoil it all by moping over Sam.

She drew back the curtains and saw that the sun was up and the shining water of the swimming pool was beckoning, cool and inviting. She checked the time. It was eight o'clock. She quickly pulled on her swimsuit, took a towel from the bathroom and set off for an early morning dip.

The complex was just coming awake. On some of the terraces, she could see people drinking coffee in their dressing gowns. A woman waved to her as she went past and she waved back. From the trees she heard the early chorus of birdsong that Betty had mentioned. She had a quick shower then dived into the cool water and struck out with a series of fast crawl strokes. She swam for twenty minutes before getting out and drying off.

The exercise made her feel wonderfully alive. Every fibre of her being tingled with the joy and promise of the morning. She returned to the apartment, made some coffee and spread honey on a croissant. She took her breakfast out to the terrace and ate in the sunlight while she thought of the day that lay ahead.

In an hour's time, Josh was going to pick her up and take her to Marbella. Until a few days ago, she hadn't set eyes on him and knew nothing of his existence. Indeed, she still knew very little about him apart from the fact that he worked in the family's electrical retail business. But there was something about him that strongly appealed to her. It had been there from the first moment she saw him that morning when he had held open the gate for her. It was his eyes that had struck her then, that beautiful soft blue colour that was so rare in a man. But in the short time she had known him she had found many other attractive qualities in him.

There was no question that he was handsome. He was at least six feet tall with a strong masculine build and he had all the charm and grace of a well-bred gentleman. Her thoughts returned to the previous evening when he had gone out of his way to be pleasant and make her feel comfortable. He had heaped attention on her so that she had been left feeling like she was the most important person at the restaurant.

But now her sense of loyalty intervened and she pulled herself up short. She was in a relationship with Sam even if it was going through a rocky patch right now. She must keep that fact in mind. Josh was a good neighbour, nothing more. She was going to have a wonderful day, she had no doubt about that, but she must remain on guard. She must do or say nothing that would give rise to any misunderstanding. With that resolution, she finished eating, returned the breakfast things to the kitchen and began to get ready for her trip.

Just before ten, Josh rang to say he would pick her up in five minutes. By now she had managed to shower, get dressed, brush her hair and apply some make-up. She gave herself a quick look-over in the wardrobe mirror and decided she looked fine. She made a last-minute check of her sunglasses, keys and money, locked up the apartment and stepped out into the sunshine just as Josh came striding down the stairs from his mother's apartment. At the sight of him, she felt her heart swell. He looked stunning in his open-necked shirt, Levis, brown loafers and cardigan tied casually around his waist. He stopped and gave her a quick peck on the cheek.

"You were up bright and early," he said. "I spotted you returning from the pool about half past eight."

"I decided to have a swim to wake me up."

"I take it you had no trouble sleeping?"

"Like a log. I conked out almost as soon as my head hit the pillow."

"That's the sign of a clear conscience," he laughed.

He took her arm and began to walk with her towards the car-park where his black Audi rental was waiting. She settled into the passenger seat and buckled her safety belt while Josh expertly manoeuvred the car out of its parking space.

"So you've never been to Marbella before?" he asked as he opened the gates with an electronic zapper.

"No, although I've heard a lot about it."

"Mum doesn't like it," he said, smiling, as he drove out onto the road. "It gets very crowded with tourists at this time of the year. I'm not overwhelmed by it myself but it's worth a visit. Do you plan to do some shopping?"

Amy shook her head.

"That's a relief. My pet hate is trailing around department stores. We'll just park somewhere and go for a stroll along the promenade then grab something to eat."

"Be my guide," Amy said, settling into the comfortable seat and watching the coast slip by.

It took Josh twenty minutes to reach the outskirts of Marbella and then the traffic began to build up. It was another fifteen minutes before he was able to find a parking space. But at least they were in the centre of the town.

"You look like the energetic type," he said. "Do you fancy a quick tour before we head off for the sea?"

"Sure."

"Okay, let's start with Orange Square."

He took her for a stroll through little narrow streets of quaint shops and cafés and ten minutes later they arrived at their destination.

The pavements of the square were planted with orange trees and every second building appeared to be a restaurant or souvenir shop.

They stopped at a café and had coffee and cake while they watched the tourists checking out the restaurant menus. It was not yet midday but already it was hot. The sun beamed down from a cloudless sky. It began to get so warm that Amy suggested they move down to the promenade where it would be cooler.

When they arrived, they found the area crowded with holiday-makers and the beach a mass of brown bodies. But it was enjoyable to stroll along by the sea past the mime artists and the busking musicians and the 'looky looky men' with their bootleg CDs and cheap watches. They walked for about a mile till they met a bend in the Paseo and saw the white outline of Puerto Banus further along the coast.

"Getting hungry?" Josh enquired.

"Mmmm, slightly peckish."

"Any idea what you would like to eat?"

"I don't mind. I'm not really fussy."

"I know several places we could try," Josh said. "There's a very good Italian restaurant just a little bit further on. I'm not tiring you out, am I?"

"Don't worry! I'll let you know when you are."

Fifteen minutes later they came across the place Josh had mentioned. It was simply called Luigi's. But the plain name did not do justice to the establishment. Amy could see at once that this was an upmarket restaurant. The tables were set out on the beach and covered with shining linen tablecloths while dark-haired waiters in black trousers and white aprons ferried drinks and food to the diners.

He turned to ask her opinion. "What do you think?"

"It looks lovely."

"Then this is where we'll have lunch," he declared.

He had a brief word with the head waiter who quickly led them along a boardwalk to a table set for two near the water's edge. The man bowed as he helped Amy into her seat then asked what they would like to drink.

"Campari and soda," she said and Josh asked for a beer.

A few moments later, a waiter appeared with the drinks and two menus.

Amy paused to take in the setting. A few yards away, the tide was lapping softly at the shore. In the distance, sailboats scudded like white moths on the placid sea while dotted along the coastline she could see palm trees sheltering the magnificent villas of the rich and famous.

"I'm very impressed. This looks like something out of a film set," she said.

Josh smiled. "I thought it might appeal to you."

"You've been to this restaurant before?"

"Yes, many times. How did you know?"

"The head waiter seemed to recognise you."

"And so he should," Josh joked. "I've spent enough money here over the years."

They sipped their drinks while they studied their menus. There was so much to choose from that Amy had difficulty making up her mind. Finally, she opted for a starter of asparagus tips in mayonnaise sauce to be followed by veal cutlet and salad. Josh ordered tortellini with pesto to start and grilled sole sprinkled with pine nuts. He asked for a bottle of Frascati to drink with the meal.

When the waiter had taken their order, Josh looked at her and said: "Let me ask you something, Amy. Are you happy?"

The bluntness of the enquiry took her by surprise. Immediately, she burst out laughing. "What a question? Why do you ask?"

"Well, Sam has gone back to Dublin and now you've been left on your own. I thought you might be missing him."

The question had thrown her completely off balance. Here was Sam back again like the ghost at the banquet. How did she answer? The last thing she wanted to do was spend the lunch moaning about her boyfriend's bad behaviour. What kind of impression would that create?

"His return to Dublin couldn't be helped. It's the nature of his job. In his business, the clients call the shots."

"Have you heard from him?"

"He texted me yesterday to say he had arrived safely."

"I'll bet he's not a happy camper."

"He's not. He's furious."

"I can't blame him. I'd feel exactly the same if I was in his position." He raised his glass to his lips and took a sip of beer. "I wouldn't want to leave a beautiful woman like you behind."

Amy felt herself blush at this unexpected compliment.

"So when is he coming back?" Josh asked.

She shrugged. "Who knows? If he doesn't get his project finished, he might not come back at all."

"Really?" he said and a strange look came into his eyes. "That's interesting."

She put Sam out of her mind. The food arrived and it surpassed Amy's already-heightened expectations. The quality, the service, the attention the waiters lavished on Josh and her – all were outstanding. She could scarcely remember a meal like it. When it came time for desserts, she shook her head, saying she couldn't eat another morsel. They sat on at the restaurant chatting and sharing experiences as the waves rose and fell on the shore and the breeze fanned the leaves of the trees along the promenade.

Finally, she picked up the courage to ask a question that had been on her mind all morning.

"You've asked me about Sam. Do you mind if I ask you something?"

"No," he replied. "Fire away."

"Are you in a relationship?"

She watched as a dark cloud came over his face and he quickly lowered his glance.

"Not right now."

Now she regretted her enquiry. Was that a note of sadness she heard in his voice, hinting at some recent unhappiness? She decided to back away from this dangerous conversation. But he surprised her by pressing on.

"I did have a girl. She was an actress called Nina Black, very beautiful, very exciting and extremely talented. We were quite fond of each other. For a while, it looked like the relationship might develop into something long-term. Then we broke up."

"What happened?"

"It's a long story. Maybe I'll tell you about it some time. But the short answer is that her work came between us."

Checking his watch, he announced that it was half past three. He quickly summoned the waiter and paid the bill.

"Are you okay for the walk back? I can order a taxi, if you're feeling tired."

"I think I have just enough energy left," she laughed.

"In that case, I know what we'll do. We'll walk back to Marbella and then I'll drive you to Puerto Banus. You have to see it and it's only fifteen minutes away. We'll find some little café at the seafront and have coffee."

It was after five o'clock when they reached Banus and the sun was beginning to lose its heat. They found the streets around the port jammed with people strolling and the bars packed with men in sailing caps and blonde women sporting fabulous tans. The port itself was a hive of activity. Every berth was taken by yachts and cruisers, their pennants fluttering in the gentle breeze.

They found a table at a bar overlooking the port and ordered coffee.

"Now that you've seen Puerto Banus, are you impressed?" Josh asked.

"It does have a certain kind of glamour," she admitted.

"But it's beginning to fade and it's far too expensive. You should check the price of property around here. You'll get a shock. Mind you, prices are tumbling because of the recession. A friend told me recently of a villa that was valued at €1.5 million just a year ago. You could pick it up now for €500,000."

"That's a very big drop."

"It's a distressed sale," Josh explained. "The owner lost a packet when the markets tanked. Now his bank has taken possession."

"How sad," Amy said.

"He's just one of many. Take my advice and stick with Magnolia Park. It's got everything you could ever want and the properties will never lose their value. Have you thought any more about buying?"

"No," Amy said.

"If you do, talk to me. I might be able to help you avoid the pitfalls."

It was almost eight o'clock when Josh finally drove the Audi through the gates of Magnolia Park and parked. They had been gone for ten hours.

"Did you have a good day?" he asked.

"I had a wonderful day. The best day of my holiday so far. I want to thank you for your generosity."

"There's no need. I enjoyed it too. Perhaps we might repeat the experience some other time? What do you think?"

She hesitated for a moment before replying.

"Okay," she said. "I'd like that."

He smiled and leaned across to open her door. As he did so, his arms fell across her shoulder and their cheeks almost touched. Amy felt a shock run through her. For a brief moment she thought he was going to kiss her. And then the moment passed. He pushed the door open and she stepped out of the car.

"Enjoy the rest of the evening," he said.

Chapter 18

Betty didn't have to wait long for her prediction about Nigel Smyth to come true. Josh had no sooner left to collect Amy for their trip to Marbella when the phone rang. When she answered, she heard Nigel's voice.

"I hope I'm not disturbing you?" he began.

"Not at all," she replied, feeling her skin tingle at the sound of his voice. "I was just having a cup of tea."

"I've been invited to a charity auction," Nigel explained. "It's been run by the Optimists Club. It's for the animal shelter. I wondered if you would like to come with me."

"Oh," Betty said, putting down her cup and saucer. She had been thinking about this phone call and how she should respond but now that it had occurred, she was suddenly in a tizzy. "When is it?"

"Tomorrow at one o'clock, I'm sorry about the short notice. I only got the invite this morning and I immediately thought of you."

"Where is the venue?"

"Los Alamos golf club. There's a lunch and then the auction. You don't have to bid unless you want to. I'll come and pick you up."

Betty hesitated. "I'm not sure," she said. She knew it sounded weak and indecisive and made her appear stupid.

"It could be a bit of fun," Nigel encouraged. "I'll make sure to get you home again by teatime."

"All right," she said, making up her mind. "I'll go."

"Brilliant," Nigel replied. "I'll call for you at midday. I'll ring in advance."

"Okay."

"I think you're going to enjoy it, Betty."

There was a click and the call ended. Betty leaned back in her chair and closed her eyes. What have I just let myself in for, she thought.

Her first reaction was that she wouldn't know anybody there. But it was immediately followed by another thought: that might be no bad thing. Betty didn't want gossip flying all over the place. She knew the way people could talk. She didn't want her friends thinking she was having an affair with Nigel just because he was bringing her to a charity auction.

But the thought of an affair sent another shiver running down her spine. A man was taking her out. How long was it since that happened? And not just any man but Nigel, who, despite his age, was still a virile, handsome, masculine specimen. Betty felt like a naughty schoolgirl who was about to do something bold and slightly risqué. But it was so exciting that it left her feeling alive and brimming with energy.

She stood up. What was she going to wear? It would have to be something smart, something youthful and feminine that made Nigel's eyes pop and the other ladies stare. But nothing outrageous, of course! That would certainly start the tongues wagging. She went into her bedroom and began to ransack the rows of dresses in her wardrobe. There was a dress in here somewhere that she had bought for Alf's sixty-fourth birthday party. But she hadn't worn it since.

It took her a couple of minutes to find it. It was a little red cocktail dress that hugged her figure tightly and came to about an inch above her knees which was quite short enough, thank you very much. Anything more would be much too daring and would make her look foolish. She quickly peeled off her dressing gown and stepped into the dress. She turned to examine herself. It still fitted her perfectly. She still had a good figure and her legs were in fine shape and would look even better with a decent pair of shoes.

She immediately turned her attention to her shoe-rack and rummaged till she found a pair of red heels. She tried them on and did a little pirouette in front of the mirror. She looked twenty years younger! She glanced at her hair. It had been cut just a few days ago but it could benefit from a rinse and blow-dry. She went back to the phone and made an appointment for three o'clock and decided to have the dress cleaned by the next morning.

Suddenly, she felt like a young girl again, just about to go to her first dance. She felt so excited that she went to the fridge and found a mini-bottle of cava and poured it into a glass. She went back out to the terrace, sat down and turned her face to the sun. It was only a quarter to twelve, a bit early to be drinking but what the hell? It was a long time since Betty had something to celebrate.

She spent the afternoon visiting old Mrs Gilbert, keeping her appointments with the hairdresser and the dry-cleaner's and doing a little shopping. At five o'clock she made a light dinner of grilled chops and salad then sat on the terrace and listened to the birds chirping in the garden.

The thrill of this morning had not diminished as the day had progressed. If anything, it was stronger now than ever. It was a wonderful feeling of being wanted, maybe even desired, by a good-looking man. It was a feeling she thought she had said goodbye to forever. Certainly, if she was depending on her husband, Alf, to rekindle it, Betty knew she would be waiting for a very long time.

It was strange the way Alf had allowed the company to take over his life and swallow him up, to the detriment of everything else. She knew it was no longer about money. They had more than enough to live comfortably for the rest of their lives. It was something else, something to do with power and achievement and success, some male thing that Betty didn't quite comprehend.

But then she had never really understood what made men tick – or a lot of women too, for that matter. Just look at what had happened to Gladys Taylor and some of the oddballs she had ended up marrying. One of them had even tried to murder her. In fairness to Alf, he had never done anything like that. In all the years they had been married he had never once raised his hand to her. Just as well or Betty would have had him in the divorce court before he could say Jack Robinson.

Thinking of Gladys made Betty ponder if she should ring her and tell her about Nigel's invitation to the charity auction. She knew that Gladys would be delighted at the news since she had brought them together. But she decided against it. It would make her sound like some giddy young girl who had been gasping for some man to invite her out. And nothing could be further from the truth.

And there were other things to consider. She barely knew Nigel yet. Who could say that in a few weeks' time they mightn't decide that they weren't really suitable for each other? Then she might end up looking silly. No, it would be better to say nothing for the time being till things had settled down. Anyway, Gladys had her own methods of finding out things and no doubt she would know soon enough.

She heard the sound of the front door opening and then Josh walked out to the terrace and kissed her gently on the cheek. She could tell at once that he was in fine form.

"Did you have a good day, dear?" she asked.

"Yes, Mum, I had a wonderful day. I took Amy to Marbella, had a lovely lunch at Luigi's and finished up in Puerto Banus with the nouveau riche."

He laughed and Betty felt her heart lift. She was so pleased for Josh that he was in such good humour.

"Did Amy enjoy it?"

"I think so. She certainly didn't complain."

"She's a nice young woman."

"She certainly is and extremely good company."

"It was very kind of you to take her out today, dear. Is she missing her boyfriend?"

"That's a very good question," Josh mused. "It's difficult to tell but I have to say she didn't appear to be exactly broken-hearted about it."

"Really?"

"That was my impression but I could be wrong. How about *you*, Mum, anything exciting to report?"

She thought it best not to mention Nigel Smyth. It would take too long to explain and Josh might get the wrong impression.

"I had a nice relaxing day. And now it's topped off by seeing you in such good spirits. Are you hungry, dear? Would you like me to make you something to eat?"

"I might have a sandwich later. Dad wasn't looking for me, was he?"

"No, why do you ask? Were you expecting him to call?"

"I've been thinking I might extend my break."

Betty couldn't believe her ears. Here was something else to celebrate. She sat up straight.

"Why, that would be wonderful, Josh. You know how much I enjoy having you with me."

Chapter 19

Sam gave a despairing sigh and bent once more to the drawings and papers that lay scattered across his desk at Burrows Advertising Executives. Outside the window, the streets of Dublin were shrouded in cloud. A handful of raindrops hurled themselves against the window pane. He thought briefly of the sunlit garden and the flowers and the clear blue skies he had left behind in Magnolia Park and wished with all his heart that he was back there. But he still had this damned advertising campaign to finish and Ron Burrows had made it clear that Sam was going nowhere till it was done.

This was his third day back at his desk and already it seemed like thirty. He felt as if he was in his own private torture chamber and his chief tormentor was the Slimline Fashions boss, Herbie Morrison. Sam had spent his first day back ringing round the city as he began the grim task of dismantling the advertising campaign he had already put in place before he went to Spain. It was like asking a mother to murder her own children. He thought of the long hours of creative energy that had gone into that work and now it was all being consigned to the wastepaper bin. It made him want to weep.

First he had to get onto the advertising managers of the magazines and TV stations where he had booked space and explain that there had been a hitch and he now needed to cancel. He expected reaction and he wasn't disappointed. He could still hear the expletives and threats ringing in his ears. He had only succeeded in mollifying them by promising that the space would be booked again the moment a new campaign was put in place.

Next he had to repeat the exercise with the billboard agencies. When that was over, he felt like he had just completed a tour of duty in Helmand province. Then he had to handle Topaz Maguire and her agent. This was like climbing Mount Everest in a diving suit. He only managed it after being subjected to a lengthy harangue about how he was insulting Topaz's reputation and endangering her career and finally agreeing to pay her half the fee they had negotiated even though she had done absolutely nothing to earn it.

That took all of the first day. He felt so washed out at the end of it that he headed straight round to the Zhivago Bar on Dawson Street where the first person he ran into was the blonde-haired Zoe Byrne who worked on reception. Zoe was only too delighted to sit with him at the counter and pour sympathy into his ear while he poured Bacardi Breezers into her.

It was after closing time when they left and Sam had only a vague recollection of how he got home. But he was absolutely shocked the following morning to find his shirt collar smeared with crimson lipstick. Thank God Amy wasn't around to see it. He was almost sick at the thought of the possible consequences. He had a shower and a quick cup of coffee and headed back into work. On the way, he dropped the shirt into a litter bin at the top of Grafton Street.

When he got into the office, he had to brace himself for the most difficult part. He had to find another model to replace Topaz Maguire and Ron Burrows had insisted that this must involve the co-operation of Herbie Morrison. It was going to be like Chinese water torture.

He began by ringing round the various agencies and asking them to send him portfolios of the models on their books. Next, he rang Herbie and invited him to drop by the offices of Burrows Advertising Executives. Half an hour later Herbie arrived, full of enthusiasm, rolled up his sleeves and sat down opposite Sam at his desk. Sam closed his eyes, uttered a silent prayer to St Jude, Patron of Hopeless Cases, and began.

"No," Herbie said when Sam showed him the first photo.

"Too fat," he said, as he rejected the second.

"Too thin," he said about the third.

"No," he said to the fourth.

It went on like this till, after an hour, Sam had exhausted all the photographs in the portfolios and Herbie still hadn't found one he liked.

"I think we need a coffee break," Sam said.

They had another go at it. This time, Herbie spent more time examining each photograph. He held it at arm's length, brought it up close his face. He even produced a magnifying glass from his coat pocket and subjected each model to minute scrutiny before rejecting her. This exercise took another two hours and they were right back where they started.

Herbie sat back and folded his arms.

"Are there any more you can show me?" he asked.

Sam shook his head. "You've seen every model in Dublin."

"You'll have to look elsewhere."

Sam felt a murderous anger surge in his heart. He felt an overwhelming desire to take Herbie Morrison by his scrawny throat and throttle the life out of him.

"It can't be done," he said, his voice shaking.

"How do you mean?"

"They'll go on strike if you try to bring in models from outside. Then you'll get nobody."

"That's ridiculous," Herbie said.

Sam shrugged. "That's the way it is. They're very protective of their local turf."

"So what are we going to do?"

"You'll have to try again."

By now it was almost lunchtime. Sam suggested that they take a break and resume again at two o'clock. In the meantime, he made a beeline for Zhivago and downed a couple of large vodkas to steel himself for the ordeal that lay ahead. On his way back to work, he ran into Ron Burrows.

"How's it going?" Ron asked.

"It's not."

"What's the problem?"

"Herbie doesn't like any of the models."

Ron's face went rigid. "You've got to stick with it," he said. "I'm depending on you. We've got to secure that contract."

"Even if it means I spend the rest of my life in prison for strangling the bastard?"

Ron Burrows considered for a moment. "Yes," he said.

Herbie was waiting in Sam's office when he got back. He looked as if he was looking forward to another four-hour session.

"Ready?" Sam said.

Herbie nodded.

Sam took his jacket off and hung it on the back of the door. He undid his shirt button and loosened his tie. He had made up his mind that he wasn't going to let Herbie Morrison out of the room till he had selected a model even if it meant tying him to the chair and starving him to death. They sat down and started again.

After ninety minutes, they had managed to narrow the field to half a dozen models that Herbie said he might consider. Sam set the other photographs aside and concentrated on the six.

"What about this one?"

He held up a photograph of a doe-eyed beauty.

Herbie shook his head. "She's too young. It's not the right image."

"This one?"

"Too old."

"What about this one?"

"Too skinny."

Sam felt his temper boil over. He could restrain himself no longer. He leaned across the desk and grabbed Herbie by the shirt collar.

"Listen, you miserable shit, if you don't pick a model by the time I have counted to ten, I'm going to start pulling your fingernails out with a pair of rusty pliers!"

Herbie stared back in terror. A vein in his head had started to throb. "You wouldn't do that?"

"Try me," Sam said.

Herbie quickly bent his face to the photographs again.

"This one," he said, picking a photo at random and holding it up.

Sam lifted the phone and rang Ron Burrows.

"I want you to come in here and witness this so there are no misunderstandings."

"Has he agreed?"

"I hope so." He stared across the desk at Herbie Morrison till he was forced to lower his eyes. "For his sake."

Now it was the third day. Sam had come into work early, determined to get this project finished by hook or by crook so he could get out of there and back down to Spain. It had been the worst job he could ever remember. It had turned into the Campaign from Hell. He hoped he never heard the words Slimline Fashions again as long as he lived.

He thought of ringing Amy to tell her he was on his way but something warned him to be cautious. He would wait till everything was securely nailed down and then he would let her know.

He spent most of the morning supervising a photo shoot with the model Herbie had finally chosen: a slim twenty-eight-year-old called Polly McCall who was a highly successful catalogue and advertising model. She was charging €500 an hour to pose in Herbie's garments but Sam didn't care. He would make sure it went onto the bill.

He had a quick break for lunch and then he spent the afternoon completing the artwork before sending it by courier for Herbie's approval. Next, he began ringing the advertising departments to rebook the space he had cancelled earlier. As the day moved on, he began to feel hope rising in his breast once more. He felt like a condemned man who is finally shown a glimpse of daylight through his prison bars. He thought of Amy and Magnolia Park. He thought of a nice grilled lobster at La Rueda restaurant. He thought of the sun sinking into the still waters of the port and the stars peeping out. Soon he would be there.

He was wakened from his reverie by the shrill ringing of his phone. It was Herbie calling back.

"You got that material I sent you?" Sam asked.

"Yes," Herbie said. "That girl I picked. She's perfect. Why didn't you go for her the first time? It would have saved us all a lot of bother?"

Sam uttered an exhausted sigh.

"So you're happy? You're ready to sign off?"

"Not quite," Herbie said.

Sam felt his heart sink once again.

"How do you mean?"

"This slogan you've come up with – *Slimline: Release the Inner You.*"

"Yes?" Sam said.

"I don't like it."

Sam sank his head onto the desk and let out a groan that could be heard all the way to the end of the street.

While Sam was enduring Purgatory at the hands of Herbie Morrison, Amy was sitting at a little café on the seafront on the Paseo Maritimo eating chocolate cake in an effort to cheer herself up. Despite the enjoyable time she had spent with Josh yesterday, she was feeling quite down. This was the third day and she still hadn't heard a word from Sam despite his promise to ring her. All she had received was the short text message to say that he had arrived safely. She was beginning to have doubts about his sincerity. She couldn't escape the unwelcome thought that as soon as he got back to Dublin, he had slipped right back into his old selfish ways.

She knew he was busy. Ron Burrows was a cruel taskmaster. But Sam wouldn't be so busy that he couldn't spare a couple of minutes to pick up the phone and ring her. It was looking very like a case of out of sight, out of mind. Even if they had never had the row, she would have expected him to call her but, considering they had, it was extraordinarily neglectful.

It sent her a very strong message. It told her she wasn't particularly high on Sam's priority list. The thought made her uneasy. She had forgiven him for his bad behaviour at the Parsons' drinks party and the terrible things he had said afterwards. And this was how he responded? By ignoring her. An uncomfortable feeling was beginning to grow on her. It looked as if Sam's apology had been just so much hot air.

At that moment, her phone gave a loud ring. She checked and saw it was her friend, Debbie Fox. At least Debbie hadn't forgotten about her.

"Hello, Debs," she said, trying to inject a cheerful note into her voice to mask her feeling. "How are you?"

"Not as well as you are, enjoying yourself in the sun. I checked the weather forecast this morning and I see it's 26 degrees down there."

"Yes, the weather has been fantastic. I haven't seen a single cloud since I arrived."

"You lucky cow," Debbie said.

Amy frowned. She wasn't sure she appreciated being referred to as a cow.

"I'm actually sitting at a little café on the promenade eating cake as we speak."

"You're making me jealous," Debbie said.

Amy laughed but Debbie's next remark completely took the wind out of her sails.

"You're not lonely, are you?"

"Lonely? Why should I be lonely?"

"Well, I see that Sam is back in town."

"What?" Amy said, momentarily caught off guard. So that was why Debbie was ringing her. Bad news travels fast.

"I saw him the other night in Zhivago."

"He had to go back to sort out some problem with an advertising campaign," Amy started to explain.

"Ah," Debbie said. "So that's the reason. I thought maybe you guys might have had a little tiff or something."

Amy felt herself starting to get angry.

"What would have given you that idea, Debbie? The reason he is back in Dublin has to do with his work."

"Of course it has. Well, just to let you know that he seemed to be enjoying himself. He had a blonde woman with him. She looked very pretty. And they seemed very comfortable together."

"What do you mean?" Amy asked, feeling her legs go weak.

"She was kissing him. How much more comfortable can you get?"

After Amy switched off her phone, she slumped back in her seat and gasped. She was overcome with shock. She couldn't believe what she had just heard. Sam out drinking in Zhivago with a pretty blonde woman? And kissing? It couldn't be true. Debbie must have made a mistake.

Another thought came crashing into her head. Of all her friends, Debbie Fox was the one she liked least. She had never fully trusted her. It was Debbie who had warned her about moving in with Sam. She had long held a suspicion that Debbie was secretly jealous because she fancied Sam herself.

That would explain it. Debbie had made it up to cause trouble and ruin Amy's holiday. But surely Debbie wouldn't risk inventing a story like this without some evidence? It was far too serious. She must have seen *something*. And what was more, she was bound to have witnesses.

Amy was plunged straight back into doubt and despair. If it had been Debbie Fox's intention to upset her and spoil her holiday then she had succeeded spectacularly. It was all Amy could do not to weep with frustration.

Sam was the real culprit in all this. Debbie was able to gloat because he had given her the ammunition.

What a fool she had been! She had harboured a picture of him moping about Dublin, feeling lonely and dejected as he tried to sort out the problem over the Slimline advertising campaign. She had felt sorry for him. She had even forgiven him for what he had said and done.

But instead, he had been enjoying the night-life, out snuggling up with some blonde woman. This was the same man who couldn't even spare a few minutes to ring her. This thought made any lingering sympathy she had for Sam melt and disappear. Something else occurred to her and made a shudder run down her spine. Was this the first time he had cheated on her? Had he done it before? She ransacked her brain for other occasions. She could recall several times when he had called to say he would be working late and wouldn't be home for dinner. Were those just excuses? Instead of working at the office, had he been off entertaining women behind her back?

And then she remembered something else. When she was moving into his apartment he had suggested a set of rules. One of them was that she shouldn't ring him at the office if he was working late. He said they had to allow each other space. They had to learn to trust each other. Was that just an excuse to give him cover while he carried on with his philandering?

There was one way to find out. She would ring him right now and confront him. She took out her phone again and called his number. She heard it ring for a few seconds before she was put through to his Message Minder.

She steadied herself and tried to speak as calmly as possible.

"Hello, Sam, this is Amy. Something has come up. You and I have got to talk urgently. Please ring me as soon as you get this."

She closed her phone and stared at the chocolate cake beginning to melt in the sun. But her appetite was gone. She couldn't touch another spoonful.

Chapter 20

Betty was in the kitchen clearing away the breakfast things when she heard the sound of the shower running in Josh's bathroom. She stopped to listen and a smile spread across her face. She was certain she could hear him humming. Ten minutes later, he came out of the bedroom with his golf bag and kissed her softly on the cheek.

"Morning," he said and poured himself a cup of tea.

"You're in very good form this morning," she said.

Josh grinned. "And why not? Who wouldn't be in good form with a mum like you?"

"Oh, get away with you!" Betty giggled. But she was pleased when he paid her nice compliments. He was her only child and she loved him to bits.

"Besides," Josh continued, "you would need to have a heart of stone not to be happy in a place like this."

"I'm very happy for you. So you're off again to the golf course. When will you be back?"

"Some time in the afternoon."

"Well, if you want lunch, you'll have to get it yourself. I'm going out too."

"Oh," Josh said. "Where are you off to – anywhere exciting?"

"I've been invited to a charity auction."

"That should be interesting."

"It's for a good cause. The animal shelter."

"Make sure to enjoy yourself. And don't come back with any antique furniture. Your apartment is quite cosy the way it is, thank you very much."

He laughed and kissed her cheek once more then carried his teacup to the sink.

"*Adiós*," he said.

She heard the door close and the sound of his footsteps retreating down the stairs.

She was relieved that he hadn't questioned her any further about the auction. She had decided not to tell him about Nigel, at least not yet. He might not understand. It would save embarrassment if she didn't have to explain.

But she was glad of one thing. So far, he seemed to be enjoying this trip and she had a suspicion it had something to do with that young Irish girl, Amy Crawford. It brightened her heart to see him in such good spirits. It might help him forget about Nina, although Betty could see dark clouds on the horizon. Amy had a boyfriend already and no doubt he would show up again one of these fine days.

Oh well, she thought, there's no point in meeting trouble halfway and anyway it's none of my business. She was surprised to discover that she was really looking forward to the auction. If anything, her excitement had grown at the prospect of seeing Nigel again.

She knew she was going to look well and had no fears that she would make a fool of herself. And besides, she was really doing nothing wrong, just accompanying a good-looking man to a lunch. It wasn't as if she had agreed to go off with him for a passionate weekend to a hotel in Malaga.

This thought brought a gleam to her eye. She had been married so long to Alf and seen so little of him over the years that she had forgotten the thrill of an occasion like this.

She was aware that someone like Nigel could easily have lots of women. She knew that most of her friends would regard him as a fine catch and not just the single ones – some of the married ones might be tempted too. But Betty wasn't interested in his money. It didn't excite her. She had more than enough to get by on. And besides, there were more important things in life, like peace of mind, for instance.

But Nigel had chosen *her*. She wondered what special quality he had seen in her. Betty didn't fool herself that she was glamorous. She was long past the first flush of youth. But at the lunch in El Toro restaurant, this hadn't mattered. Nigel had spent the entire time focused on her. No-one had ever paid her such attention in the last thirty years. And now he wanted to see her again.

It made her think of her marriage to Alf. It was sad to admit but it had really been rather dull. Alf had been a good provider and he had been faithful and they rarely argued or had disagreements. But he had no passion. When she heard some of her friends talk about the exciting sex lives they had, it made her blush. She could remember nothing like that. Of course her friends could be exaggerating. But they couldn't *all* be telling lies.

Betty smiled to herself. At last a little bit of romance had come into her life. What harm could it do? She would go along to this auction today with Nigel and see if the magic was still there. And if he wanted to see her again, she would keep that option open too. It was a bit like setting out on an adventure. Who could tell where she might end up?

Nigel had promised to call for her at midday. By eleven thirty, she was ready. She had retrieved the red dress from the cleaner's and now it looked brand new. She had decided not to wear any jewellery apart from a pair of gold earrings. She had put on a little make-up but not too much. She wanted to look good but still appear natural. She didn't want to give Nigel the impression that she had spent time or money preparing for this event.

At ten to twelve, he rang to say he was on his way and would meet her at the gate in five minutes. Betty sprayed a little perfume on her wrists then checked that all the switches were off and the plugs were taken out of the sinks. She had heard a terrible story one time about someone who had left a plug in the kitchen sink and came home to find the entire apartment flooded. Ever since, she had been very careful. When she was satisfied, she locked up the apartment and set off.

As she passed through the garden she could feel her heart beginning to beat and by the time she got to the gate it was pumping with excitement. Nigel was already there, waiting in his shiny black Mercedes. He was dressed in a neat grey suit with a blue tie. When she got into the car, he presented her with a single red rose.

"What am I supposed to do with this?" she asked.

"Put it in your hair, if you like."

He leaned closer and smiled into her eyes.

"You look wonderful," he whispered.

Los Alamos golf club was set on rolling green sward in the hills above Marbella. Betty had never been there before but she had heard a lot about it. It was supposed to be one of the most exclusive clubs on the Costa. It took them half an hour to get there.

"Are you a member here?" she asked as Nigel swung the car in through the gates.

"No, but some of my friends are."

"It looks magnificent. The membership fees must be expensive."

"I've checked. They're twenty grand a year."

"My God, that's a lot of money just to play golf. I'd expect to own a piece of the course for that sort of cash."

Nigel seemed to find this funny and started to laugh.

"Do you play golf?" he asked as they got out of the car.

"No but my son does. He's staying with me at the moment."

"Maybe we can have a game together," Nigel said.

Betty immediately regretted her remark.

"I'm sure he'd enjoy that but I don't think he's going to be around much longer. He has to go back to the UK in the next few days."

"I'll get him the next time he's out," Nigel said and pressed a zapper to lock the car and set the alarm.

The clubhouse was only a short distance away. Nigel offered his arm and they began to walk. As they approached, they could see a group of people on the terrace standing around sipping drinks.

"Do you know the people who have organised this auction?" Betty asked.

"No, I hardly know any people down here. I'm only beginning to find my feet. But a friend asked me to come and I agreed."

"What's your friend's name?"

"Johnny Carstairs."

"What does he do?"

"He sells time-share."

"Will he be here?"

"I sincerely hope so," Nigel said. "Otherwise we won't know a sinner."

They ascended a stairway to the terrace and a waiter offered them wine from a tray. Betty accepted a glass. She clung closely to Nigel's arm. She could see some of the women casting inquisitive glances in their direction.

A man in a white suit approached and introduced himself.

"Hello, I'm Charles Norton," he said. "I'm the chairman of the organising committee."

"I'm Nigel Smyth and this is my companion Betty Parsons."

Charles Norton consulted a clipboard that contained a list of names and ticked off Nigel and Betty.

"You're very welcome," he said and shook hands. "We'll be sitting down to lunch in half an hour. You'll find the seating plan at the entrance to the dining room."

"Are you expecting a large turnout?" Nigel asked.

"We've sold two hundred tickets but I don't expect they will all come. But we'll make a success of it, you needn't worry. I hope you have a good time."

He made a polite bow to Betty and returned to the group further along the terrace.

There was a table and chairs nearby and Nigel suggested they sit down and take the air.

"Thanks for coming," he said.

"Thank you for inviting me."

He smiled. "I wouldn't have felt comfortable with anyone else."

"What a nice thing to say!"

"Well, it's the truth. I've only been in Spain a short time but I'm finding it difficult to make friends. The problem is I don't know who to trust. But I feel I can trust you, Betty."

She felt a blush creep into her cheeks.

"Thank you, Nigel. It's true what you say. You *do* meet some strange people down here from time to time. There are quite a few fraudsters and people like that."

"Tell me about it," Nigel said. "I've already met one man who wants me to invest in a restaurant."

"Be very careful," she warned, "Make sure to check it out before you do anything. You should always get professional advice."

"Don't worry. I've already told him I'm not interested."

"The problem is that a lot of people are running away from something. They think they can come to Spain and begin a new life in the sun and all their problems will disappear. But often they just bring their problems with them."

"You sound like a psychiatrist," Nigel said with a grin. "What are *you* running away from?"

"Nothing, I just like the lifestyle and the nice weather. That's the reason I came."

"I'm only joking," Nigel went on. "Why doesn't your husband retire and join you?"

"He likes his work too much."

"He should be careful that he doesn't mislay you. A good-looking woman like you could be snapped up by some smooth-tongued Casanova type. I know if you were my wife, I wouldn't leave you alone on the Costa del Sol."

At that moment people began to leave the terrace and drift into the main club. Nigel put down his drink and stood up.

"Looks like they're about to start," he said. "Shall we go in?"

At the entrance to the dining room, the seating plan had been pinned onto a large board.

"Well, that's a relief," Nigel exclaimed, when he had examined it. "Table 18. We're sitting with Johnny and his wife."

Inside was a large room with tables spread out. A stage had been set up and the items for auction had been arranged for display with numbers attached. Some people were already examining them.

As they entered the room, Betty could see more women staring her way as if trying to figure out who she was and what she was doing with such a handsome man.

They were crossing the floor when they heard a loud bellow and saw a burly man in a red jacket waving frantically.

"There he is," Nigel said and steered Betty in that direction.

A slim, heavily-made-up woman was seated beside the man. She was grinning like a Cheshire Cat.

"This is the guy who roped me into this caper," Nigel said to Betty. "Meet Johnny Carstairs and his wife, Vi. This is Betty Parsons."

They all shook hands and Johnny summoned a waiter and ordered a round of drinks.

"Find the place all right?" Johnny asked.

"I've been before."

"Here, I've got you some catalogues."

He gave them each a booklet then whispered: "Just between ourselves, a lot of the stuff they're auctioning is junk. But there's an interesting cruise for two around the Med on offer." He winked. "Might go cheap."

Vi turned her smile on Betty. "Where do you live?" she asked.

"Fuengirola. And you?"

"Puerto Banus. Been out here long?"

"Thirty years," Betty replied.

This seemed to bring Vi down a peg. "That's a long time," she said.

"Yes, the place was very different back then, not so many foreigners. And it was very cheap. You could buy an excellent meal for a fiver. How long have you been out?"

"Three years. Friend of Johnny's got him an opening in the time-share business."

"Don't you find property in Banus very expensive?"

"We're renting," Vi said.

At that moment, the waiter arrived with their drinks. Johnny raised his glass.

"Here's mud in your eye!" he laughed and swallowed a mouthful of gin and tonic.

Vi moved closer to Betty and lowered her voice. "How long have you known Nigel?"

"Just a short time."

"Are you divorced?"

"Oh no," Betty said quickly. "My husband's working in London. Nigel and I are just friends."

Vi looked doubtful. "I'm very fond of Nigel," she said. "You know he's getting divorced?"

"Yes, he told me."

"I've a feeling that he won't be single for very long. He's too hot." She grinned again. "Know what I mean?"

The meal was served: vegetable soup and roast lamb with vegetables followed by a chocolate flan. Johnny wolfed it all down. Then the auction began.

Betty had taken the opportunity to study the list. Johnny was quite right. A lot of the stuff on auction *was* junk: some old paintings, a couple of ornaments, the contents of some fashion queen's wardrobe, a signed copy of the life story of the captain of Los Alamos golf club.

The auctioneer was a thin man in a black blazer who sported a small military moustache. He kept up a steady spiel laced with hoary old jokes as he rapidly shifted the goods for the best possible price.

Finally, it came to the major item of the day – the Mediterranean cruise. This was what everyone was waiting for. The bidding opened at €500 and quickly climbed to €700. Nigel and Betty took a lively interest in the proceedings. The auction had been progressing by bids of €50. Now the bids jumped by €100.

There were three men involved – the few women who had been bidding earlier had dropped out by this stage. The bidding reached €1000 when one of the men conceded, leaving just two still in contention. One of them was a short man wearing what looked very like a brown toupee. The other was taller. He wore glasses and was dressed in a black pullover with a golfing crest. They eyed each other furiously like rivals in a love contest.

"€1000, I'm bid," the auctioneer intoned. "Any advance on €1000?"

He glanced from one man to the other like a tennis umpire till the small man nodded.

"€1100, any advance on €1100?"

The man in the pullover lifted his hand and the bidding reached €1200. People fell quiet and watched intently to see which of them would be first to give up.

There was another furious round of bidding till the price eventually reached €2000.

"€2000, I'm bid for this fabulous cruise. Ten days sailing around the Mediterranean, top-class dining, entertainment every evening, pampered like royalty, everything taken care of including on-shore tours. Any advance on €2000?"

The man with the golfing pullover raised his bid to €2100.

The auctioneer turned his attention to the man with the toupee.

"Any advance on €2100? This would make a wonderful wedding present for someone. Any advance? €2100, I'm bid."

The man with the toupee seemed to hesitate and then he shook his head. The auctioneer gave him a pitying glance. The man with the pullover struggled to contain a smile.

"€2100 . . . going once . . . going twice . . ."

He was about to bring down his gavel when Betty became aware that Nigel had raised his hand. The auctioneer's face lit up with pleasure. There was more gas in the tank yet.

"The gentleman in the grey suit has bid €2200. Any advance?"

The room had become so silent that you could have heard a pin drop.

The auctioneer turned to look at the man in the golfing pullover. The smile had drifted off his face and now he was glaring daggers at Nigel. He glanced at the auctioneer for a moment then he too shook his head and sat down.

The auctioneer brought his gavel down. "One Mediterranean cruise sold to the gentleman in the grey suit for €2200!"

With the conclusion of the bidding, the tension in the auction room seemed to evaporate like air going out of a balloon. A buzz of conversation quickly spread around the tables. People leaned across to clap Nigel on the back and congratulate him on his success. He walked quickly up to the stage, produced his credit card and a few minutes later returned to his seat with a voucher for the cruise tickets in his pocket.

"You got a bargain there," Johnny Carstairs remarked. "Those tickets must be worth at least three grand."

"Maybe more," Vi said. "You're a lucky sod. I'd give my right arm to go on a cruise like that. Well done, Nige."

"You managed it like a poker player," her husband continued. "The way you let those guys knock each other out before you swooped in for the kill. You could sell them for a profit. I know a bloke who would buy them off you."

But Nigel just smiled and said nothing.

Now that the auction was over, people began to drift away and the staff came in to start clearing up.

"Want to go home?" he asked Betty.

She nodded and they stood up. Johnny had a large brandy in his hand and looked as if he was settling down for the afternoon. He waved goodbye while Vi insisted on hugging Betty and saying she had a great time and they must all get together again soon.

Once they were outside, Nigel turned to her.

"That wasn't so bad now, was it?" he said.

"It was quite enjoyable," Betty replied.

"Grub okay for you?"

"It was very nice. But the portions were on the large side. You may not have noticed but I didn't finish the dessert."

Nigel laughed. "I noticed all right. You have a dainty appetite, Betty."

"It's a lady's appetite!" she laughed.

"But that's why you have such a dainty figure."

Betty liked it when he said nice things about her but she wasn't sure yet how she should respond. There was a question she was dying to ask but she couldn't summon the courage.

"Where did you meet Johnny?" she said.

"I was introduced to him in a bar in Marbella. I'd only been here a couple of weeks. He gave me his card and insisted we keep in touch. He's a wheeler-dealer."

"I gathered as much."

"But he can be useful. He knows people. I needed a locksmith for my house and he put me in touch with this guy from Liverpool who did a very good job and didn't rip me off."

"Vi thinks you're hot," Betty said.

Nigel laughed again. He seemed to be in fine form after securing the cruise tickets.

"Does she now?"

"I'm told a lot of women think so."

"Well, I can't help what they think," Nigel said. "It's what *you* think that interests me." He looked at her. "Do *you* think I'm hot, Betty?"

She blushed with embarrassment.

"You're not supposed to ask a thing like that. It's fishing for compliments. It's not a very polite thing to do."

"You haven't answered my question."

"I think you're quite attractive. And just as important, I find you a very interesting man. But I don't know you very well, do I?"

"Well, now you have an opportunity to know me better."

He reached into his pocket and withdrew the cruise tickets.

"I'm inviting you to come on the cruise with me."

"*Me?*" Betty gasped.

"Who else? Why do you think I bid for them?"

They travelled back to Magnolia Park in virtual silence. Nigel had just confirmed what she had feared and had been afraid to ask. The reason he had bid for the cruise tickets was because of her. She knew she should be grateful but somehow that wasn't how she felt. Nigel had just landed her with another dilemma.

He dropped her at the gates and said he would ring again in a day or two. Betty thanked him for the offer of the cruise and said she would need time to consider it. That seemed to satisfy him. He waved from the car window as he drove away and Betty made her way back through the gardens to her apartment. When she got there, she found that Josh had still not returned from his golf outing. She poured a gin and tonic and went to sit on the terrace.

She was in a state of confusion. Her dalliance with Nigel had gathered speed like a runaway train. It was in danger of running completely out of control if she wasn't careful. This was only the second time she had been out with him and he had proposed taking her away on a ten-day cruise. What was she supposed to do?

The cruise was scheduled to leave Malaga in August and stop at Valencia, Palma Majorca, Sardinia, Naples, Sicily and Malta. Betty had never been on a cruise before but it sounded marvellous and she had heard stories from some of her friends about the wonderful times they had enjoyed on similar excursions. She was certain she would love every minute of it. But it wasn't that simple, was it?

She wished with all her heart that he hadn't done it. She wished he would slow down and take things easy. What was his hurry? Betty didn't like being rushed, particularly with something as important as this. It was a pity because she was beginning to grow fond of him. He was an intelligent man and he possessed what Betty thought of as 'character'. She could tell he was a man with principles. Now he had placed her in an impossible position. She was afraid if she turned him down he would be offended and she didn't want to hurt his feelings.

But if she accepted his offer she would really be stepping over an invisible line. It would be what was known as a bridge too far. It was one thing to accompany him to a charity lunch like today. That was harmless and could be easily explained to any reasonable person, including her husband Alf – although Betty had no intention of telling Alf any time soon. But going on a Mediterranean cruise with Nigel would propel her into a different scenario altogether.

For one thing, they would be in each other's company all the time. They would be on a boat. There would be no escape, no hiding place. They would be together all day long, from breakfast right through till dinner. They would even be together when the boat docked and the passengers went ashore on excursions. And there was another grim thought that had been lurking in the back of her mind since Nigel made his announcement. *They would have to sleep together.*

Betty almost choked on her gin and tonic. She raised a hand to her throat and caught her breath. She took out a handkerchief and wiped her eyes. She had arrived at the kernel of the problem. She had known when she started down this road with Nigel Smyth that sooner or later sex would raise its head. She had sat here on this very terrace just a few days ago and thought about it. But she had no idea it would happen so soon. Nigel certainly didn't waste time. He was proving to be a very fast worker indeed.

She wondered if he had planned this auction lunch deliberately. Had he known in advance that the cruise would be one of the items on offer? Was that why he had asked her to come? She hoped not because it would reveal a scheming side to his personality that she wouldn't like. But however it had come about she wished it hadn't happened. Now she was faced with the consequences.

What was she going to do? She could always tell him that the cruise clashed with her wedding anniversary and her husband was coming out to celebrate. That would certainly put an end to it. And it would also serve to remind him of her status as a married woman in case he had forgotten. But it was a feeble excuse and he would see through it right away. And besides it was a lie and Betty didn't like telling lies because they always tripped you up.

No, the best thing would be to ring him tomorrow and tell him she had thought about his offer and decided that it wasn't appropriate. He could sell the tickets or give them to someone else. It would leave no room for misunderstanding about the nature of their relationship. And if Nigel didn't like it, tough! He was the one who was pursuing her. She had agreed to a platonic relationship that would involve lunches and social functions. She certainly hadn't signed up for sex orgies on the high seas.

After coming to this decision, she felt better. Nigel was a businessman like Alf and was used to making snap judgements. But this time he had gone too far. She would ring him in the morning after Josh had left for golf and give him her answer. And to let him down gently, she might suggest they go to a concert in the Cultural

Centre later in the week. She had seen an advert for an Andalusian flamenco troupe. She wondered if he liked that sort of thing.

She felt so relieved at resolving her dilemma that she had another gin and tonic. On the whole, it hadn't been a bad day. Before he made his startling announcement, things had been coming along very nicely although she hadn't cared too much for Johnny Carstairs and Vi. Johnny was a wheeler-dealer. She was wary of people like that. And Vi with all her slap and make-up, had reminded her of a character out of *EastEnders*.

But Nigel had been very kind. And he had said some really affectionate things. He had told her she looked marvellous. He had said he only felt comfortable with her. He had presented her with a red rose. She couldn't remember Alf ever doing that. He had even said if he was married to her he wouldn't leave her alone down here. Nigel really was a very nice man and he was definitely fond of her. She just wished he would slow down and not try to rush everything.

She sipped her gin and stared out at the sky and the small wisps of clouds drifting like candy-floss on the horizon. She hoped Nigel wouldn't be too disappointed when she told him. She hoped he wouldn't think she was being ungrateful. Thoughts of the cruise came creeping into her mind once more. If it wasn't for the fact that they would have to sleep together, she knew she would enjoy every moment. She wondered if there might be some way round this problem.

Would it be possible to have separate cabins? That would certainly remove the immediate threat although it wouldn't eliminate it altogether. But at least they wouldn't have to sleep together. If the tickets specified a double-room would the cruise company be prepared to change them? They might demand a surcharge but that wouldn't be an impossible obstacle.

By now, Betty was completely muddled and the gin and tonic wasn't helping. It might have calmed her earlier but now there was a danger it would put her to sleep. What she really required was a second opinion. She needed to talk to someone who could advise her. She thought of Gladys Taylor. She hadn't intended to tell

Gladys that Nigel had asked her out. She had planned to wait till things had settled down a bit. But this was an emergency.

Gladys answered the phone immediately.

"Hello, ducks," she began. "How are you today?"

"I'm okay."

"You don't sound okay," Gladys said. "Have you been drinking?"

"Just a couple of G and T's. There's something I want to talk about. I need your advice."

"Go ahead. I'm all ears."

"It's about Nigel Smyth."

She heard Gladys chuckling.

"I knew it. He's a wolf that one. What's he gone and done, ducks?"

"He hasn't done anything *yet*. He took me to a charity auction at Los Alamos golf club today."

"Ooooh. That sounds very cosy. So things are progressing smoothly between you two?"

"Well, yes and no. We had a nice lunch and then he bid for a pair of cruise tickets and he got them."

"Where's it going?"

"Round the Med. Ten days, all expenses paid."

"Sounds lovely," Gladys said. "I went on one of them one time. Made me feel like the Queen of Sheba, it did. So what's the problem?"

"He wants me to go with him."

She heard Gladys's earthy laughter crackling through the ether.

"He wants you to go with him and you're ringing me for advice? What planet are you living on, Bet?"

"Well, you see, I have issues with that," Betty said. "I've only just met him. Mind you, he has been very nice, a proper gentleman, I think you'd describe him. But this is all a bit sudden. And then there's the main problem. I'd be expected to share a cabin with him."

"Of course, ducks. That's why he bid for the tickets!"

"But I keep telling you, Gladys. I'm a married woman."

She heard Gladys give a loud sigh like she was dealing with a difficult child.

"The trouble with you, Bet, you've lived a very sheltered life. How many men have you known in your life?"

"Just a few and then Alf."

"Well, you should know that when most men invite you out to dinner and make a fuss over you, they usually have some objective in mind."

"Not all men."

"I said most."

"What about a platonic relationship?" Betty asked.

"Platonic? What language is that?"

"It means just being friends, meeting because you enjoy each other's company but no physical involvement."

"Never heard of it," Gladys said.

"So should I go on the cruise or not?"

"That's entirely up to you, ducks. But I know what I would do."

"You're not really very much help," Betty said.

"I introduced you, didn't I?" Gladys said, sounding miffed.

"I don't mean that. But I feel like I'm getting out of my depth here."

"If you don't go, I can tell you one thing. There'll be plenty of women lining up to take your place."

"Well, that's their business. They don't have husbands to consider."

"Oh, some of them do, ducks."

"So what should I do?"

"Why don't you have a think about it?" Gladys suggested.

"I already have."

"Well, think some more. You don't have to make up your mind right away. In fact, a strategic delay might be good tactics. Make him think you're not jumping into bed with every bloke that comes along."

"I beg your pardon," Betty said.

"Why, what did I say wrong?"

"You don't know me very well or you wouldn't say that."

"You asked for my advice and now I've given it. But remember, if you go on this cruise, you'll have to drop this modesty lark. And one other thing: put the cap back on that gin bottle, ducks, unless you want to have a hangover in the morning."

Chapter 21

By one o'clock, Josh had finished his round of golf. He came in from the course, had a shower and thought about lunch. His mother had said she was going off to a charity auction and wouldn't be home till later. That left him with the option of eating a snack at the clubhouse or going off to a restaurant somewhere for a proper lunch. He got into his car and drove the short distance to La Cala and a little place he knew called La Solera.

When he entered, he found the restaurant filling up but he was able to secure a table beside the window where he could look out at the tide gently rising and falling on the beach. He ordered a dish of paella with clams and chicken and a green salad. While he ate, his thoughts turned to his mother.

A change had come over her in the last few days. At first he believed it was because he had come out to join her. He knew how much she enjoyed his visits and she always cheered up when she saw him. But he was starting to believe it might be something else. This morning she had seemed particularly excited. And she had acted rather oddly, as if there was something she was trying to hide. He wondered if there was some business going on in her life that she wasn't telling him about.

Ever since he was a little boy, Josh had maintained a very close relationship with his mother. She was the one who had spoiled him and protected him and let him have his own way. Over the years they had grown particularly close. She knew about the break-up with Nina, of course. His mother had liked her and the two women got on well together. But she had never questioned him about it. Betty Parsons was not the type of person to probe.

Josh had always wondered what went on between his parents. Their relationship was strange to say the least. It seemed as if they had developed separate lives. But it had nothing to do with any friction between them. And as far as he could figure out, they had remained faithful to each other. His father was too consumed with work to have any energy for anything else whereas Betty seemed content to spend her time happily in the sun with old Mrs Gilbert and her friends in the theatre society.

But perhaps that was changing. Josh had definitely noticed a shift in her mood. He wondered if it might be a good idea to sit down with her some evening and have a little chat. He would have to approach it diplomatically, of course. But she might welcome the opportunity. It would be like the old days when he was a little boy. Only this time, their roles would be reversed.

The other person on his mind was Amy. She had succeeded in doing something that he hadn't thought possible – driving Nina Black from his thoughts. Since Amy had come on the scene, his obsession with Nina had almost disappeared. He was surprised to discover that he had barely thought of her at all in the past few days.

There was some mysterious quality that was drawing him to Amy. She was pretty of course and that was what had first caught his attention. But it was more than that. It was her personality. She was bright and intelligent and cheerful. And warm. That was it. He had discovered that she had the ability to lift him out of himself. Being in her presence was like a tonic. On the few occasions when they had been together, Josh had found himself increasingly attracted to her.

Yesterday, when he brought her home from Marbella, there was a brief moment when he had been tempted to kiss her. It would have been a simple matter to press his lips to hers. How would she have reacted? Josh had a sneaking suspicion that she might not have objected. In fact she might even have welcomed it. But at the last moment, he had drawn back. He had thought of what that kiss would mean and where it might lead.

Nothing was ever simple. Amy already had a boyfriend and Josh was loath to interfere in an established relationship. He had personal experience of the anguish it could cause. He only had to think of Lorenzo Morelli and Nina. Yet, there was something which had struck him as strange – since Sam had returned to Dublin, Amy had barely mentioned him at all and only volunteered information when she was asked.

He wondered if they'd had a serious fight. His mind went back again to the drinks party and the sound of raised voices as he passed their apartment. And the following morning, Sam was gone. Had they had a bust-up? Was that the real reason Sam had gone back to Dublin? If it was, then perhaps the relationship was less secure than he had thought? He would like to get to know Amy better. But he had to act quickly. He didn't have much time. Sooner or later, his father was going to ring and demand that he get his ass back to work.

He finished his meal, paid the bill and started back for Magnolia Park. He parked the Audi and as he was passing the courtyard near the gates, he decided to stop off and have a glass of wine.

The bar was empty. He sat at a little table looking out over the courtyard. It was all so peaceful. In a doorway, a fat cat lay sleeping in the shade. Since leaving La Solera, his thoughts had been consumed with Amy. He came to a decision. He took out his phone and rang her number.

By the time Amy returned to Magnolia Park, half an hour had passed and Sam had not returned her call. It just reinforced her growing conviction that Debbie Fox had not been lying when she said she had seen him kissing some blonde woman in the Zhivago Bar. If he had nothing to hide why didn't he ring her back? Unless he was tied up at a meeting. She checked her watch. It was half past two. She would give him another couple of hours and if he still hadn't called, she would draw her own conclusions.

She took her book, sat on the terrace and tried to read. But she couldn't concentrate. Her mind kept drifting back to the conversation with Debbie Fox. No doubt she was busy spreading the story all over town. She wondered how many other people had seen him with that blonde woman. Had he so little concern for her that he was prepared to flaunt his affair in public?

How was she going to face everyone when she returned? How was she to put up with the insincere condolences and the pity? That was going to be the hard bit. She knew that some of her so-called friends would be secretly delighted at what had happened.

By now she was feeling really sorry for herself. Since this holiday began, Sam Benson had revealed a side to his personality that she hadn't known existed. It was a very nasty side. At the Parsons' drinks party he had been rude, arrogant, jealous and possessive. And now it looked as if he was also a cheat. How easily she had been taken in. What a fool she had been to trust him! There was only one small grain of comfort in this whole sorry mess. It was better that she should learn the truth about him now and not later, when God forbid, she might have married him.

But she wasn't just feeling humiliation at Sam's betrayal. There was also sadness. She had invested a lot of time and effort in this relationship. She thought of the good times they had spent together, particularly in the early days when she had been head over heels in love with him. Now it looked as if all that promise had crumbled into dust.

She wondered if she should cut her losses and go home after all. She would miss the sun and the peace of Magnolia Park. But at home there were people she could rely on for support and encouragement. The problem was, it would look like a defeat having to trail back to Dublin with her tail between her legs.

As she was turning these matters over in her mind, she noticed a young woman with dark hair come out of one of the adjoining apartments and carry a sun-bed onto the lawn. Amy didn't remember seeing her before. And her skin was white as a sheet which suggested she must have just arrived. The woman spotted Amy, waved her fingers in a friendly greeting and Amy waved back.

She wondered if she should go and talk to her, welcome her to Magnolia Park and give her some tips in the same way that Betty Parsons had welcomed her. But just then her phone rang. The sound made her jump. This would be Sam at last.

She opened the phone and clamped it to her ear.

"So you finally picked up the courage to call me, you two-timing prick?"

There was silence.

"Do you hear me? I know exactly what you've been up to so don't start lying to me."

"Amy? Is that you?" a voice asked.

Her heart jumped into her mouth. She had made a gigantic mistake. This wasn't Sam. It was Josh.

"Oh my God," she said and clapped her hand to her mouth.

"Have I got the right number? Is that Amy Crawford?"

"Yes," she replied in a small voice, feeling totally mortified.

"Well, that's a relief!"

"I apologise. I was expecting someone else. And I didn't check to see who was calling."

"That's okay," he laughed. "What were you doing anyway? Practising for a part in a gangster movie?"

"No, I was baring my claws to sink them into someone's throat. But you can relax. It wasn't you."

"Well, I'm very relieved to hear that," he said. "Look, I've just come back from a round of golf and I'm sitting at the bar in the courtyard near the gates. – it overlooks the main courtyard of the complex – I'm enjoying a glass of wine and the thought occurred that you might like to join me."

For a brief moment, Amy thought she was dreaming.

"I'm sorry for not giving you more notice," he continued. "But I'd really like to see you."

She could think of nothing that would give her greater pleasure right now than to have a drink with Josh Parsons.

"I'm on my way," she said. "I'll be with you in ten minutes."

She frantically gathered her belongings from the terrace. Then she dived into the bathroom and had a quick shower. It took five minutes to brush her hair and apply some lipstick and a little scent. Finally, she rummaged in her wardrobe for something to wear, settled for a loose white sun dress, stuck her feet into a pair of sandals and set off. She found Josh sitting alone in the shade wearing a pair of Ray Bans. He took them off as she approached, stood up and kissed her lightly on the cheek.

"Thanks for coming."

"Not at all, I was just finishing a book I've been reading."

"You look lovely," he said, running his eyes over her in admiration.

Amy felt her pulse quicken. "Thank you, what a nice thing to say."

"What would you like to drink?"

"I'll have a glass of mineral water."

"Coming up," Josh said and waved to a figure behind the bar.

The waiter hurried over to take the order and a few minutes later reappeared with the drinks and a little dish of olives.

Josh stretched his legs and gave a contented sigh. "You know something? My mother is absolutely right. Why would any sane person want to swap this life for the frantic hustle of London or Dublin?"

"You tell me," Amy said.

She let her gaze wander over her surroundings. The courtyard was perfectly still and the shade of afternoon was beginning to creep across the cobbled stones. The flowers were a blaze of colour and the only sound to disturb the peace was the water splashing into the basin of the fountain.

"Have you heard any more from Sam?" Josh enquired.

At the mention of the name, she felt herself tense. "No."

"I'll bet he's missing the sun, poor devil."

She hoped Josh hadn't brought her here to talk about Sam. It was making her uneasy.

He reached out and gently took her hand. "You can tell me to mind my own business but there is something I really must ask you, Amy. Have you two had a fight?"

"Why do you want to know?"

"I'm interested."

She took a deep breath.

"The short answer is yes, we did have a fight."

"I guessed as much. That's why you exploded on the phone earlier. You thought I was Sam calling. What did he do to make you so angry?"

She put down her glass. Should she tell him everything? It was so embarrassing. But talking to Josh might help her get it off her chest.

"Where do I start? I've known Sam for almost two years and I've lived with him for the past twelve months. It took me a while to figure him out. But he is extremely self-centred. He likes to get his own way."

"That's not unusual. We all do."

"But some of us have consideration for others. Remember the afternoon when your mother invited us for drinks?"

"Of course."

"I was relaxing. You were telling me about China. I was enjoying our conversation and I wanted to stay longer. But Sam suddenly decided he'd had enough and wanted to go. He practically dragged me out of the apartment."

"I think he felt excluded."

"I think he was jealous."

"Really?"

"Yes, he was jealous of you because he thought I was paying you too much attention. When we returned to our apartment, we had a flaming row. I told him I had been insulted and embarrassed. He said some very hurtful things. I did too. I completely lost my temper. He ended up by storming out."

"And that's why he went back to Dublin?"

"No, he was recalled because some clients weren't happy with an advertising campaign he had been working on."

"Let me ask you something else," Josh said. "Were you guys planning to get married?"

Amy gave a rueful smile and held up her fingers. "Do you see any engagement ring?"

"Do I take it that means you weren't?"

"That's exactly what it means. The subject of marriage was never discussed."

"But it has been a serious relationship?"

"So far, yes."

He shrugged. "People always fight on holidays. You'll get over it. He'll apologise and you'll make it up."

"I haven't told you everything. This morning, someone called to give me some bad news. She told me she had seen Sam in a bar in Dublin with another woman."

"Oh dear," Josh said. "But it could be innocent, you know. Perhaps you should let him explain himself."

"She was kissing him."

Josh averted his gaze. "That doesn't sound too good."

"It sounds terrible," Amy said. "It sounds like treachery. It sounds like he has been deceiving me. And it makes me wonder if he has done it before."

Josh took a sip of wine and slowly drew his hand across his chin. "I'm sorry for grilling you like this but I had a good reason to ask. You can tell me to butt out now if you wish. But the truth is, I've been thinking about you a lot, Amy. I'd like to spend more time with you while we are both here. But I didn't want to interfere if you were involved in a serious relationship. I didn't think it would be fair. But now that I know what has happened, I'd like to ask you something else."

"Yes?"

"You've had a pretty miserable holiday so far, haven't you?"

"I think you could safely say that."

"Well, we might be able to change that for the better."

"How do you mean?"

"I was due to return to London in the next few days. But now I think I'll tell my father I'm going to stay here for another week. I've got a car. I can take you on trips to places you might like to visit like Seville and Granada. So what do you say? Would you be interested?"

She checked her watch. It was now half past four. It was more than three hours since she had called Sam and left her message and he hadn't called back. She had given him enough leeway and now he had run out of road.

She looked into Josh's cornflower blue eyes that had attracted her from the very first moment she saw him. Right now, there was nothing she would like more than to spend the rest of the holiday with him.

"Yes," she said. "That sounds like a wonderful idea."

Chapter 22

The sound of the door opening woke Betty. She was sitting on the terrace and must have dozed off in the heat. It was so unlike her. Gladys Taylor was right. She would have to lay off those gin and tonics. She glanced at her watch and saw that it was almost five o'clock.

Josh came in carrying his golf clubs. And most surprising, he had brought Amy with him. He strode out onto the terrace and kissed his mother's cheek.

"Fell asleep, did you?" He glanced at the empty glass on the table beside her.

Betty sat up straight. "Hello Amy," she said. "It's lovely to see you."

"You too, Mrs Parsons."

"Would you like a cup of tea, dear? I'm just about to make some."

"I'd love a cup of tea."

"Amy is looking for something to read," Josh explained. "She's finishing the novel she was reading. I told her you had loads of books."

"Oh certainly," Betty said. "What sort of books do you like?"

"I'm not fussy – something with lively characters and an interesting plot. It doesn't have to be Charles Dickens."

Betty laughed. "Those are my very own sentiments. Well, have a rummage through the bookshelf. You can borrow as many as you like."

She went into the kitchen and put on the kettle.

"How did your charity auction go?" Josh called after her.

"It went very well. They raised a good deal of money for the animal shelter. And there was a nice lunch."

"Meet any interesting people?"

"Just the usual, dear, I'm sure you'd find them all very boring."

Josh smiled and Amy drifted off to the bookshelf in a corner of the lounge. She came back with two books and sat down at the terrace table as Betty began to arrange the tea things.

"You really do have a lot of books, Mrs Parsons."

"You don't have to be so formal, dear. Just call me Betty. Now let me see, what did you pick?"

"*Chocolat* by Joanne Harris and *Howard's End* by EM Forster."

"You have very good taste," Betty said. "Those are excellent novels. I'm sure you'll enjoy them. They were made into films, you know. Are you a big reader?"

"I don't get much time. But I like to read on holidays."

"I love a good book." Betty had produced a walnut cake and proceeded to cut it into slices. "Now sit down and drink your tea. Are you enjoying your holiday?"

Amy exchanged a glance with Josh.

"Yes."

"Well, that's good. And how about Sam? When is he coming back?"

But before Amy could reply, Josh cut in.

"I've something to tell you, Mum. I'm extending my stay for another week. I'm going to ring Dad and let him know. I'm sure he'll be able to manage without me for a while longer."

Betty put down her teacup. "Another week?"

"Yes. I'm taking Amy sight-seeing in the car. We're off to Granada tomorrow."

"Why, that's marvellous. You'll love Granada, Amy. It's beautiful, all that lovely Moorish architecture. And you must visit the

Alhambra Palace. You'll have a great time but make sure to take a hat. The sun can get very strong."

"I'll do that," Amy promised.

Eventually they finished the tea and Amy stood up.

"I have to go now," she announced. "I've got things to do."

Josh accompanied her to the front door.

"I'll pick you up in the morning at nine o'clock. The sooner we're on the road, the better."

"Nine o'clock will be fine. I'll be ready."

He bent towards her and, this time, their lips met. Amy felt a charge of electricity run through her. Eventually, they drew apart.

"Tomorrow at nine, okay?"

When he returned to the terrace, Betty was gazing out over the garden. She turned to look at him.

"You and that young lady are getting quite familiar."

"She's on her own. I thought we agreed to take her under our wing."

"But she's got a boyfriend. You'll have to be careful, Josh."

He laughed. "I don't think you need to worry about that, Mum."

"Well, I just hope you know what you're doing."

Chapter 23

The following morning, Josh was up early. By half past eight, he had taken a swim in the pool and had a shower. Betty found him in the kitchen, drinking coffee and eating toast while the morning sun poured in through the window.

"So you're off to Granada?"

"Yes. I thought we'd make an early start."

"When will you be back?"

"Early evening, I expect. You don't mind? You don't think I'm neglecting you?"

"Oh, not at all," Betty said. "In fact I'm quite pleased."

"You can come with us if you like."

She made a face. "You don't want an old fogey like me. Besides, I've already seen Granada more times than I can count."

Josh finished his breakfast, kissed his mother and set off. Betty waited till she heard the front door close. Then she went out onto the terrace and listened to the sound of the birds chattering in the bushes.

She had been right about Josh. There was definitely something going on between him and Amy. She had noticed the change in him, how upbeat and perky he was. And now he had decided to extend his stay for another week and take Amy driving all over the countryside. Well, if these weren't clear signs that there was something going on, her name wasn't Betty Parsons.

But she was glad. Josh needed a lucky break after his bad experience with Nina and perhaps Amy was the very woman to deliver it. She seemed a nice, lively young person and she was quite pretty though not as pretty as Nina. *She* was a raving beauty. She had men stopping in the street to stare after her. But look how it had all ended – with poor Josh getting his heart broken.

Betty just hoped that there wasn't any trouble when Amy's boyfriend found out. But there was nothing she could do about it. And anyway, it was none of her business.

She was relieved that Josh was going off for the day. It would give her an opportunity to tackle the big problem that was bothering her – what to do about Nigel and this cruise. She had been thinking about very little else since he made the invitation. But the phone call with Gladys Taylor yesterday had convinced her. There was no way she could go on that cruise without ending up in bed with him. She had slept on the issue overnight and woken with her mind made up.

She sat down, took out her phone and rang his number.

"Betty," he said. "I was just thinking about you."

"And I've been thinking about you too. We have to talk."

"What about?"

"This cruise."

"What about it?"

"I don't think I can come."

There was a brief pause.

"Where are you now, Betty?"

"I'm at home."

"So why don't you meet me for coffee? I have to drop into Fuengirola to pay some bills."

"When?"

"Eleven thirty. I should be finished by then. I'll meet you at Constitution Square. I'll take you to Sonia's Bar."

"All right," Betty said.

Amy and Josh were approaching Malaga along the motorway. In the distance, they could see the city shining in the bright morning light.

"How long is the journey to Granada?" she asked.

"That depends on the traffic – about two hours, maybe slightly more." He turned to smile at her. "Are you excited?"

"Yes, Amy," said. "This is one of the places I most wanted to visit."

"I think you're going to love it. Mind you, it *will* be hot."

"I took your mum's advice and brought a hat."

She fished in her bag and took out a yachtsman's canvas cap and put it on.

"I found it in the wardrobe. What do you think?"

"It suits you."

"It doesn't make me look stupid?"

"No comment."

She took off the hat and swiped him with it.

"Stop," he laughed. "Do you want me to crash the car?"

Once they had left Malaga behind, they joined the A92 and travelled east. Amy watched as the Spanish countryside flashed by: olive fields, orange groves and fields planted with vines. Occasionally, they came upon tiny whitewashed villages, surrounded by wide open fields. At last, they saw Granada in the distance, shimmering in the heat.

After talking to Nigel on the phone, Betty had spent the next half hour getting ready. She wanted to look her very best for this particular encounter. She had a quick shower, dried herself and began searching for something to wear. She wanted to look elegant but not too formal. She chose a lilac dress which she thought looked fresh and stylish.

It was hot this morning and she knew it would get hotter still as the day wore on so she brought a parasol and a fan. She kept them both closed as she walked slowly down to the railway station, making sure to stay on the shady side of the street. It took her fifteen minutes to reach Constitution Square and when she got there she could see no sign of Nigel. But she knew he would turn up so she chose a seat, opened her parasol and sat down.

The square was the centre of the town. At one end, was a beautiful church and at the other a busy *tapas* bar with tables and chairs spread out along the pavement. People used the square as a meeting point just as she was doing and now there were dozens of them sitting about, with children playing and groups of old ladies in black dresses chattering together as they relayed the local gossip.

She gave a start when she heard Nigel's voice.

"You gave me a fright!" she laughed.

"Sorry, Betty! And my apologies for being late."

"You're not late. I've only just arrived."

He bent and kissed her cheek then offered his arm as she stood up.

"There was a queue in the bank," he explained.

"There's always a queue at this time of year," Betty explained. "It's the tourists changing money. You have to get there early."

"I'll remember that," Nigel said as they set off through the little side-streets till they came to Sonia's Bar.

Sonia was a thin, vivacious, dark-haired woman in her mid-thirties who seemed to be always on duty any time Betty dropped by.

They sat outside beneath an awning and Nigel ordered two *café con leches*.

"How about something to eat?" he asked.

She shook her head. "No, thanks."

"Mind if I have something? I didn't have any breakfast."

"Fire away," Betty said.

When Sonia returned with the coffees, Nigel ordered a ham and cheese roll.

"You look lovely this morning," he said. "Like a spring flower."

"Oh get away. You're a flatterer," Betty replied, opening her fan and beginning to cool herself with it.

"But you like it," he grinned.

"Of course I do. Show me a woman who doesn't enjoy being told that she looks good."

"Men aren't much different," Nigel said.

She sipped her coffee. She had been dreading this conversation with Nigel but now that she was sitting down and they were chatting, it didn't seem quite so bad.

"So you don't want to come on the cruise with me?" he asked.

"No," Betty said.

"You don't have to make up your mind right away. It's not for several months."

"It doesn't matter. I don't think I can go. It doesn't feel right."

"Oh well, I'll just have to find someone else. Is there anyone you can recommend?"

"How about Gladys Taylor?"

Nigel smiled. "Gladys is good fun but she wouldn't do. She's far too loud. We'd never get on."

"Oh, I don't know. She's got loads of admirers."

"Well, I'm not one of them," Nigel said firmly. He took a bite out of his roll. "Why won't you come on the cruise?"

"I think you know very well," Betty replied.

"I'm afraid I don't."

"I have to remind you that I'm a married woman," she replied, aware that she sounded very stuffy. "I still have a husband. He's alive and lives in London."

"I'm well aware of all that."

"So why are you persisting with this notion that I'm single and available for rumpy-pumpy at the drop of a hat. I think you've misjudged me, Nigel."

He put down his coffee and began to laugh. Soon his shoulders were shaking with mirth.

Betty flushed, feeling quite offended by his laughter. "I'm fond of you Nigel. I think you're a very nice man. You're kind and considerate and I enjoy your company. You're easy to talk to and you have a good sense of humour. But I only agreed to see you because I thought we could be friends. I certainly never envisaged jumping into bed with you at the first opportunity."

Nigel eventually stopped laughing and wiped his mouth with a paper napkin.

"Who said anything about jumping into bed?"

"You did."

"No, I didn't. I never mentioned it."

"You implied it."

"I'm afraid you're letting your imagination run away with you, Betty. I have no intention of luring you into bed."

She snapped her fan shut. "How are we supposed to avoid it if we're sharing a cabin?"

"There you go again," Nigel said, starting to laugh once more. "Jumping to conclusions."

Betty stared at him. "What do you mean?"

"The tickets are for separate cabins. They're not even on the same deck. Here, check them for yourself."

He reached into his pocket and took out the envelope.

Betty opened it and removed the tickets. He was right. They were single cabins, one on Deck A and the other on Deck C. Her face went bright red.

"Please forgive me," she said, giving the envelope back, feeling a fool. "I don't know how to begin to apologise."

"You wouldn't make a very good detective, Betty. You should always go on the evidence."

She tried to hide her blushes. "I'm sorry, Nigel. You must forgive me."

"I'll just have to give these tickets to Johnny and Vi. She said she'd give her right arm for a cruise like this. Palma Majorca, Napoli."

"Don't," Betty said as her hand went out and touched his sleeve.

"So what do you want me to do?"

"Nothing. I'm afraid I've got this whole thing mixed up."

Nigel smiled as he put the envelope back in his pocket. "Are you changing your mind?"

"I might be," Betty said. "Give me a few more days to think about it."

It took twenty minutes for Josh and Amy to descend into Granada as by now the traffic had built up.

Josh found a municipal car-park near the Alhambra Palace and they walked the remainder of the way. They arrived in time to catch the last guided tour of the morning. He purchased tickets and they set off with an intense young student guide leading the way.

The guide certainly knew her stuff and could speak excellent

English. She took them round the various attractions, explained the history and culture and drew attention to details of the magnificent Moorish architecture. By the time the tour came to an end, Amy's head was swimming with information and her feet were sore from walking up and down all the steps.

"I think it's time for lunch," Josh said.

"And a drink," Amy added. "I'm parched."

They strolled into the town till they came across a little bar that was offering a *menu del dia* for €10 which included bread and a drink.

They paused and studied the board. It offered three courses. Josh translated.

"First course is mixed salad, macaroni with tomato sauce, *gazpacho* which is a cold soup, or meat-balls. Second course, you can have chicken and chips, *calamari*, spare ribs or grilled sea bream. Dessert will be custard or cake. What do you think?"

"All this for €10?"

He nodded.

"I don't think we'll do better than that."

They trooped into the cool interior and found a table at the back. There were diners already seated at several tables but the place was largely empty. A young woman quickly appeared to take their order.

Amy asked for a beer and then gave her food order: soup and chicken. Josh opted for macaroni and sea bream and a glass of red wine.

"So," he said. "How would you rate your morning?"

"Wonderful!"

"We've still got a lot of the city to see. It's not too hot for you?"

"Not yet. But don't worry, I'll let you know when it is."

They finished the meal. By now the bar was crowded as a tour bus deposited more visitors at the door. Amy took out her purse but Josh insisted on paying.

"It's my treat. I invited you."

In the course of the afternoon, they climbed to the Mirador de San Nicolas which gave spectacular views across the city. Next, they visited the Cathedral and the Royal Chapel where the Catholic monarchs, Isabella and Ferdinand, were buried. Then they wandered around the narrow streets of the old Moorish quarter with its quaint little houses and shops. By now the temperature had risen steeply and Amy was beginning to wilt. Josh suggested they stop for something to drink. They found a café and ordered glasses of cold freshly-squeezed orange juice.

"I think you've walked enough," he said.

"Is there more to see?"

"Lots more, but not today. We can always come again another time."

"If you say so. I don't suppose there's any point coming down with sunstroke!"

Betty made her way home in the afternoon heat with a feeling of joy in her heart and lightness in her step. Nigel was such a nice man. He was so unlike any man she had met – so kind and considerate and well-mannered, yet so strong and resolute and dependable. Her little talk with him had lifted a weight from her mind and now she felt a wonderful sense of freedom. It all went to show how foolish it was to make snap decisions. Nigel had been right. She *would* make a terrible detective. She would probably end up arresting the wrong people while the culprits went free.

Suddenly, the world seemed a much nicer place. The sun was shining. The sky was a clear unbroken expanse of blue. Everyone she passed on the street had a smile on their lips. Even the beggars outside the train station seemed happy. As she went by, she opened her purse and gave each of them some coins before crossing the road and proceeding towards Magnolia Park.

It just proved how wrong she had been to rely on advice from Gladys Taylor. Gladys was a good sort but she'd had a terrible time with men and it had coloured her judgment. They weren't all scoundrels and cheats out to get everything they could from a woman. They weren't all trying to lure you into bed. Nigel was the living proof. She would tell Gladys so the next time they spoke.

Her mind turned to the promise of the cruise. Ten days sailing around the calm blue waters of the Mediterranean, eating lovely food and meeting interesting people. Nigel had told her they even had a cinema on board where you could watch the latest movies and a theatre with nightly entertainment. And every couple of days, they would dock in some exotic port and go ashore to visit wonderful places that she had only read about in books. It would be a magical experience. It would be the holiday of a lifetime.

She had told him she needed more time to think about it but already she was making up her mind. She'd be crazy to pass up an opportunity like this. Her friends would think she was gaga. The whole problem had been solved by the fact that they had separate cabins. Now she would have some privacy and wouldn't have to worry about sharing a bed. And to think she had doubted Nigel's intentions. It made her feel so ashamed of herself.

She ought to have known that he was too much of a gentleman to pull a sordid trick like that. He had simply regarded the cruise as an opportunity to relax and to get to know each other better. And he was right. It was perfect. There would be plenty of occasions to sit and have little talks and all those lovely shore excursions not to mention ballroom dancing and the theatre and dinner at the captain's table.

Already, Betty was beginning to look forward to the cruise. Their little chat this morning had removed the last remaining doubt. She could accept his invitation. And she could do so with a clear conscience. But before she gave Nigel her final decision, she had one more thing to do.

She arrived at Magnolia Park in high spirits and went in through the gate. On her way past the gardens, she decided to call on Mrs Gilbert. She knocked but there was no answer. She pushed open the door and found the old lady sitting in her lounge with the curtains drawn, watching a soap opera.

"You should lock that door, you know," Betty said. "Anyone could walk in. I could have been the Yorkshire Ripper."

"You'd be wasting your time," Mrs Gilbert chuckled. "There's not much left of me to rip."

"You've got a very morbid sense of humour," Betty said, smiling to herself. "But it would be safer, you know."

"If I locked the door I would probably mislay the keys. Then I wouldn't be able to get out."

"Well, I hope you lock it at night," Betty said. "Now, how are you keeping? Is there anything you need?"

"I don't think so."

"You've got enough groceries? What about medication?"

"I'm fine," the old lady said. "Stop fussing over me."

"Why aren't you sitting on your terrace getting fresh air?"

"I'd miss my soaps. Sit down. Would you like a cup of tea?"

"No, thank you. I've just had coffee."

"Were you out meeting someone?"

"Yes."

"Anyone I know?"

"I don't think so," Betty said. "Just a friend."

"How is Josh?"

"He went off to Granada today with Amy."

"Is that the young Irish girl who was at your drinks party?"

"That's right," Betty said.

"I enjoyed that party. Although I think Josh gave me too much to drink. Every time I turned round he was topping up my sherry glass. I think it made me tiddly. I slept for sixteen hours."

"I didn't hear you protesting too much."

"I don't like to be impolite. Good manners are very important, you know."

You're so right, Betty thought.

"Where's that young woman's boyfriend, the one who didn't have much to say for himself?"

"He had to go back to Dublin."

"Oh indeed," Mrs Gilbert said, leaning forward to peer at Betty. "When the cat's away, the mouse will play."

Betty frowned. "You've got a very suspicious mind."

"Not at all. It's only human nature, isn't it? That's the way of the world. She's an attractive young woman and Josh's a good-looking fellow. Why shouldn't they go off to Granada together? I know if I was a young woman again, I'd jump at the chance."

She cackled with mirth.

"He's just being friendly, that's all," said Betty.

"I wouldn't bet on that. I wouldn't be at all surprised if there's more than friendliness going on there. And Granada is such a romantic city. There's something in the air. Maybe they'll fall in love."

Betty smiled to herself. The same thoughts had been going through her own mind.

"Well, if you're sure you've got everything you need, I'll be off. I'll call again tomorrow. And take my advice. Keep the front door locked."

"Bye," Mrs Gilbert said and turned up the sound on the television.

Amy and Josh were in the car again and driving out of the city. Josh turned on the air conditioning and flooded the interior with cool air. Amy dozed for a while but suddenly came awake as they were passing Malaga.

"I thought we might stop and get some dinner," Josh said. "I'm hungry again. How about you?"

"Yes, I think that's a good idea."

Josh knew Malaga well and after parking the car he led Amy the short distance to a fish restaurant where they ate a delicious meal of grilled hake and sliced potatoes.

They lingered a while over coffee and it was almost eight o'clock when he finally drove the car in through the gates of Magnolia Park and stopped.

"Home sweet home," he said. "You look whacked."

"I am. So what do we do for our next adventure?"

"We take it easy," Josh replied. "If you have recovered sufficiently by tomorrow, we might take a trip up to Mijas. It's only fifteen minutes away. You can't leave without having a donkey ride."

Suddenly she felt the urge to fling her arms around his neck.

"Thank you, Josh, my *caballero*! I've had a wonderful day."

He laughed. "I didn't know you could speak Spanish."

"I know what *caballero* means. It means horseman or knight. I looked it up in my phrase book."

Josh smiled and his blue eyes sparkled with affection.

"I've been called a whole lot worse, I suppose."

They paused for a moment to gaze into each other's eyes. Next moment, their lips were joined in a deep embrace.

"Whooo," she said at last. "I'm feeling faint."

He left her at the door of her apartment and promised to ring in the morning.

"What are you doing for the remainder of the evening?"

"I'm going to have a long hot shower and then I will make a cup of cocoa and curl up on my terrace with one of those novels your mother loaned me and watch the stars come out."

"That sounds like the perfect way to end the day," he said as he turned and walked off into the night.

It was only after he had left and she was getting undressed that the thought came to her. Sam still hadn't called. It underscored the truth of what Debbie Fox had told her. And it confirmed her earlier decision. He was guilty as hell. But the way she was feeling now, Amy didn't care if she *never* heard from him again.

Chapter 24

It was a quarter past eight when Betty heard the apartment door open. She was sitting on her terrace reading. But she hadn't been able to concentrate. She had been thinking about what she had to say and how she was going to phrase it.

Josh came in. He looked happy and contented despite the long day. He bent to kiss her cheek.

"Feeling okay?" he said.

"Yes. I've been watching the sun go down. It's very relaxing at this time of the evening. How was your trip?"

"Brilliant. We did a lot of sight-seeing and got a lot of exercise climbing up and down those hilly streets. But it was very hot."

"I did warn you. I hope Amy took my advice and brought a hat."

"Oh yes, she did, a very fetching boating cap she found in the wardrobe."

"Did she enjoy the trip?"

"She had a wonderful time."

"And where are you going tomorrow?"

"Not far, just up to Mijas."

"That will be nice. I haven't been to Mijas for a long time. Are you hungry? Would you like me to make you something to eat?"

"Thanks, Mum, but we had dinner in Malaga."

"Well, in that case, why don't you get yourself a drink and sit beside me? I've got something to tell you."

Josh went into the kitchen and came back with a beer. He lowered himself into the empty chair beside his mother with an expectant look on his face.

"Okay, Mum, what's the big secret?"

"Something has happened and I want you to know."

By now, she had got Josh's full attention.

"I've met a man," Betty said. "And he wants me to go on a cruise with him."

Josh stared at his mother in surprise. So he had been right. There *was* something going on. But never in a hundred years would he have suspected anything like this. He put down his beer.

"Does Dad know about this?"

"No," Betty said.

"Are you planning to tell him?"

"I haven't decided. You see, I don't want to upset him."

"How long have you been seeing this man?"

"Not very long. His name is Nigel Smyth. He's a retired motor trader. I only met him recently. We were introduced by a friend and then he asked me to go with him to this charity auction. That's where he got the tickets for the cruise."

"What do you know about him?"

"Just what he told me. He's separated from his wife. They're going through a divorce. He only moved down here to live a short time ago."

Josh picked up his glass again. This was a shock. His mother was the last person he would have expected to come out with something like this.

"Is it a romantic relationship?" he asked, as diplomatically as he could.

"Oh no," Betty said, quickly. "It's just friendship. It's platonic. He's lonely and looking for some company. He's a really nice person. He's got very good manners. He's a gentleman. If you met him you'd see for yourself."

"Nevertheless, you need to be careful," Josh said. "There are plenty of so-called gigolos down here but I suppose you're aware of that."

"Nigel's not a gigolo."

"But you don't know that, do you? Who else have you told about this?"

"Only Gladys Taylor, she introduced us."

"Do you trust this man?"

"Oh yes."

"Do you want to go on this cruise?"

"I had doubts at first but I was speaking to him this morning and we've got separate cabins. That puts a whole new complexion on it."

"So you think you might accept?"

"Yes, but I haven't told him yet."

Josh sipped his beer. What was he supposed to say? His mother was a mature woman of sixty. If she wanted to go on a cruise with this man, how could he stop her? She was old enough to make up her own mind. His major concern was that it didn't upset his father.

"I've always thought that Dad neglected you," he said. "He should come down here more often. In fact, he should retire and live here permanently. I suppose you must get lonely too?"

"Not in that sense. I've got lots of acquaintances and plenty of things to do. But I just thought it would be nice to have a gentleman friend. There's a difference you know between women and men friends. They have different things to offer."

Josh nodded. She seemed to know what she wanted.

"I've no doubt that's true," he said.

"Oh, I know it is. So what do you think? Am I doing the right thing?"

"If you're sure you know what you're getting into. But I think you should tell Dad. You don't want him hearing about this from someone else. It wouldn't be fair."

After Amy had showered, she wrapped herself in a bathrobe, made a cup of drinking chocolate and went to sit on the terrace with

Howard's End, one of the novels she had borrowed from Betty. Out in the garden, she could hear the chirping of the cicadas and smell the heavy scent of the roses drifting up from the flower beds. It was pleasant to sit like this with the evening coming down. The temperature had dropped but it was still warm.

Once more, she thought how wonderful it would be to live here all the year round, to watch the seasons come and go and the leaves fall from the trees. But it *was* a pipe-dream. In little more than a week, she would have to leave, climb aboard the plane and go back to Dublin and the humdrum life of the insurance office.

She was not looking forward to it. It would mean moving out of Sam Benson's apartment and finding somewhere else to live, probably back in the family home in her old bedroom. She hoped her mother would have the good grace not to remind her of the warning she had issued when she decided to move in with Sam in the first place.

The one bright light in this whole sorry mess was Josh. She could feel the tingle of his parting kiss still fresh on her lips. She closed her eyes and thought of the wonderful day they had just spent together. It was a day to remember, one she would cherish for the rest of her life.

In a week's time, he would be leaving too to go back to his job in London. What would happen then? Would they keep in touch? Would she see him again? Or was this just one of those fleeting holiday romances she remembered from her schooldays when she would meet some boy and they would pledge undying love and then they would go back home. There might be one or two letters, maybe even a phone call and eventually it would all fizzle out as other distractions took over. Was that what would happen to Josh and her?

She hoped not but there was one thing that made her curious – the mysterious Nina Black. Josh had spoken of her only briefly and never mentioned her again. Amy was intrigued by Nina and wanted to know more about her. She wanted to know what she was like. In particular, she wanted to learn what had happened to cause the break-up between them.

She began to feel drowsy. It had been a long day and now she felt tired. Her eyelids drooped. Eventually, she shook herself awake, locked up the apartment and slipped under the cool sheets. Perhaps tomorrow on their trip to Mijas, she might get an opportunity to ask him more about Nina.

Chapter 25

But as events turned out, they didn't get to talk about Nina Black. The following morning started well. Amy woke at seven thirty to find that the sun was coming up. She got dressed and walked the short distance to the train station and had a breakfast of coffee and *churros* – strips of deep-fried dough sprinkled with sugar. On the way back, she called into the market and bought some fruit, a pot of home-preserved marmalade and a packet of good-quality tea in a little shop that sold British products such as kippers and HP sauce. When she got back to the apartment it was nine o'clock.

Today they were going to Mijas but Josh hadn't mentioned any time. She was debating whether to go for a quick swim when her mobile rang. When she answered it and heard his voice, she thought that he sounded upset.

"We've got a problem," he said.

"What sort of problem?"

"The car won't start."

She felt relief that it wasn't something more serious. "What are you going to do?"

"I've been on to the car-hire company and they've promised to get it repaired by tomorrow. They have offered to provide me with a replacement car. But it won't be delivered till this afternoon."

"That's all right," Amy replied. "If you're concerned about me, I don't mind waiting."

"Well, I was planning to have lunch in Mijas. There is one other possibility if you don't mind slumming."

"What's that?"

"We could go by bus. It's only a short journey and the view is fantastic."

"That's not slumming," Amy said. "I like bus journeys. When do you want to go?"

"There's a bus leaving at eleven o'clock which would get us up there in perfect time."

"That's fine," Amy said. "I'll be ready."

"Well then, I'll dispense with the replacement. I like the Audi and they've promised to have it repaired and returned to me by tomorrow. They have also knocked off a day's rental charge."

"That sounds reasonable," Amy said.

She had her swim, got dressed, got ready to leave, then settled down with *Howard's End*. Once she got into the story, she found the novel gripping. She was so engrossed in it that the time flew by. Before she knew, it was a quarter to eleven and Josh was ringing to say he was leaving his apartment. She put the book away, slung her bag over her shoulder and got ready to meet him.

Mijas was what was known as a 'white village' – a collection of small whitewashed houses and some expensive designer homes, perched on a hilltop about six miles above Fuengirola. It had stunning views over the surrounding countryside and the coast.

It took the bus twenty minutes to make the steep climb. When they descended into the square, the restaurants were getting ready for lunch and the bars and cafés were conducting a lively trade for the tourists. Josh suggested they make a tour of the town, see the points of interest and then find a good place to eat. Amy was happy to fall in with his plans.

They climbed the little winding street past the ancient bullring till they came to another pretty little square dotted with restaurants and souvenir shops. Amy made sure to ask a passing German tourist to take their photograph. Josh suggested coffee and then they started downhill again till they arrived at the *mirador* – a vantage point which provided breathtaking views over the entire coastline.

They had fun trying to pinpoint Magnolia Park in the jumble of toy buildings that represented Fuengirola. After several attempts, Amy gave up. From this distance, everything looked the same. But Josh came to the rescue.

"The trick is to find a landmark and work from there. Let's start with the Miramar shopping complex."

This was quickly identified.

"Now the railway station."

After a few moments, Amy found this too.

"You're almost there. Don't take your eye off the station for a moment. Just work your way past the market and you're almost there."

"I've found it!" Amy shouted in excitement. "There it is, right there."

Josh grinned. "If I ever take up exploring, I'll make sure to bring you along."

Their next stop was the tiny grotto to the Blessed Virgin where they posed for more photographs till it was time to move on. They stopped at an art gallery and a souvenir shop where Amy bought some postcards and then they found themselves back in the main square again. It was now five to one.

"Do you fancy a donkey-ride?" Josh pointed to the row of donkeys waiting patiently with their owners outside the tourist office.

But she shook her head. "Not really!"

"So, will we go for lunch?"

"Okay." All the walking and climbing had made her hungry.

Close by, was a restaurant with a terrace. It catered mainly for tourists and the available tables were quickly being snapped up. They sat down and a waiter soon appeared to take their orders. As they ate their meal Amy could feel a sense of peace steal over her. The anger she had felt with Sam had almost completely disappeared. Now she was happy. Just being in Josh's company seemed to calm her. As they were finishing dessert, he reached out and stroked her hand.

"Are you enjoying your holiday now?"

She looked into his eyes. "You know I am."

"I will have the car again tomorrow. Where would you like to go?"

"Don't you want to play golf any more?"

"I can play golf any time. But it's not every day I have a beautiful woman like you to keep me company."

She entwined her fingers in his. "Do you mean that?"

"Absolutely. Before I met you I was feeling very low. You've cheered me up. But this holiday will come to an end sooner than we realise and then you'll be gone."

"You'll be gone too."

He lowered his eyes. "Unfortunately, that's true. But we can still see each other. I have to come to Dublin from time to time to check on our store in Dundrum. And you can hop over to London on a Ryanair flight. You can stay at my apartment if you like. You'd love it. It's in the Docklands. You can see over the entire city skyline." He hesitated. "That's if Sam is out of the picture, of course."

Ignoring his implied question, she said, "It won't be the same. I will always remember these days as a magic time in my life."

"You might change your mind when you go back home. You might forget me."

"No," she said, quickly. "I won't forget you. Ever!"

They sat for a moment in silence looking into each other's eyes, trying to read each other's thoughts. Their reverie was finally interrupted when the skinny waiter presented the bill.

They set off again across the square to the bus stop.

"I've just had a brainwave," Josh said. "There's another bus we can get. This one goes to Arroyo de la Miel. It's a lovely little town further along the coast. It's a short journey. We can have coffee there and catch the train home." ·

"Okay, let's do that," Amy said.

The Arroyo bus was departing in five minutes. They bought their tickets and sat at the front to get the best view as the bus travelled the narrow, winding roads down from the hills. The journey took half an hour. They wandered round Arroyo in the late afternoon sunshine and found an English tea-shop where they had tea and currant scones. It was almost eight o'clock when they finally reached her apartment. She took out her keys and opened the door.

For a moment they paused as if neither of them wanted the magic to end. Then Josh drew her close and pressed his lips to hers. She felt herself melt in his arms.

"Not here," she whispered. "The neighbours might see us."

She drew him inside and closed the door. Next moment, they were locked in a passionate embrace. They moved to the bedroom as one. Her hands were all over him, frantically undoing the buttons of his shirt to reveal a muscular torso covered with a fine coating of down-like hair.

"Slow down," he whispered.

He stood up and undid his belt and his shorts slid to the floor. He stood naked before her. Her hands reached out and drew him down beside her and her mouth devoured him.

Chapter 26

Betty sat in the cool of the apartment lounge and took out her phone. All day, she had been practising how she would do this and what she would say. Part of her didn't want to do it at all but she had talked to Josh and he had said she should and she respected his advice. It was the right thing. If she didn't do it, it would be unfair and she could end up hurting Alf. And Alf didn't deserve to be hurt.

She had finally made up her mind. She would go on the cruise with Nigel. But she didn't want him to get the idea that she was bursting to go off with him, even if she was. The thought of the cruise was too tempting. She was even more excited by the glossy brochure that Nigel had given her. It contained pictures of elegant couples relaxing at the ship's luxurious bars or playing roulette in the casino.

It had photographs of the spotless dining room, the ballroom, the swimming pools and the comfortable cabins. There was even a photograph of the staff lined up on the deck in their smart uniforms, several chefs in the middle in their white jackets and hats. They were all smiling as if they couldn't wait for Betty to step on board so they could lavish attention on her. *A Holiday to Dream Of*, the slogan read, and for Betty every word was true. There was no way she was going to allow this wonderful opportunity slip through her fingers.

She sat with the phone in her lap and thought about her husband. They had been together for a long time. Her mind went back to the first time they met. It was 1971 at a dance in the Clapham Palais in south London. Betty was only twenty years old and very impressionable. Until that evening, she'd had only three boyfriends.

But Alf was more than just a boy. He was twenty-five. In Betty's eyes, he was a mature man of the world with his smart suit and suede shoes and slicked-back hair. When he asked her to dance, she was thrilled. The band was playing a slow dance number. As she walked out onto the floor, she glanced over her shoulder and saw her friends staring at her with envy and this made her feel even better.

When the dance was over, Alf invited her to have coffee with him in the café. They talked for a while and he told her he was a sales assistant at an electrical store in Brixton. But he had no intention of remaining there. Alf said his ambition was to have his own shop some day. Betty was impressed and said she admired a man with ambition. This seemed to please Alf. They danced some more and then he took her home and they agreed to meet again the following evening.

At the time, Betty was living with her parents and two sisters in a council flat in Tooting and worked as a trainee cashier in the local Woolworths store. On their next date, Alf took her to the cinema to see *The French Connection* with Gene Hackman. He bought popcorn and soft drinks and afterwards they went to a burger bar. Betty thought this was all very sophisticated.

When they had been going out for several months, he brought her home to meet his mum, dad, sister and his gran who was living with the family. She was an old lady who was deaf and kept getting Betty's name mixed up and calling her Kitty. The following week, she brought him to meet her family. Her mum made a big fuss of Alf and insisted that he stay for tea which was curry and rice from the Indian takeaway.

Soon they were going steady and everyone expected them to get married. Betty used to daydream about what life would be like as a married woman with her own home and children. But Alf hadn't proposed just yet. He told her he wanted to wait till he had saved enough money. Betty's mum said this was very sensible and showed that Alf was a reliable man and would make a good husband. Even then, he was thinking ahead.

But she had to wait for another eighteen months till her twenty-second birthday before he bought her an engagement ring. Betty didn't mind waiting. One of her friends told her too many girls got married in haste and repented at leisure. And she was enjoying the fuss that the engagement ring had created among her colleagues at work and the customers who came into the store. Besides, by now she knew Alf was in love with her and wasn't likely to run off with anyone else.

A year later, they were married by the local vicar and then everyone went back to her mum's flat for tea and sandwiches before she left with Alf to spend the weekend in Southend-on-Sea. He said it would be a shame to waste good money on an expensive honeymoon and promised to make it up to her when he became a successful businessman.

When they returned, they moved into a one-bed apartment near her family and Betty continued to work at Woolworths. She enjoyed being a married woman and keeping house and making sure that Alf was happy while he worked like a slave to save money for his shop. But a few years later she got pregnant and Josh came along and she had to stop working to look after the baby.

By this stage, Alf was almost ready to open his own shop. He had managed to save several thousand pounds with the local bank and the manager agreed to advance him a loan once Alf presented him with his business plan. He spent several months looking for a place until he finally found an empty shop on Tooting High Street. It had plenty of space, a basement for storage and a good position next door to the post office.

The owner was looking £300 a month for the rent but Alf negotiated him down to £200. He spent another six weeks getting the shop ready, putting up shelves and display counters and hiring two assistants. At last he was ready to fulfil his ambition. He threw an opening party and got the local newspaper editor to provide publicity and photographs by bribing him with a new washing machine. The following day he opened for business.

This was when Betty's life began to change dramatically. Alf had always worked hard but now he went into overdrive. He worked fifteen hours a day, six days a week. He began to disappear on trips to source new products and when he came home he would be exhausted and fall into bed and sleep for ten hours. But the shop was remarkably successful. Alf's prices were very competitive and he provided an excellent back-up service for customers with complaints.

Eventually, they moved to a fine big house in Wandsworth and Alf equipped it with beautiful furniture and all the latest appliances for the kitchen. They were very comfortably off. Alf's business was prospering. He had a good management team in place. But he still wasn't satisfied. He wanted more. Instead of relaxing and enjoying the money he was earning, he worked even harder.

Their sex life had never been very good but now it became almost non-existent. It wasn't that Alf had lost interest in her or was out chasing other women – he just hadn't the time or the energy for lovemaking. But by now Josh was growing up and that kept Betty occupied.

Josh started school and Betty had time on her hands. She began to grow restless. She went through a period when she felt that her life had no purpose any more. Then they came down to Fuengirola on a holiday and she discovered Magnolia Park.

Eventually Betty moved down to Spain to live permanently. At first, she missed her husband but she told herself that even when she was at home, he was never around. Gradually, she made new friends. She had good neighbours. She grew to love Magnolia Park. She had a fine life down here on the Costa del Sol. She knew that her situation wasn't perfect. In fact it wasn't even normal. But Betty had remained faithful to her man. She had everything she wanted except one thing and now that Nigel had come on the scene, she thought she had found it.

She got Alf's number on her mobile. She heard the phone ring for a moment and then his voice answering.

"Alf, it's me."

"Betty, how are you? When is Josh coming back? Tell him I need him here. The work is piling up."

She took a deep breath.

"I've got something important to tell you."

"What is it, dear?"

"I've met a man. His name is Nigel Smyth. I'm going on a cruise with him."

At last, she finished her call. It had taken so much out of her that she felt the need for a gin and tonic. She didn't care what Gladys Taylor might think. She fixed the drink and took it out to the terrace and sat looking out over the garden. By now the sun was beginning to set and dusk was descending. Just then, she heard the phone ring. Her first thought was that it was Alf calling her back. But when she answered, she heard a woman's voice. She felt herself go tense. She knew this voice.

"I'm looking for Josh," the caller said. "I was told he was visiting you in Fuengirola."

"That's correct," Betty said quickly. "But he's out just now."

"When will he be back?"

"I don't know."

"Would you mind passing on a message? Would you tell him I'm back in London and need to talk to him urgently?"

Chapter 27

Sam sat at the zinc counter of the Zhivago Bar and heaved a sigh of despair so deep that it seemed to come from the tips of his toes. He felt as if all the cares of the world were conspiring to weigh him down. In the past week, everything he had touched had gone belly-up. He thought of what he had left behind in Magnolia Park – the sun, the flowers, the peace, and of course Amy. He wished he was there right now and not here in Dublin being slowly tortured to death by Herbie Morrison and Slimline Fashions.

"Herbie Morrison is an idiot," Zoe Byrne said.

Sam turned to look at the blonde receptionist who was perched on a stool beside him.

"But he's a rich idiot," he said. "And that's why Ron Burrows jumps when he says so."

"Ron Burrows is a pretentious prat!" Zoe said with vehemence. "I'm disgusted with him. He should defend his staff. He should tell Herbie Morrison to go and take a running jump."

"I couldn't agree more," Sam said wearily.

"You're too loyal," Zoe continued. "That's your problem. Ron takes you for granted. He thinks he can walk all over you. You know what it is? He doesn't appreciate your talent. And you know why? Because he has no talent himself."

This sounded like music in Sam's ears. Zoe was a woman after his own heart. She is so right, he thought. This beautiful creature who was sitting beside him was the only person who understood him. She articulated his grievances perfectly. He *was* unappreciated. He *was* loyal. Since coming back, he had sweated his guts out for this damned Slimline campaign. And what thanks did he get? None. His boss was continuing to side against him with that moron, Herbie Morrison who wouldn't recognise a creative idea if it walked in and bit him on the arse.

Now he was stuck in Dublin instead of relaxing on the Costa del Sol. He thought of the countless phone calls he had made, the arguments with advertising managers, the hours he had spent with Herbie Morrison while the idiot tried to select a suitable model for the campaign. And then, just when he thought everything was finally sewn up, Morrison had come up with a last-minute problem. He didn't like the slogan and wanted a new one. It was enough to make an angel weep.

The injustice made Sam's blood boil. He had given everything he had to this damned project. He had been dragged back from his holidays to satisfy the whim of this miserable cretin who hadn't the intelligence of a flea. He had worked his heart out and Herbie Morrison still wasn't happy. And instead of telling him where to stick his bloody campaign, Ron Burrows had caved in and ordered Sam to stay till it was finished. What sort of boss was that?

He was beginning to suspect that Morrison was a sadist who derived some secret pleasure from humiliating people. Particularly creative people like Sam who had taste and discernment and intelligence. How else could you explain his behaviour? Sam had worked on hundreds of advertising campaigns during his career including major ones that were worth multiples of the fee they were earning from Slimline. And he had never come across anyone as utterly stubborn and ignorant as Herbie Morrison. It was an insult to his creative integrity that he was being forced to put up with it.

If he had any gumption, he would walk. He would write out his resignation letter and give it to Ron Burrows in the morning. And he would issue a press statement explaining exactly why he was doing it. That would force them all to sit up and take notice.

But Sam knew this wasn't a runner. He understood the way the industry worked. Word would go out that he was a prima donna who couldn't stand the heat. One or two of his colleagues might support his courageous stand but most of them would snigger at him behind his back. Some of them would even be on the blower immediately looking for his job.

He gave a hopeless sigh. He could see no way out but to stick with this damned campaign till the death. And the way he was feeling right now, it might come to that – but it would be Herbie Morrison's death. If he raised one more objection, Sam would throttle the life out of his miserable carcass and throw it off the roof. And he would take great pleasure in doing it.

Zoe was tugging at his sleeve.

"Cheer up," she said. "Don't let them get you down."

He turned to her and tried to smile but it came out as a lop-sided grin. He was tired. He was angry. And now he could feel himself getting drunk.

"They're not worth it," she said. "I wouldn't waste my breath on them."

"How right you are," he said, drawing her closer and planting a wet kiss on her mouth. "They should make you the MD. *You* wouldn't stand for any nonsense from Herbie Morrison."

Zoe giggled. "You bet," she said. "I'd have him off the premises quicker than shit from a duck's ass."

Sam glanced at his watch. It was ten past nine. He should really go home, try and get a good sleep and prepare for the trials of tomorrow. But he liked it here in the Zhivago Bar. He liked listening to Zoe as she bolstered his battered morale. She really was a gorgeous woman and so sympathetic and loyal. She had stood with him through the trials he had been forced to endure, offering succour and understanding.

He turned to her. She was smiling at him.

"One more for the road?" she asked as her eyes filled with mischief and the promise of more to come.

"I'm not sure. I've got to be back at my desk in the morning bright and early. Ron wants this campaign wrapped up by lunch-time."

"Hump Ron," she said. "What does he care about you?"

She was right of course. She understood. "Okay," he said. "Another Bacardi Breezer and a large whiskey."

He raised two fingers and the barman nodded.

"And you can stay at my place tonight," Zoe said. "I'm in Ballsbridge. It's closer for work in the morning."

Amy leaned over Josh and let her tongue roam across the mass of fine blond hairs that covered his chest. When she came to his right nipple she sucked it into her mouth and gently bit down with her teeth. Immediately, she felt his body squirm beneath her and his strong arms grasp her shoulders.

She raised her head, looked down into his face and smiled.

"You like that, don't you?"

Without waiting for a reply, she lowered her head again and took his left nipple between her lips. She heard him moan with pleasure. Next minute, he had drawn her face to his and their mouths were locked together. She felt his wet tongue dart past her lips and his palm brush against her breast. Now it was her turn to squirm as a surge of passion swept through her.

She felt his hand moving across her belly and down to her thighs. She held him close, and gave a shudder as he entered her. She closed her eyes and was carried away on a wave of pleasure. They made love and afterwards she lay in his arms in the tangled sheets listening to the beating of his heart.

"You're a very sexy man," she said. "You certainly know how to please a woman."

"Thank you. You're not exactly a novice yourself."

"I just follow my instincts. So, you enjoyed it?"

"Of course, what man wouldn't?"

She ran her fingers through his hair and looked into his face.

"You know, I've been attracted to you since the first day I saw you. Do you remember? You held the gate open for me."

"You didn't even know who I was."

"It was your eyes. That's what drew me."

She moved her hot body closer and kissed his eyelids.

"And now here we are, together at last."

He stroked her face and she snuggled close to him.

After a while, they made love again, slower this time, the sensation slowly building till she exploded in climax. They lay drenched in sweat, sated by their passion until finally Josh got up, went into the bathroom and she heard the shower running. He came back wrapped in a towel and began to get dressed.

"I have to go now, see how my mum is getting on. She'll be wondering where I am." He grinned. "You know, she doesn't miss a thing!"

Amy didn't mind releasing him back to Betty. She'd had a wonderful day with this magnificent man.

"I was thinking we might take a trip to Seville tomorrow," he continued. "If I get the car back. What do you say?"

"That sounds fantastic."

There was a tantalising smile on his face.

"It's quite a distance. We might have to stay overnight, share a hotel bedroom."

"Better still," she said.

"That's what I hoped you would say."

He buttoned his shirt and bent to kiss her. She held him close, savouring the last moments of the passion that had recently overwhelmed her. At last, she let him go and he walked to the door.

"I'll call in the morning around ten. Sleep tight."

He waved and was gone.

Amy lay back on the bed and savoured the memory of what had just occurred. It had been the most passionate encounter she had ever experienced – much more exciting than anything she had known with Sam. She could not remember a time when she felt so satisfied and completely and deliriously happy. She had made love with a gorgeous man and it had been so beautiful that she thought her body was going to burst with pleasure.

She was falling in love with Josh. It wasn't just the beautiful sex.

It was everything to do with him: his sense of humour, his consideration and kindness, his whole being. The feeling she had for him was more intense than anything she had ever felt for another man. And the most fantastic thing – she believed he felt the same way about her.

She let her mind drift back over the events of the past twelve hours. It had been a magical day. She thought of the trip to Mijas, the bus ride to Arroyo, the train journey home and then the passionate lovemaking as they lay naked in each other's arms on this very bed. And tomorrow she would enjoy his company all over again. They would set off to visit the exciting city of Seville, they would eat some nice food, drink some good wine, and tomorrow night they would fall asleep in each other's arms, tucked up snugly in bed in some small hotel. She uttered a sigh of gratitude and pleasure.

She had a shower and changed the sheets then got back into bed. She was tired and her body ached with a delicious fatigue. She listened to the stillness in the garden outside disturbed only by the gentle hum of the night insects. She felt her eyelids grow heavy as the waves of sleep washed over her. She couldn't wait for the morning with its promise of more pleasure to come. Within minutes she was fast asleep.

Josh climbed the stairs to his mother's apartment, carrying with him a tinge of regret at leaving Amy. He would have been happy to spend the rest of the night in her warm embrace. But he had to consider his mother's feelings and, besides, he had tomorrow to look forward to.

When he came in, he found Betty waiting for him. She was sitting in the lounge with a book in her lap.

"Why aren't you in bed getting your beauty sleep?" he joked.

"I spoke to your father," she said. "He wants to know when you're returning to London."

"Did you tell him about the cruise?"

"Yes."

"And how did he react?"

Betty shrugged. "He didn't. It didn't seem to matter to him."

Josh frowned. He was about to question her further when she got up and approached him.

"There is something else."

He looked at her. Her face was sombre. It told him at once that something was wrong.

"What?"

"There was a phone call when you were out. Nina is back in London. She wants you to call her urgently."

Chapter 28

Josh felt a tremor run through him. He stared at his mother in disbelief.

"Nina called?"

"Yes," Betty replied.

"When?"

"About half an hour ago."

"What did she want?"

"She said she was back in London and wanted you to call her."

He looked stunned. He sat down on the nearest chair and sank his head into his hands. Betty got up and went to him.

"You don't have to call her just now. Why don't you leave it till the morning? You look tired."

He glanced at his watch. It was ten thirty which meant nine thirty back in London.

He turned to his mother again.

"How did she sound?"

"I thought she was upset. She seemed very anxious to speak to you."

"How did she know I was here?"

"She didn't say."

For a moment, Josh seemed paralysed with indecision as he

206

wrestled with this unexpected news. Then he quickly made up his mind.

"She left a number?"

Betty handed him the piece of paper where she had jotted the information down. He took it from her and walked out onto the terrace. He opened his phone and took a deep breath. Then he pressed in the number and heard it ring. His call was answered almost at once.

"Nina, it's Josh. My mother said you were looking for me."

"Oh Josh, thanks so much for calling back! I need to talk to you. You're the only one can help me."

His fingers tightened around the phone. "What is it, Nina? What's the matter?"

"When are you coming back from Spain?"

"I don't know. It could be a week."

"Can't you come sooner?"

"Why, Nina? What's happened?"

"I've left Lorenzo. I'm back in London. I'm staying with a friend but I don't know where to turn. I need you, Josh. You must come back."

"I can't, Nina."

"I'm really desperate, I've no money, I've no job. I've got nothing."

So Nina was in trouble. She was asking for his help. It was the moment he had dreamed might happen. Nina had come back to him. He heard her begin to cry, heart-wrenching sobs that echoed in his ear.

"Please," she begged. "You must help me. If you won't help me, I don't know what I'm going to do."

"Shhh," he said, in a comforting tone. "Try to calm down."

"I can't calm down," she sobbed. "You've no idea how desperate I am. I feel so depressed I think I'll kill myself."

"Don't be a fool. You can't do that. Do nothing till you hear from me again. Do you understand?"

"Yes," she said.

He heard her sniffle.

"I'll ring you again in the morning. In the meantime, go to bed and try to get some sleep."

"Okay."

She sounded calmer now.

"Wait till you hear from me," he said.

"Okay. I need you, Josh."

"Go to sleep. I'll ring you in the morning."

After Josh had gone to bed, Betty sat alone on the terrace, turning her thoughts over in her mind. She had known that phone call from Nina would not be good news. And she had been right. She knew that something bad had happened by the look on his face after he had finished talking to her. But all he had said was that Nina was in trouble and needed help.

A week ago, she might have welcomed Nina's phone call. Then, Josh had been down in the dumps. And she knew it had to do with the break-up of his relationship with Nina. But in the meantime, his mood had changed again – ever since he had taken up with Amy.

Since meeting her he had been like a different person. Instead of going about restless and discontented, he was cheerful and bright. The gloomy cloud that seemed to follow him about had lifted. He had a smile on his face and a spring in his step. He had even extended his stay here in Magnolia Park by another week. Whatever impact Amy had on him, Betty could see it was for the better. Josh had become a new man. Now his attitude had shifted again.

Her mind was in turmoil. Her cosy little existence had suddenly been turned upside down. And it wasn't only Josh. Her talk this evening with Alf had been another bombshell. When she told him she was going off on the cruise with Nigel he hadn't even paused for breath. He had simply said: "That sounds like an excellent idea, Betty. A holiday will do you the world of good."

She had been shocked. She had expected something stronger. She had been prepared for Alf to argue with her, perhaps even forbid her to go. She had been expecting him to ask more about Nigel and how she had met him. She was waiting for him to demand to know about the state of their relationship and whether she had any romantic feeling for Nigel. But Alf hadn't even asked where the cruise was going. He had simply told her it was an excellent idea.

If a junior employee in one of his shops had said he needed to take a few days off, he would probably have given him the same response.

That conversation with Alf had upset her. She couldn't shake off the strange feeling that he was losing touch with reality. Try as she might, she couldn't escape the startling conclusion that Alf was so consumed with his business that nothing else mattered to him – even her. This realisation struck her with such force that it shook her. She had always believed that Alf loved her in his own strange way. But now she wasn't sure.

Would a man who loved his wife allow her to go off on a holiday with another man without at least asking some basic questions, even a man as detached and unsuspecting as Alf? Wouldn't he want assurances that it was innocent and that there wasn't something more sinister involved? Either Alf had the trust of a saint or he just didn't care. Betty was beginning to think it was the latter.

All these years when she had fretted about spending so much time in Spain while he slaved to build up the company, Alf had been blithely unconcerned. While she suffered pangs of guilt about leaving him behind in the cold and damp of the London winters, it hadn't bothered him at all. He had been glad to get her out of the way so he could concentrate on what he really loved: Parsons Electrical.

This was a shocking thought. But the more she considered it, the more she was forced to concede that it had always been like that – right back to when they first met. While Alf was working hard to build up the company, Betty had believed he was doing it for her and Josh. Now she could see that the company was an end in itself. She was a part of Alf's life but only a small part. It occurred to her that if he had to choose between Parsons Electrical and her, the company would win hands down.

She must have been blind not to see what was staring her in the face for all these years. Other people must have seen it. Gladys Taylor certainly had. That was why she had set her up with Nigel. But then, Gladys was a woman of the world and had been knocked about by it in her lifetime. While Gladys had her eyes wide open, Betty had been sleep-walking, insulated in her snug little cocoon in Magnolia Park.

She wondered if Josh had seen it too. He was a bright young man. He must have known. And thinking of Josh brought her right back again to that phone call from Nina tonight. It was bad news. It would bring trouble. Betty knew it in her bones.

She sighed. It was time to go to bed. But she knew she would have difficulty getting to sleep. She had received too many shocks in the last twelve hours. She knew she was in for a restless night.

Chapter 29

The sun filtering through the curtains in the bedroom woke Amy. She caught the fragments of a dream, quickly dissolving in the clear light of day – she was naked and wrapped in Josh's arms and they were in a cosy little hotel in Seville.

She glanced at her watch and saw it was ten minutes to nine. She had slept for nearly eleven hours which was clear proof of how tired she must have been after all the vigorous activity of yesterday. That activity had certainly been very pleasant. A smile broke on her face when she thought again of their lovemaking. But now it was time to get up and prepare for another busy day. Josh would be calling shortly and they would be repeating the experience.

She jumped out of bed and went into the kitchen to put on the coffee percolator. Then she decided to nip out and have a quick swim in the pool. There was no better way to shake away the cobwebs than a vigorous splash in the cool blue water.

When she returned there was a rich aroma of percolating coffee drifting through the apartment. She made toast and took it out to the terrace with her coffee, some tomatoes and cheese and the jar of marmalade she had bought at the market a few days ago. Then she sat down to enjoy her breakfast.

Today was to be the highlight of her holiday. She was going to Seville with Josh and they would be staying overnight. While she ate her breakfast, she took out her guidebook and leafed through the pages which described the attractions that awaited her: the cathedral where Christopher Columbus was entombed, the Royal Palace, the Giralda Tower and the Alcazar.

As she read, her imagination took flight. She thought of all wonderful sights that this beautiful city had to offer. And at the end of the day, there would be dinner in a little restaurant in a quiet little square followed by a night of passion, wrapped together in each other's arms. She couldn't wait to set off.

She quickly packed an overnight bag and made a final check that everything was in order: money, credit cards, phone, camera, hat and shades for the hot sun she expected to encounter. Then she had another cup of coffee and settled down on the terrace to wait for Josh's call. While she waited, she picked up *Howard's End* and began to read.

The time ticked away. She was engrossed in the novel and when she checked her watch again, she saw it was a quarter past ten. Josh should have called by now. She wondered what was delaying him. Had the car not arrived? She was beginning to get uneasy. Surely nothing could have happened. She was so looking forward to this trip that she couldn't bear the thought of being disappointed. But when half past ten arrived and there was still no call, she could stand the uncertainty no longer. She picked up her phone and rang him.

He answered immediately.

"It's me – Amy," she said. "I was wondering if there was a problem with the car."

"No, it's not the car, something's come up. I won't be able to go to Seville today. I've got to return to London at once."

She felt her heart sink. "Why? What's happened?"

His next words chilled her to the bone. "Nina is back and she's in trouble."

Chapter 30

Amy stared at the phone till the buzzing sound told her the call had been terminated. She was stunned. She felt as if Josh Parsons had just slapped her face. One moment she was expecting him to say they were leaving for Seville and the next second he was announcing that he was off to London to see his old girlfriend. It was as if the ground had just opened up and swallowed her.

Suddenly, she felt disappointment overwhelm her and the tears welled up in her eyes. Damn, she thought. Weeping is the last thing I want. She got up from her seat on the terrace and hurried inside the apartment for fear that someone would see. She closed the door, lay down on the bed and buried her face in the pillow. Josh's voice was still ringing in her ears: *"Nina is back and she's in trouble."*

With those brief words, Amy's hopes had faded into dust. She had been wary of the mysterious Nina Black ever since she first heard her name. She knew she had exerted great power over Josh in the past. But she never suspected she would return so swiftly and snatch him away from her.

She glanced at the overnight bag standing beside the door, packed and ready for the trip to Seville. She had set her heart on that trip. It was to be the highlight of her holiday, just the two of them together in that romantic city. But she had been a fool. She had allowed her heart to rule her head, just as she did with Sam Benson. The thought of the cruel way that Fate had turned against her once again brought on a fresh burst of self-pity and soon the tears were flowing once more.

As she lay with her face buried in the pillow, she thought of what she was losing. Josh was the best man she had ever met. He was everything she desired. And now it looked as if he had deserted her to run back to Nina. It was just so, so sad. Here she was, all on her own again. Eventually, she got up from the bed and went to the bathroom and washed her face. Then she opened the overnight bag and put everything back into their drawers. She wasn't going to need them now.

She had a week of her holiday left. But the sparkle had gone out of it. The joy she had been experiencing had vanished like morning dew in the heat of the sun. Now the days stretched ahead of her, barren and lonely. She got undressed, put on her swimsuit and carried her sun-bed out to the garden. As she approached her favourite spot, she saw that someone else was already there.

As she drew near, a young woman with dark hair raised her head and smiled at her. Amy recognised her. It was the same woman she had seen in the garden a few days before.

"Hi," the woman said and waved.

"Hello," Amy replied.

"Do you live here?" the woman asked.

"I wish. I'm just here on holiday."

"Me too."

"Are you on your own?" Amy asked.

"Unfortunately. I was supposed to come with my boyfriend but at the last minute his mother took ill and he had to pull out."

"Well, join the club," Amy said, adjusting her bed to catch the sun. "I'm on my own too."

The young woman sat up and stretched out her hand.

"I'm Carly O'Brien."

"You're Irish?" Amy asked in surprise.

"Yes, I'm from Wexford."

"Well, it's good to meet you, Carly. I'm Amy Crawford and I'm from Dublin."

Betty sat in the cool lounge of her apartment and took out her phone. Josh had gone off to London and now she was alone. She had thought about this matter long enough. Now it was time to take action.

It was the conversation with Alf last night that had clinched it. It had brought home to her a truth that she had hidden from herself for far too long: her husband didn't really care about her.

But the strange thing was, she felt relieved. Alf's attitude had put a completely new complexion on things. She didn't have to feel guilty about going on this cruise with Nigel. Alf had actually given his blessing. She could go off sailing around the world for six months if she liked. And she could do it with a clear conscience.

She found Nigel's number and listened to the ringing tone with the phone pressed tight against her ear.

"Hello, Betty."

She gave a little start at the sound of his voice. "How did you know it was me?"

"Your number comes up on my screen."

"Oh," she said. "So that's how it works. I'm still trying to get the hang of these mobile phones."

She heard Nigel laughing and it cheered her up. He is always in good form, she thought. He always sees the bright side of life.

"How are you this morning?" he asked.

"I'm a little bit sad to tell you the truth. My son, Josh, has just gone back to the UK in a dreadful hurry."

"Business?" Nigel asked.

"No, some young woman he was involved with. She rang last night to tell him she's in trouble."

"You mean she's pregnant?"

"Well, if she is, it's got nothing to do with him. He hasn't seen her for over a year."

Nigel laughed again. "So if you're sad, why don't you let me take you for lunch to cheer you up? We'll have a glass of wine and a chat."

"That would be nice. I'd enjoy that."

"Where would you like to go?" Nigel asked.

"I don't mind. It doesn't have to be anywhere expensive."

"I'll tell you what, I'll drive into Fuengirola at one o'clock and we can go somewhere local."

"That's a very good idea," Betty said. "There's something else I wanted to say."

"Yes?"

"I've decided to go on that cruise with you."

There was a momentary pause.

"Well, that's excellent news," Nigel said. "That has made my day. Now we really have got something to celebrate."

For their lunch appointment, Betty decided to go to a restaurant called Sin Igual which was on the road into Los Boliches, the adjoining town to Fuengirola. In English, it meant 'without equal'. She had first been taken there by a solicitor called Felipe Gonzalez who had carried out the legal work when she was buying her apartment.

That was a long time ago but the quality of the food and the excellent service had remained constant. So when Nigel arrived in his shiny Mercedes, Betty suggested he leave the car in Magnolia Park and they walk the short distance to the restaurant.

Once they had been seated and had given their orders, he took her hand.

"You look lovely today, Betty. You look radiant."

She giggled. She was coming to enjoy these compliments from this attractive man. She had been missing them. When was the last time Alf had paid her a compliment?

"You look good too, Nigel. I think your jacket is very smart. Where did you get it?"

"This?" he said and fingered the blue linen jacket. "I bought it in Cortes Inglés."

"It fits you very well. And you've had your hair cut."

He laughed. "You're very observant."

"I notice things," Betty remarked. "I think women are more observant than men, don't you?"

"I've never thought about it," Nigel confessed.

"Well, I've noticed that you take very good care of yourself. I admire that. A lot of single men are untidy. They've no women to keep them in order!" She threw him a laughing glance. "But you're always well turned out. You're not vain, are you?"

"I don't think so."

"I can't stand vain men. I think vanity has a lot to do with insecurity. They're always looking for attention. They're like children."

"I'm pleased you've not put me in that category! And I'm delighted you've decided to come on the cruise. Now I don't have to give the tickets away."

"You could have gone without me."

He shook his head. "I could never have done that. I got them for you, Betty. I told you that. What made you change your mind?"

"I decided it was a good idea after all. Now, I'm quite looking forward to it."

"Are you sure it didn't have anything to do with the sleeping arrangements?"

"That certainly was a factor. You see, I thought you were being presumptuous and I didn't like that."

"I'd never presume anything with you, Betty. I'm not a wolf. I respect you. You know, I could get women who would be very happy to come on that cruise with me *and* share a cabin."

"I do know that."

"But that's not what I'm looking for."

"What *are* you looking for?"

"A companion – someone intelligent, someone who can make me laugh, someone who can make me happy."

"And you believe I can do that?"

"Oh, I know it, Betty. Every time we meet, it convinces me more. Why do you think I spend time with you?"

The wine came and the first courses of salad and pasta. They kept up a stream of conversation above the loud buzz of voices in the little restaurant. Betty asked Nigel about his wife. What was she like, what was she going to do when the divorce came through?

"She may get married again, I don't know. I told you she's got another man."

"Yes, you did tell me. It was the first time we met at the theatre lunch at El Toro restaurant."

"Of course I remember. You had bacon and cheese salad to start and then sole."

Betty smiled. So Nigel must have had her under observation right from the very start.

"My wife is a lovely woman," he continued without bitterness. "It's just that we don't have much in common. But we have remained good friends. She'll be coming down to stay with me for a few days."

"When?" Betty asked, anxiously.

"Next week. Perhaps you'd like to meet her?"

"Oh, no," Betty shook her head. "Wouldn't she regard me as a rival?"

"Not at all. I told you the divorce is very amicable. I think she'd like to meet you."

"I wouldn't feel comfortable."

"There's no reason. And it would give you an opportunity to see my house. You haven't been there yet."

It was true. And Betty was curious to see this ten-room villa which Gladys Taylor had said was fantastic and had magnificent views all the way to North Africa. Although, privately, she thought it was far too big.

"Perhaps I will. Why did you break up?"

"We got married too young."

"I did too."

"It's the luck of the draw, I suppose. What about your husband, what's his name?"

"Alf."

"Do you love him, Betty?"

She hesitated before replying. Nigel was watching her closely across the table.

"You're not really sure, are you?"

Betty didn't reply. Instead, she quickly changed the subject.

"I've been reading that brochure you gave me about the cruise.

There were pictures of people dressed up for the ball. I don't have a ball gown."

But Nigel dismissed her doubts with a wave of his hand. "That doesn't matter. You don't have to go to the ball if you don't want to."

"But I do want to go. I've never been to a ball. I think I'd enjoy it. It's all part of the experience."

"Then we'll get you a ball gown. I'll take you to Marbella and you can pick one. I'll help you choose."

Betty giggled again. She was really enjoying this lunch with Nigel.

"You know, I'm beginning to get excited about this cruise," she confessed.

He reached out and took her hand in his. "You'll love it, Betty. You'll never forget it. You'll remember it for the rest of your days."

It was after three o'clock when they left the restaurant to walk back to Magnolia Park. They parted at the gates but, before they said goodbye, Nigel drew her close.

"Do you mind if I kiss you, Betty?"

She lifted her face, expecting a chaste peck on the cheek. But instead he kissed her full on the lips. She felt a shock run up her spine. But before she could react, Nigel stepped back and smiled.

"Now, Betty, what do you think of that?"

He had taken her completely by surprise and now she was flustered.

"I think I enjoyed it."

He grinned. "There's plenty more where that came from," he said as he got into the Mercedes and drove away.

Betty walked back to her apartment through the garden, still savouring the memory of that kiss. Nigel was turning out to be a very intriguing man. His personality was growing on her by the day. Every time they met, she liked him more.

As she approached her apartment, she saw two people reading beside the fountain and as she drew near, she realised one of them was Amy. She stopped to speak to her.

"Hello, my dear," she said.

Amy sat up suddenly and took off her sunglasses. "Oh Betty, you startled me," she said.

"Are you enjoying that novel? You seemed really engrossed."

"Yes, I am. And Betty, I'd like you to meet someone. This is Carly O'Brien. She's a visitor and she's Irish too."

The young woman smiled up at Betty.

"I'm delighted to meet you," Betty said and took her hand. "At this rate, you Irish people will be taking over Magnolia Park."

"You better watch out!" Carly O'Brien quipped and they all laughed.

"I have to go," Betty said and made her way back to the apartment.

As she went, a thought began to grow in her mind. Poor Amy had put on a brave front just now but Betty knew she must be feeling low. Josh had just disappeared back to London and left her on her own again. That made two men who had left her in the course of a single week. She must have a little chat with her soon, try to cheer her up.

Josh had caught the midday flight out of Malaga airport and arrived at Heathrow at one thirty local time.

Since speaking to her last night, Nina had hardly been out of his mind. She was in trouble and she needed him. This was an emergency. She could be in danger. When he spoke to her last night she had sounded desperate and had talked of suicide. He had no alternative but to go to her.

He told himself he must get to her quickly and offer what help he could. She had split up with Lorenzo. He wondered what had happened between them. Josh had never forgiven Lorenzo. He blamed him for breaking up his relationship with Nina. He had lured her away to Rome with promises of a glittering film career. Now she was back in London, penniless, jobless and in need of help. What sort of man would he be if he didn't go to her in her moment of need?

As soon as he alighted from the plane, he rang Nina to tell her he had arrived. He could hear the relief in her voice.

"Thank God," she said.

"How do you feel?"

"Much better now that you are here."

"Okay, sit tight. I'm on my way. I'll be with you shortly. We'll try to sort everything out."

He switched off the phone, hurried through Customs and Immigration, and out into the vast arrivals hall. In the plane he had separated his sterling from his euro notes. He had enough sterling to pay for his fare but he was going to need more. He spotted an ATM machine in a corner of the arrivals hall, inserted his credit card and withdrew some cash. Satisfied that he had sufficient money, he walked outside and caught a cab to take him into the city.

The address Nina had given him was in west London, near Hammersmith. He gave the directions to the cab driver and sat back and watched the familiar landmarks flash by. The journey took half an hour. It was half past two when the cab finally pulled up outside a terraced house in a rundown street. The number 63 was barely discernible on the fading paint of the door.

The house had been divided into flats. The address Nina had given him said Flat 3. He pressed the buzzer and waited. After a moment he heard her voice on the intercom.

"Is that you, Josh?"

"Yes."

"Come on up, it's the third floor."

There was a click. He pushed open the door and went in. A musty smell greeted him. The hall was shabby – a worn carpet covered the floor, there were damp patches on the walls, stains on the stairs and a pile of junk mail on a table. When he came to the third floor, he saw a door was open. He knocked and entered.

It was a dismal, depressing room. There was an empty grate, a scuffed dining table, a couple of chairs and a worn settee. Nina was sitting in a chair by the window wearing a faded silk dressing gown. She was smoking a cigarette. She put it out, stood up and turned to face him.

He looked at her in shock. She was nothing like the beautiful woman he remembered. Her hair was unkempt and unwashed. She had lost weight, her face was pale and there were dark smudge-marks beneath her eyes where she had been weeping. She walked towards him and buried her head in his chest.

"Oh Josh, thank you for coming. You've no idea what this means to me."

She began to weep again.

He smoothed her hair and tried to comfort her. "Shhh," he said. "It's all right. I'm going to take care of you. Everything is going to be all right."

After a while he released her.

"Have you eaten anything?" he asked.

"I had some toast for breakfast."

"Get dressed, I'll wait. I'll take you for lunch. You can tell me everything that has happened."

While she went off to the bedroom to get ready, Josh lowered himself onto the settee and looked around. He had forgotten how awful some London accommodation could be. He had seen similar rooms. They were not places for living but mere staging posts on the way to somewhere else. But not since his student days could he remember a more dismal room than this. He wondered at the circumstances that had led Nina to fall so far.

Eventually, she reappeared. She had made an effort to tidy herself up. She had put on a skirt and clean blouse and jacket and had tried to brush her hair into some semblance of order. She had also applied some red lipstick to her mouth.

The pub at the corner of the street was serving bar food. Nina found a table and, after they had both chosen beef, Josh paid and carried the food back to the table. He went off again to the bar and returned with glasses of red wine.

"You look very well, Josh," Nina said as he sat down.

He nodded. It would be a lie if he returned the compliment. Nina seemed to know this. He changed the subject.

"The flat you're staying in, whose is it?"

"It belongs to an actress friend. She's not working at the moment, 'resting' as we say. She's letting me sleep there till I get back on my feet." She lifted a fork and began picking at her food.

"When did you get back from Rome?"

"Two days ago."

"What went wrong? How did you end up like this?"

She sighed and made a gesture with her fork. "Where do I begin?"

"Why don't you tell me," he said.

Nina took a sip of wine and wiped her mouth with a paper napkin. She hesitated for a moment. "It's a dreadful story. I don't know if you want to hear it."

"Let me be the judge of that," he said.

"When I left you, Lorenzo took me to live with him in this fabulous apartment he owned on the Via Veneto in the centre of Rome. It was an amazing place, marble baths, modern art, crystal chandeliers, not to mention fabulous views right across the Roman skyline. I've never seen anything like it.

"At first, life was wonderful. While we were waiting for the film to be released we had a ball. Lorenzo was as good as his word. He bought me nice clothes, took me to parties every night and introduced me to all these important people in the film industry. He kept telling everyone that his film was going to be the sensation of the year. I was a dazzling new talent he had discovered and he was going to turn me into a star.

"He had some sort of arrangement with the paparazzi. I don't know if he was bribing them but, everywhere we went, photographers would be waiting. Our photos appeared in all the papers and magazines as if we were minor royalty. For those first few months we had a marvellous time: parties all night long, champagne breakfasts at the Eden Hotel and sleep all day. It was the sort of lifestyle you only read about in the celebrity magazines."

"Then what happened?"

"Don't you read the film reviews?" Nina asked.

"I'm too busy. I don't have time."

It was only partly true. After the break-up of their relationship, Josh had studiously avoided reading anything that might mention Nina's name.

"The film bombed. The critics hated it. I suspect some of it might have been spite or jealousy because Lorenzo had an arrogant side that got up a lot of people's noses. Perhaps if he had cultivated the critics a bit more, they might have been kinder. But when the film was released the knives came out with a vengeance. It was like the Saint Valentine's Day massacre. And it couldn't have been worse from my perspective. They preferred Maggie Bolton to me. One of them described me as raw and unsophisticated."

Nina finished her wine and Josh ordered more. She pushed her plate away. She had barely touched her food.

"How did Lorenzo react?"

"At first he tried to pretend it wasn't happening. He kept saying that the next reviews would be better. But sometimes there is a herd mentality which takes over the film critics and once a bandwagon starts to roll, they all jump on board. At any rate, the reviews just continued to get worse. I don't think the film got a single decent review that gave it more than two stars.

"Lorenzo then went into a period of denial. He said the critics didn't know what they were talking about. They weren't intelligent enough to capture the subtle nuances of the film. Industry insiders would see it for the great work of art that it really was. And the audiences would love it. In time it would become a classic that would be remembered for years to come.

"He used to say that he was looking forward to proving the critics wrong. He even kept a file of clippings which he was going to quote back at them when the film was hailed as a masterpiece. He said he would enjoy rubbing their noses in the dirt and watching them squirm with embarrassment at the stupid things they had written.

"But when the film went on general release, the audiences stayed away in droves. It was a box-office disaster. It had to be taken off after only a four-week run. Lorenzo had put a lot of his own money into the production so of course he stood to lose a packet. That was when the reality began to dawn on him. He knew he was facing a catastrophe. That's when things turned really bad."

So far, Nina had managed to maintain her composure. Now she began to weep once more.

"Would you like a glass of water?" Josh asked.

She shook her head. "It's all right. I'll be fine in a moment."

She lifted her wine and took another mouthful then blew her nose on a handkerchief and started again.

"He needed a scapegoat, so he blamed me. The critics hadn't liked my performance so he held me responsible for the hostile reaction. I was too wooden. I lacked empathy. I didn't interpret the story properly. My delivery was faulty. On and on the criticism went. I was no good. I couldn't act. I had wormed my way into his affections. I had deceived him. He didn't know why he had hired me. It got so bad that I thought of escaping and running away. But I had nowhere to go.

"I rang Harry Pender and asked him to help but he didn't want to know. The film was a failure so Harry didn't want to be associated with it because the bad reaction would rub off on him. He washed his hands of me. Now I was entirely on my own. I thought things couldn't get any worse but I was wrong. Lorenzo started beating me."

"The bastard," Josh muttered under his breath.

"Yes, he *is* a bastard. But I wasn't to know that. The time I went off with him, I thought he was a genius who was going to transform my career. It was only later that I came to see his true nature."

"What happened next?"

"He started drinking heavily. He became a recluse. He holed up in his apartment and refused to go out in public. People kept ringing him and calling at the door looking for money he had borrowed to finance the project. There were shouting rows and arguments. Threats were issued. It began to get really scary. When he was drunk, he started screaming at me, calling me a cow and a whore and other names I won't mention. He would fly into a tantrum and beat me with his fists. I was a curse. I had misled him and dragged him down. I was responsible. I was to blame. It got so bad that I locked myself in one of the bedrooms and didn't come out for three days. That's when I finally decided I had to get out of there before he killed me."

As Josh was forced to listen to her tale, his heart began to melt.

No matter what Nina had done to him, she hadn't deserved this fate.

"I thought of going to the police but I spoke hardly any Italian and I knew no-one in Rome. I decided that I had to escape. I had my passport and my clothes but I had no money. What I am about to tell you is shameful but I didn't have any choice. I waited till he passed out drunk one night and stole his wallet. I had already packed a bag. I got down to the street and caught a cab and asked the driver to take me to the airport. I bought a ticket on the first available plane out of Rome. It took me to Paris and from there I made my way back here to London.

"Once I arrived, I rang my friend and told her of my plight. She offered to let me stay at her flat. That was two days ago and I've been there ever since. But I didn't know where to turn. Then I thought of you. I rang your number but got no response."

"I changed my phone," Josh said.

She nodded. "I rang the company and someone told me you were in Spain. I told them I was a close friend and they gave me your mother's number." She shrugged. "You know the rest."

They sat for a while in silence. By now the pub was beginning to empty. A dozen thoughts were cascading through Josh's head. But the immediate thought was what to do about Nina.

"Have you contacted your parents?" he asked.

She vigorously shook her head. "I don't want them to know. It would break their hearts."

"So what do you plan to do, Nina?"

"I'd like to get back into the theatre. It's my career. But it's not going to be easy. I've no agent and everyone will know about the film disaster. It's a small world and as you know, bad news travels fast." She paused and stretched out a hand to stroke his wrist.

"I thought we might . . ." She broke off. "Can you find it in your heart to forgive me?"

"I already have, Nina."

"Could we get back together again? Pick up the threads where we left off? Could we put this nightmare behind us and start all over again?"

He looked into her beseeching eyes and, somewhere in that haggard face, he saw again the Nina he had once fallen hopelessly in love with.

"I made a dreadful mistake by leaving you," she said. "I can see that now and I know it hurt you terribly. I'm not going to make excuses because nothing can justify what I did."

"We have all made mistakes, Nina."

"If we were able to get together again, I'm sure I could rebuild my career. With your support, I could pick myself up, claw my way back. I know I've got talent."

"I know that too."

"I would have to go back to playing small parts but I'm not proud. In time I could find another agent. But I'm not sure I can do it on my own. I want you back again, Josh. I want us to be together the way it used to be. We were a good team, you and me."

"Yes, we were."

"That's what I want. That's where I see my future. But without you . . ." She waved her hand and let the sentence hang in the air.

He was silent because he didn't know what to say. He looked at her then slowly took out his wallet and gave her most of his money.

"Take that. It will tide you over for a few days. This has all come to me as a shock and I need time to think. I have your number. I'll contact you again in a few days' time."

They left the pub and he walked back with her to the front door of her house. There was an awkward moment while they stood together. She turned to face him and leaned her head on his shoulder.

Next moment, she had drawn him close and their lips met in a hot embrace.

Chapter 31

Josh strode purposefully through the bustle of the London streets but he was barely conscious of his surroundings. His mind was elsewhere, back in the pub where he had sat with Nina while she poured out the horror she had endured at the hands of Lorenzo Morelli. Josh's gut instinct had been correct. Morelli had stolen her away and in the end he had destroyed her. He thought of the grimy little flat where she was living with its all-pervading air of poverty and defeat. Nina was in a very bad way. He had been shocked by her appearance – the pale thinness of her frame, the frightened look in her eyes. She was a shadow of the beautiful woman he had known. She had lost weight and she looked ill and now he regretted that he hadn't insisted that she see a doctor.

Inevitably, his mind travelled back to the first time they met and the period they had spent together. That had been a glorious time. He remembered thinking that he would never be happier. Nina just had to walk into a room for his heart to lift. She had the ability to transform a situation with her mere presence. She seemed to radiate energy, to trail clouds of joy and optimism in her wake.

He recalled the walks by the river, the intimate meals in romantic restaurants, candles flickering, shadows dancing on the walls, the stolen moments of pleasure before she rushed off to some rehearsal or to meet some director. It had been a frantic time but the hours they had spent together had been all the more precious for that – because they had been snatched from the busy lives they both were living.

Josh had been in love with her. He had thought it then and he knew it now. He had been in love with her almost from the beginning, from the first meeting in the pub in Notting Hill when he had walked in on a blind date not knowing what to expect and this glamorous creature had swept him completely away.

That was the Nina he wished to remember, not the bedraggled creature he had just left in that grotty flat. It broke his heart to see her like that. But he knew that Nina could pull herself out of this mess. She was a fighter. She would claw back her career. She had talent, regardless of what the critics might have said. And she had courage. All she needed was support, a helping hand to pull her out of the mire into which she had sunk.

She still had the power to captivate him. The memory of that kiss on the doorstep as he left her had brought desire flooding into his heart. He thought again of the wonderful times they had spent in bed together in her flat in Fulham, lost in passion for each other. He could have all that back again. He could have the theatrical parties, the shows, the intimate dinners, the mornings waking up with her naked body warm beside him and her dark hair spread like a raven's wing on the pillow.

She had begged him to take her back, to resume their relationship where it had left off before Morelli had come along to mesmerise her with his promises of stardom and success. Another man might draw pleasure from her dilemma, might lay down conditions and force her to grovel and apologise.

But Josh felt none of these impulses. She had made a mistake. It was easy to understand why. Her head had been turned. Any young woman in a similar situation could have made the very same choice. But Josh did not believe in nursing grudges and storing resentments. Let the past bury the past. It was time to move on.

At last, he found a taxi rank and asked the driver to take him to his apartment in the Docklands. He entered the gleaming foyer and rode the silent elevator to his penthouse apartment on the tenth floor. When he opened the hall door and let himself in, he could smell stale air in the rooms. He opened the sliding doors to the terrace and a cool breeze rustled the curtains.

He stood for a few moments looking out over the London skyline. It was late afternoon and the sun was bathing the city in a bright light, glinting off rooftops and spires and the glassy water of the Thames. Eventually, he went back inside and rang his father.

"Where are you?" Alf asked when he heard his voice. "Did your mother tell you I've been looking for you? Your phone's always engaged."

"I'm back in London," Josh said. "I got in a couple of hours ago."

"When are you coming back to work? Things don't stand still, you know. I need you to go up to Scotland on a reconnaissance mission for me. I've heard of a site in Glasgow that's come on the market. It would be perfect for another store."

"We already have two stores in Glasgow," Josh reminded him.

"And there's room for a third. Glasgow is a big city, the population is almost 600,000. That's plenty of customers for our products. When can you go?"

"I need another few days to sort out some personal business."

"Haven't you had enough time? You seem to have spent forever in Spain knocking golf balls around."

"I'll be in Glasgow next Monday morning. Get somebody to type up the info and send it to me."

"How is your mother?" Alf asked.

"You should know. You were talking to her."

"She mentioned something about going off on a cruise with some man she had met."

"And what did you say?"

"I told her to go and enjoy herself. A holiday will do her good. I think she gets bored down there on her own all the time."

Josh was about to say that if she was bored it was because his father had neglected her for all these years. But he held back.

"Would you transfer me to Olivia, Dad? I need to talk to her."

"I expect you in Glasgow on Monday and no excuses," Alf said before he put Josh through to his secretary.

When she came on the line, Josh asked if any messages had been left in his absence. She read them to him but there was nothing so urgent that it couldn't wait.

"I have to go to Glasgow on Monday morning. Would you organise a flight and accommodation for me and email the details?"

"I'll do it right away," Olivia said.

He put down the phone. He went to the mahogany drinks cabinet and poured a large measure of Scotch into a cut-glass tumbler. He lowered himself into a comfortable armchair by the window and stared out across the London skyline. He had some big decisions to make that would decide the future direction of his life. And he only had a short time to do it.

Amy drew her chair closer to the table and examined the menu the waiter had just given her. What would she have to eat? She didn't really have much appetite but she had skipped lunch and she had to eat something or else she'd get ill. Across the table from her, Carly O'Brien was studying her menu with the air of a woman who was looking forward to a good feed.

They were sitting outside a restaurant in a little square in the heart of the old town. It was seven o'clock and already the restaurant was beginning to fill up with people coming for early dinner.

Carly glanced up from her menu to admire the window boxes filled with bright red geraniums and the sun beginning to cast shadows on the cobblestones of the square.

"It's beautiful here, isn't it?" she said. "So romantic."

She was right of course but Amy wasn't feeling particularly romantic right now. All day, she had been struggling to keep thoughts of Josh and what he might be up to in London out of her mind. The idea of having dinner together was Carly's suggestion and Amy had seized on it as an opportunity to avoid having to spend a night feeling sorry for herself alone in her apartment.

Out of the corner of her eye, she could see the waiter hovering with his notepad at the ready.

"Have you decided what you'd like to eat?" she asked Carly.

"Yes, I think I'll have the chicken in lemon sauce."

"That sounds good."

She beckoned the waiter and gave their order, chicken for Carly and a mushroom omelette and salad for herself. She asked for a half carafe of wine to accompany the meal.

"I'm glad I met you," Carly said. "I didn't really fancy the idea of spending two weeks here on my own. But we'd paid for the holiday so when Brian's mum got sick, I decided I might as well come, anyway. What happened to you?"

"I came with my boyfriend but he had to go back to Dublin on emergency business. It's all very complicated."

"What a bummer. So how long have you been here?"

"A week."

"You seem to be enjoying yourself."

Do I? Amy thought. It's certainly not how I feel.

"It's really lovely in Magnolia Park, the gardens and the fountains and everything, real peaceful. Don't you think so?"

"Yes, I do," Amy said.

"It's sort of magical. And there's the sun shining all day long. Look at you. You've got a great colour. You're as brown as a berry."

"Thank you," Amy said, brightening up a little.

The wine arrived and they filled their glasses. The girl sitting across from her was bright and cheerful. Amy knew she would be sympathetic. It would be a great relief to come clean about Sam and Josh and get it all off her chest.

But something held her back. She barely knew Carly O'Brien. She had only met her today and she didn't have the courage to spill out her heart to a complete stranger. But just sitting here talking to her and having her company was comforting. She was glad now that they had met.

The waiter was back with their food. They began to eat.

"This chicken is very good," Carly said. "Have you been to this restaurant before?"

"No, this is my first time."

"You seem to know your way around."

"It's not too difficult," Amy said. "You'll soon get used to it. Most of the restaurants are pretty good. There are a few dumps but you can spot them very quickly. And if you go to the Tourist Office, they'll give you a free map of the town."

"Will we eat together again tomorrow? We could have lunch."

"If you like," Amy said. "I'll be glad of your company."

Carly smiled. "That's good. You can give me some tips and when you go back to Dublin, I'll be able to manage better on my own."

Just then, Amy's phone began to ring. When she pressed it to her ear, she was surprised to hear Betty's voice.

"Hello, dear," she said. "I hope I'm not disturbing you?"

"Not at all," Amy replied, grateful to hear yet another friendly voice. "I'm just having an early dinner with my friend, Carly. Remember, you met her in the garden today?"

"Oh yes. She seems a nice young woman. She'll be a companion for you."

Betty seemed to have the ability to read Amy's mind.

"I was wondering if you might be free to call and see me when you get home," Betty said. "I want to talk to you about something. It won't take long."

"Sure," Amy replied. "I'd like that. I'll call on you when I get back. Say about eight thirty?"

"That'll be perfect," Betty purred like a cat. "I'll be waiting."

Amy switched off her phone and put it back in her bag. Betty is up to something, she thought. I wonder what it can be.

Chapter 32

Amy stood outside Betty's apartment in a mood of bemusement and expectation. The meal with Carly had gone very well. They had chatted about holidays and boyfriends but Amy had been careful to keep her lip buttoned even when Carly confided that she had some doubts about her own boyfriend, Brian, who wanted them to get engaged, and asked for Amy's advice. They finished the wine and Carly insisted on ordering two glasses of liqueur to finish off the meal and now Amy was feeling a little light-headed.

On the way back, she called into her apartment and picked up a little gift she had bought for Betty the previous day, then made her way up the stairs.

She pressed the bell and heard footsteps approach and next thing Betty's blonde head was peeping out at her.

"Come in, Amy. I was just sitting out on the terrace doing the crossword with my reading lamp on. I don't suppose you do the crossword, do you?"

Amy shook her head. "I find they take too much time and I can never figure out the clues."

"Well, I enjoy them. They keep my brain sharp. I read a newspaper article that said crossword puzzles are a good way to ward off dementia."

Amy found herself smiling. "I don't think that's likely to happen to you."

"Well, let's hope not."

Betty led her through the apartment and out to the terrace.

"I brought you a present," Amy said and pressed a plastic bag into Betty's hand.

Betty opened it and drew out a packet of tea.

"My goodness, real tea-leaves?" She gave Amy a kiss on the cheek. "That's very thoughtful of you."

"I know how much you enjoy your cup of tea," Amy said.

"I certainly do. Where did you get it?"

"There's a little shop at the market near the train station."

"I must remember that," Betty said. "Now why don't we have some? You just make yourself comfortable and I'll go and put the kettle on."

Amy sat down and looked out over the garden. The lights had come on around the fountain and illuminated the water splashing into the basin. Carly had been right. There *was* a magical quality about Magnolia Park. She was going to miss it when she went home.

Betty was back with a tray of cups and saucers and a plate containing a cake. She went off again and returned with a teapot and stand.

"Let it draw for a minute," she said. "It will taste better." She cut the cake and passed a slice to Amy. She had refused dessert at dinner but now her appetite seemed to have revived. "It's coffee cake. It's very good."

Amy lifted a piece with her fork and tasted it. "Mmmm," she said, appreciatively. "You're right. It *is* good."

Betty smiled. "I think we can pour the tea now."

She poured two cups and gave one to Amy. She added a little drop of milk to her own cup and stirred it. "I like my tea almost black," she said.

"I do too."

Betty cut a piece of cake for herself and relaxed back into her chair.

"Now my dear, why don't you tell me exactly what's on your mind?"

Amy looked at her in surprise. It was as if Betty Parsons could see right into her heart. She felt herself blushing. "Is it so obvious?"

"Well, you do strike me as a wee bit gloomy," Betty said. "Although you're putting on a brave show and I admire that. But there is an expression I used to hear: *a problem shared is a problem halved*."

"I'm feeling pretty miserable," Amy confessed.

"Is it because of Josh?"

Amy hung her head. "Yes, but not just Josh. I had been looking forward to this holiday for months but since I got here it's been one calamity after another. I had a row with Sam and he went back to Dublin. Then I heard he was carrying on with another woman."

"Oh dear," Betty said.

"It gets worse," Amy went on. "Did you know that Josh and I were supposed to be going to Seville today?"

"No," Betty said. "I didn't."

"And then he rang at the last minute and said he had to go back to London in a hurry. That really floored me. He sounded so brusque on the phone. I couldn't believe it."

"Nina Black," Betty said.

"Yes, Nina Black."

Betty topped up Amy's tea. "I don't mean to pry, my dear, but have you grown fond of Josh?"

"Yes," Amy blurted out. "Very fond, and I thought he felt the same way about me. So you can imagine how I felt when he told me the news."

"I know exactly how you felt. It's perfectly understandable. He should have handled it much more diplomatically. It was extremely insensitive. I have to say, he doesn't usually behave like that."

"Perhaps she is seriously ill?"

"I spoke to her," Betty said. "She didn't say she was ill – but she did say she needed to see him urgently."

Betty paused.

"Let me tell you about Josh," she said.

Amy sat forward in her chair and listened attentively while the older woman spoke.

"Josh is an only child," Betty began. "I suppose I spoiled him when he was a little boy. He was used to getting his own way. But at the age of thirteen he was sent away to boarding school. He hated it. He was badly bullied by the other boys. There was a lot of snobbery at that school. It wasn't very pleasant for him. But the point is, by the time he left school, I was living out here most of the time and his father was working like a lunatic as he always did. Josh has never had what you might call a proper family life. He missed that. I think he still does."

"Has he told you this?" Amy asked.

"No dear, it's purely observation. I think Josh would like nothing better than to settle down with some woman he loves and have his own little family. I think he craves the security he missed as a child. I don't think he wants to spend his life working all the time like his father. He's been unfortunate with women. And with Nina in particular. She is very beautiful – long black hair, vivacious. He brought her out here one time. They seemed a perfect couple. He was infatuated with her. I thought they were going to get married. In fact, I was waiting for an announcement any day. Then something happened. They broke up suddenly and it all fell apart."

"He said her work came between them."

"So he's talked to you about her?"

"No, he just mentioned her in conversation."

"She is extremely ambitious. She wanted to get into films. But the upshot of the break-up was that Josh was plunged into the dumps. He was very unhappy until you showed up. Then he suddenly came alive again. You had a very good influence on him."

"Do you think so?" Amy asked.

"Of course, he was like a new man. He was happy again. He even extended his holiday to spend more time with you. You had a very positive effect on him."

237

"But now he's gone."

"Yes, but I have a feeling he'll be back."

At these words, Amy felt herself brighten up. "Why do you say that?"

"I'm his mother, dear. You see, people are slow to change. Whatever setback Nina has encountered, she will remain basically the same. Who's to say she won't take off again? She's an actress. She will go wherever her career takes her. And that is not a recipe for stability."

"It doesn't mean it couldn't work."

"Of course it doesn't."

"Perhaps he's still in love with her."

Betty looked at her. "Who knows what love is? He found you sufficiently attractive to change his holiday plans to spend more time with you. Love can grow, you know. And it can also die. It's like a plant. It has to be nurtured with care and affection in order to thrive. Do you want him back?"

Amy lowered her glance and stared at the floor. "Yes," she said.

"Then you should be patient. I will be speaking to him later."

Betty sat back in her chair and smiled.

"Do you feel better?" she asked.

"Yes."

"You see, I was right about sharing your feelings instead of bottling them up. I'll call you tomorrow if I have any news for you. Now why don't we have another piece of cake?"

It was an hour later when Amy left Betty's apartment. She was in much brighter spirits than when she had arrived a few hours earlier. The chat had been like a tonic. Betty had spoken a lot of sense and it had helped Amy put things in perspective and shake off the feeling of disappointment that had gripped her all day.

She would have an early night. Perhaps tomorrow she would go shopping with Carly O'Brien. There was a big shopping mall up near the castle which she had been meaning to visit. Shopping was always a good way to cheer you up. She went into the bedroom to get undressed when she heard the bell give a sharp ring.

Who can this be, she wondered as she walked out to the hall and pulled the door open.

Immediately, she felt her blood freeze.

Sam Benson was standing on the doorstep.

Chapter 33

Sam had woken that morning with a noise like a concrete mixer churning in his head and a mouth that tasted like the Sahara desert. It took him a couple of minutes to realise he was in bed somewhere.

But there was something not right. *It wasn't his bed.* He didn't recognise any of his surroundings. There was a dressing table where the wardrobe should be, the windows were on the wrong side of the room and they had blinds instead of curtains. And the pictures on the walls were all wrong.

He gave a start. He had heard a story one time about a man who drank so much that he began to see snakes coming out of the ceiling. Was that what was happening to him? Had Herbie Morrison finally driven him over the edge and into insanity?

Slowly, he let his glance travel around the room. There were clothes scattered across the floor. He looked closer and saw a white bra and beside it a pair of what looked like boxer shorts. His trousers were lying in a heap in a corner as if they had been flung there by force. He saw his shirt, rolled in a ball beneath the window.

Just then, something moved in the bed and he felt his heart jump into his mouth. He lay still, afraid to breathe. The movement started again and this time the bedclothes began to rise up in a heap. It was accompanied by a deep growling sound like a wild animal was about to pounce. Sam sat bolt upright, prepared to strike if anything attacked him. A tousled blonde head began to emerge from under the sheets and a pair of black smudged eyes peered at him like cinders in the snow.

By now, Sam was terrified.

"Don't come any closer," he warned.

Zoe Byrne yawned and stretched her arms.

"Calm down. What's the matter with you? You look like you've seen a ghost."

Sam blinked and recognised his partner of the night before.

"Where am I?" he said.

"You're in my apartment. You came back with me in a taxi last night. Don't you remember? Zhivago Bar?"

By now, Sam's heart was racing and his face had broken into a cold sweat. The concrete-mixer in his head had gone into overdrive. He looked at his hands and saw they were shaking.

"I need a drink," he said.

"There's beer in the fridge," Zoe said.

It was ten minutes before the shaking finally stopped and his heart began to slow down. In the meantime, Sam had managed to shower, drink a cup of black coffee, swallow a couple of aspirins and get dressed in his crumpled clothes. He found his mobile phone and checked for messages. There were none.

Zoe was still curled up in bed, watching him.

Through the fog in his brain, a few thoughts were beginning to emerge. He had spent the night with Zoe Byrne. If Amy ever found out, she would go ballistic. She would never take him back. Please God Zoe would keep her mouth shut.

But he had even more pressing matters to worry about. He had to concentrate on getting into work. Ron Burrows had given him an ultimatum. The accursed Slimline campaign had to be finalised today. But first he had to get a fresh change of clothes.

"I'll have to go back to my own place," he said. "I look like a tramp."

"Suit yourself."

"What's the nearest cab company?"

"Emerald Cabs. The number's on the door of the fridge."

He went back to the kitchen and rang the number. The man who answered said they'd have a cab round to him in five minutes.

He returned to the bedroom. "Thanks for everything. See you later at the office," he said. "You were fantastic."

"As if you remember," Zoe said contemptuously. "Who are you kidding?"

Sam sat in the back of the cab and made up his mind. That experience had scared the living daylights out of him. He'd never had shakes like that before. His holiday had been ruined and now his very sanity was at risk. He had done all he could with the Slimline campaign. He could bring it no further. If Herbie Morrison still wasn't satisfied, Sam was walking away.

It would mean giving up a promising career built up by hard work over many years. But there was a limit to what he could take and now it had finally arrived. If necessary, he would find another job. Coming to this decision brought some relief. He felt a fragile peace settle over him. At last, the cab drew up outside his apartment. He paid the driver and stepped out.

The place looked cold and neglected. There was a pile of dirty dishes in the sink and the waste bin was overflowing. He went into the bathroom and shaved then splashed some cologne on his cheeks. Immediately, he felt fresher. He brushed his teeth and examined himself in the mirror. He looked terrible. He had seen better-looking corpses. There were bloodshot lines in his eyes and his face was the colour of concrete. But at least he wasn't sweating any more.

He went into the bedroom and dug out a clean shirt and fresh underwear. He changed his socks and found a new pair of shoes. Finally, he selected a fresh suit from the rack. He turned and examined himself. At last he was beginning to resemble a human being.

Just then, his phone started to ring. He sat down on the bed and clamped it to his ear.

"It's Ron," the voice said.

Immediately, Sam felt himself go tense.

"How are you this morning?" Ron asked.

"Okay," Sam lied.

"I'm about to make you a happy man."

Sam wondered if he was being ironic. Please, he thought, don't let him tell me that Herbie Morrison has signed up for another campaign. I'll go straight out and throw myself under the first bus.

"What?" he asked cautiously.

"I had Herbie Morrison on to me this morning."

Sam felt his left knee start to tremble.

"And?"

"He's finally accepted the Slimline package."

It took a minute for the information to register.

"He's accepted?" Sam cried.

"Yes, in fact he's delighted with it, the whole campaign, the model, the slogan, the art work, everything! He said once you guys had ironed out the initial hiccoughs, you were a fantastic team. He's a great admirer of your talent, Sam."

Sam felt a great wave of relief wash over him.

"That's very good to know. Has he signed off on it? Remember what happened the last time?"

"He's doing that this morning along with paying up. It's in the bag, Sam. He says he's looking forward to working with you again."

"Well, I'd need to think about that. Don't promise him anything. Does this mean I'm free to resume my holiday?"

"Of course and I'm paying you a bonus in consideration of the disruption all this has caused."

"Thanks, Ron. That's very decent."

"So I'm just calling to wish you *bon voyage*. Your work here is finished for the time being. Go off and enjoy yourself with the lovely Amy."

"Will do," Sam said.

He switched off the phone and punched the air with his fist.

"Yessss!" he said.

He immediately sat down with his laptop, went online and began searching for flights to Malaga. There was one leaving that afternoon. He paid for his ticket by credit card and printed out his boarding pass. He wondered if he should ring Amy and let her know he was coming. No, he decided. I'll surprise her.

He quickly packed his travelling bag and rang for another cab to take him to the airport. Then he took his mobile phone and locked it away in a drawer. He wasn't going to make that mistake again. Now he was incommunicado. He still didn't trust that bastard Herbie Morrison not to come up with some last-minute hitch. He locked up the apartment and went down to the street to wait.

The last week had been an absolute nightmare and now the next hurdle was to mend his fences with Amy. It was going to require some soft soap and a little sackcloth and ashes. It was going to require a lot grovelling and apologising. But Sam was confident he could do it. He was so looking forward to seeing her once more and relaxing again in the sun. He thought of La Rueda restaurant and a nice fat grilled sole and fried potatoes. Hell, he deserved it after what he'd just gone through!

The taxi from Malaga airport deposited him at last outside the gates of Magnolia Park. Sam walked through the cool gardens with their scent of roses drifting on the night air. He felt like a completely different person to the terrified creature who had woken up in Zoe Byrne's bed this morning. He shivered at the memory. But that was the past. He had turned over a new leaf. Once he was reconciled with Amy there would be no more philandering with floozies in the Zhivago Bar.

When he arrived at the apartment, he saw a light on in the bedroom. He paused for a moment to straighten his tie. Then he pressed the bell and fixed a contrite smile on his face. He heard footsteps approaching, the door opened and there she was standing before him.

"Hello, Amy," he said. "I'm back."

Amy stared at him as if she was seeing an apparition. The breath left her body and it took a few seconds before she was able to speak.

"What are *you* doing here?" she managed to say.

Sam gave a hearty laugh. "What do you think I'm doing? I've returned to you. I've sorted out the problems back in Dublin and now I'm here to continue my holiday."

"You can't come in," she said and made a move to shut the door but he quickly stuck his foot in the jamb.

"Not so fast," he said. "I'm fully entitled to be here. My name is on the rental agreement."

He was right. His name *was* on the damned agreement along with hers. But that didn't mean she had to share the same roof with him. If he insisted on his rights, then she was moving out.

Meanwhile, Sam had brushed past her and strode into the apartment. She had no option but to follow. He dropped his bag on the floor, heaved a satisfied sigh and turned to her.

"Come on, Amy, you're not still carrying on that stupid argument, are you? It's ridiculous." He reached out to hug her but she quickly pulled away.

"Don't touch me," she said.

"Amy, I've apologised to you. You've made your point and now it's time to move on. It won't happen again, I promise. I'll be on my best behaviour. Now why can't we just be friends again and stop this silly nonsense?"

He sat down on the settee and glanced around the room.

"It's great to be back," he said. "You've no idea the time I've had with that moron, Herbie Morrison. The man has the intelligence of a fruit-fly. But I fixed him in the end. And do you know what he told Ron? He's looking forward to working with me again. Can you imagine? I'd rather cut my wrists than be in the same room again with that imbecile. Now where do you fancy eating tonight? I'm really looking forward to some decent grub."

Amy folded her arms and stared at him. "I won't be eating anywhere with you."

"So what are you going to do? Go on hunger strike? Don't you think you're carrying this martyrdom act a bit far?"

"It's not a martyrdom act. I'd be sick all over the table if I had to eat a meal with you."

"That's a rather nasty remark," he said.

"It's the truth. You can remain here simply because I have no legal means of removing you. But I don't have to eat with you. Or sleep with you either. And if you stay here, I'm moving out."

"Where will you go?"

"I'll get a hotel room."

Sam let out a groan. "What *is* the matter with you, Amy? I've been working my ass off – ten and twelve-hour days to sort out that bloody advertising campaign. I've busted a gut to get here. I only had a sandwich to eat on the plane. And this is the welcome I get?"

"You should have thought about that when you went smooching with blonde bimbos in the Zhivago Bar!" she snapped.

His mouth fell open. So she had found out about Zoe Byrne. How the hell had that happened?

"I don't know what you're talking about."

"You're not a very convincing liar," she retorted. "I have a witness."

His face went pale. "You've had someone spying on me?"

"Don't flatter yourself," she said. "I wouldn't waste my time spying on you."

"Some little sneak carrying tales, is that it?"

"Someone saw you in Zhivago snuggling up to some blonde wagon and thought it was in my interest to know."

He attempted to laugh but didn't quite manage it. "I'm afraid your informant has got this all wrong."

"Really?"

"Yes. I can explain it."

"I wouldn't waste my breath if I was you."

"I did have a drink in Zhivago but it was totally innocent. The blonde woman I was with is Zoe Byrne. She's a colleague. She works on reception. You've met her. It was totally above board."

"I was told you were kissing her."

Sam made a quick decision to brazen it out.

"Well, your informant has got her facts wrong. Has it occurred to you that this is a case of malicious gossip? Someone who wants to cause trouble between us?"

"You're the one who's causing the trouble. I rang you two days ago and asked you to reply urgently. Do you realise you never called me once in all the time you were away? And now you turn up on the doorstep and you expect a hero's welcome."

"I've just explained, Amy. I was working flat out."

"You still found time to go carousing with this Zoe Byrne creature."

"I'm apologising again," he said. "I should have called you. Now why don't we put the past behind us and enjoy the remainder of our holiday?"

Amy gave an exhausted sigh. Arguing with Sam was like wrestling with an octopus. "I'm afraid it's not that simple any more."

"Why not?"

"I've met someone else."

Chapter 34

"You've met someone else?"

Sam looked at her in stunned disbelief.

"Yes."

"I should have known," he said, angrily. "It's that blond guy, Josh, isn't it?"

"Yes."

"So I was right. And you have the nerve to accuse *me* of being unfaithful?"

Amy shrugged. "These things happen. I fell for him. We'd had the argument and you said those cruel things. Then you went home and you never once bothered to ring me I was feeling lonely and Josh and his mother took me under their wing. It just grew from there."

"Don't be stupid."

"That's what happened, Sam. And, when I heard you were enjoying yourself in Zhivago with Zoe Byrne, that was the killer blow. I decided it was the end."

"Nothing just happens like that."

"What are you suggesting? That I came out here looking for romance? I had never seen Josh before in my life. I didn't even know he existed. I've just told you, I fell for him."

"And it never occurred to you to let me know? You could have phoned."

"I did phone and you never replied."

"Where is he?" Sam growled. "I'm going to wipe the smirk off his pretty blond face."

"Don't be an idiot. Anyway, he's not here. He's in London."

"I'll knock his teeth down his goddamned throat. He doesn't know who he's tangling with." Another thought seemed to occur to him and he turned on her again. "Have you had sex with him?" he demanded.

Amy stared back at him. "I beg your pardon?"

"You heard me? Have you been to bed with him?"

"That is absolutely none of your business. And I think you have a damned cheek to even ask."

"It *is* my business. I'm supposed to be your boyfriend, remember? We've been living together for the past year."

"Not any more."

"What the hell do you mean?"

"Isn't it obvious? Our relationship is over. When I return to Dublin, I'm moving out of your apartment."

He gasped. "Now I really know you're off your head. You can't move out."

"Why not?"

"Where will you live?"

"With my parents. I've still got a bedroom there."

He moved towards her but she pushed him away.

"You can't do this, Amy."

"I *am* doing it."

"Just give me one more chance to prove myself."

"No, Sam. It wouldn't work. My mind is made up."

By now, he was looking desperate.

"You're not thinking straight," he said. "This is a silly holiday romance. It happens all the time. People come out here and they get blinded by the sun. They leave their brains on the plane. But once you get back to the reality of Dublin, you'll change your mind. He lives in London. How do you propose to carry on your love affair? Phone calls and text messages? That won't get you very far."

She shook her head. "You don't understand, Sam. I don't love you any more. The love I once had for you is gone. Our relationship is finished. Now you can behave like an adult and accept it or you can kick up a fuss and make things difficult for both of us. But nothing you can do or say will make me change my mind."

He stared at her as the reality of the situation began to sink home. "So you're serious about this?"

"Yes, I am."

He gave a weary sigh. "I suppose I'll have to find a spare room somewhere."

He stooped and picked up his bag. At the front door, he paused and turned to her again. "I hope you're not making a giant mistake here, Amy, something you will regret for the rest of your life."

The front door closed and she heard his footsteps retreating along the path. She flopped down on the settee. They had come to the end of the road and there was no turning back. But his last words were still echoing in her mind.

What if she had made a mistake and Josh decided to stay with Nina? That was something she *would* regret for the rest of her life.

In his penthouse apartment high over the city, Josh sat staring out over London as the daylight began to fade. His tumbler was empty, the whiskey long consumed. Through his mind, images and memories flitted and danced. He had always accepted that Nina held a powerful spell over him but he hadn't realised till now just how strong it really was.

The rational part of his brain told him he should let her go. She had left him once and there was no guarantee that she wouldn't do it again. Her lifestyle made it almost inevitable. It was completely disruptive. It involved long periods of rehearsals, sudden changes of plan, rushing from one end of the country to the other at a moment's notice. Did he want to put himself through all that again?

A relationship with Nina would bring excitement but it would not provide security.

Yet part of him couldn't let her go. The part of his mind where pleasurable memories are stored kept recycling those images of them together in the early days of their romance when they were so carefree and happy.

The ringing of his phone shattered his reverie. When he picked it up, he heard his mother's voice.

"Josh, it's me. How are you?"

He sat up. "I'm fine, Mum."

"Have you spoken with your father?"

"Yes, we talked this afternoon. He wants me to go to Glasgow to look at a site for another store."

"He will never change," Betty said. "Did you see Nina?"

"Yes."

"How is she?"

"Not good. She's had some very bad experiences. She looks terrible and hasn't a penny to her name. She has asked me to help her. She wants us to get together again."

"And what are you going to do?"

"I don't know. I'm trying to make up my mind."

"There is something I should tell you," Betty went on. "I know this is none of my business but I feel I must speak."

"What is it, Mum?"

"I've talked to Amy."

"How is she? Is she all right?"

"No, she's not all right. She's upset, poor girl. She's a brave young woman so she tried to conceal her feelings but I have to tell you that you've hurt her by the way you behaved."

"I'm sorry. I thought I explained to her that I had to rush away."

"She was expecting to go to Seville with you today. She was very excited about it. Couldn't you have been more gentle with her?"

Immediately he felt a stab of conscience. His mother was right. He should have handled the matter more sensitively. And the terrible thing was, while he had been sitting here worrying about Nina, he hadn't once thought about how Amy might be feeling.

"You're right, Mum. I'm sorry. I was in a terrible hurry and I wasn't thinking straight."

"You know she cares about you, Josh?"

"Yes, I do know."

"So perhaps you should take that into account in whatever plans you decide."

"I'm sorry," Josh said again.

"Now I've said my piece. You may regard me as an interfering busybody if you like but I had to get that off my chest."

"No, Mum, you're not a busybody. I'm glad we talked."

"So when can I expect to hear from you again?"

"Soon. I have some business to take care of and I have promised Dad to be in Glasgow on Monday morning to commence work. But I will be in touch with you before then."

Josh put down the phone. His mother had the uncanny knack of always spotting the essential part of any problem. Now, he would have to start all over again and view the situation in a new light.

Betty put down the phone with a feeling of satisfaction. She was glad she had spoken to Josh and pointed out the error of his ways. He *had* been insensitive. He hadn't stopped to think. Now, she had put Amy back in the frame. Betty liked both women and she hoped Josh would come to the right decision. But she knew that whichever way he turned, one of them was going to get hurt.

Betty hated to see people getting hurt – even people she thought might deserve it. But many things were outside her control and this was one of them. She had done her bit and now she had to stand aside and let matters take their course.

By now the garden was in shadow, filled with the scent of the flowers. It hung like perfume on the evening air. A thought came to her. She picked up her phone again and dialled.

"Hello, Betty," a voice said.

"Nigel, I was thinking of you."

"That's nice."

"I wanted to tell you again how much I enjoyed our lunch today."

"I enjoyed it too."

"I was thinking we should do it again. Only this time, I'm going to pay."

She heard him laugh.

"I could never allow that, Betty. It would never do. A gentleman always picks up the tab for a lady."

"You're old-fashioned, Nigel. That has all changed now. Haven't you heard of women's liberation?"

"Of course, but some things never change and this is one of them. If I invite you to lunch then I must pay."

"What if I invite you to lunch?"

"I still must pay."

Betty giggled. She was enjoying this banter with Nigel. "I hope we're not going to have our first falling-out over this."

"I hope so too!"

"What if we split the bill? Wouldn't that do?"

"You're very determined, Betty."

"Yes, I can be."

"I'd need to think about it. When are you planning to have this lunch?"

"As soon as I'm free, I have a lot going on here just at the moment."

"Then I'll be at your disposal, Betty."

"And afterwards, you must come back for coffee. You've never seen my apartment and my son is away."

"Now you have me intrigued," Nigel said. "Good night, Betty. Sleep well."

"You too."

She turned off the phone. It was lovely having Nigel as a friend. Now she need never feel lonely. He would always be there at the end of the phone if she felt like a chat. She looked at her watch and saw it was ten thirty. She would take a book and read on the terrace and then to bed. It had been a busy day. And she was tired.

Chapter 35

The following morning, Josh was up early. Outside the window, the morning was bright, although not as bright as the mornings in Spain. He went into the kitchen and put on the kettle to make coffee and while he waited for it to boil he went into the bathroom, shaved, showered and got dressed in a pair of dark trousers, casual shirt and grey linen jacket. He made the coffee and took it onto the terrace.

It was a clear day. He could see for miles across this city that housed millions of living, breathing human beings drawn from all corners of the world. In a room in one of those houses, Nina was coming awake – if she had slept at all. She needed a period of rest and recuperation, good food and fresh air before she could recover her former beauty and be in a fit state to approach an agent and resume her acting career. But Josh had faith in her. He had absolutely no doubt it could be done.

He finished the coffee and went into a dark-panelled room dominated by a large desk. There were several phones, a telex machine, filing cabinets, bookshelves, a desktop computer and printer. This was his office where he did most of his work from the comfort of his home. He sat down in a leather chair and checked the time. It was now nine o'clock. Nina should be up by now. He lifted the phone and rang her.

"Hello, Nina," he said.

He heard the grateful sound of her voice.

"Oh, Josh, thank God you called. How are you this morning, my darling?"

"I'm fine, Nina. But, more to the point, how are you?"

"I'm all the better for hearing your voice."

"Were you able to sleep?"

"Just a little. But you know me, I don't need much sleep."

"I beg to differ, Nina. I think you need all the rest you can get. In fact, I think you need to see a doctor. I'm going to recommend someone to you."

She began to protest. "I don't need a doctor, Josh. I need to get working again. That's what I require to get back on my feet."

"We'll see. Would you like to go for lunch today?"

"I've got nothing to wear."

"I'll take you some place where that won't matter. I'll call for you at midday. I'm looking forward to seeing you again, Nina."

"You too, my sweet. I'll be waiting."

He finished the call and dialled another number. When it was answered he gave his name and asked to be put through to Mr Osborne. When the man came on the line, Josh introduced himself again.

"Good morning, Mr Parsons, what can I do for you?"

"I'll be calling to see you at ten o'clock," Josh said.

"Very good, sir."

"In the meantime, there are some things I would like you to do."

For the next few minutes, he spoke to Mr Osborne while the man carefully took down his instructions.

"Is that everything, Mr Parsons?"

"Yes."

"Very good, sir. I will see you at ten o'clock."

He made several more calls before he was finished, including one to his father to confirm the trip to Glasgow. At last, he replaced the phone, stood up and left the room. He had a lot of business to complete this morning. He had better make a start. He locked the apartment, rode the elevator to the basement and settled into the driving seat of his car. A few minutes later, he drove up the ramp and out into the bright London morning.

It was exactly five minutes to twelve when he turned into the rundown street where Nina lived and parked outside Number 63. He pressed the buzzer for Flat 3 and heard her welcoming voice.

"Josh?"

"Yes."

"Come up."

He climbed the grotty stairs till he came to her landing. The door was slightly ajar. He knocked politely and pushed it open. Nina was standing at the window wearing the same faded dressing gown as last time. She was smoking and staring down into the street. She turned and immediately crushed out her cigarette and rushed into his arms.

"My darling," she whispered. "I've been waiting patiently since I got your call."

He caressed her hair and kissed her cheek.

"You're shivering, Nina."

"It's just a chill."

"Can't you light the fire?"

"I've no money for gas."

"Then you should wear more warm clothes."

He looked at her. She was like a bag-woman who tramped the streets and slept at night in shop doorways. It was difficult to find any trace of the beauty that had once shone out of those dark eyes. Yet he knew it was still there beneath the surface, waiting to blossom into life again with care and attention.

He gently eased her down onto the couch.

"I told you I was taking you to lunch," he said. "Why aren't you dressed?"

She waved her hand. "I've changed my mind. I've got no appetite. You'd only be wasting your money."

"At least let me go out and buy you some provisions."

"No," she said, firmly. "You can do it later."

She began to cough and drew a handkerchief from the pocket of her dressing gown to wipe her mouth.

"You should stop smoking, Nina. Those cigarettes are killing you. Think of the harm they're doing to your lungs, not to mention your voice. You will need your voice when you resume your career."

"You're right," she said. "I will stop but not just yet. I'll do it as soon as I get back on my feet again."

He paused. "I said you should see a doctor. You need a thorough medical check. I think you're ill."

"I'll be fine once I find somewhere else to stay. I just need to start working and earning money. It's hanging around this bloody flat that is making me depressed."

"I want you to see the doctor at once, today. I'll give you money to cover the expenses."

A look of defiance sprang into her eyes but she quickly changed her mind.

"All right, I'll do it."

"There is something else I'd like you to do."

"What?"

"I want you to contact your parents. I think you should go and stay with them for a while till you get better."

"No," she snapped. "It isn't possible. I would never let them see me like this. It would hurt them too much."

"You must," he insisted. "You won't get better if you stay here. Your parents are waiting for you."

Her face fell as this last statement began to sink in. "How do you mean?"

"I spoke to them this morning. I explained the situation to them. I didn't tell them everything but I let them know you are in a bad way and need somewhere to rest and recuperate till you are well enough to return to London and pick up your career. They will be very happy to take you in and look after you."

She stared at him. A look of fear had now entered her eyes.

"And what are you going to do in the meantime?" she asked.

"I have other plans."

"But they don't involve me?"

Josh paused then slowly shook his head.

"No," he said. "Unfortunately they don't."

She sprang out of her seat and flung herself on him. She began to pummel and punch him with a strength that belied her frail condition. Exhausted at last, she slid onto the floor and began to weep.

"You bastard," she said. "I might have known. You've deserted me too now that I need you most. Why are you doing this? I thought you said you had forgiven me?"

Josh picked her up in his arms and gently laid her down again on the couch. He knelt beside her.

"I *have* forgiven you. And I'm not deserting you, Nina. It was you who deserted me. So I am not taking this course out of any motive of revenge. I am doing it because I still care deeply about you. You are a talented actress. You still have a successful career ahead of you. But you can't even attempt to make a comeback till you have recovered your health and strength and the best place to do that is with your parents."

"I hate you," she screamed. "You rat, you low-life! You're abandoning me. You're every bit as bad as Lorenzo Morelli."

Josh waited till she had spent her fury then spoke again in a quiet voice. "I'm not abandoning you, Nina. I've given this matter a lot of consideration. I've thought of nothing else since you rang me two nights ago. But I've reached my conclusion."

He reached into his pocket and drew out an envelope. He placed it on the table beside the couch.

"There's two thousand pounds in that envelope. It is to enable you to buy new clothes and pay your fare back to your parents and also to open a bank account. I assume you don't have an existing one?"

She shook her head.

"Once you have opened the account, I have made arrangements with my bank to lodge a further sum of £2000 into it every month for the next six months to help you get back on your feet. It will also provide you with the capital to make a fresh start on your career when you have sufficiently recovered."

He bent over her and stroked her face.

"Do this, Nina. Realise the potential that is in you. Prove the critics wrong. Show them what a wonderful actress you can be."

"But I can't do it without you."

"Yes, you can. You must. I'm sorry."

She began to weep again. "Why won't you take me back?" she pleaded. "Why can't we just pick up where we left off before I ever met Lorenzo Morelli?"

"Because it would never work out between us. We would only make each other miserable."

"No," she said and grasped his arm. "You are only saying that because I hurt you."

"I'm saying it because it's true."

"We were happy once. I made a silly mistake but we can be happy again. Just give me one more chance, you'll see."

He gently removed her arm. "It's not so simple, Nina. Nothing stands still. If you had come back to me a month ago, even a week ago, it might have been different. But in the meantime, I have met someone else."

She drew back and the remaining colour drained from her face. "What are you saying?"

"When you left me, I was miserable. I thought I would never be happy again. You broke my heart, Nina. But I went to visit my mother in Fuengirola and that's where I met another woman. I have become very fond of her and I think she shares my feelings. I left her in a hurry to come to your side. Now I must go back to her."

Nina looked distraught. "So there is no hope for us?"

"Not in the way you want. We can still remain friends if you wish but we can never be lovers again."

She reached up and put her arms around his neck and kissed him. "You're a good man, Josh, and I threw you way. If only I could turn back the clock."

"It can't be done, Nina. You must put the past behind you and look to the future. Open that bank account. Go back to your parents. Get well again."

He gently freed himself from her arms and walked to the door where he paused briefly before turning back.

She was sitting on the couch with her head sunk on her chest in a mood of total dejection.

"Goodbye, Nina."

She didn't answer. Josh closed the door and started down the stairs.

Chapter 36

Amy carried her sun-bed out to the garden and settled down to read. She had a few hours to herself. At one o'clock she was going for lunch with Carly O'Brien who that morning had taken off to the weekly outdoor market where she hoped to pick up some bargain gifts for her friends back home.

Amy stretched her body to the sun. She was developing a good tan – her face, arms, legs and body were covered in a beautiful dark chestnut hue. At least she would be taking something back to Dublin at the end of the holiday even if it wasn't the partner she came out with.

She had heard no more from Sam since their confrontation the previous evening and she hoped it would stay that way. She had finished with him and this time it was final. Thankfully, he appeared to have got the message. But she also hoped he had found somewhere to stay – she didn't like the thought of her former boyfriend wandering the streets of Fuengirola looking for a place to lay his weary head.

Her chat with Betty last night had improved Amy's mood and the departure of Sam had brightened it further.

And then there was Carly. It was a stroke of luck that Amy had met the young woman from Wexford. Now she had a companion.

Yet a feeling of uncertainty continued to grip her. She couldn't help thinking of Josh and what might be happening between him and Nina in London. She had one big advantage over Amy in the contest for Josh's affections. She had known him longer. They had lived together. And Josh would have memories of those happy times they had spent with each other – memories that would keep drawing him back.

She was just opening her book when the phone rang. She checked and saw her mother's number.

"Hi, Mum," she said.

"I thought I'd give you a call," her mother said.

"That's nice."

"Everything all right down there?"

"Why do you ask?"

"Somebody said they saw Sam in town a few days ago. What's he doing here? Why isn't he down there with you?"

Amy bit her lip. So word had now reached her parents. What was she going to say? She had better tell her mother the truth. She would have to do it eventually. "We've broken up."

"What?" Mrs Crawford exclaimed. "That was very sudden, wasn't it?"

"I suppose it was."

"So what happened?"

"It's a long story. And there's another thing. I'm going to need my old bedroom back again."

"It's waiting here any time you need it. I hope you're not broken-hearted over this?"

"No. I think it's all for the best."

"Well, if you say so. Anyway, what is the weather like?"

"The weather is marvellous," Amy replied, happy to get away from the dangerous subject of Sam.

"At least that's some good news. And what about your accommodation, are you pleased with it?"

Amy let her eye travel round Magnolia Park – at the beautifully trimmed, lawns, the fountain, the roses, the pool, the white apartments gleaming in the bright morning sun.

"It's beautiful, Mum. It's the sort of place you see in travel books. I wish I could stay here for ever."

She heard her mother laughing.

"You were always a bit of a dreamer, Amy. What would you live on? Fresh air?"

"There's no harm in dreaming, Mum."

"I suppose not," Mrs Crawford said. "You'll be back to harsh reality soon enough."

They chatted for a few more minutes and then her mother said she had to go because the postman was at the door. Amy ended with a promise to call again in a few days' time.

She settled down once more with her book. At least, she had got that bit out of the way. But a few minutes later, the phone rang again.

This time, she got a shock when she pressed it to ear.

"Hi, Amy, is the sun still shining down there?"

"Josh!"

"That's right. I'm ringing to apologise for my abrupt behaviour. I should have explained things better. Nina was in trouble and I had to help her. I'm calling to say that I'm catching the 2pm flight from Heathrow. I should be at Magnolia Park around six o'clock, your time. Are you free to have dinner with me tonight?"

Amy could scarcely believe her ears. Josh was coming back. *And* he had invited her to dinner.

"You're coming back today?"

"Yes, and there is something I need to talk about. So are you free to have dinner or not?"

"What do you think, Josh? Of course I am."

Josh finished the brief conversation by agreeing to pick Amy up at seven at her apartment. Then he excused himself, saying he had to call his mother.

Amy tossed her novel in the air and let out a whoop. Old Mrs Gilbert, who was passing by, stopped to stare.

"Are you all right, my dear? Do you require assistance?"

Amy ran to her and wrapped her in a hug. "No, Mrs Gilbert. I'm perfectly all right. If I felt any better, I'd burst."

"Oh, don't do that, dear. Just sit down and rest and I'll get you a glass of brandy. It will soon revive you."

"But there's nothing wrong with me, Mrs Gilbert. I'm just happy, that's all."

"Are you sure?"

"Perfectly sure. I've just had the most wonderful news."

"Well, I'm very pleased for you," the old lady said. "Good news is always welcome. And I like to see people happy."

She toddled off and Amy quickly scooped up her belongings and hurried back to her apartment. Her head was in a tizz. There were so many things she had to do in advance of her dinner date with Josh. Top of the list was a visit to the hairdresser's. With all the sun and the swimming, her hair was like a rat's nest. But would she be able to get an appointment at such short notice?

She was rifling through the phone book when she heard footsteps coming along the path and when she looked out she saw Carly O'Brien approaching with her arms laden with bags from her trip to the market.

Damn, Amy thought, I'd completely forgotten about our lunch appointment.

Carly stopped when she saw her. "You look very excited. Something happened?"

"Yes," Amy replied. "But I'm afraid I won't be able to go for lunch today. You see, I've been invited out to dinner and I need to find a hairdresser. Like immediately!"

"Dinner with a man, is it?" Carly said with a playful grin.

Amy stared. "How did you know that?"

"Oh c'mon, Amy, why else would you get yourself all tied up in knots?"

"It is a man. But it's not the man I came here with."

"Ohhh," Carly said, her eyes widening at the prospect of a juicy scandal. "Who is it?"

"It's a man I met here, in Magnolia Park. A wonderful man. His name is Josh and he is Mrs Parsons' son. He had to go off to London but now he's back again and he's taking me to dinner tonight."

"That's so exciting. It's like something out of a movie. But what about your chap, the one who had to return to Dublin on business?"

"He's back here too. But it's all over between us."

"My God. Is he upset?"

Amy nodded.

"Very."

"It sounds extremely complicated," Carly said.

"It *is* complicated. I would tell you all about it but I don't have time. I've got to get organised for this dinner date."

"I see what you mean. Okay, let me have a look at your hair." She studied Amy's head for a moment then said, "Ummm, it could do with a trim and a good shampoo, all right."

"But where am I going to get a hairdresser at such short notice?"

"You're looking at one," Carly said and started to laugh.

"You?"

"Yes. I'm a hairdresser. That's my job. Now just let me leave these bags in my apartment and I'll be back to you at once. We'll soon have you looking immaculately groomed and ready to knock this guy for six."

"I wish," Amy said.

Carly went off and returned twenty minutes later with her scissors and brushes and combs. She sat Amy at the bathroom sink and draped a large towel around her shoulders then began vigorously shampooing her hair. When she was satisfied, she towel-dried it and then began snipping and cutting and tweaking.

"This Josh fella, is he handsome?"

"He's very handsome. He's about six feet tall with blond hair and the most dishy blue eyes you've ever seen. But it's not just his looks, Carly. It's everything about him, his personality, his kindness, his charm, his sense of humour."

"He sounds like a hunk."

"He is. Maybe you'll get a chance to meet him. Then you can decide for yourself."

"I can't wait. Are you in love with him, Amy?"

Amy paused for a moment.

"You know something, Carly. I think I might be."

Forty-five minutes later, Carly had finished. Amy looked in the mirror and saw that her hair had been transformed. Instead of looking tired and drab, it now shone with vitality.

"You've done a wonderful job," she said. "I'm delighted with it. You're a very good hairdresser, I'll say that."

"Thank you."

"Now, how much do I owe you for your work?"

"Get away with you!" Carly said. "I don't charge my friends. You've been very kind to me. You rescued me when I was alone."

I also rescued myself, Amy thought. We rescued each other.

"Now what are you going to wear?" Carly continued.

This was Amy's next dilemma. She had brought several dresses but she wanted something really eye-catching. She opened the wardrobe door and the two women rummaged through the racks but Amy could see nothing that suited.

"I'll tell you what," Carly said. "We're about the same size. I've got several dresses that might do – you could borrow if you like."

"Are you sure?"

"Positive. C'mon, you can have a look."

They walked quickly to Carly's apartment and began examining the dresses in her wardrobe. After a few minutes, Amy drew out a black cocktail dress with a low V-neck and held it against her body. It looked smashing.

"Why don't you try it on?" Carly encouraged her.

Amy quickly stepped out of her sundress and put on the little cocktail number. It fitted her like a glove. She turned to examine herself from behind. The dress reached several inches above her knees and would show off her legs to excellent effect.

"You look fantastic," Carly said.

"You think so?"

"I'm telling you. When he sees you tonight, his head is going to spin."

"And you don't mind if I borrow it?"

"Didn't I offer?" Carly said. "And you can borrow these black shoes as well. They're a match."

She picked up a pair of black heels and thrust them into Amy's hands.

"Try them on. They should fit."

Amy slid her feet into the shoes. They were a little bit tight but she wouldn't be walking very far. The combination of the shoes and the dress had transformed her appearance. She could meet Josh tonight feeling totally confident.

She turned to Carly and gave her a squeeze.

"You're very generous. How can I thank you?"

Carly laughed and glanced at her watch.

"You can pay for the lunch. C'mon, it's almost one o'clock. We had better get a move on if we want to get a good table."

Chapter 37

It was three thirty when Amy got back to Magnolia Park. This time they had gone to a British bar on the seafront because Carly said she was getting an urge for some familiar comfort food. There, she devoured a plate of roast beef and Yorkshire pudding with three veg while Amy contented herself with a seafood salad and one glass of wine.

When they got back to Magnolia Park, the sun was boiling in the heavens and sucking the energy out of everything that moved. Amy left Carly at the swimming pool and went into her own apartment where she immediately turned on the air-conditioning and lay down on the bed.

During the lunch, she had managed not to think too much about tonight's dinner with Josh. But now that she was alone, it surged back to the forefront of her mind. She was dying to see him again but her excitement was tinged with an element of caution. In the past week, she had been tossed hither and thither by the caprice of fortune. Now, some instinct warned her not to set her hopes too high. Josh had said nothing about what happened in London between himself and Nina. This dinner might not turn out to be a celebration. It might become a farewell.

But whatever happened, it would bring matters to a head and put an end to the unbearable uncertainty. She had fallen head over heels for Josh. It had been sudden and unexpected and had taken her completely by surprise. It was as if she had been swept along by a swift current that washed her straight into his arms.

At six o'clock, she started to get ready. First, she went into the bathroom and took a long shower and, once she had dried herself, she sat down in front of the dressing table and began to apply her make-up. She used it sparingly, just applying a little eye-liner and mascara and a thin veneer of lip gloss to her mouth. When she was finished, she sat back and examined the results.

She was quite pleased. She took Carly's black dress from the closet, zipped it up and ran her hands down her thighs to straighten it out. She smiled at her reflection in the mirror. Whatever else happened tonight, she was going to look stunning.

Finally, she sat down on the edge of the bed and slipped on the black shoes. Then she stood up and applied a little spray of scent to her wrists and neck. She was reaching for her jacket when she heard the doorbell ring. She took a deep breath. This was it, she thought, the moment of truth. With her heart thumping, she walked out to the hall and pulled open the door.

Josh was standing on the doorstep, dressed in a white lightweight suit and open-necked shirt. His blond hair gleamed in the evening sun. In his hand was a single red rose.

"I missed you," he said and kissed her cheek.

He had the car waiting at the gates. They got in and started up the hill for Mijas. From time to time, as he chatted about the flight, she caught him sneaking glances at her. At last he turned into a car-park and stopped the engine and announced that they had arrived.

Amy let her eyes take in the breathtaking scene. The restaurant was set in a garden looking down over the town and the coast. Pots of flaming geraniums and trellises of roses perfumed the evening air with their delicate fragrance. A light breeze stirred the leaves of the overhanging trees. It was idyllic.

A waiter appeared and led them to a table on the terrace where they could view the rolling countryside. He gave them menus and asked if they would like a drink. As soon as he was gone, Josh took her hand and stared into her eyes.

"You look beautiful," he said.

"Thank you."

"I'd like to apologise again. I rushed away to London without properly explaining the situation. I'm very sorry."

Amy lowered her eyes.

"It's important that you understand the background," Josh continued. "I told you about Nina Black but I didn't tell you everything. I was madly in love with her. I was crazy about her. I thought she was the one woman in the whole world who was destined for me. And then she left me and it broke my heart.

"She made a film in Ireland for an Italian director and when it was finished she went off to Italy with him. She told me she had to do that for the sake of her career. That was a year ago. But I always harboured a secret hope that some day she might return.

"Then, two nights ago, she called me out of the blue. She said she was now back in London. She had no money and she was desperate. She even talked about killing herself. She pleaded with me to help her. I felt I had no option but to go to her. I met her and she asked me to take her back and resume our relationship. A week ago, I would have jumped at the chance but something had happened in the meantime."

He paused.

"I met you, Amy."

She felt her pulse begin to race.

"I went to see Nina and she wasn't exaggerating. She was in a terrible state. Her career is in ruins, her director turned against her after bad film reviews and her agent has deserted her. She is penniless and she is living in this awful flat in Hammersmith belonging to one of her actress friends.

"I have to tell you that my heart went out to her. But her plight forced me to look at my own situation and I realised that I didn't love her any more. If I went back to her, it would be a disaster. The truth is, Nina can't give me what I want, Amy. But you can."

He paused and his eyes seemed to penetrate into her soul.

"Do you know what I want, Amy?"

"Yes," she replied. "I think I do. You want permanence and stability in a relationship with someone you love."

He smiled. "How did you know?"

"Because it's what every sane person wants."

"Is it what you want?"

"Of course."

He hesitated before speaking again. "Do you mind if I ask? What is happening between you and Sam?"

"It's over," she said. "He came back and I sent him away."

His expression showed surprise but there was also relief.

"How did he react?"

"Not very well. I don't think his ego could handle it but I told him in the end that there was nothing left between us."

"So it's final?"

Amy nodded. "As far as I'm concerned, it's final. He left and I haven't heard from him since. And now you're back again."

She saw a light come into his eyes.

"In that case, I have a proposal I want to put to you."

At that moment, there was a rustling sound behind them and the waiter appeared with their drinks. They had been so immersed in conversation that they hadn't even had an opportunity to look at the menus. But right now, food seemed the least important thing on their minds. They asked the waiter for his recommendation and he suggested roast lamb.

"For two?"

"Yes," they both nodded.

The waiter left and Josh resumed the conversation.

"Before I go any further, I want to let you into a family secret. My father is a workaholic. He has spent his entire life building up Parsons Electrical. He has put in twelve and fourteen-hour days, rarely took holidays, worked weekends. And he has been very successful. But his success has come at a price. The marriage between my parents exists in name only."

Amy lowered her head. It was rarely pleasant when family secrets came out of the cupboard. But Josh pressed on.

"My mother has been living here for years. She enjoys the climate and the lifestyle and she has made her own circle of friends. But my father rarely visits and when he does, he spends the time

271

playing golf or watching television. She might as well be a single, unmarried woman.

"My father is still expanding his business empire. I have to return to Glasgow on Monday to look at a site for another store. And the company already has two stores in the city. Meanwhile, I am coming under increasing pressure to take on more responsibility. My father doesn't like travelling and because he is getting older, that area has been delegated to me. But at the same time, he refuses to retire and allow me to take control of the company.

"If I had control, I would do things differently. I would put management structures in place so that I didn't have to work around the clock. You see, Amy, I don't want to end up like him. When I get married I want to live a normal life. I want to have the security of a wife and family. For me, work is only a means to an end. It isn't an end in itself. So when I was home, I took the opportunity to put a proposition to him. I told him I wanted to move to Spain and work from here."

"From *here*?" she said in surprise.

"Why not? Most of my work is done on the phone and when I have to travel, I can do it just as easily from Malaga as from London. And if my work takes me back to the UK, I can be there in a couple of hours."

"Where would you live?"

"Right here in Magnolia Park."

"With your mother?"

He laughed. "I think my mother might have other ideas. No, I'd buy a place of my own."

She shook her head in amazement.

"Just between ourselves," he went on, "there is a beautiful property coming on the market in the next few weeks. Mum has heard about it on the grapevine. It's a three-bed top-floor apartment overlooking the pool. I would probably get it at a good price. I could convert one of the bedrooms into an office and work from there."

"What would you do with your apartment in London?"

"I'd keep it. I'll always need somewhere to stay when I'm back and, besides, this is not a good time to sell property."

"You seem to have it all figured out. Do you think your father will go for this proposition?"

He shrugged. "I don't see why not. As long as the work gets done, it doesn't matter where I'm based. And I know that Mum would be delighted. Anyway, he has promised to consider it and give me a decision soon."

"You said you wanted to put a proposal to me."

"Yes, but before I do that I must ask you another question."

He took a deep breath then plunged ahead.

"What are your feelings towards me?"

She paused and looked him straight in the eye.

"I think you know that, Josh."

"Tell me."

"I've fallen in love with you."

He drew her close and kissed her and Amy felt her heart melt with passion.

At last he released her.

"That is what I was praying you would say. I love you too, Amy. And now that I know where we stand, let me tell you my proposal."

She held her breath.

"I want you to come and live with me here in Magnolia Park. I want to offer you a job as my personal assistant."

Chapter 38

Amy gasped. Everything was happening too quickly. She wished time would slow down so she could savour the significance of all she had just heard. But before she could reply, the waiter was back with their food. It came on a silver platter, a whole roast leg of lamb adorned with sprigs of rosemary and cooked with potatoes, onions, garlic, broccoli and peppers.

She waited till the waiter had gone then turned to Josh again.

"Do I understand you correctly? You want me to work with you?"

"Yes."

"But I know nothing about the electrical business. What would I do?"

"What I said. You'd be my PA. You'd manage my affairs, make hotel reservations and book airline flights when required. You'd arrange meetings, log telephone calls, keep unwanted callers away from me. It would be a busy job. I'm offering it to you and I'll pay you well."

"But you already have a secretary, don't you?"

"Yes, I've got Olivia but she's married and has two young children. She won't want to move to Spain. Olivia won't lose her job. She'll be redeployed within the company. So what do you think?"

"I'm bowled over. I wasn't expecting anything like this. I don't know what to say."

"Say yes, for God's sake! Think of the advantages. We've just expressed our love for each other. It means we can be together, in Magnolia Park. Remember that day in Mijas when we talked about what would happen when the holiday comes to an end? Well, now you know."

She closed her eyes and thought of all he was offering her. To be with this gorgeous man all the year round, here in Magnolia Park with its gardens and pool, the fountain, the rose gardens and its peace and serenity. It was a dream come true.

She opened her eyes and took in her surroundings. Darkness was beginning to fall. All over the valley, lights were coming on and they shone like fireflies in the gathering dusk. It was like something from a picture postcard. And he was offering her this and much more, not just for a fortnight's holiday but all the time, seven days a week, fifty-two weeks of the year.

"So what's your response, Amy?"

She turned to look into his beautiful blue eyes. They were appealing to her.

"Yes," she said. "Of course, I agree. Nothing would make me happier."

It was eleven o'clock when they returned to Magnolia Park. The lights glittered round the fountain and the balmy night air was filled with the chirping of the cicadas. A full moon hung in the cloudless sky. Amy's head was spinning with all that had occurred in the past few hours. The course of her life had been transformed and she was giddy with thoughts of the tantalising prospect that had suddenly opened before her.

At the door of her apartment, they paused and Josh took her in his arms. She felt herself shudder at his touch. Next moment their mouths were locked in a deep embrace.

All the events of the evening conspired to make her delirious with passion. Josh pressed her body to him and she felt his fingers travel along her spine and down to her thighs.

"I need you," he whispered.

Next moment Amy had opened the apartment and together they stumbled into the bedroom. He drew her dress up over her head and in an instant they were clawing at each other, frantically locked in each other's arms. They fell onto the bed and she felt his tongue caress her neck and her breasts while his hands explored her body till she was weak with pleasure. When at last he entered her, she exploded with pleasure.

Afterwards, she lay cradled in his arms while he stroked her face and hair.

"That was so good," he whispered.

She held him tight. There was no need to say anything. The response of her body to his lovemaking was testament enough.

After a while he began again and this time the pleasure was even greater than before.

It was two o'clock when he finally got up from the bed and went into the bathroom to shower.

"I've got one more day before I return to London," he said. "Why don't we take in that trip to Seville?"

Amy could think of no better way than to spend the time in the company of this wonderful man, the one person she loved above all others.

"I'd really enjoy that."

"I'll call for you at eight o'clock. I'll ring beforehand in case you're still sleeping."

"Okay."

She put on her dressing gown and accompanied him to the door. He took her in his arms for one last passionate farewell and then he was gone, slipping into the shadows of the night.

Amy had a shower and got in under the cool sheets. It had been a momentous day. Her mind travelled over all the events that had taken place and all the astounding news she had heard. There was so much she would have to do – inform her parents, give notice to her employers. And there would also be legal forms to fill in and a work permit to secure if she was going to take up employment as Josh's personal assistant.

But all that could wait. Tonight she wanted to luxuriate in the warm memories of the lovemaking that had just taken place.

Still thinking of that passionate encounter, she finally drifted off to sleep.

Chapter 39

The following morning, they set off on the trip to Seville that had been abandoned so dramatically a few days before. Amy made sure to bring her camera so she could get some photos. They departed Magnolia Park soon after eight for a journey that Josh said could take between two and three hours depending on the traffic. And, because he had so little time left, he proposed that instead of stopping over as they had planned the first time, they make this a one-day visit and return to Fuengirola that evening.

Amy was happy to fall in with his plans. If everything came to pass, she would spend many more nights with Josh's warm body pressed beside her.

They bypassed Malaga and started on the motorway for Seville.

Josh turned to her and smiled.

"I spoke to my father when I got home last night. I think he's coming round. I think he's going to say yes."

She could hear the excitement in his voice. She was excited too. She couldn't wait for it to happen.

"Won't I need to get a residence permit and stuff like that?"

"Sure. I will too. But let's not rush our fences. Once Dad has agreed, I'll get Mum's solicitor to sort it out for us."

"And you really think your dad is going to give his approval?"

He turned to her and smiled. "I think so, Amy. I think it's in the bag."

"When are you going to Glasgow?"

"Tomorrow evening."

"Then let's make the most of the last day."

It was half past ten when they finally saw Seville in the distance, its spires and turrets shining in the morning sun. Fifteen minutes later they left the motorway, made their entry into the city and Josh found a place to leave the car.

Amy was eager to see the city. She had been disappointed once before but now she was determined to enjoy this visit.

Already, she could see it was a magnificent place with its gilded towers and glistening steeples and narrow, winding cobbled streets. Josh had brought a guidebook and a map and he spread it out on his lap while together they planned their itinerary. They decided to begin at the cathedral. He slung his camera over his shoulder, handed Amy a bottle of water, locked the car and they set off.

The guidebook said that the cathedral was the largest of its kind in the world and dated back to 1401. They paid their entry charge and entered the gloomy interior. It was a hive of activity with tour groups and their guides making their way around the vast church. Josh and Amy followed in their wake, pausing occasionally to admire the grandeur of the architecture, the rich furnishing and impressive paintings that adorned the walls.

They finished at the magnificent tomb of Christopher Columbus, his casket carried on the shoulders of four medieval knights in armour, representing the Spanish kingdoms of Aragon, Leon, Castille and Navarre.

They spent almost an hour in the cathedral and could have stayed longer but there was so much more to see. In quick succession they visited the Giralda Tower, the Torre del Oro and Calle Feria with its craft shops and pretty balconies with hanging baskets of flowers. Here they found a market in progress and even greater crowds than they had encountered in the cathedral.

By the time they had managed to navigate the street, the heat was becoming intense and they had finished their bottles of water. At last they found a little bar where they gratefully slumped down at a table in the shade and ordered cold beers.

"How are you holding up?" Josh asked.

"Not very well. This heat is draining my energy."

"Now you understand why everything shuts down in the afternoon for the siesta," he said. "I think we have an important decision to make. We can go looking for a place to have lunch or we can have some *tapas* here. Which would you prefer?"

Amy was content to sit where she was and sip her beer in the cool shade of the bar.

"Let's stay here," she said.

They proceeded to the counter and ordered portions of potato salad, meatballs, stuffed peppers, tortilla and grilled sardines. The meal came with a basket of bread and, together with a couple of glasses of wine, it made a quick and tasty lunch.

"*Mucho calor*," Josh said when the waiter came to take away their plates and leave the bill.

He replied in a rapid outburst of Andalusian Spanish.

"What did he say?" Amy asked.

"He was complaining about the heat. He says it's already twenty-eight degrees Celsius."

"That is hot, no wonder I'm wilting."

"You're right. The best time to come here is in the spring and autumn. I'll tell you what. Why don't we spend another hour seeing some more of the city and then we'll drive back home."

"Are you sure you want to do that? There's still an awful lot to see."

He kissed her cheek and smiled.

"You're forgetting something, Amy. We're going to have all the time in the world to see Seville. We're going to be living here."

They made the next stage of their tour by horse-drawn carriage but not before the driver had obligingly photographed them standing together beside the horses. Then it was off for a short canter to the Plaza de España, another of the city's major tourist attractions.

They spent half an hour admiring the huge square with its fountain and mosaics but were happy to retreat to the nearby Maria Luisa park with its shady trees and lakes to sip cold bottles of Lucozade while they took a breather.

Eventually, they made their way back to the car.

"It's like Granada all over again," Josh remarked as he started the engine and turned on the air-conditioning. "We only managed to see a portion of Seville. Are you tired?"

She nodded.

"Do you want to take a nap?"

"No, it will pass."

"Hungry?"

"I will be in an hour or so."

"If you can hold out till we get to Malaga, we can have dinner there again. Then we won't have far to get home."

She snuggled closer and kissed his cheek. "You think of everything," she said.

But by the time they approached Malaga, the heat had taken its toll and Amy was exhausted. And her appetite had gone as well.

"Do you mind if we don't have dinner?" she asked.

"Not hungry?"

She shook her head. "Just tired."

"Well, in that case, we'd better get you home."

Amy slept like a baby, exhausted after the trip to Seville, while Josh spent the night at his mother's. But when she woke the following morning, she had retrieved her strength. Josh was flying out to Glasgow that evening and the prospect of losing him when he had only recently returned, caused a tinge of sadness. But this time, it was for a business trip and she knew she would see him again.

She started the morning with a refreshing fifteen-minute swim in the pool. As she ploughed through the cool water, her thoughts drifted to the wonderful new life she would have when she moved down here to work with Josh. It would not be such a major disruption. Her family and friends were only a couple of hours away by plane and she could maintain easy phone and email contact with them. She would have a job and a steady income. But most of all – she and Josh would be together.

She would make new friends, take up new hobbies. Maybe Josh would teach her to play golf. They would have their own apartment, they could give dinner parties, go out the theatre with Betty, drink coffee at pavement cafés and wake each morning to the sun warming the geraniums in the window-boxes. It would be a fantastic life.

She was still smiling at the thought as she got dried and returned to her apartment. She was putting on the percolator to make coffee when her phone gave a buzz and she heard Josh on the line.

"Hi," he said. "I saw you in the pool. Very impressive. You have obviously recovered from the rigours of Seville."

"I fell asleep the moment my head hit the pillow and slept for ten solid hours."

"You must have been really tired. What are you doing about breakfast?"

"I am just about to make some coffee."

"Why don't you nip up to our place? Mum and I are having breakfast on the terrace. It's scrambled eggs and smoked salmon. Does that suit you?"

"I think I could force myself to eat some," she laughed. "I'll be with you in five minutes."

She pulled on a tee-shirt, shorts and sandals and made her way up to Betty's apartment. When Josh opened the door, he took her in his arms and swung her round.

"Now," he said, planting a kiss on her lips, "you look radiant. Why don't you join Mum while I get your breakfast?"

Betty was waving frantically from the terrace where she was seated at the table with a large pot of tea.

"Come and sit beside me, dear. Josh has just been telling me all about your plans. Oh, I think it's marvellous. I'm just as excited as you are. The thought of having you two as neighbours, I can't get over it! It's the best news I've heard for a very long time."

"I'm having trouble coming to terms with it myself," Amy admitted.

"Well, I'm delighted you have agreed. You don't mind uprooting yourself and coming to live here?"

"I'll miss my family and friends but it's not like I'm going to live in Australia. I can be back in Dublin quite easily if I need to. And there is the small matter of the weather to consider."

"And the lifestyle, my dear. You'll love it here and I'll introduce you to lots of people. But of course you're the sort of person who will have no trouble making your own friends. You'll take to it like a duck to water."

At that moment, Josh appeared with plates of salmon and scrambled eggs. He returned to the kitchen and came back with a basket of crusty bread rolls. Betty poured the tea and they started to eat.

"Tell us about this apartment that's coming up for sale," Josh said to her.

"It belongs to the McArthurs," Betty replied. "You must remember them. He's in his late fifties, plump. His wife is a younger, thin, bottle-blonde woman. She was always sunbathing at the pool. Well, apparently his business is in trouble, something to do with the recession. They have to sell."

"Do you know what price they want?"

"Four hundred I should think but you will get it for less. Mrs Kingston has their telephone number. I could get it from her and you could call and talk to them."

"No," Josh said. "Do nothing for the time being. I have to get Dad's agreement before we make a move. I intend to have another chat with him when I get back."

"Assuming he agrees – and we get the apartment – how long would it be before we could move in?" Amy asked.

Josh glanced at his mother. "If we can arrange a price with the McArthurs, we could get the sale completed within four to six weeks. Give another two or three weeks for reconstruction work and decoration. We could be living in the apartment in less than three months."

"I will have to tell my employers," Amy said.

"How much notice do you have to give?"

"A month, I think. I'd have to check."

"Okay, so there's no rush."

"I also have clothes and personal stuff to bring out."

"Would you need to hire a van, do you think?"

"Oh no, I think I could bring the important stuff in a couple of suitcases. I can always bring the rest at a later stage."

"So, in order of priority, I have to get Dad on board, then we have to purchase the apartment, then you give notice to leave your job." He sat back, took a sip of tea and waved his hand. "It's a piece of cake. Nothing can go wrong."

After breakfast, Betty suggested they go on a reconnaissance mission to check out the apartment. They went through the garden to the swimming pool. The McArthurs' flat was on the top floor of Block Two. It was south-west facing which meant it got the sun all afternoon. It also had a long terrace with commanding views of the complex and the town and probably also of the sea. Already, Amy liked the look of it.

"Have you ever been inside it?" Josh asked his mother.

She shook her head. "They did give a party one time but I couldn't go because I had a meeting of the theatre group."

"So you've no idea what condition it's in?"

"No, but they only use it for a few months each year and they never rent it out so I imagine it's in pretty good shape."

He turned to Amy. "What do you think?"

"It looks marvellous. I'd love to get a peep inside."

"So would I," Josh agreed.

She felt his arm slip around her waist and his lips brush her cheek.

"You're every bit as excited as I am, aren't you?" he said.

"You bet," she replied.

Josh said they should have lunch this afternoon to celebrate and Betty said she knew the very place. They would go to Sin Igual. She said she had recently been there and it had been very enjoyable.

"Okay, give them a ring and tell them we'll be there around two. Now you'll have to excuse me, ladies. I've got some business matters to take care of."

He gave Amy a quick peck on the cheek and left.

Betty reached out and took Amy's hand.

"You have no idea how much this means to me," she said. "My greatest desire is that Josh should be happy and I know he will be happy with you."

Amy's thoughts were drawn back to the last occasion when she had talked with Betty just a few nights ago.

"Do I detect your hand in this somewhere?" she asked.

Betty's face became a mask of innocence. "Me?" she replied, looking shocked. "I don't know what you're talking about, my dear."

Lunch was at two so Amy was free till then. She dropped Carly O'Brien's dress into the dry cleaner's and, when she returned, took her novel and chair and went out to the garden. Josh had said they must wait but Amy knew this wouldn't be easy. Patience wasn't one of her strong suits. She looked up when she heard a cheery voice nearby and saw Carly come struggling out onto the lawn weighed down with her sun-bed, bag, towels and magazines.

"Let me give you a hand with some of that," Amy said, getting up and taking the bag and magazines and carrying them to a spot beside her.

"So," Carly said, settling down, "I'm just dying to find out. How did your dinner-date go?"

"It went very well, thanks to you. I'm having your dress cleaned and I've set the shoes aside. You'll have them back tomorrow."

"There was no need for that."

"Yes, there was," Amy insisted. "You dug me out of a hole and I'm very grateful."

"You shouldn't have! But forget about the dress – tell me about the evening! I'm dying to hear. Was the restaurant nice?"

"It was beautiful."

Amy began to tell her about the magical setting, the flowers and the wonderful perfume and the lights twinkling like stars as dusk began to fall.

"It sounds fantastic. And the food, what did you eat?"

"Roast lamb."

"Oh," Carly sighed. "I just love roast lamb. Why doesn't someone take me to places like that? And Josh – tell me more about him."

"Well, he was just as handsome and gallant as ever."

"It sounds so romantic," Carly sighed.

Amy wondered if she should tell her more. She was bursting to tell her all about the fantastic proposal Josh had made that was set to change her life. But there were several hurdles to overcome, particularly regarding the purchase of the McArthurs' apartment, so she was forced to restrain herself.

"You're right, Carly," she replied. "I think it was the most romantic evening of my entire life."

The morning ticked away till Amy said she had to go. She packed up her belongings and returned to her apartment. She had just finished dressing when Josh rang to say he and Betty would call for her to walk the short distance to Sin Igual. It was hot and they had to stay in the shade. But Betty said she didn't mind a little stroll now and again because she needed the exercise.

They had no sooner arrived when Josh insisted on ordering a bottle of champagne to mark this special occasion.

"You know, I've been thinking," Betty said. "None of this would have happened if I hadn't spoken to you the day you arrived."

"And it wouldn't have happened if I hadn't picked Magnolia Park out of the holiday brochure," Amy added.

"Ummm," Betty said, thinking of herself and Nigel Smyth, "Magnolia Park does have a sort of magic, doesn't it? It makes people do strange things. I'm going to propose a toast."

They laughed and filled their glasses and touched them together.

"To Magnolia Park!" Betty said.

"To Magnolia Park!" they replied.

The afternoon passed in a cheerful buzz of laughter and goodwill. Amy got out her phone and Betty took photographs of Josh and Amy with their arms wrapped around each other. Amy took photographs of Josh and his mother. Finally they enlisted the assistance of the waiter to take photographs of them all together. It was five o'clock when they paid the bill and left to return to Magnolia Park.

As they were leaving, Amy felt the sadness tugging again at her heart. The holiday was drawing to a close. That evening, Josh was flying off to Glasgow and a few days later, she would have to return to Dublin and leave this peaceful place behind. And then the waiting would begin in earnest.

Josh's flight was at eight thirty and they had agreed that Amy and Betty would accompany him to see him off. At seven o'clock he turned up with his travelling bag and put it in the boot of the hired Audi. He had to return the car to the rental company and Amy and Betty would come back by taxi.

They set off along the motorway and twenty minutes later they were at their destination. Josh had already printed out his boarding pass and a quick check of the information board showed that his flight was leaving on time. He returned the car and Betty and Amy walked with him to the security gates where they would have to part.

He kissed his mother and then he turned to Amy and took her in his arms. Despite her resolve, she felt her eyes fill up with tears. He was leaving and she didn't know when she would see him again.

"I'll ring you every day," he said. "I'll let you know what is happening." He gently wiped the tears away from underneath her eyes with his fingers. "You must be strong, Amy. You must believe. Promise me you won't be sad."

She nodded her head. "I promise."

She felt his soft lips touch hers. Then he was walking away to the security barriers. He turned one last time and waved goodbye. Next moment he was swallowed up by the crowd.

Chapter 40

Four days later, Amy arrived back in Dublin to an overcast sky and a stiff breeze tossing the leaves of the shrubs beside the taxi rank. She felt shivery in her light summer clothes. She sank gratefully into the back of the cab and asked to be taken to her parents' home in Raheny.

The last couple of days had been hard. No sooner had Josh departed than she began to miss him terribly. He kept his promise and rang her every day. But instead of cheering her up, the sound of his voice only made her miss him more. A tide of loneliness swept her up. She also had to steel herself for the unpleasant tasks that lay ahead. She had to move her belongings out of Sam Benson's apartment and she also had to face her friends and work colleagues who would be sure to question her about the break-up. At least her mother had taken the news in her stride. Amy had a suspicion that she might even be secretly pleased. Sam had never been her favourite person.

As the taxi skirted the roads around north Dublin, Amy rehearsed the tasks that still lay ahead. Until Josh came through with the green light, it would be better if she said nothing about the move to Spain. She would have to conduct herself carefully in the days that lay ahead.

Her mother came out to meet her when the taxi finally drew up outside the Crawfords' semi-detached home on Myrtle Avenue. While Amy was paying the driver, her mother lifted her suitcase and quickly carried it into the house.

"What did you do that for?" Amy asked, once they were inside and the front door was closed.

"I didn't want the neighbours to see," her mother explained.

"See what?" Amy asked.

"That you are back living with us. You know the way they talk around here."

"I didn't know it was something to be ashamed about. Anyway, it's none of their damned business where I live."

"Calm down," her mother said. "Do you want a cup of tea? I suppose you're tired after the flight. Your bedroom is ready. Why don't you go upstairs and unpack while I put the kettle on?"

"Thanks, Mum. I'd love a cup of tea."

Amy manhandled the heavy suitcase up the stairs to her single room. Already she was beginning to feel the restrictions of living with her parents again. Her room looked exactly as she had left it: the single bed with the duvet, the dressing-table and wardrobe which her father had built years ago when she was small, the pink carpet that stained too easily, the flowered curtains across the windows which gave a view of the front-garden and the street.

She was right back where she had started. The room looked small and old-fashioned compared with the bedroom she had shared with Sam in his modern apartment at Sutton but at least she would be alone here and that was a huge relief.

Thinking of Sam gave her an uneasy feeling. She had to go downstairs and explain to her mother who would want to know exactly what had caused them to break up. And later she had to confront him again and arrange to get her belongings out of his apartment.

She quickly unpacked her clothes and put them in the laundry basket then washed her face with cold water. She put on a little make-up then brushed her hair and descended the stairs.

Her mother was waiting in the kitchen. She had prepared a plate of ham sandwiches and an apple-tart from the local Centra store.

The teapot was sitting on a stand in the middle of the table. Two cups and saucers and spoons were laid out and two places set.

"Sit down," Mrs Crawford said. "I'm sure you're hungry after all that travelling."

"Thanks, Mum," Amy replied. She sat and took a sandwich from the plate as her mother poured out the tea.

"Where's Dad?"

"He had to go to the doctor. His back is hurting him again."

"It's not serious, is it?"

"It *is* for him. But if you mean is it going to kill him, I don't think so. Well, how was the holiday?"

"It was fine."

"Nice weather?"

"The weather was marvellous. The sun shone every day. We hardly ever saw a cloud."

"So what happened between you and Sam?"

Amy lowered her head. "I discovered he wasn't the man I thought he was, certainly not the man I wanted to live with any more."

"Well, if you want my opinion and I'm sure you don't, you're better off without him. Sam Benson was always too flashy for my liking. And I did warn you about moving in with him but I won't go on about it."

"I've something else to tell you, Mum. I've met a new man. His name is Josh Parsons."

Mrs Crawford blinked. "That was certainly fast. You don't waste time, do you?"

"I'm hoping to go back to Spain to be with him."

"What? When is this going to happen?"

"Soon, I hope. But it depends on certain things working out. I'll tell you all about it once I'm sure."

Mrs Crawford shook her head. "You young people today. I hope you know what you're doing."

"I think so, Mum. This time I know I've met the right one."

"Well, you're very welcome to stay here in the meantime. You can live here as long as you like."

"I'll give you some money for food and bills," Amy said.

Mrs Crawford made a tutting sound with her tongue. "You'll do nothing of the sort. A bird would eat more than you. This is your home, Amy. We're your parents. We're glad to have you back."

Amy finished the tea and returned to her room. She sat down on the bed, took out her phone and rang Sam. He answered immediately.

"You got back okay?" she began.

"I've been back for days," he said coldly. "Thanks to you, I had to cut my holiday short."

"Can we keep this civil? I want to arrange to get my stuff out of the apartment."

"What's stopping you? You've got a key, haven't you?"

"I want to do it without any hassle so I'd prefer if you weren't there when I call."

There was a sharp intake of breath. "Am I hearing right? You want me to vacate my own apartment for your convenience? This is the same woman who dumped me out on the street in a foreign country without a bed to sleep in? You really have a brass neck, Amy."

She bit her tongue. The last thing she wanted was another fight with Sam with her mother downstairs where she could hear everything.

"I said I wanted to do this without any hassle."

"Come whenever you like," he said. "I'll be in town all day."

There was a click and the phone call ended.

Amy checked the time. It was four o'clock. If she went now, she could get her stuff and be out of the apartment before Sam returned from work. She checked the number of the local taxi company and called them. The woman at the base promised to have a cab at her address within ten minutes. Amy put on a jacket, checked that she had her keys and cash and went back downstairs.

"Where are you off to?" her mother asked when she reappeared.

"I'm going to get my stuff out of Sam's apartment."

"Do you need me to come with you?"

Amy shook her head. "I think I'll be able to manage on my own."

From the window, she saw the cab enter the street and slow down. She walked out to the hall and opened the front door.

"I'll be back in an hour," she said.

She sat in the back seat and gave the driver directions. It was only a short journey. Ten minutes later, the cab pulled up outside the apartment and Amy asked the driver to wait.

The apartment was on the ground floor. She turned the key in the lock and went in. The place was quiet. She walked into the kitchen and found the sink filled with unwashed plates and the refuse bin overflowing with empty pizza boxes. Sam didn't seem to be managing too well on his own.

She grabbed a roll of bin bags from a cupboard, went off to the bedroom, opened the wardrobe and began to stuff clothes and dresses into the bags. She pulled out the drawers and emptied them of underclothes and socks. She was starting on her CD and book collection when she heard a footfall. Her heart jumped into her mouth. She turned and saw Sam standing in the doorway.

"Hello, Amy," he said. "So you're really going through with this?"

She froze. For a moment, she found herself unable to speak. He stood framed in the doorway with a strange smile on his face.

"You told me you'd be in town."

"And you believed me? You really can be very naïve at times, Amy." He walked towards her, took the bag out of her hand and put it down on the bed. "Now why don't you come into the kitchen and have a glass of wine and we'll talk this thing over?"

"No," she said, firmly. "We've already had our talk. There's nothing left to say. Our relationship is finished and I'm here to remove my property. If you don't mind that's what I intend to do."

She picked the bag off the bed and resumed her packing.

Sam gave a loud sigh. "Oh dear, oh dear, you really are very stubborn, Amy. You and I both know that in a week or two when your blond friend loses interest in you and stops ringing, you'll come back to me like a little lost puppy. Why not save yourself the embarrassment of moving back in again? I'm prepared to forgive you and draw a line under the past. But you have to meet me halfway."

Amy gasped in disbelief. Despite everything that had happened, Sam hadn't grasped the gravity of the situation at all. He was still as arrogant as ever. "You are prepared to forgive *me*?"

"Of course, I'm a reasonable person. You meet some guy on a starry night and you get a rush of blood to the head and you think you're in love. I'm not holding it against you."

"You're crazy," Amy said. "You don't understand a thing, do you? It's over between us."

She pushed past him and began to stuff books into the bag. Suddenly, she heard a sob. She turned to find Sam sitting on the bed. Tears were streaming down his face.

"Don't leave me, Amy. Please. I don't think I can live without you."

In a flash, her heart went out to him. This was the man she had once loved and had shared her life with and now he had been reduced to a frightened little boy.

"It's no good, Sam. Our relationship was in trouble even before we went to Spain. If I returned to you, it would only be a matter of time before we were both unhappy. Don't you see that?"

"I'll change," he pleaded. "I'll do anything you want."

"You won't change, Sam. You might try to but you are the way you are. This is for the better, believe me. You'll soon get over me and get on with the rest of your life." Just then there was a knock on the door. When she opened it, Amy found the taxi-driver standing in the hall.

"Are you all right, Miss? Do you need any help?"

"Yes," Amy said. "You could carry those bags out to the cab for me, if you don't mind."

She stuffed her laptop into a box and turned back to Sam. He had taken out a handkerchief and was wiping his eyes.

"So this really is the end?"

"Yes," she said.

Sam looked as if he was about to burst into tears again.

She turned and hurried down the stairs.

The following morning, Amy went back to work. She was dreading it.

She knew that her friends would want to hear all the gory details of the end of her relationship. As luck would have it, the first person she encountered when she entered the office was Debbie Fox. She was seated at her desk near the door as Amy came in.

"Welcome back," she said, getting up and giving her a big hug. "My God, you look fantastic. Look at that fabulous tan. I'm jealous already. So how was the trip?"

"It was brilliant," Amy replied. "Everything was perfect – the weather, the food, the complex where we were staying. If I'd had my way, I would never have come home."

Debbie gave a tight little smile. "But all good things must come to an end, Amy. So what about Sam? Did he enjoy it too?"

Amy had already figured out how to deal with this situation. The best way was to get it over fast.

"You'd have to ask him about that, Debbie."

Debbie's face showed mock surprise. "How do you mean?"

"We're no longer an item." She pushed past, walked to her own desk and sat down. Debbie quickly followed her. "Did I hear right? Did you say you've split up?"

"There's nothing wrong with your hearing, Debbie."

"Oh my God!" Debbie clasped a hand to her mouth. "You poor thing, you must be heartbroken to lose a hunk like Sam. What are you going to do?"

Amy looked her straight in the eye. "I didn't say I'd lost him. I broke it off."

"Broke it off?" Debbie almost shrieked and several heads looked up from their desks. "What happened?"

"Keep your voice down," Amy said. "I suddenly realised that Sam and me were not really suited to each other. So rather than waste any more time on a lost cause, I called it a day."

"And-and how did he take it?"

"Like I said, you'd need to ask Sam about that."

She gave her colleague a sweet little smile, picked up the phone and pretended to dial. Debbie slunk away but not before giving Amy a look that said she hadn't believed a word she'd been told.

The rest of her friends eventually turned up for work and Amy saw them gossiping at the water fountain and their eyes sneaking pitying glances in her direction. At coffee break they descended on her desk in a posse and bore her away to the canteen on the pretence of consoling her.

"This is terrible," Lorraine Clancy said, once they were sitting at a table with coffees and muffins. "This is the worst news I've heard for months."

"What's terrible about it?" Amy demanded.

"How long were you together?"

"About twenty months in total."

Lorraine shook her head. "What a terrible waste!"

"You could probably get him back again," Tara Brady said. "I would be quite happy to act as a peace envoy, if you like."

Amy sat quietly and drank her coffee till they had all finished speaking. "Look guys, I appreciate your concern. But it really is over between me and Sam Benson. I don't want him back. We're finished."

"Really?" Debbie Fox said.

"Yes, Debbie, really."

Time went by and Amy was lonely. Each morning she left for work. Each evening she returned to her home in Raheny and the meal her mother had prepared for her. Sometimes she watched television or retired to her room and read a book. Other times, she went for a walk. One evening she went to the cinema on her own. But she kept up her spirits by thinking of the wonderful future that lay ahead once Josh's plans went into action. They would be together again in Magnolia Park.

He rang every day. He always sounded upbeat but the news she desperately wanted to hear didn't arrive.

The first week passed and by now Amy was growing impatient. What was taking Alf Parsons so long to make up his mind? Surely it wasn't so difficult to come to a decision?

Then on the morning of the tenth day, as she was on the train into work, her mobile rang. She quickly dug it out of her bag and clasped it to her ear.

"Hello," she said.

It was Josh. "Amy, I've got bad news."

She felt herself go cold.

"Is it what I think?"

"Yes. My father has turned us down."

Chapter 41

For a moment, she thought she might be sick. It was all she could do to keep her voice steady.

"Turned us down? Why?"

Josh gave a weary sigh. She could tell he was just as shattered as she was.

"He wants me close to him in London. And he says he doesn't see why we should incur the expense of buying another apartment in Spain and hiring one more secretary. I've tried arguing with him, Amy. We've had some furious rows but he won't budge. I'm sorry."

She was completely lost for words. "Don't blame yourself."

"I was sure he would agree," Josh continued. "I'm devastated, Amy."

She wished she was with him now so she could put her arms around him and comfort him. "So where do we go from here?"

"I don't know. I've tried every argument but he just digs his heels in. But we won't give up. I'm sure I'll think of something."

She heard the hopelessness in his voice.

"Thanks for calling, Josh. I'm on the train now. We'll talk again later. And remember, whatever happens I will still love you. We'll find a way to be together."

She closed her phone.

She was stunned. She thought of the bright hopes that now lay in ruins and the dreams which had turned to ashes. She was jolted back to reality as the train came thundering into the station.

Amy tried hard to keep hope alive but it was difficult and every day she felt herself sink deeper into a pit of despair. She saw the dream she shared of living a new life in Spain with the man she loved dwindle and flicker till it was barely alive. Josh rang every day in an effort to cheer her up. But she could tell that he was no longer the confident man he once was. His father had blocked them and Josh could see no way out of the cul-de-sac they now found themselves in. Meanwhile, her friends had noticed the change in her mood and, mistaking it for sadness at the break-up with Sam, they kept inviting her out for drinks or to clubs and parties. She just wished they would leave her alone with her misery.

Her life became a dull plod between the office and home. There were days when she had to force herself to go into work and when she got home she locked herself away in her bedroom and rarely came out. Even her mother believed her melancholy was related to the break-up with Sam and tried to comfort her.

Then one morning, Amy received an unexpected phone call at work. When she answered, she was surprised to hear Betty Parsons' voice at the other end of the line.

"Hello, my dear," she began. "I hadn't heard from you so I thought I'd give you a call. How are you keeping?"

"I'm well," Amy lied.

"And what is the weather like in Dublin?"

"Not as nice as Spain."

She heard Betty laughing.

"That would be difficult now, wouldn't it? Mind you, it's getting quite hot down here. You know the temperature was up to 25 degrees on Monday. And it's only the beginning of June."

"That's hot."

"Too hot, my dear. Old Mrs Gilbert doesn't like it. It drains her energy and God knows she hasn't much energy to begin with."

"Please tell her I was asking for her."

"I will, of course. Now I know you're probably very busy and I" don't want to take up your time. I'm ringing on a personal matter. When I've spoken to Josh recently, I can't help noticing that he has been very out of sorts. I wondered if you and he were having a little tiff?"

"You mean he hasn't told you?"

"Told me what, dear?"

"About his father."

"What about him?"

The thought occurred to Amy that she might be straying too far into the family's private business. Perhaps Josh had a good reason to withhold the news of Alf Parsons' decision from his mother.

"Well, he . . ."

"Yes, my dear?"

"He turned down Josh's plan to move to Spain."

She heard a sharp intake of breath come down the line. "He did *what*?"

"He turned down the plan that Josh had to buy the McArthurs' apartment and relocate to Spain. That's why Josh is in bad form."

There was a pause before Betty spoke again.

"So now you won't be coming out here to live? I won't be having you as neighbours?"

"It doesn't look like it."

"Well, that is outrageous. I've never heard the like. It can't be money because Alf is absolutely rolling in it. I'm – I'm flabbergasted."

"I'm sorry to break the bad news," Amy said.

"Not at all, dear. You were perfectly correct. Don't tell Josh we were speaking. Just leave this matter with me. I think I'll have to look into it a bit more."

Amy terminated the call with an uneasy feeling that she might have said too much.

On the terrace of her apartment in Magnolia Park, Betty stared down at the garden where the roses were drooping in the heat. Beside her was a huge umbrella and an electric fan. She had dispensed with her usual pot of tea, and a jug of iced lemonade stood on the table with a glass beside it.

She was in shock at the news she had just heard. She had been married to Alf Parsons for almost forty years but in all that time she had never known him to reveal such a mean, nasty side to his character. To turn down the young couple's dream of a life together and for what reason? So he could keep control over Josh.

Betty had never interfered in her husband's business decisions but this time Alf had gone too far and she was not going to sit idly by without letting him know what she thought of it.

She lifted the phone again, dialled the head office of Parsons Electrical in London and asked to be put through to Mr Parsons. A minute later she heard the shrill voice of Alf's secretary.

"Who shall I say is calling?"

"*His wife!*" Betty bellowed.

She heard the secretary give a start.

"Right away," she said and Betty found herself speaking to her husband.

"Well, this is a pleasant surprise," Alf began cheerily. "What's the reason for this unexpected call?"

"Business," Betty replied in a grim voice.

"How do you mean?"

"Let me explain. I've been married to you for a long time, Alf Parsons and I've stood by you through thick and thin even though you have neglected me sorely and never visit me in Spain so that sometimes I wonder if we're really married at all."

Alf had never heard Betty use this tone of voice and something warned him that he had better treat her seriously.

"What is the problem, Betty?"

"I'll tell you exactly what the problem is. It has come to my attention that you have blocked a proposal by Josh to locate here in Magnolia Park and employ his young lady friend as his secretary. Is that true?"

"Yes," Alf said.

"And might I enquire why?"

"Because there's no need for it. It's a waste of money. And besides, I want him beside me here in London."

"Alf, let me tell you some home truths. You have blighted our marriage because of your obsession with work. Now you're intent on blighting Josh's life and turning him into a clone of yourself. He has a chance of happiness with this young woman. I've met her and I can tell you that she's a very nice, genuine person. I've no doubt that she and Josh will be extremely happy together. They're in love, although I doubt if you will understand what that means. And I want to tell you that I will not allow you to stand in their way."

"But it's not your decision, Betty. This is a business matter for the company to decide."

"Really? Then let me remind you that I am a director of the company. Or had you forgotten?"

"But you've never played any role in the company!"

"Well, I'm starting now. I am warning you, Alf Parsons. If you persist with this nonsense, I will go to the papers and tell them the whole story. I have a friend down here whose son is an editor with the *Mirror*. I'm deadly serious, Alf."

"You don't want to do that, Betty. Think of the publicity!"

"That is exactly what I'm thinking about. Parsons Electrical, *The Friendly Store*? There's nothing very friendly about the way *you* are behaving."

"Hold on, Betty. Don't get carried away."

"I'm not carried away. I've never been more rational in my life. If it's the only thing that will make you see sense then I won't hesitate."

"All right, all right," Alf said. "Let me see what I can do."

"You can advance Josh the money to buy that apartment and you can agree to put Amy Crawford on the payroll. Those are my demands. Anything less and you'll be reading about this in the *Mirror*. Have I made myself clear?"

"Yes," Alf said, meekly. "Very clear."

Chapter 42

Shortly after Amy's talk with Betty, several things occurred in quick succession.

The following day at work, she got a call from Josh.

"You're never going to believe what's happened!"

"Tell me," Amy said, catching the note of excitement in his voice.

"Dad has changed his mind."

"About your relocating to Spain?"

"Exactly."

She caught her breath. "You mean we can go ahead with the plan?"

"Yes. Dad just called me into his office this morning, asked me to close the door and said he had been thinking things over and had decided that moving to Spain was an excellent idea. He said it would allow me to gain a fresh perspective on the company's requirements whatever that means. I don't know what has come over him but I wasn't going to question him. He told me to go ahead and start initiating proceedings."

This was fantastic news. Suddenly Amy's world was starting to look bright again.

"Oh Josh, I don't know what to say I'm so happy. You won't believe how low I have been for the past couple of weeks."

"I haven't exactly been on Cloud Nine either. I never thought that Dad would raise any objections to the plan. So, I was bowled over when he vetoed it. But now, he's come round. I'm just so thrilled. It means we can be together again. And this time, we will stay together."

Amy closed her eyes. She was so excited that she had to stop herself from jumping up and shouting the good news all over the office. "Keep me informed," she said. "I want to know everything that happens."

"You bet," he said.

She put down the phone and her lips formed a silent prayer. "Thank you, God," she said.

Now that the project was back on the road again Amy felt all her old enthusiasm return. Suddenly she was bustling around with a smile on her face and pep in her step. It became so obvious that Tara Brady asked her one day if she had got a new man in her life that she wasn't telling anyone about.

"As a matter of fact, I do, Tara, you've guessed right."

"Anybody I know?"

"I don't think so. His name is Josh and he lives in London."

"Where did you meet him?"

"In Spain."

"Oh, that's wonderful news. Are we going to meet him?"

"That might be difficult but I can show you a photo."

She got out her phone and showed her colleague the picture that Betty Parsons had taken the day they had lunch together at Sin Igual restaurant.

"My, he's handsome," Tara said. "He's so sexy I could eat him. You're a lucky woman, Amy."

Amy smiled. "I know, Tara," she said.

She was tempted to tell her friend all about her plans to go and live with Josh in Spain but she had just recovered from one setback. There was no point tempting Fate a second time. It would be much safer to wait a little while longer till everything was watertight. Then she would tell the whole office.

But now she felt her confidence grow by leaps and bounds and it was bolstered a few days later by more good news. This time Betty came on the phone to say she had been talking to Mrs Kingston and had got the McArthurs' telephone number. She had called to make preliminary enquiries and they were very anxious to do business with Josh. They had sent instructions to the management company to let him have the key. Josh was planning to come down and look over the apartment.

"I think you should come too, dear. You must have a say in this. And besides, another opinion is always valuable."

"I'd better to talk to him," Amy said. "Thanks for keeping me posted, Betty. I'll stay in touch."

She had barely finished speaking when the phone rang again and this time it was Josh with the same news.

"I'm thinking of going out this weekend. I'd like you to come with me. We should look at the apartment together."

"I'd love to come, Josh – let me check flights from Dublin. I'll get back to you right away."

She immediately went onto the internet. There was a flight leaving Dublin on Friday evening at 8pm which would get her to Malaga at 11.30pm and another returning on Sunday evening. They could view the McArthurs' apartment on Saturday and spend the rest of the weekend discussing it and coming to a decision. But before she did anything she had to co-ordinate her plans with Josh.

He agreed with her at once. "The sooner we view the better. I'll book right now."

"There's something else," she said. "Where are we going to stay?"

"The obvious place, Amy – we'll stay with my mum, where else?"

Next she had to break the news to her mother and, naturally, she asked questions.

"You're going back to Spain. Has this got something to do with Josh, by any chance?"

"Yes. We're going to look at a place to live."

"So your plans are working out?"

Amy took a deep breath and nodded her head.

"Yes," she said. "It seems so."

The days dragged by till Friday morning when she arrived into the office with a weekend bag, ready for a quick exit to the airport at close of work at five. This led to a spate of fresh enquiries from her friends but she stuck to her resolution to stay silent till all the details were firmly in place and nothing could go wrong.

At lunchtime, she spoke to her supervisor who agreed to allow her leave early when Amy explained that she had a plane to catch. So at four thirty she picked up her bag, said goodbye to her colleagues and set off, leaving them scratching their heads in bafflement about what on earth she was up to.

As her taxi approached the airport, her excitement began to mount. She was going back to Spain, to the sun, to Magnolia Park, to the fountain and the rose garden. But most of all, she was going back to Josh, the man she now knew she loved beyond any possible doubt.

The plane left on time. Amy opened her paperback novel and tried to relax. But she couldn't concentrate. Her mind kept projecting forward to the wonderful new life that was opening up for her. As hard as she tried to keep it under control, her imagination insisted on soaring ahead. In the end, she gave in, put the novel aside, closed her eyes and dreamt of the brilliant future that awaited her.

There was a tailwind and they arrived in Malaga fifteen minutes before schedule. Amy hurried off the plane, through Immigration and Customs and out into the arrivals hall. There was a small crowd at this late hour and it wasn't difficult to spot Josh. He was standing at a pillar just outside the gates. He rushed forward at once, held her at arm's length and stared at her.

"You look even more beautiful than ever, Amy. Welcome back to Spain."

Betty was waiting for them when they arrived at Magnolia Park and despite the late hour she had the teapot ready – Josh had phoned to say they were on their way.

"Sit down, sit down," she fussed, ushering the pair out to the terrace like an anxious mother hen. "How was the flight?"

"It was very smooth."

"Well, you must have a cup of tea to perk you up. Travelling is a very tiring business."

"There's one thing I want to do first," Amy said, walking to the rail and gazing down at the garden.

She took a deep breath and filled her lungs with the clean night air laden with the scent of flowers. She turned to the others and smiled.

"Now I know I'm back. Nothing has changed."

"One thing has," Betty said. "I told you it was warmer. I hope it's not too hot for you."

"I think I can live with that. Now tell us the news about the McArthurs' apartment."

Betty reached into her pocket and took out a bunch of keys and placed them on the table. Then she proceeded to pour out the tea.

"I picked them up today and I don't have to return them till Monday. We can view the apartment first thing in the morning."

Amy was so anxious to see it that she was prepared to go right now but she knew the apartment would have to be viewed in daylight to see it properly.

"You spoke to the McArthurs?" Josh said.

"Yes, and they are very keen on a quick sale."

"Did they mention a price?"

"What I thought – €400,000."

"We can easily manage that," Josh said.

"You'll get it for less. I got the distinct impression that they want it off their hands as quickly as possible. I understand from Mrs Kingston that they bought it for £80,000 ten years ago, so anything over that is profit."

"Okay, let's see it first and then we can decide what to offer."

"Mrs Kingston keeps an eye on it when they're away. She said it's in very good condition."

Josh drank his tea and smiled.

"So everything is coming together at last. I wonder what happened to make Dad change his mind."

There was silence around the table. Amy glanced at Betty but her face gave nothing away.

Chapter 43

They sat chatting on the terrace till two in the morning. As the time approached for bed, Amy began to grow anxious about the sleeping arrangements. She knew that Betty was broadminded but she still felt uncomfortable about sharing a bed with her son under his mother's roof.

But the difficulty was solved by Josh who gallantly went off to get pillows and sheets and spread them out on the couch, signalling she could have the bedroom to herself and thus save embarrassment. It was with relief mingled with some regret that Amy finally went off to bed. Five minutes later, she was fast asleep.

The sun streaming in from the terrace woke her the following morning at eight o'clock. She felt wonderfully rested and anxious to greet the new day. She put on her swimsuit and took a towel from the bathroom. From the kitchen, she could hear the sound of someone moving about and guessed that Josh was already awake. He was on the terrace drinking coffee when she emerged with her towel to go for a swim.

"Sleep well?" she asked with grin.

"Very well – at least I had no distractions."

He put his arms around her, drew her close and gave her a deep, passionate kiss.

"Mind you, I can't guarantee that I won't be overcome with lust tonight. So maybe you should lock your bedroom door."

"You might break it down."

"I might," he said.

"And I might like that," she said with a smirk.

She made her way down to the garden and along to the pool. It was quiet and the only sound was the morning chorus of the birds and the occasional purring of a car passing on the road outside. Already, she could feel the pull of Magnolia Park drawing her back.

The sun was getting strong now and it was going to be a very hot day. But the water was cool and inviting. She swam for half an hour and when she returned she discovered that Josh had already been down to the bakery for rolls and pastries and Betty was also up. They sat around the table on the terrace and chatted while they ate breakfast.

When it was over, they set off for the McArthurs' apartment. Amy was very keen to see it. If anything, her excitement had increased since she returned to Spain. If everything turned out the way she hoped, this apartment could be her new home. She couldn't wait to open the front door and walk in.

They went up in the lift to the top floor and found the apartment directly facing them. Betty produced the keys and quickly undid the locks. She pushed open the door and invited Amy to enter first.

They were immediately in a spacious lounge with white walls, white furniture and a long window with sliding doors which gave a view out over the town. Amy opened the doors and stepped out onto the terrace, which ran the entire length of the lounge. There was a collection of pots with pink and crimson geraniums which had been recently watered, presumably by Mrs Kingston.

She ran to the rail and gazed out. The entire neighbourhood lay exposed beneath her gaze as far as the sea and the views were breathtaking. Josh and Betty quickly joined her on the terrace and uttered gasps of admiration at the sight that lay before them.

"This is absolutely stunning," Josh said.

Betty was rapidly nodding her head in agreement. "It must be the best view in the entire complex."

They stood for a while admiring the fantastic sight till Josh suggested they go and inspect the rest of the apartment.

They stepped back into the lounge and Betty locked the door. To the right was another door that led into a fully-equipped kitchen with a breakfast bar in the centre. To the left was a large bathroom with bath, shower and bidet.

Josh tried the taps and flushed the toilet.

"Plumbing seems to be working fine," he said.

Next were the bedrooms. The first was a huge master-bedroom with wardrobes, dressing-table and another, en suite, bathroom. The doors led out to a second terrace which looked down on the gardens and pool. The next two bedrooms were smaller guest-rooms.

As they made their way around the apartment, Josh's eyes kept glancing about in search of work that might need to be done or facilities that weren't functioning properly. Occasionally, he would pause and tap a wall. It took half an hour before they had completed their inspection. They went back into the lounge and sat down around the coffee-table.

"It appears to be in very good order," Josh said. "What do you think, Amy?"

She looked from one to the other. "You want my honest opinion? I think it's fantastic. I could move in here right away and be happy to do it."

"What about you, Mum?"

"I agree with Amy. I wouldn't change a thing."

"One of the guest bedrooms has to be converted into an office," Josh reminded them.

"But nothing else needs to be touched," Amy said. "It's in much better condition than I expected. Once we're living here we might find small things that need to be changed but nothing major."

"What about the furniture?"

"There are some new pieces I'd like to buy but, on the whole, the furniture is excellent. I can't find fault with the McArthurs' decor. Besides, I'll probably spend most of my spare time on that wonderful terrace."

Betty laughed. "I think Amy and I are on the same wave-length on this one."

"So you think I should bid for it?"

"Yes!" they chorused.

"Well, in that case, why don't I do it right now?"

He glanced at his watch. It was eleven o'clock which meant ten back in the UK. It wasn't too early to call. He took out his phone and punched in the number his mother had given him. It rang for a bit and then he heard the phone being picked up.

"Mr McArthur," he began, "my name is Josh Parsons. My mother has been speaking to you about your property in Magnolia Park. We've just had a look at it. I'm calling to say that we're interested in purchasing."

"Good. I take it you've been informed about the price? €400,000."

"That's one of the things I hoped we could talk about," Josh replied.

The conversation continued for another fifteen minutes. This was the first time Amy had listened to Josh negotiate and she was impressed by what she heard. But it was still a nail-biting experience. The apartment was perfect. She knew they weren't going to find anything better in Magnolia Park or anywhere else in Fuengirola. It would be a pity to lose it over the matter of a few thousand pounds.

At last, Josh snapped his phone shut. He turned to them and smiled.

"I take it you heard most of that?"

"We heard you offering €320,000," Amy said.

"Well, he drives a hard bargain but I've got him to accept €350,000."

Amy jumped out of her chair and flung her arms around his neck. "There's a saving of €50,000 right away, you clever, clever man," she yelled. "I can't believe it. Hooray!"

Josh looked pleased with his performance. "He's contacting his solicitor first thing on Monday morning to prepare a contract. And what's more, he has agreed to get the whole business completed within three weeks."

They decided to go for lunch to a nearby bar but Amy was in such a state of excitement that she had no appetite and only managed to pick at a tuna salad. Her mind was swimming with all the things that still had to be done.

"Will he stick to the three-week deadline?" she asked.

"I should think so. He needs the money."

Betty was less optimistic. "The solicitors are the bogey," she said. "They can take forever. I'd be more inclined to think four or five weeks."

"Well, I'll make sure there are no hold-ups on our side," Josh said. "I have to lodge a deposit with his solicitor. I'll ask Dad to forward the cash first thing on Monday morning when the banks open."

"What about the conversion work?" said Amy. "You can't do that till we've got possession."

"But you can line up a builder to be ready to start once you get the keys," Betty added. "And I might be able to help. I know some reliable people. Is there much work involved?"

"Not really," Josh said. "Just some shelving and cupboards to be erected and cables installed for the electronic equipment. I'll also have to order a desk and office furniture. It shouldn't take more than a week."

Amy's face was now glowing with anticipation.

"So we really could be living here in six weeks' time?"

"Maybe sooner, if there are no hiccoughs."

"Then I'd better give notice to quit my job as soon as I get back."

Once they were alone, Amy drew Josh aside.

"There's something on my mind that I'd like to talk about."

A look of concern passed over his face. "What is it?"

"I've been thinking. I want to make a contribution to the cost of buying this apartment. I've got some savings and I want to give them to you."

"You don't have to do that."

"I do, Josh. It's for my own peace of mind. If I don't make a contribution I'll feel like a kept woman and I can't accept that."

"You won't be a kept woman, Amy. You'll be a paid employee of the company. And besides, I'm not buying the apartment. The company is. The deeds will be in the name of Parsons Electrical."

"In that case I insist on paying for the new furniture."

He laughed. "Well, go ahead if it keeps you happy."

"It does, Josh."

The rest of the weekend flew past. There was only one topic of conversation – the purchase of the McArthurs' apartment and the imminent move to Magnolia Park. Now that they had succeeded in buying the property, Amy could barely contain herself. Her mind kept replaying images of the life she would enjoy here when she moved to live permanently in Spain.

Betty was equally animated at the prospect of having Amy and Josh living beside her. It looked as if all their dreams were coming true. Amy was returning on Sunday evening but Josh had decided to stay till Monday to leave instructions with Betty's solicitor and give him power of attorney to act on their behalf.

On Sunday afternoon, Amy said goodbye again and Josh drove her to the airport. But this time she had no regrets about leaving. The next time she came out here she would be staying for good.

The first thing she did when she got home was to confirm the news to her parents.

"When is all this taking place?" her father wanted to know.

"Very soon, I expect to be moving down there within the next six weeks."

"Does it mean we won't be seeing you again?"

Amy laughed. "Oh, Dad, this isn't like the bad old days when parents kissed their children goodbye at the emigrant ship and never heard from them again. I'll be able to nip back whenever I want. Plus I'll be on the phone. And you can come out and stay with us whenever you like. We've got a spare bedroom. You'll love it."

"We might take you up on that," her father said.

The following morning when she went into work she gave

written notice to leave her job. Her supervisor was surprised but, when she learned where Amy was going, her attitude immediately changed.

"My God, how I envy you! That sounds fantastic. Congratulations."

The next task was to tell her friends. This was something she had been looking forward to for a long time. She waited till they were gathered for morning coffee in the canteen before tossing the bombshell into their midst.

At first, there was a stunned silence then they all started talking at once.

"You're leaving?"

"You're going to live in Spain?"

The questions came thick and fast. Amy did her best to answer them without appearing smug or superior. She showed them photographs of the apartment and a picture of Josh and they all agreed he was a hunk.

"Some people have all the luck," Debbie Fox said. "A handsome man and a new job in the sun, why don't things like that happen to me?"

"Has he got any brothers?" Lorraine Clancy asked.

"Afraid not," Amy replied. "He's an only son."

Josh rang every day to keep her up to date with developments. At first, things moved very quickly. The contract was signed and the deposit was paid. Then everything slowed down again while the solicitors set about checking the deeds and making sure there were no loose ends that might cause problems later on. Amy resigned herself to waiting. She was getting used to it by now. But at least this time, there was no question of Alf Parsons changing his mind. Josh told her that his father now seemed to be as keen on the move as they were.

Betty also kept in regular contact. She reported that the McArthurs had been out to remove their personal possessions from the apartment and were very happy with the deal and the price they were receiving.

"So, it looks like a win-win situation," Amy remarked.

"What does that mean, dear?"

"It's a situation where there are no losers."

"That's right. That's exactly what it is."

One evening after work, Amy sat down at her computer and sent an email message to Carly O'Brien. She had never forgotten how kind and helpful she had been the day of her momentous dinner-date with Josh. She uploaded a photo of him and typed the message: *Here is Josh, the man who took me to dinner. I'm going back the Spain to live with him.*

Carly's response was completely different to all the others. *Isn't he a lucky man to get you?* she wrote and wished her well.

A few days later, she received the phone call she had long been waiting for. Josh called to say he was going down to Fuengirola the following day to sign the final papers.

"Is that it? Does this mean the company will own the apartment then?"

"That's exactly what it means. And the day after that, the builders are going in to carry out the renovation work. I've given them strict instructions that it must be finished within a week."

"So when will it be ready for occupation?"

"In ten days' time. You can book your ticket now, Amy."

Suddenly everything gathered speed again. Amy spent the next few days selecting the clothes and other items she wanted to take with her. When she had finished, she had packed three suitcases. There was plenty more stuff she wanted to bring but it would have to wait till the next trip home.

She was due to leave work on Friday and depart for Spain the following Wednesday. Friday arrived at last and with it the farewell party. First there was a presentation in the office where her supervisor made a little speech saying Amy had been an ideal employee and they were sorry to lose her. But she would be happy to swap places with her in the morning. Everyone laughed and applauded.

Amy felt her eyes brim with tears. She'd had ups and downs with some of her colleagues but, on the whole, they were a good bunch and she knew she would miss them. She was given a new laptop computer as a going-away present then people started taking pictures and finally they all adjourned to the pub across the street for drinks.

It was a mad night. Everyone kept saying how much they envied her. They kissed and hugged and promised to come and visit at the first opportunity. Then Debbie Fox fell into conversation with some guys up from Cork for a rugby match and in no time the party had moved across the bar to the rugby supporters. It was Amy's cue to leave. She slipped away with her new laptop, caught a cab at the top of the road and went back to her parents' house.

Chapter 44

Wednesday couldn't come quickly enough. Amy had said all her goodbyes and had assured everyone that she would only be a short distance away and could be back in Dublin in less than three hours if circumstances required. By now her parents had adapted to the news of her departure. They had taken the sensible view that she was an adult and if this move to Spain made her happy then it was a good thing.

At ten o'clock, Josh rang to confirm that the builders had finished, the apartment was cleaned and ready for occupation. He was in it now, installing his computer and fax machine and getting the office ready to start work.

"What time does your flight get in?"

"Four thirty."

"I'll be waiting in the arrivals hall. *Bon voyage.*"

At eleven the taxi arrived to take her to the airport. Her father helped her carry her luggage and stow it away in the boot. Then she kissed her parents and made her farewells. She felt no sadness at leaving, only joy at what lay ahead. She was going where her heart was leading her and she knew that only good could come of it. But she also knew that this was a momentous occasion as she waved to her parents from the window till the cab turned a corner and the house disappeared from view.

Dublin airport was packed with holidaymakers but she had given herself plenty of time. She checked in her luggage then made her way through the security barriers and out to the departure lounge. The flight was leaving on schedule and she only had a short time to wait before boarding. Twenty minutes later, they were flying out over the sea and leaving Dublin behind.

Josh was waiting as promised when the plane touched down at Malaga and quickly whisked her out to the car to complete the journey to Fuengirola. The first thing to strike her was the intense heat. It was like opening the door of a furnace. She was glad when they were out on the motorway and Josh had switched on the air conditioning.

"How is your mum?" she asked.

"She can't wait to see you again. Now that we are going to be neighbours, she's like a child whose Christmases have all come at once."

"I'm looking forward to it too. Your mother is a very shrewd woman. She'll be good company for me when you're away on business trips for your father."

"She has another reason to be happy," Josh said.

"Oh? What is that?"

Josh turned to her.

"Did you know she has a gentleman friend?"

"No."

"Well, she has. And he is taking her on a cruise of the Mediterranean."

Amy's mouth fell open. "I don't believe you."

"It's true."

"Is this a romantic involvement?"

"I'm not sure. She's told my dad and he doesn't seem too concerned."

"When is this cruise?"

"It starts tomorrow. So she will barely have time to welcome you before she has to take off."

"But when she returns, we will still be here," Amy said. "We're not going anywhere. We've got to get used to the idea that from now on Magnolia Park will be our home."

Josh laughed.

"Isn't it marvellous?" Amy said. "We're going to wake every morning to the sun shining and the flowers in bloom and every day we'll be together."

She turned to look from the window. The coast was coming into view and the sparkling ocean and the little white houses dotted along the hillside. She was overtaken by a feeling of fulfilment and satisfaction. She closed her eyes and let the feeling take her over.

Betty was waiting for them. She had dressed in a light summer dress that hugged her figure. Amy could see that she had also got her hair styled for the occasion. The two women greeted each other like long-lost friends.

"Let me see you," Betty said. "My, you look like a princess!"

"I couldn't put it better," Josh added.

"Thank you," Amy replied. "You look very well too, Betty."

"Did Josh tell you that I'm off tomorrow on my cruise?"

"Yes, are you excited?"

"You bet, this is the first holiday I've had since I came here. And the ladies in the theatre society are green with envy. My friend, Gladys Taylor, tells me they haven't recovered from the shock. But neither of you has met Nigel, have you? I must introduce him when I get back. You'll like him. Maybe I'll give a little dinner party."

"That would be fun," Amy said. "Now I want to have a quick inspection of my new home."

Betty came with them as they trooped from room to room. Josh was particularly keen for her to see his office with its gleaming new furniture and the view out over the gardens and the pool. They finished up on the terrace.

"I've had the cleaners in and they did a superb job. They said they can call once a week if you want. I've got their number," Betty said.

Josh had produced a bottle of champagne in a bucket of ice and poured three glasses.

"A toast," he said. "To our new life in Magnolia Park!"

"Hear, hear!" Betty said and they raised their glasses.

Amy thought how everything had been transformed in the space of a few short months. She had come here for a two-week holiday in May and now it was August and she had come to stay.

Betty said she had to be up early in the morning and wanted an early night so she took her leave. Once she was gone, Josh wrapped Amy in his arms.

"I've waited so long for this," he whispered as his lips kissed her neck and his fingers slid along her back and down to her thigh.

Amy felt her body flame with passion as she frantically kissed him back. He gathered her in his arms, carried her into the master bedroom and deposited her on the king-sized bed.

"Now," he said, as he quickly began to undress her. "Remind me what I've been missing."

Chapter 45

It was the second day of the cruise and the ship had left Valencia en route for Palma Majorca. Betty and Nigel sat on the deck and listened to the strains of the orchestra drifting out from the ballroom. It was a balmy night. A big moon hung in the sky and lights twinkled from the towns and villages along the coast. Betty heaved a sigh of contentment. So far the cruise had far exceeded all her expectations.

This evening they had eaten dinner at the captain's table. It meant dressing up but Betty had enjoyed it although there was far too much food. Mind you, that hadn't stopped the plump man who sat next to her whose name was Colonel Baxter. He had demolished everything that was put in front of him and had even looked enviously at the food Betty had left on her plate, as if he could eat that too.

She could see that food was going to be a problem. From breakfast right through to the midnight buffet, the staff were encouraging you to eat, eat, eat. It was if the organisers were determined that no-one would leave the ship until they had gained at least half a stone in weight.

Then there was the entertainment: flower arranging, art classes, yoga, ballroom dancing, bridge classes, clay-pigeon shooting, deck bowls. And if that wasn't enough, there was the cinema, the casino, the theatre, the three swimming pools, the gymnasium, the seven bars and the library for those exhausted from all these activities who just wanted a quiet refuge to sit and read a book. And all this was before they even set foot on dry land to visit the various ports on their itinerary.

Betty sipped her Bailey's Irish Cream and turned to Nigel who sat beside her, nursing a glass of brandy while they watched the waves roll by.

"I got a text this evening from Josh."

"Oh," Nigel said. "How is he?"

"He's fine. They're both fine. They're settling in very well. You haven't met them yet. I was thinking of having a little party when we get home so you can all get to know each other."

"That sounds like a good idea."

"I think you will like them. You know, I'm very happy for Josh. He had a bad experience with a young woman but Amy seems perfect for him. At heart, Josh is a home bird. I'm glad he's not taking after his father with his obsession for work."

"Everyone is different, Betty. Some people can't relax. They have to be working."

"He doesn't have to. He's got all the money he needs."

"It's got nothing to do with money. Maybe in the beginning it does. Ambition is good. It's what gets you out of bed in the morning. But sometimes work can become all that matters."

"He's not going to change – it's too late." She smiled at Nigel. "But it doesn't matter any more."

Nigel took her hand. "Happy?" he asked.

"Yes. I'm very glad I came."

He gently squeezed her hand.

"How is your cabin?" Betty asked. "Is it comfortable?"

"I've got no complaints."

"Does it have a porthole?"

"Yes."

"Mine doesn't."

"We could swap if you like," Nigel said.

"Oh no, there's no need for that."

They sat for a while staring out at the ocean.

"You know," Betty said. "I wouldn't mind having a look at your cabin sometime."

"That's no problem. When would you like to see it?"

"How about right now?"

They looked at each other and Betty began to giggle.

"I suppose you think I'm a Jezebel?"

Nigel smiled. "Not at all, Betty. I was wondering when you were going to ask."

If you enjoyed

Magnolia Park by Kate McCabe

why not try

Casa Clara also published by Poolbeg?

Here's a sneak preview of Chapter One

CASA
Clara

KATE McCABE

POOLBEG

Fuengirola

Chapter 1

Every morning when Emma Frazer threw open her window at Casa Clara she was greeted with a scene that warmed her heart. Directly below her was a little cobbled courtyard with a fountain that splashed water from the gaping mouths of four bronze horses. And all around was a vista of flowers: pink and yellow roses, trailing purple wisteria, flaming blood-red geraniums spilling from their brown terracotta pots and pushing their bright heads to the sun. If she lifted her eyes a little higher, she could catch a glimpse of the sea beyond the pines, the morning mist rising like a pall of smoke towards the sky. It was a scene that never failed to uplift her and fill her with energy for the tasks that lay ahead.

Mornings were the best time but the evenings had their magic too. Then the air was cool and heavy with the intoxicating scent of the flowers, and the lights from the lanterns danced and sparkled off the water in the fountain. This was a peaceful time when Emma liked to sit and reflect on the day that had passed. And often she thought too of the transformation that had taken place in her life since she first arrived at Casa Clara four short months before.

Sometimes when she looked back she shivered at the terrible risk she had taken and how it could all have ended in disaster. There were times when she thought she must have been crazy – to pack a single bag and leave everything behind with no clear idea of where she might end up or what she might do. But she had no choice. She felt her life was being squeezed out of her. She had to escape. And in the end, she had found the Casa and everything had turned out fine.

The existence she had at Casa Clara was so different to what she had left behind. She thought of Dublin with its grey skies and rain-swept streets. She thought of her workplace with its mind-numbing boredom that was slowly driving her to distraction. But none of these things had been responsible. What had forced her to flee was the sense that a knot was tightening around her and the certain knowledge that unless she went, she would end up doing something she would regret for the rest of her life.

Casa Clara was a small hotel at the edge of the sea in Fuengirola, a thriving holiday town in southern Spain. It had once been a fine mansion with sturdy walls and gates and beautiful trees to provide shade from the unforgiving sun. It had been the home of a wealthy wine merchant but after he died the house gradually fell into decline until a local man, Miguel Ramos, had seen its potential and bought it for a song.

Miguel borrowed money from the bank and renovated the old house. He called it Casa Clara, in honour of his mother who he adored. He installed new plumbing. He hired landscape gardeners to replant the grounds which had become wild and overgrown with the passage of time. Out of the mansion's vast rooms, he constructed eighteen cosy bedrooms with en-suite bathrooms. He turned the former mansion into a successful business and then, a few years later, he suddenly died and left it all to his glamorous young widow, Concepta Alvarez.

*　*　*

Emma had first set eyes on Señora Alvarez late one evening in the previous April when she'd turned up at the reception desk with a single bag and nowhere to stay. She had earlier arrived at Malaga airport on a flight from Dublin, hailed a taxi and asked the driver to take her to a hotel in Fuengirola. And that was when she'd encountered her first setback. The young taxi-driver took her to several large tourist hotels only to find they were fully booked. Emma began to get nervous. She knew absolutely no one in Fuengirola, or the whole of Spain for that matter. She began to have terrible visions of ending up sleeping on a park bench or under a boat on the beach.

But the taxi-driver had come to her rescue.

"There is one last place we can try. It is small hotel, a bit old-fashioned. But it is right on the beach."

"What is it called?"

"Casa Clara, *Señorita*!"

He took her straight to the Casa. A glamorous creature with flashing eyes and coal-black hair sat behind the reception desk and checked the computer before announcing that they had received a last-minute cancellation and a room had become available. Emma thanked her lucky stars and gave the taxi-driver a generous tip. After she had signed the register and paid her deposit, Paco, an old man who seemed to double as concierge and general factotum led her up the narrow, winding stairs and along a corridor before pausing to lift a heavy bunch of keys from the chain fastened to his thick leather belt. He opened the door and showed her into the most charming little room that Emma had ever set eyes on.

The walls were bare whitewashed stone. At one end was a comfortable wooden bed covered in crisp white sheets. Beside it, a heavy chest of drawers stood with a vase of fresh flowers on top. In another corner, a large mahogany wardrobe sat beside a writing desk and chair. Paco pushed open another door to reveal a small bathroom with shower, bidet and toilet. Emma was overcome with relief.

She tipped Paco and the old man beamed with pleasure. She waited till he was gone then walked quickly to the window and flung it open. She was on a balcony looking down into the courtyard – her first sight of the scene that she would grow to love. The light was fading and a new moon was riding high in the sky but she could see the fountain and smell the heady scent of the flowers. She turned back and looked once more around the little room. It was perfect. It was snug and cosy and clean. But most of all, it was safe. She sat down on the bed and silently thanked God for directing her here.

After she had unpacked and had a shower, Emma began to feel hungry. She had been so relieved to find a room that she had forgotten to ask about meals. So she went downstairs again and inquired at reception where she was told that the hotel only served breakfast. Feeling slightly disappointed, Emma set off to explore the town. She had been here once before with a group of school friends to celebrate the end of their exams and she had pleasant memories of long, sunny days and star-filled nights, and the scent of orange blossom on the air. She strolled along the sea front past the fish restaurants and pavement cafés till at last she came to the Castillo. Now that it was evening, the old Moorish castle was lit with lamps. It looked majestic where it perched at the edge of the ocean, guarding the town. Emma climbed the winding path beside the walls till at last she stood, breathless, looking down at the dark, heaving ocean.

As she watched the lights of the ships passing on their way to Malaga, she thought of what the future might hold as the days unfolded. She would have to find work of course and somewhere permanent to stay. The small amount of money she had brought wouldn't last forever. But all that could wait till tomorrow. This evening she would relax and enjoy her first day of freedom.

At last she turned away and headed back to the town. Soon she was in a maze of narrow little streets that were bustling with life and filled with the aroma of cooking. She had eaten practically nothing all day and now she was ravenous. She came to a restaurant in a pretty little square and found a table outside.

She sat down and ordered a dish of prawns and rice and a half carafe of chilled white wine with a basket of crunchy bread. Above her, the sky was a bright canopy of stars. She could feel a cool breeze waft up from the sea. A wonderful feeling of contentment began to steal over her. No one would find her here. For the first time in months, she felt truly happy.

* * *

She woke early next morning to find the sunlight pouring in through her bedroom window. She glanced at her watch. It was almost eight o'clock. She had slept for seven hours and now she felt rested and full of energy. She would celebrate her first morning in Fuengirola by taking a swim in the sea. She wondered if there was a gate from Casa Clara down to the beach.

She pulled her swimsuit out of her bag and put it on, then quickly slipped into a pair of baggy pants and a cotton top. She took a towel from the bathroom and made her way down to the reception desk. But when she got there, she found it was deserted. She rang the bell but no one came. After waiting for a few minutes, she wandered out into the courtyard and found Paco and a young man setting up tables for breakfast.

"I want to go for a swim," she explained in her halting Spanish. "Is there a gate that will take me to the beach?"

"*Sí, sí,*" Paco replied and spoke rapidly to his young companion who stopped what he was doing and gestured for Emma to follow him. He led her past the fountain and down to the end of the garden where he showed her how to open the gate by tapping in a security code.

"What is your name?" she asked as she scribbled the numbers on a piece of paper so she would remember them.

"Tomàs."

Emma smiled. "*Muchas gracias, Tomàs.*"

The young man blushed. "*De nada, Señorita.*"

She skipped lightly onto the beach. It was deserted. She got undressed and stepped carefully into the water. It felt wonderful to be in the sea, to feel the cold, clean water envelop her. She felt so alive, so invigorated. She swam for twenty minutes, occasionally lying on her back and gazing up at the bright sun as it climbed higher in the morning sky. Then she got out and dried herself.

On her way back to the Casa, she saw that a buffet had been set up in the courtyard on a long trestle table. On it were urns of coffee and fresh rolls and plates of cheese, ham, boiled eggs and fruit. Emma sat down at a table near the fountain and had breakfast under a tree. Above her, she could hear the birds singing in the branches and the lazy hum of the bees as they foraged among the flowers. It was so tranquil, so peaceful. So different to what she had left behind.

She thought of the things she had to do. First of all, she had to get a job. She had no idea what she might do, but she was prepared to work at anything that would provide her with an income. And she would also visit some estate agents and see if she could rent a small apartment. If she was going to remain in Fuengirola, she would need a permanent base. By now, the courtyard was filling up as more people turned up for breakfast. But, as she drank her coffee, she became aware that an air of confusion appeared to have overtaken the staff. They seemed disorganised, rushing about as if no one was in charge. It was odd; last night when she arrived everything had been so orderly. She wondered what had happened to disturb the calm.

On her way back to her room, she met Paco again as he was carrying suitcases down the stairs to the hall. The old man had a glum look on his face as he stopped to let her pass.

"Is everything all right, Paco?" she asked.

He slowly shook his grey head. "Señora Lopez is no more."

"Who is Señora Lopez?"

"She is the lady works the reception."

"Was she the lady who checked me in last night?"

"No, that was Señora Alvarez. She is the owner. Señora Lopez works reception and now she is gone."

A terrible thought struck Emma. "Do you mean she is dead?"

"*No, no. Resignada.*" He waved his arms. "This morning she leaves. She says she can take no more of the pressure. Now we have no one in charge. Everything is confusion."

So that was the cause of the panic Emma thought, as she continued up the stairs to her room. The receptionist had resigned. Well, she hoped they would have the problem sorted out when she returned this evening. She preferred Casa Clara as it had been when she first arrived – a haven of peace and tranquillity.

She set off for the town and spent the day checking out employment possibilities. But this was when she suffered her second setback. Several of the souvenir shops had notices for staff but they wanted people with fluent Spanish and Emma knew that her grasp of the language was certainly not good enough. She sought advice at a little restaurant where she ate lunch and the kindly waiter explained that many bars and restaurants hadn't opened yet. Until the tourist season got fully under way, her chances of restaurant work were not promising.

She inquired at a few bars and got the same response. So it was with a heavy heart that she made her way back to Casa Clara that evening. And here she found another cause for concern. The situation had got worse since she had left that morning. Now the place was in utter disarray. Suitcases were piled in the hall, new arrivals stood patently waiting to register, but the staff seemed totally disorganised. She found the glamorous owner, Señora Alvarez, sitting at the reception desk looking very cross as she tried to cope with the myriad demands of running the little hotel.

Emma went up to her room, got undressed and took a shower. She could see that in a small place like this, every person would count. It just took one employee to be sick or fail to turn up for work and the smooth running of the operation would be thrown into confusion. And the receptionist played a key role in the whole business. She could understand why Señora Alvarez was looking so cross. And then a strange thought entered her head. She could do the job herself!

She shook her head. She was allowing her imagination to run away with her. But why not? She was desperate for work and prepared to roll up her sleeves and tackle anything. And here was a job staring her in the face. She tried to think of the tasks the receptionist would have to perform: answering the phone, taking bookings, making out bills and probably one or two other small chores. She could easily do it. She had some Spanish but, what was equally important, she could speak English and most of the guests appeared to be British tourists.

She had nothing to lose by asking. The worst that could happen was for Señora Alvarez to say no. But if she said yes, then Emma would have a job and an income and might even be able to live here at Casa Clara where after just twenty-four hours, she was already beginning to feel at home. There was only one way to find out. She would go right now and speak to the proprietor.

She quickly dressed in a sober skirt and blouse, brushed her long dark hair and put on a little lip-gloss. She examined herself in the mirror. She looked the image of respectability. Summoning all her courage, she went back down the stairs again to the reception desk.

Señora Alvarez was on the phone and Emma could see that the strain had already got to her. She was tense and irritable and small beads of perspiration stood out on her dark forehead. At last, the conversation ended. She put down the phone and looked up at Emma.

"*Sí, Señorita*?" she asked, quite curtly. "Your room is to your satisfaction?"

"Oh yes," Emma replied. "I'm very pleased."

"So what can I do for you?"

Emma took a deep breath.

"I understand you have a problem."

Señora Alvarez stared. "Problem? No. We are under a little pressure that is all. But everything is in order."

"I understand you need a receptionist," Emma pressed on, putting on her most winning smile. "I'd like to apply."

Señora Alvarez looked surprised. "*You* want the job?"

"Why not? I'm looking for work. We might be able to help each other."

"Have you any experience?"

"No. But I think I could pick it up quite quickly. And I know I would be good."

Señora Alvarez considered for a moment. She looked Emma over and then her mood seemed to change. She quickly summoned the startled cleaning girl and instructed her to take her place behind the desk. Then she indicated for Emma to follow her to a small office where they both sat down.

Emma composed herself and took a good look at Señora Alvarez. She was about thirty-two with a shapely figure, ample bosom and a handsome face. She had jet-black hair and dark, flashing Spanish eyes. And she was clearly fond of jewellery. Her fingers and wrists were cluttered with rings and bracelets and a heavy gold chain adorned her slender neck.

"This is not an easy job," Señora Alvarez began. "You must always have the calm head."

Just like you, Emma thought mischievously but kept the thought to herself.

"Let me explain your duties," the proprietor went on.

For the next fifteen minutes, she outlined the responsibilities of the receptionist. In addition to taking the bookings, greeting the guests and keeping the register and the accounts, Emma would be expected to oversee the entire staff. She would be in charge of the cooking, cleaning, housekeeping and gardening staff. In fact, she would be responsible for the smooth running of the entire operation, although Señora Alvarez retained the official title of manager.

"So, do you think you could do this job?"

"*Sí*," Emma said, without a moment's hesitation.

"There would have to be a period of probation, of course. Shall we say one month?"

"One month seems reasonable," Emma replied.

"And we must also get you a permit to work. But we can arrange that."

"Thank you."

"Now as for your salary," Señora Alvarez continued with a serious look in her eye.

Ten minutes later they both stood up again and shook hands.

Emma was the new receptionist at Casa Clara. Her salary was to be €250 a week and Señora Alvarez had agreed that she could live in at the hotel. The Señora had a smile of relief on her handsome face. Emma could barely contain her joy.

* * *

She started her new job the following morning, determined to be a success. Her working day began at eight o'clock and didn't finish till nine or ten in the evening. She was supposed to have every Saturday off but when the first Saturday came along she was compelled to work because of pressure of business. After a fortnight, she began to understand why her predecessor, Señora Lopez, had left in a hurry. But she loved the work and there were many compensations. Señora Alvarez left her alone and didn't interfere. The staff were loyal, cheerful and hardworking and clearly delighted that someone was in charge once again. Very quickly Emma settled down and began to run Casa Clara efficiently. Señora Alvarez, who lived in a large house on the edge of the town, led a busy social life and she couldn't be bothered with the hundred little details that demanded attention. She was happy to let someone else run the place while she partied with her society friends.

This arrangement suited Emma perfectly. She soon discovered she had a talent for managing people and getting the best out of them. Even though she worked hard, she got enormous satisfaction from her job. She had practically no outlays and most of her salary went straight into her bank account.

Gradually her Spanish began to improve till she could converse quite easily with everyone. Her probation period ended and she was kept on. She even persuaded Señora Alvarez to employ a young assistant called Cristina, an eager twenty-year-old from Seville who was keen to learn the hotel business. And this allowed Emma more free time. She could enjoy the beautiful weather, the lovely food and the tranquillity of the garden and the courtyard where she loved to sit and relax in the evening when her shift was finished. It was bliss.

Time moved quickly and before she knew, four months had passed. Coming to Fuengirola had worked out far better than she had dared to hope. She had not only found peace but also fulfilment. She loved being here and her life had changed out of all recognition.

But a cloud was gathering over Emma's happy life. This morning when she threw open her window, the scene that lay before her failed to work its usual magic. Last night, she had received a message that brought bad news. Emma had a foreboding that her tranquil existence was about to come to a sudden end.

If you enjoyed this chapter from
Casa Clara by Kate McCabe
why not order the full book online
@ www.poolbeg.com

POOLBEG WISHES TO

THANK YOU

for buying a Poolbeg book.

If you enjoyed this why not
visit our website:

www.poolbeg.com

and get another book delivered straight
to your home or to a friend's home!

All books despatched within 24 hours.

POOLBEG

WHY NOT JOIN OUR MAILING LIST
@ www.poolbeg.com and get some
fantastic offers on Poolbeg books